Mrs. Oliphant

The Primrose Path

A Chapter in the Annals of the Kingdom of Fife

Mrs. Oliphant

The Primrose Path
A Chapter in the Annals of the Kingdom of Fife

ISBN/EAN: 9783337173210

Printed in Europe, USA, Canada, Australia, Japan

Cover: Foto ©Andreas Hilbeck / pixelio.de

More available books at **www.hansebooks.com**

A Chapter in the Annals of the Kingdom of Fife

By MRS. OLIPHANT

AUTHOR OF

"THE CHRONICLES OF CARLINGFORD" "AGNES" "A SON OF THE SOIL" "CARITÀ"
"FOR LOVE AND LIFE" "MISS MARJORIBANKS" "INNOCENT" &c.

"A violet in the youth of primy nature,
Forward, not permanent, sweet, not lasting,
The perfume and suppliance of a minute;
· No more."

— "the primrose path of dalliance!"
HAMLET, *Act I., Scene III.*

NEW YORK

HARPER & BROTHERS, PUBLISHERS

FRANKLIN SQUARE

1878

By Mrs. Oliphant.

TO

THE VERY REVEREND THE PRINCIPAL:

THE RIGHT REVEREND

THE MODERATOR:

ONE OF THE CHIEF LIVING ILLUSTRATIONS OF FIFE:

FROM

THE HUMBLE CHRONICLER OF THE KINGDOM

Greeting!

JUNE, 1878.

THE PRIMROSE PATH.

CHAPTER I.

THE old house of Earl's-hall stands on a long strip of land between two rivers, in that county affectionately known to its inhabitants as the kingdom of Fife. It is not a great house, but neither is it an insignificant one, though fortune has brought the family low which once held some primitive state in it : a quaint, gray dwelling, not formed for modern wants. To make an ordinary dining-room and drawing-room in it would be as impossible as to content an ordinary band of modern servants with the accommodation provided in the low vaulted chambers below, which are all the old house possesses in the way of kitchen or servants' hall ; but when you see its gray gable and turret projecting from among a cloud of trees, the old Scotch manor-house looks as imposing as any castle. The belt of wood round the little park, or what in Scotland is called "the policy," is old too, and as well-grown as the winds will permit. . It is true that a great turnip-field, reaching up to the walls of the garden which lies on the southern side, has been thrust in between the house and the wood, and the policy is as ragged as a poor pony badly groomed and badly fed ; but these are imperfections which a little money could remedy very quickly. The house itself is very peculiar in form, and consisted once of two buildings built on two sides of a court, and united by a mere screen of wall, in which is an arched door-way surmounted by a coat of arms. Probably, however, the second of these buildings, which has now fallen into ruins, was a modern addition, the other being the ancient body of the house. It is of gray stone, three stories high, with a round turret at the western side, which rises higher than the rest by one flight of the old winding stone staircase, and has a little square battlement and terrace at the top, from which you look abroad upon a wide landscape, not beautiful, perhaps, but broad and breezy, rich fields and low hills and vacant sea. To the right lies the village, with its church built upon a knoll in the rich plain, and its houses, gray, red, and blue, as the topping of chill bluish slate or rough-red generous tile predominates, clinging about the little height. Cornfields wave and nestle round this centre of rural population, and behind are the hills of Forfarshire, and a farther line of the Grampians, half seen among the mists. The softly swelling heights of the Lomonds lie in the nearer distance, and in the foreground the Eden sweeps darkly blue, with a line of breakers showing the bar at its mouth, toward the low sand-hills and stormy waters of St. Andrews Bay, a place in which no ship likes to find itself ; while over the low sweep of the sands St. Andrews itself stands misty and fine, its long line of cliff and tower and piled houses ending in the jagged edge of the ruined castle, and the tall mystery of St. Rule's—the square tower which baffles archæology. Such is the scene, rural and fresh and green, with a somewhat chill tone of color, and many a token of the winds in the bare anatomy and shivering branches of the trees, and with no great amount of beauty to boast of : yet ever full of attraction and suggestion, as such a width of firmament, such a great circle of horizon, such variety of sea and land and hills and towers must ever be.

Through the door-way in the wall, which is rich with rough but effective ornamentation, boldly cut string-courses, which look as if there might once have been some kind of fortification to be supported, you enter a little court, from which the house opens—a square court, turfed and green, and containing a well and an old thorn-tree. The ruined portion of the house, roofless and mouldering, is on the east side ; the habitable part on the west, an oblong block of building ; and at the well, on the day when this history opens, two figures, one old, one young, both full in the gleam of westering sunshine which breaks over the wall. One-half of the court is in deepest shade, but this all bright, so bright that the girl shades her eyes with one hand, while with the other she pumps water into the old woman's pail, who stands with arms a-kimbo, shaking her head, and giving vent to that murmur of remonstrative disapproval, inarticulate yet very expressive, which is made by the tongue against the palate.

"Tt-tt-tt," says old Bell. "If ever there was a masterful miss and an ill-willy, and ane that will have her ain way!"

"How can I be masterful and a miss too?" said the girl, laughing. Her arm grew tired, however, with the pumping, and she left off before the vessel was half full. "There!" she said, "I'll cry on Jeanie to do the rest for you. I'm tired now."

"Oh, Miss Margret! but you need not cry upon Jeanie. I am fit enough, though I'm old, to do that much for mysel'."

"It's the sun has got into my eyes," said the

girl; and she strayed away into the shade, and seated herself upon a heavy old wooden chair that had been placed close to the door. The sun would not have seemed unbearably hot to any one accustomed to his warmer sway; but Margaret Leslie was not used to overmuch sunshine, and what she called the glare fatigued her. Such a mild glare as it was—a suffusion of soft light, more regretful at giving so little than triumphant in delight over its universal victory! It had been rainy weather, and the light had a wistful suddenness in it, like a smile in wet eyes. Margaret withdrew into the shade. She was a girl of seventeen or so, the only daughter of this old gray house, the only blossom of youth about it except Jeanie in the kitchen, whom she did not "cry on" to help old Bell—not so much because old Bell declined the help, but because she herself forgot next moment all about it. Margaret had no idea that to say she would "cry upon" Jeanie was not the best English in the world. She was as entirely and honestly of the soil as her maid was; a little more careful, perhaps, of her dialect; not "broad" indeed, in her use of the vernacular, because of the old father up-stairs, but with an accent which would make a young lady of Fife of the present day shiver, and a proud and determined aversion to the "high English" which only disapproving visitors ever spoke—ladies who looked with alarm upon her, suggesting schools and governesses. Nowhere could there have been found a more utterly neglected girl than Margaret, whom nobody, except old Bell, had ever taken any care of, all her life. Bell had been very careful of her—had kept her feet warm and her head cool, had seen that she ate her porridge all the mornings of her childhood, and that there were no holes in her stockings; but what more could Bell do? She discoursed her young mistress continually, putting all kinds of homely wisdom into her head; but she could not teach her French, or to play the "piany," which were the only accomplishments of which Bell was even aware.

"It's no my fault," the old woman said, putting out her open palms with a natural gesture of mild despair. "If I were to speak till I was hoarse (and so I have), what would that do to mend the maitter? The mainster he turns a deaf ear, though I was to charm ever so wisely; and Miss Margret hersel'—oh, Miss Margret hersel', if she could learn a' that a young leddy should, in twa minutes by the clock, it might be done; but hold her to one thing I canna—it wants somebody with more authority than me; and a bonny creature like that, and with a fortune coming till her from her mother! How is she ever to learn the piany, or a word but broad Scots out here?"

Little Margaret cared for such lamentations. She sat softly swinging the heavy chair against the wall, which was not an easy thing to do. She had not the aspect or physiognomy adapted for a hoyden; her features were small and refined; her color more pale than warm, lighted up by evanescent rose-flushes, but never brilliant; her hair singularly fine in texture and abundant in quantity, but of no tint more pronounced than brown, the most ordinary and commonplace of shades. Her face was a cloudy, shadowy little face, but possessed by a smile which came and went in the suddenest way, brightening her and

everything about her. No particular art of the toilet aided or hindered the prettiness of her little slight figure. If she was not as God made her, she was at least as Miss Buist in the village made her—in a dress of blue serge, as near the fashion as possible, of which the peculiarity was that it was rather tight where it ought to be loose, and loose where it ought to be tight. But Margaret's soul had not been awakened to the point of dress, and so long as it did not hurt, she minded little. Her shoes were made, and strongly made, by the village shoemaker; everything about her was of the soil. When she had swung her chair to the wall, she let it drop back again to its place, and swallowed a little yawn as she watched the water brim into the pail. "What will I do, Bell?" she said. "What will I do next, Bell?"

(If any one thinks that Margaret ought to have said, "What shall I do?" they are to remember that this is not how we use our verbs in the kingdom of Fife.)

"Oh, Miss Margret! if you would but do one thing, just wan thing, without changin' for wan hour by the clock!"

"You've been saying that as long as I can mind. You, you never change, and that's why I like to be aye changing. There are so few things to do in the afternoon. The morning's better—there's something in the air. I'm always content in the morning."

"Eh ay! you're very content, flichterin' about like the birds among the trees, wan moment on this branch, the ither on that; but the afternoon, Miss Margret, the afternoon's the time for rest—if you've been doing onything the fore part of the day."

"If you want to rest," said Margaret; "you, perhaps, Bell, that are getting old, and papa—I've seen him sleepin'. Figure such a thing! Sleepin'! with the sun in the sky!"

"I can figure it real well," said Bell; "it's no often a poor body gets the chance: but just to close your eyes in the drowsy time, when a's well redd up, the fire burning steady, and the kettle near the boil, and pussy bumming by your side, ah, that's pleasant! it's a kind o' glimmer o' heaven."

"Heaven! the kettle on the boil, and pussy—that's a funny heaven," said Margaret, with a laugh.

"Weel, maybe it's ower maiteerial an image; but we're poor fleshly creatures; and I was meaning a Sawbath afternoon, when you've come hame from the kirk, your Bible at hand, and a' sae quiet," said Bell, amending her first flight. "Jeanie stepping saft about the place, waiting till it's time to mask the tea, and auld John on the other side of the fire, and nothing to do but to thank your Maker for a' his mercies and think upon the sermon—if it was a sound sermon," Bell added, after a pause, taking up her pail; "for I wouldna say they're a' of the kind that ye would like to mind and think upon in a Sawbath afternoon in the gloamin'. Miss Margret, what do you say to run up the stair and see if your papaw's wanting onything? That would aye be something to do."

"Oh, Bell, if you only had more imagination! You always tell me to run and see if papa is wanting anything: and he never wants anything, except, perhaps, a book from the high shelf, where they're all Greek, and I have to climb up upon the steps, and get no good."

"And whase fault's that?" said Bell, reproachfully. She had set down the pail again and paused, looking with mournful eyes at the young creature seventeen years old, who did not know what to do with herself. "Whase fault's that? Did I no beg ye on my bended knees to learn your French book?—a' wee words, as easy! I could have learned it mysel'; and then ye would have had a' the shelfs and a' the books open to you, and your papaw's learnin' at your finger's-end."

"Do you think French and Greek are the same?" cried Margaret. "Why, they're different print even—the a b c 's different; they are no more like the same thing than you and me."

"I'm no saying they're just the same," said Bell, a little discomfited. "One thing's aye different from another. When I was learnin' it was aw, bay, say that they learned me, no clippit and short like your English. But the creature kens something after a'," she said to herself as she went in-doors with her pail. "A thing like that, with a' her wits about her, canna be near a learned man without learning something. But no a note o' the piany!" Bell said, with a real sense of humiliation. For that want what could make up?

Margaret was left alone in the little court, and she soon tired of being alone. When she had remained there for about five minutes, watching the sun shine upon the ruin opposite to her, and print all the irregularities of the wall which connected it with the house upon the broken turf of the court, she got up suddenly and went upstairs. Musing and dreaming were the only things upon which she could spend with pleasure more than "twa minutes by the clock," as Bell said. She would read, indeed, as long as any one pleased, but that was an unprofitable exercise, and tended to nothing; for what was it all but foolish stories and daft-like poetry, and play-acting and nonsense? These things were naught in the estimation of the people in the house who were anxious about Margaret's education. The only member of the household who took no thought of her education at all was the master, who sat up-stairs in solitary state. Even Jeanie, the handmaiden in the kitchen, was very anxious on Miss Peggy's account. She wanted to see her young mistress go to balls, and have pretty dresses from Edinburgh, and enjoy herself. What was the use of being bonny and young if you stayed aye in one auld house and nobody saw ye? Jeanie asked herself. And this was a question which much disturbed and occupied her mind. Old John, too, who was Bell's husband, and the male factotum, as she was the female, had his anxieties about Miss Peggy. When she began to want to have pairties and young folk about her, what should they all do? John demanded. He would be willing, and so would Bell, to "put themselves about" to the utmost; but what was to be done for chiney and plate? Wan dozen of everything might be enough for the family, but what would that do for a pairty? So that John's mind was disturbed also. But old Sir Ludovic, what did he mind? Give him a book, and ye might mine the cellars, and throw your best bomb-shells at

the tower, and he would never hear ye. Such was the general opinion of the house.

There was no entrance-hall in this primitive house; but only a little space at the "stair-foot," the bottom of the well through which the spiral staircase wound its narrow way; but though it was dark, and the twist of the unprotected steps a little alarming to a stranger, Margaret ran up as lightly as a bird. At about half the height of an ordinary flight of stairs there were two doors close to each other, forming a little angle. One of these Margaret pushed open softly. It led into a long room, running all the length of the building, panelled wherever the wall was visible, and painted white, as in a French house: one side, however, was covered entirely with book-shelves. The depth of the recesses in which the small windows were embedded showed the thickness of the wall. One at each end and one in the middle were all that lighted the long room, two or three others which had belonged to the original plan having been blocked up on account of the window tax, that vexatious impost. In the centre of the room stood a large old japanned screen, stretched almost across the whole breadth, and dividing it into two. On the south side, into which the door opened, a large writing-table was placed upon the old and much-worn Turkey-carpet which covered the middle of the floor; and seated at this, but with his back to the sunshine, which was pouring in, sat an old man in a chair, reading. The window behind him and the window in the side each poured its stream of sunshine between the deep cuttings of the ancient walls, five or six feet thick, but neither of these rays of warmth and light touched this solitary inhabitant. He was so much absorbed in his reading that he did not hear the door open. Margaret came in behind him and stood in the sunshine, the impersonation of youth —the light catching her at all points, gleaming in her eyes, bringing color to her cheek, making her collar and the edge of white round her hands blaze against the darkness of her dress. But no ray touched the old man in his chair. He was as still as if he had been cut out of gray marble, his face motionless, the movement of his eyes as he read, the unfrequent movement necessary to turn the page, being all the sign of life about him. The book he was reading was a large old folio, propped up upon a sort of reading-desk in front of him. A large wide garment, something between a long coat and a dressing-gown, of dark-colored and much-worn velvet, and wrapped round his thin person, gave it some dignity; and he wore a little black velvet skull-cap, which made his fine head and thin white locks imposing. Margaret stood breathless, making no sound for a moment, and then said, suddenly, "You look like Archimage in the cave, papa!"

The old man made a faint movement of surprise; a wrinkle of impatience came into his forehead, a momentary smile to his lip. "Yes, yes, my little Peggy; go and play," he said. She stood for a moment behind him, hesitating, looking round her with eager eyes in search of something, anything, to interest her. She was neither surprised nor wounded to find herself thus summarily disposed of: she was used to it. Finally, seeing nothing likely to interest her, Margaret turned lightly away, and disappeared through a second door which was close to the one by which she had entered. This brought her into a small rounded room, with one window, a little white-panelled Scotch-French boudoir, with a high mantel-piece and small antique furniture —a little square of Turkey-carpet on the floor, a pretty old marquetry cabinet, and some high-backed chairs of the same covered with brocaded silk from some great-grandmother's gown. Margaret knew nothing about the value of these old furnishings. She thought the walnut-wood table, with its elaborate clustered legs, a much finer article, though it was often in her way. There were some old pictures on the walls, some books, and more ornament and grace than in all the rest of the house put together. What did Margaret care? She sang an old tune to herself, drumming with her fingers upon the window-sill, and thinking what she should do. Then she drew open a drawer in the cabinet and took from it some old fancy-work, faded but fine, with a bundle of wools and silks in the same condition. It was the relic of some old lady's industry (Lady Jean, old Bell said; but how should she know?) which had been found in one of the periodical routings out of old presses and drawers in which Margaret delighted. The linen on which the work was half done was yellow and the colors faded, but it had struck the girl's fancy, and she had carried it off with her to finish (this time a hundred years, Bell said, satirically). Margaret took it out now and laid it on the table; then she went flying up the stone stairs, and all over the rooms, to find her thimble and her scissors, which were not to be found.

And while she tries to find these, what can we do better than let the reader know who old Sir Ludovic was, and how he came to have so young a child? Margaret's foot flying up-stairs, and the sound she made of doors and drawers opening, and now an impatient exclamation (for the way thimbles hide themselves and refuse to be found!) and now a little snatch of song, was all that was audible in the still old house. Bell and John and Jeanie in the kitchen had their cracks, indeed, as they took their tea; but sounds did not travel easily up the spiral stair, and the long room with its one inhabitant was as void of all movement as was the vacant little white-panelled chamber with Lady Jean's old work thrown on the table. All silence, languor, stillness; and yet one creature in the house to whom stillness was as death.

CHAPTER II.

THE Leslies had been settled at Earl's-hall since before the memory of man. Now they were related to other Leslies in Fife; and out of it, I do not pretend to say. But this family itself was old enough to have carried any amount of honors, much less the poor baronetcy which was all it had got out of the sometimes lavish hand of fame. The family was old enough to have supported a dukedom, but not rich enough. Sir Ludovic had got but a moderate fortune from his father, and that which he would transmit to his son would be considerably less than moderate. Indeed, it was not worth calling a fortune at all. When the Baronet began his life, the policy was a real policy, a pretty small park enough, with its girdle of hardy trees. No tur-

nip-field then thrust its plebeian presence and odor between the house and its own woods; the garden was kept up with care, the other part of the house was still habitable and inhabited, and the greatest people in the country did not scorn to dine and dance in the rooms so well adapted for either purpose. But of all these good things, the rooms and old Sir Ludovic were all that remained. He had not done any particular harm at any time, nor had he wasted his means in lavish living, and nobody was so much surprised as he when his money was found to have been spent. "What have I done with it?" he had asked all his life. But nobody could tell; he had no expensive tastes—indeed, he had no tastes at all, except for books, and his own library was a very good one. It was true, he had indulged in three wives and three families, which was inconsiderate, but each of the wives had, greatly to the comfort of her respective children, possessed something of her own. Time went and came, however, taking these ladies away in succession, but leaving Sir Ludovic still in his great high-backed chair, older, but otherwise not much different from what he had ever been. The eldest son, also called Ludovic, was the only one now surviving of the first marriage. He was a man of forty-five, with a family of his own; a hard-working lawyer in Edinburgh, with no great income to keep up his position, and little disposed to welcome the burden of his father's little title when it should come. A baronetcy, and an old house altogether uninhabitable by a family, and entirely out of modern fashion— what should he make of these additions when his father died? He had made his own way as much as if he had been a poor school-master's son, instead of the heir of an ancient and important family. He could not even take his children home to the old place, or give them any associations with it, for there was no room at Earl's-hall. "Your father might as well be in Russia," his wife sometimes said when she wanted a change for a little boy who was delicate. And privately, Mr. Leslie had made up his mind to sell the place, though it had been so long in the family, when Sir Ludovic died.

Of the second family there were two remaining, two daughters, one of whom had been married and had settled in England; the other, who had not married, living with her. They were twins, and some five years younger than their elder brother. And neither did they come often to Earl's-hall. The same objection was in everybody's way—there was no room for them. And Sir Ludovic disliked letter-writing. They came occasionally to see their father, and to hold up their hands and shake their heads at the way in which little Margaret was being brought up. But what could these ladies do? To live at Earl's-hall was impossible, and to go and stay in a little cottage in the Kirkton, all for the sake of a small step-sister, and without even any security that they could really be of any use to her, was something more of a test than their lukewarm family affection could bear. And they hesitated about recommending a governess; for with an old gentleman so much addicted to marriage, who could tell what might happen? Though he was seventy-five, he was the same man as ever, and very fascinating when he chose to exert himself; and to have a new Lady Leslie would be a still greater horror than to have a young rustic for a step-sister. And then the child would be rich. It does not require much learning, as Mrs. Hardcastle says, to spend fifteen hundred a year.

So that Margaret was left alone. Her mother had been the richest of all Sir Ludovic's wives. She had been — more wonderful still — a young beauty, courted and flattered, and how it was that she passed over all her younger admirers and fixed upon a man of fifty-five, a poor old Scotch baronet, nobody could divine. But she did so, and came home with him to Earl's-hall, and brightened it a while with her youth and her wealth, and would have done wonders for the old house. Nothing less had been intended than to rebuild the ruin, though Sir Ludovic himself discouraged this, as the house, he reminded her, must pass into other hands. But poor Lady Leslie's fine projects came to a premature end, by means of a bad cold which she caught just after her little girl was born. She died, and the last gleam of prosperity died away with her. Margaret, it was true, was rich, and the allowance her trustees made her was no small help even now to the impoverished household; though, indeed, the trouble these trustees gave, her father thought, was more than the money was worth. They wrote to Sir Ludovic about her education till he was roused to swear at, though not to profit by, the perpetual remonstrance.

"Education! what would they have at her age? A mere child," he said.

"Eh, Sir Ludovic! but she's sixteen," Bell said, who was the only one in the house who ever ventured to keep up an argument with her old master.

"Pshaw!" the old man said; for what is sixteen to seventy-five? And besides, did he not see her before him a slim stripling of a girl, flitting about in perpetual motion, a singing voice, a dancing step, a creature never in the same place, as Bell said, for "twa minutes by the clock?" What does that kind of small thing want with education? Sir Ludovic liked her better without it, and so perhaps would most people; for are not the fresh wonder, curiosity, and intelligent ignorance of a child its most captivating qualities? If we could but venture to take the good of them with a clear conscience and no thought of what the child will say to us when it ceases to be a child! Sir Ludovic had this courage. He did not think much of his duties to Margaret. She had duties to him—to be always pretty and cheerful, not to speak too broad Scotch, to get his books down for him when he wanted them, to put everything ready on his table, pens, pencils, and note-book, in case he should want to write something (which he never did), and to be neat and in order at mealtimes. In this one particular he certainly did his duty. Margaret had not the privilege of being untidy, which is allowed to most neglected heroines. Sir Ludovic required scrupulous neatness, hair that shone, and garments that were spotless, and ribbons as fresh as the day. Should not we all like just such a creature about us, fair as a new-blown rose, with a voice so toned and harmonious, a step with rhythm in it, a pair of eyes running over with understanding and interest, and no education to speak of? If only the

creature would not arise upon us after and upbraid us for its want of knowledge! But of this risk Sir Ludovic never dreamed. She could read, he supposed, for he saw her reading; and she could write, he knew, for he had seen her do it. What could they want more?

Thus they lived, not uncontented, from year to year. No one told Margaret to read, but she did so, perhaps with all the more pleasure because nobody told her. She read all the best poetry that is written in English, and a great deal that was not the best. She was so great in history that she had been a Lancastrian and taken an active, even violent, part on the side of her namesake, Margaret of Anjou, as long as she could remember—a more violent part even than she took for Queen Mary, though to that also she was bound as a true Scot. She had read Clarendon and Sir Thomas Brown, and Burton on "Melancholy" (not caring much for that) and an old translation of Froissart, and "Paul and Virginia," and Madame Cottin's "Elizabeth," and "Don Quixote," all in translations; so that her range was tolerably wide; and everything came natural to Margaret, the great and the small. Needless to say that all Sir Walter was hers by nature, as what well-conditioned Scots person of seventeen has not possessed our homelier Shakspeare from his or her cradle? Whether she loved best the Spanish Don, or Lord Falkland, or Sir Kenneth in the "Talisman," was not to her mind perfectly clear. In this respect she was not so sure about Shakspeare. His lovers and heroes did not satisfy her youthful requirements; she loved Henry the Fifth, and Faulconbridge, and Benedick, but was not at all satisfied about the relations between Hamlet and Ophelia, naturally standing by her own side, and thinking that poor maiden badly used: which is as much as to say that the spell of story was still strong upon her, though the poetry went to her head all the same. These were the books Sir Ludovic saw her reading—but he took no notice and no oversight. He did not think of her at all as a responsible creature to be affected one way or other by what she read, or as undergoing any process of training for the future. The future! what is that at seventy-five? especially to a man who amiably and without evil intention has always found himself the centre of the world! It is like the future of a child—to-morrow. He did not want to pry any farther. What was to come, would come without any intervention of his. Had his child been penniless, probably he would have thought it necessary to remember that in all probability (as he expressed it) she would survive him. But she was rich, and where was the need of thinking? The great thing was that there was no room. The bedrooms in the house were so few. Where could they put a governess, he asked Bell; and even Bell, though full of resources, could not reply. There was one good-sized room which Sir Ludovic himself occupied, and another quaint small panelled chamber in which Margaret was very snug and cosy, but beyond these scarcely any bedchamber in the house was in a proper state of repair. What could any one say against so evident a fact? "We could dine fifty folk," Bell said, half proudly, half sadly, "and we could gie a grand ball after that up the stair; but pit up one single gentleman that is no very particular, that's all we could do beside."

It was a curious state of affairs. The two long rooms, one above the other, were the whole house.

Of the wealth which Margaret was to inherit, she knew absolutely nothing. There was a house "in England," a vague description which the girl had never much inquired into, seeing that till her twenty-first birthday it was very unlikely that she would have anything whatever to do with it. In the mean time it served a very pleasant purpose in her life. It was the scene of so many dreams and visions of that future which was everything to Margaret, that it could not be said to be an unknown place. She built it and furnished it, and planted trees and invented glades about the unrevealed place, such as in reality it could not boast of. Everything that she thought most beautiful in her small experience of things, or which she found in her considerable experience of books, she placed in this distant mansion, where all manner of pleasant verdure was, which was not to be found in Scotland, flowers and fruits, and green lawns, and abundant foliage, and sunshine such as never shone in Fife. She made pictures of it, and dreamed dreams, but no troublesome dash of reality disturbed the vision. She was the lady of the manor, a title which pleased her fancy hugely, and which she wove into many a fancy; but it was all as visionary as if she had found the Grange in a novel and appropriated it.

If anything could have been more unlike an English manor-house than the quaint old dwelling in which her childhood had been passed, it was the dreams Margaret wove of her future home. Claude Melnotte's palace was more like that sunshiny fancy. No castle in Spain or in the air was ever more unreal. There wants no education to teach a girl how to dream, and the less she knows, the more gorgeous and delightful becomes the imagination. But naturally this was a branch of her training totally unknown to everybody connected with her. Sir Ludovic knew a great deal, but had not a notion of that branch of human effort; neither, it may well be supposed, did Bell, though her instincts were clearer. When she saw her young mistress sit abstracted, her eyes far away, a half smile on her lips, Bell knew that there must be something going on within the small head. What was it? There were no young men, or, as Bell called them, "lauds," about that could have caught her youthful eye. Bell knew that the romance of life begins early, and had some glimmering of recollection that before any "lauds" appear on the horizon in reality, there are flutters of anticipation in maiden souls, dreams of being wooed like the rest, "respectit like the lave." But Margaret had seen none of the rural wooings which are a recognized institution in Scotland, those knocks at the window and whispers at the door, which add the charm of mystery to the never-ending romance. Bell had taken care even that Jeanie's "laud" and his evening visits should be kept out of the young lady's notice. But then, if it was not the glimmer of poetic love that flickered on the horizon, what was it? And except Bell, and perhaps Jeanie, no one had noticed the soft abstracted look that sometimes stole into Margaret's eyes, or knew her capacity for dreams. Mr. Leslie, when he came, took but little notice of his step-sister. He had a daughter who was older than she, indeed Margaret had become a great-aunt, to the amusement of everybody, during the previous winter. Her brother took very little notice of her. When he looked at her, he breathed a private thanksgiving that she was provided for, and would not be an additional burden upon him when his father died. It was only when Sir Ludovic was ill or in difficulty, that Mr. Leslie came, and the reflection, "Thank Heaven I have not the lassie to think of," was the foremost sentiment in his breast. He had plenty of his own to exhaust all the fund of interest in his heart. She had no business ever to have been, this young creature whose presence in the old house made a certain difference naturally in all the arrangements; but, being there, the chief fact was this fortunate one that she was provided for. So far as Margaret was concerned, this was the only thing in his thoughts.

As for Mrs. Bellingham and her sister, Miss Leslie, they lived a long way from Fife. They were ladies who travelled a great deal, and spent all they had to spend in making their life pleasant. Mrs. Bellingham was childless, and a widow, so that her married life did not count for much, though she herself regarded the elevation it gave her with much contentment. Now and then, instead of going to Switzerland or the Italian lakes, they would come to Scotland, making expeditions into the Highlands, and preserving everywhere their character as British tourists. Once there had been some question between them of inviting Margaret to accompany them on one of these expeditions, which it was thought might do her good and improve her manners, and give her a little acquaintance with the world. But on more mature reflection, it became apparent that the maid whom the two ladies shared between them, when on their travels, was by no means disposed to undertake the packing and toilet of a third.

"Many a girl would be glad to give a little assistance herself rather than trouble, for the chance of such a treat," Miss Leslie said, who was the weak-minded sister; "and in that way I really think we might manage—if dear Margaret was a sensible girl."

"Margaret is not a sensible girl, and we could not manage at all, and I won't have Forrester put about," Mrs. Bellingham said, who took the management of everything upon her. "Besides, a girl—she would be an endless trouble to you and me. We should have to change our route to let her see this thing and that thing, and you would be afraid she did not enjoy herself, and the Lord knows what besides. There are many things in conversation even that have to be stopped before a girl. No, no; it would never do."

And thus one hope for Margaret's improvement came to an end. A similar failure happened about the same time in Edinburgh. When Mrs. Ludovic got that German governess, who was at once her pride and her dread, she was so much affected by the grandeur and superiority as to suggest an arrangement to her husband by which his little sister might be benefited.

"It appears to me that we, who have such advantages, ought, perhaps, to share them a little with others that are not so well off. There is little Margaret at the Hall. What do you think? Sir Ludovic might send her to us to share the children's lessons. Fräulein is an expensive luxury, and a little help with her salary would be no harm. And if Margaret had six months with our girls, it would do her a great deal of good ; if it was only to learn German—"

"What does she want with German? What good would it do her to learn German?" said Ludovic, testily.

"Well, I'm sure, Ludovic, that's not an easy question. I never thought you were one to ask for an immediate result. I am sure you all say learning anything is an advantage, whether the thing they learn is any use or not. I do not always see it myself," said Mrs. Leslie ; "but many is the time I've heard you all say so. And if we could do Margaret a good turn, and at the same time save something on our own expenses—"

"Do Margaret a good turn! I do not see what claim she has on me. She has plenty of people to look after her if they would do their duty. Trustees of her money, and her mother's relations, not to speak of my father himself, who has plenty of energy left when you cross him. Indeed, if you come to that, Jane and Grace are nearer to her than I."

"Because the second is nearer the third than the first is," Mrs. Ludovic said, who had some sense of humor. But she added, "Well! I never make any attempt to fathom you Leslies but I was baffled. I think there was never a set of people like you. I hope I'll never be so left to myself as to try again."

"We Leslies! The most of the Leslies nowadays are your own bairns."

"That's true, and more's the pity," said the lady, discharging an arrow as she went away.

And thus another attempt to do something for Margaret came to nothing. Everything failed. It was nobody's business, perhaps. The trustees were strangers who did not know. Her father was old, and did not care to be troubled, and liked her best as she was. Her brothers and sisters, what had they to do with it? They were not their little sister's keeper. So between them all she was left to grow as she pleased, like a flower or a weed, nobody responsible for her, whatever might happen. Even a School Board, had there been one in the parish, what right would it have had to interfere?

CHAPTER III.

MARGARET searched a whole half-hour for her thimble, which was found at the end of that time in the pocket of a dress which she had not worn for a week ; but when she had found it, she no longer thought of Lady Jean's work. That purpose had faded altogether from her mind. She forgot even what she wanted the thimble for, and being seized with a sudden fancy for remedying the disorder of her drawers, immediately set to work to do so, with a zeal more fervent than discreet ; for as soon as she had turned the top drawer out, scattering all her light possessions, her collars and ribbons and bits of lace, out upon her bed, she was summoned by the bell for dinner, and thought of them no more. Margaret hastily arranged her hair, put on a bit of fresh ribbon, and rushed down-stairs ; for to keep Sir Ludovic waiting was a sin beyond excuse. On the other side of the great japanned screen which divided the room into two, stood the table, laid with scrupulous care, and served by John in his rusty but trim and sober "blacks," with a gravity that would not have misbecome an archbishop. Sir Ludovic had put down his book, he had washed his hands, and he was ready. He stood dignified and serious, almost as serious as John himself in the centre of the room, by the edge of the screen. *J'ai failli attendre* might be read in the curve above his eyebrows ; and yet he received his erring child with perfect temper, which was more than could be said for John, who gloomed at her from under his heavy eyebrows.

"Oh, papa, I am sorry," Margaret began. "I was busy—"

"If you were busy, that is no reason for being sorry ; but you should not forget hours—they are our best guide in life," said her father. But he was not angry ; he took her by the hand and led her in, handing her to her seat with stately ceremony. This daily ceremonial, which Margaret hated, and would have done anything to avoid, was the means by which Sir Ludovic every day made his claim of high-breeding and unforgotten courtliness of demeanor, in presence of men and angels. Whosoever might think he had forgotten what was due to his daughter as a young lady and a Leslie, and what was due to himself as a gentleman of the old school, not a modern man of no manners, here was his answer. John looked on at this solemnity with gloomy interest ; but Margaret hated it. She reddened all over her youthful countenance, brow and throat. Between the two old men she moved, passive but resentful, to her seat, and slid into it the moment her father released her, with ungrateful haste to get done with the disagreeable ceremony. They were "making a fool of her," Margaret thought. Though it occurred every evening, she never got less impatient of this formula. Then Sir Ludovic took his own place. He was not tall, but of an imposing appearance, now that he was fully visible. In the other half of the room, where all his work was done, he sat invariably with his back to the light. But here he was fully revealed. His white locks surrounded a fine and remarkable face, in which every line seemed drawn on ivory. He had no color save in his lips, and the wonderful undimmed dark eyes, darkly lashed and eyebrowed, which shone in all the lustre of youth. With those eyes Sir Ludovic could do anything—"wile a bird from the tree," old Bell said ; and, indeed, it was his eyes which had beguiled Margaret's mother, and brought her to this old-world place. But Margaret was used to them ; perhaps she had not that adoring love for her father which many girls have ; and especially at dinner, after the little ceremony we have recorded, she was more than indifferent to, she was resentful of his attractions. At that age he might have known better than "to make a fool," before John, day after day, of his little girl.

This day, however, the dinner went on harmoniously enough ; for Margaret never ventured to show her resentment, except by the sudden angry flush, which her father took for sensitiveness and quickly moved feeling. He talked to her a little with kind condescension, as to a child.

"You were busy, you said; let us hear, my little Peggy, what the busy-ness was."

"I was doing—a great many things, papa."

"Ah! people who do a great many things all at once are apt to get into confusion. I would do one thing, just one thing at a time, my Peggy, if I were a little girl."

"Papa!" said Margaret, with another wave of color passing over her, "indeed, if you would look at me, you would see that I am not a little girl."

"Yes, you have grown a great deal lately, my dear. I beg your pardon. It is hard to teach an old person like myself where babyhood ends. You see, I like to think that you are a little girl. Eh, John? we like something young in the house; the younger the better—"

"No me, Sir Ludovic," said John.

He was very laconic, wasting no words; and Margaret felt that he disapproved of her youth altogether. But this restored her to herself, and she laughed. For John, though morose in outward aspect, was, as she very well knew, her slave actually. This made her laugh, and the two old men liked the laugh. It brought a corresponding light into Sir Ludovic's fine eyes, and it melted a little the morose muscles about John's closely shut mouth.

"But I am not so very young," she said. "Jeannie's sister, who is just my age, has been in a place for a long time; and most people are considered grown-up at my age. You ought not to make a fool of me."

"My little Peggy," said Sir Ludovic, "that is an incorrect expression. Nobody could make a fool of you except yourself. It is Scotch, dear, very Scotch, which is a thing your sisters Jean and Grace have already often warned me against. You are very Scotch, they tell me."

"Set them up!" ejaculated old John, under his breath.

Margaret reddened with ready wrath.

"And I am Scotch," she said. "How could I speak otherwise? They were always going on about something. Either it was my shoulders, or it was my hair, or it was my tongue—"

"Your tongue! My Peggy, your idioms are strange, it must be allowed; but never mind. What had they to say against your hair? It is very pretty hair. I don't see any ground to find fault there."

"Oh, it was not in the fashion," said Margaret. "You know, papa, you like it smooth, and that is not the fashion now; it ought to be all towzy, like my little dog, and hanging in my eyes."

"The Lord preserve us!" said old John. He was in the habit of giving utterance to his sentiments as constrained by some internal movement *plus fort que lui;* and no one ever interfered with this habit of his. "What next?" said the old man, with a shrug of his shoulders behind his master's chair.

"Then you must continue to be old-fashioned so long as I live," said Sir Ludovic. "Your sisters are very well-meaning women, my Peggy; but even when you are as clever as Mrs. Bellingham and as wise as Miss Leslie, you will not have fathomed everything. We'll leave the

philosophy to them, my little woman, and you and I will manage the hair-dressing. That is evidently the point in which our genius lies."

Margaret looked up, somewhat jealously, to see whether she was again being made "a fool of;" but as no such intention appeared in her father's face, she returned to the consideration of her dinner. It was not a heavy meal. A little fish—"haddies," such as were never found but in the Firth, little milk-white flounders, the very favorites of the sea, or the homely herring, commonest, cheapest, and best of fish. But then, perhaps, they require to be cooked as Bell knew how to cook them. No expensive exotic salmon, turbot, or other aristocrat of the waters ever came to Sir Ludovic's table. Let them be for the vulgar rich, who knew no better. The native product of his own coasts was good enough, he would say, in mock humility, for him. And then came one savory dish of the old Scotch *cuisine* now falling out of knowledge; no vulgar dainty of the haggis kind, but stews and *ragoûts* which the best of *chefs* would not disdain. This was all; the *plat doux* has never been a regular concomitant of a Scotch dinner; and Sir Ludovic was a small eater, and had his digestion to consider. It was not, therefore, a very lengthened meal; and as six o'clock was the dinner-hour at Earl's-hall, there were still several long hours of sunshine to be got through before night came.

Now was the time when Margaret felt what it was to be alone. The long summer evening, loveliest, most wistful, and lingering hour of all the day, when something in the heart demands happiness, demands that which is unattainable one way or another—is it possible to be young, to be void of care, to possess all the elements of happiness, without wishing for something more, a visionary climax, another sweetness in those soft, lingering, visionary hours? Margaret did not know what she wanted, but she wanted something. She could not rest contained as her father did, to sit over a book and see through the west window (when he chanced to look up) the flush of the sunset glories. To feel that all this was going on in the sky, and nothing going on within, nor anything that concerned herself in earth and heaven, was not to be borne.

The little withdrawing-room—the East Chamber, as it was called, though its window faced to the south—was already all dim, deserted by the sunshine. Lady Jean's work lay on the table, where Margaret had thrown it in the afternoon, but nothing living, nothing that could return glance for glance and word for word. It was but seven o'clock, and it would be ten o'clock, ten at the earliest, before night began to fall. Margaret got her hat and ran down-stairs. She did not know what she should do, but something she must do. The little court was by this time quite abandoned by the sunshine, the body of the house lying between it and the west; but all the sky overhead was warm with pink and purple, and Bell was seated outside, with her knitting dropped upon her lap. Jeannie had gone out to milk the cow; and even old John had strolled forth with his hands behind him, to see, he said, how the "pitawties" were getting on. The "pitawties" would have got on just as well without his supervision, but who could resist the loveliness of the evening light?

"Our John he's awa', like Isaac, to meditate among the fields at even-tide," Bell said. "Eh, but it's an auld custom that! and nae doubt auld Sawra, the auld mither, would sit out at the ha' door, and ponder in her mind just like me."

"But John is not your son, Bell," said Margaret, with the literal understanding of youth.

"Na, I never had a son, Miss Margret, naething but wan daughter, and she's been married and gone from me this twenty years. Eh, my dear, we think muckle of our bairns, but they think little and little enough of us. I might as well have had nane at all but for the thought."

To this Margaret made no reply, her mind not taking in the maternal relation. She stood musing, with her eyes afar, while Bell went on:

"They say a woman has no after-pain when her first bairn's born, because of the Virgin Mary, that had but wan. But ay me, I've had mony an after-pain, and her too, poor woman, though no the same kind. I think of her mony a day, Miss Margret, how she would sit and ponder things in her heart. Eh, they would be so ill to understand—till the time came."

Still Margaret said nothing. The old woman pondered the past, but the girl's brain was all throbbing and thrilling with the future. The sound of something coming was in her ears, a ringing, a singing, a general movement and flutter of she knew not what. To Bell the quiet was everything; to Margaret, she herself was the universe, and all the horizon was not too big to hold the rustling pinions and approaching foot-balls of the life to come.

"I think I will take a walk down the road," she said, suddenly, over Bell's head.

"Take a hap with you, in case it should get cauld. Sometimes there's a wind gets up when the sun goes down. And you'll no bide too long, Miss Margret," Bell called after her as she ran lightly away.

Margaret did not care for the wind getting up, nor foresee the possibility of the evening chilliness after the warmth of the day. It was always chilly at night so near the sea; but seventeen years' experience to the contrary had not dispelled Margaret's conviction that as the weather was at one bright moment, so would it always be.

The road down which Margaret went was not very attractive as a road. The hedges were low and the country bare. It is true that even the rigor of Fife farming had not cut down the wild roses, which made two broken lines of exquisite bloom on either side of the way. Long branches all bloomed to the very tips waved about in the soft air, and concealed the fact that the landscape on either side was limited to a potatofield on the right and a turnip-field on the left. But the wild roses were enough for Margaret. Were they not repeated all over the skies in those puffs of snowy vapor tinted to the same rose hue, and in the girl's cheeks, which bloomed as softly, when the exercise, and the flowering of the flowers, and the reflection of the sunset reflections had got into her young veins? The color and sweetness rapt her for a moment in an ecstasy, mere beauty satisfying her as it does a child. But human nature, even in a child, soon wants something more, and in Margaret the demand came very quickly. She forgot the love-

liness all at once, and remembered the something that was wanted, the blank that required filling up. She turned aside into a by-way, along the edge of a cornfield, with a sigh. The corn was not high, as it was but June, and when she turned her face away from the sunset, the world paled all at once all around her.

Margaret went on more slowly, unconscious why. She went on hanging her young head till she came to a brook at the end of the field, over which there was but a plank for a bridge. The brook (she called it a burn) ran between two fields, and on one side of it grew an old ash-tree, its trunk lost among the bushes of the hedge. Here a post, which had been driven into the ground to support the homely bridge, made a kind of seat upon which the wayfarer might pause and look at the homely yet pretty Kirkton, with its old church on the brae. Margaret herself had intended to rest upon this seat. But when she was half-way across the plank, a sudden sound so startled her that she lost her footing; and though she saved herself from plunging into the burn altogether by a despairing grasp at the bushes, yet she got her foot fast imbedded in the damp bank, and there stuck, to her infinite embarrassment and disgust. Some one started from the seat at the sound of the suppressed cry she gave, and rushed to the rescue. It was, need it be said, a young man? yet not exactly of heroic guise.

Margaret, crimson to the hair, and feeling herself the most gawky, the most awkward, the most foolish of distressed damsels, her ungloved hand all torn and pricked with the thorns of the branch which she had caught at, her foot held fast in the tenacious clay, did not know what kind of hoyden, what rude village girl, red and blowzy, she must have looked to the stranger. She looked a nymph out of the poetic woods, a creature out of the poets, a celestial vision to him. He sprang forward, his heart beating, to offer his hand and his assistance. Was it his fault? He feared it was his fault; he had startled her, moving just when she was in the act of crossing the plank. He made her a thousand apologies. It was all his doing; he hoped she would forgive him. He expended himself so in apologies that Margaret felt it necessary to apologize too.

"It was me that was silly," she said. "Generally, I never mind a sudden sound. What should it matter? Nobody would do me harm, and there's no wild beasts, that I should be so silly. Oh, it's nothing; and it was all my fault."

"You are the queen in your own country. There should be nothing in your path to startle you."

"Oh no, I'm not the queen," said Margaret, laughing. "I have to take my chance like other folk. You are a stranger here," she said, with friendly innocence. The fact that she was, if not the queen, as she said, yet at least a princess, the first young lady hereabouts, and known to everybody as such, made her friendly and made her bold. Supremacy has many agreeable accessories. The young man, who had taken off his hat and held it in his hand, half in respect, half in awkwardness, here blushed more deeply than she had done when she saw him first.

"I am not a stranger, Miss Margaret. I am Robert Glen, whom you used to play with when you were a little girl; but I cannot expect you to remember me, for I have been long away."

"Oh, Rob!" she cried. Margaret was delighted. The vivid color came flushing back to her cheeks out of pure pleasure. She held out her hand to him. He had not been so respectful when they had parted, which was ten years ago. "Indeed, I mind you quite well, though I should not have known you after all this long time; but how did you know me?"

"The first moment I saw you," he said, "and there is nothing wonderful in that. There are many like me, but only one Miss Margaret, here or anywhere else."

The last words he murmured in an undertone, but Margaret made them out. She laughed, not in ridicule, but in pleasure, just touched with amusement. How funny to see him again, and that he should know her; and still more funny, though not disagreeable, that he should speak to her so.

"I was vexed," she said, "very vexed that a stranger should see me so, my shoe all dirty and my hand all torn—it looked so strange; but I am not vexed now, since it is only you, and not a stranger. Just look at me—such a figure! and what will Bell say?"

"You have still Bell?"

"Still Bell! who should we have but Bell?" cried Margaret, the idea of such a domestic change as the displacement of Bell never having so much as crossed her fancy. Then she added, quickly, "But tell me, for I have not heard of you for such a long, long time. You went to the college, Rob?"

She said his name unadvisedly in the first impulse; but looking up at him, and seeing him look at her in a way she was unused to, Margaret's countenance flamed once more with a momentary blush. She shrank a little. She said to herself that he was not a little boy now as he used to be, and that she would never call him Rob again.

"Yes, Miss Margaret, I went to the college. I went through all the curriculum, and took my degree sometime ago."

"Then are you a minister now?"

Margaret spoke with a little chill in her tone. She thought that to be a minister implied a withdrawal from life of a very melancholy and serious description, and that she might not be able to keep up easy relations with poor Rob if he had passed that Rubicon. She looked at him earnestly, with a great deal of gravity in her face. Margaret had not known many ministers close at hand, and never any so nearly on a level with her own youthful unimportance as Rob Glen.

"No," he said, shaking his head. "No. My poor mother! I will never give her the pleasure I ought. I am not a minister, and never will be. I say it with sorrow and shame."

"Oh!" cried Margaret, growing so much interested that her breast heaved and her breath came quick. "Oh! and what was that for, Mr. —Rob? You have not done anything wrong?"

"No," he said, with a smile; "nothing wicked, and yet perhaps you will think it wicked. I cannot believe just what everybody else believes. There are papers and things to sign, doctrines—"

Margaret put her hands together timidly and looked into his face.

"You are not an infidel?" she said, with a look of awe and pain.

"No; I am—I don't quite know what. I don't examine too closely, Miss Margaret. I believe as much as I can, and I don't think anybody does more; but I can't sign papers, can I, when I do not know whether they are true or not? I cannot do it. I may be wrong, but I cannot say I believe what I don't believe."

"No," said Margaret, doubtfully. This was something entirely out of her way, and she did not know how to treat it. She made a hurried sweep over her own experiences. "I always think it is because I don't understand," she said; and then, after another pause, "When papa says things I don't understand, I just hold my tongue."

"But I am obliged to say yes or no, and I can't say yes. I hope you will not blame me, Miss Margaret; that would make me very unhappy. I have often thought you were one that would be sure to understand what my position was."

Margaret did not ask herself why it was that she was expected to understand; but she was vaguely flattered that he should think her approbation so important.

"Me! what do I know?" she said. "I have not been at the college, like you. I have never learned anything;" and, for almost the first time, it occurred to Margaret that there might be some reason in the animadversions and lamentations over her ignorance, of her sisters Grace and Jean.

"You know things without learning."

"Oh!—but you are making a fool of me, like papa," cried Margaret. "And what are you doing now, if you are not a minister? You have never been back again till now at the Farm?"

"I am doing just nothing, that is the worst of it. I cannot dig, and to beg I am ashamed."

"Beg!" She looked at him with a merry laugh. He was what Bell would have called "very well put on." Margaret saw, by instinct, though she was without any experience, that Rob Glen could not have been a gentleman; but yet he was well dressed, and very superior to everybody else about the Kirkton. "I suppose you have come home on a visit, and to rest."

"Yes; but, Miss Margaret, all this time your foot is wet and your hand is scratched. Will you come to the house? Shall I go and get you dry shoes from Bell? What can I do?"

"Oh, nothing," said Margaret; "do you think I never got my feet wet before? I will change them when I get in. But I think I will go home now. What have you been doing? Oh, drawing!" she exclaimed, with a cry of delight. She seized the book which he half showed, half withdrew. "Oh, I should like to see it—it is the Kirkton! Oh, I would like to draw like that! Oh," cried Margaret, with a deep-drawn breath, and all her heart in it, "what I would give!" and then she remembered that she had nothing to give, and stopped short, her lips half open, her eyes aflame.

"Will you let me show you how to do it? It would make me so happy. It is as easy as possible. You have only to try."

Margaret did not make any reply in her eagerness. She turned over the book with delight. The sketches were not badly done. There was the Kirkton, breezy and sunny, with its cold tones of blue; there were all the glimpses of Earl's-hall that could be had at a distance; there was the estuary and the sand-banks, and the old pale city on the headland. But Margaret had never come across anything in the shape of an artist before, and this new capability burst upon her as something more enviable, more delightful than any occupation she had as yet ever known.

"I have a great many more," said the young man. "If you will come to the house, or here to the burn to-morrow, I will show you some that are better than these."

"Oh yes, I will come," said Margaret, without hesitation. "I would like to see them. I never saw anything so beautiful. The Kirkton its very self, and Earl's-hall, old Earl's-hall. Papa says it will tumble down about our ears; but it never can quite tumble down and come to an end while there's *that*!" the girl said. If the artist had been Turner himself he could not have had finer praise.

And she let him walk the length of the field with her, telling her about his wonderful art—then ran home, her heart beating, her mind roused, and amused, and delighted. The slow twilight was just beginning to draw a magical silvery veil over earth and sky. Margaret ran home hurried and breathless, occupied to the full, conscious of no more deficiencies.

"Have you been out all this time, Miss Margret?" said Bell, just rising from her seat by the door, "and you've had your foot in the burn. Go quick and change, my bonnie pet. I've been ower lang in the court, and the dew's falling, and a' the stairch out o' my cap. We're twa fuils for the bonny gloamin', me and you."

CHAPTER IV.

MARGARET went up-stairs with her heart and her feet equally light. She was full of excitement and pleasure. It was true that she had not many excitements in her life, especially of a pleasurable kind; but those she had encountered had not been straightway communicated to some one, as the happy privilege of her age in most cases. Out of sheer inability to contain her sentiments and sensations in one small bosom, she had indeed often poured forth innocent disclosures into the ear of Bell. And when these concerned anything that troubled her, specially the remarks and criticisms of her sisters, Bell had been the best of confidants, backing her up steadfastly, and increasing her indignation by the sympathy of warm and strong resentment. But of other troubles and pleasures, Bell had not been equally understanding. And she was the last person, Margaret felt, to whom she could tell the story of this evening's encounter. Bell would not have been amused and interested like Margaret. She would have opened great eyes of astonishment and exclaimed upon the audacity of Rob Glen in venturing to approach Miss Margaret. "Rob Glen! who was he to proffer his acquaintance to the young lady of Earl's-ha'?" Margaret knew as well how Bell would have said this, as if she had actually delivered the tirade. Therefore the girl made no mention of her new friend. She ran up-stairs,

where she found Jeanie lighting a pair of candles on the table in the East Chamber.

"I've lighted Sir Ludovic's lights, and will you want anything more the nicht, Miss Margaret?" said Jeanie, her fair fresh face giving out more light than did the candles.

"Oh, Jeanie!"—the girl began, but then she checked herself. No, she would not tell any one, why should she? Better to keep it in her own mind, and then there would be no harm. Margaret was not often scolded, but she had a misgiving that she might come in the way of that unusual discipline were she too communicative on the subject of her long conversation with Rob Glen.

She sat down in the East Chamber alone, her face and her eyes glowing. How pleasant it was to have an adventure! The little white-panelled room was but poorly lighted by the two candles. The window still full of twilight, clouds of gray here and there, with a lingering tinge upon them of the sun or its reflections, hung like a great picture on the wall. There were one or two actual pictures, but they were small, and dark, and old, not very decipherable at any time, and entirely invisible now. On the table, in the speck of light which formed the centre of the room, of itself a picture had there been any one to see, lay Lady Jean's old work, with its faded colors, in pretty harmony with all the scene around; and centre of the centre, Margaret's face, not faded, but so soft in its freshness, so delicate in girlish bloom. She sat with her elbows on the table, her face set in the palms of her hands, her eyes looking into the light, making the two little flames of the candles into stars reflected in their clearness. A half-formed smile played about the soft curve of her lips. How pleasant it was to have an adventure at all! And how agreeable the kind of the adventure! Rob Glen! yes, she remembered him quite well when she was seven years old. He had been twelve, a big boy, and very kind to little Miss Peggy.

The farm, which was a small farm, not equal to the large farms of wealthy Fife, a little bit of a place, which his mother had kept up when she became a widow, was close to Earl's-hall; and Margaret recollected how "fond" she had been of her playfellow in these old days, very fond of him! before he went into St. Andrews to school, and then away to his uncle in Glasgow (it all came back upon her) to college. She remembered even, now she came to think of it, the scoffs she had heard directed by Bell and John at the Glens in general, who had not thought St. Andrews good enough for their son, but had to send him to Glasgow, to set him up! And here he was again. Margaret remembered how he had carried her across the ditches and muddy places, and how she had kissed him when he went away; she blushed at the thought, and laughed a little. And now he had come back! and he could draw! That was the most interesting of all. He could make beautiful pictures of everything he saw.

The Kirkton, poor little place, had never looked so attractive before. It had been only a little village of no interest, which sisters Jean and Grace held in the utmost contempt, driving Margaret wild with suppressed rage by the comparison they made between the Scotch hamlet and their English villages; and now it was a picture! She wondered what they would think of it now. Margaret gazed into the flame of the candles and seemed to see it hanging upon a visionary background. A beautiful picture: the gray old church with its rustic tombs, and all the houses clustered below, where people were living, waiting their advance and preferment into the grassy graves above. Here was the real mission of art accomplished by the humblest artist—to make of the common and well-known a dazzling undiscovered glory. Only the Kirkton, yet a picture! and all the doing of the old friend equally glorified and changed—Rob Glen. Margaret was more pleasantly excited, more amused, more roused in mind and imagination than perhaps she had ever been in her life.

A stirring in the long room close by roused her to a sense of her duties. That windowful of sky had darkened; it was almost night: as much as it ever is night in Scotland in June—a silvery night, with no blackness in it but a vague whiteness, a soft celestial reflection of the departed day. Evidently it was late, time to go to bed. Margaret pushed the door open which led into the long room. Sir Ludovic was closing his book. He kept early hours; for it was his habit to wake very early in the morning, as is so usual to old people. He turned to her with a smile upon his face.

"My Peggy, you are late; what has kept you amused so long to-night? It is you generally who let me know when it is time for bed. What have you been doing?"

"Nothing, papa;" but Margaret blushed. However, as she blushed so often this was nothing to remark.

"Put it up upon the shelf," he said; "I have done with that one. It is heavy for you to lift, my dear. It is a sign that I am an old man, a very old man, my little Peggy, that I allow you to do everything for me; but at the same time there is a suitability in it. The young should learn to serve. When you are a full-blown lady, it is then that all the men you meet will serve you."

"I want no men to serve me, papa. When I am middle-aged, as you say, I will have no servants but women. Is not Jeannie better to hand you your plate and fill you your wine than old John?"

"Old John and I have grown old together, my Peggy; but I think your taste is very natural. A young woman is a pleasanter object than an old man."

"I did not mean that," she cried, with compunction; "you, papa, you are the handsomest of us all. There is no one to match you; but the like of Jeannie looks so clean and fresh, and John in his black clothes—"

"Looks like an old Cameronian minister, that is true; but, my Peggy, you must not judge by appearances. Before you are—middle-aged, as you say, you will learn that appearances are not to be trusted to. And, by-the-way, what is it to be middle-aged? For my instruction I would like to know."

Margaret paused to think. She stood looking at him with the big book in her hand, leaning it against the table, embracing it with one arm; then, naturally, as she moved, her eyes sought the uncovered window, and went afar out into the silvery clouds to find her answer. As for her father, he sat with his ivory hands spread out on the arms of his chair, looking at her with a smile. Her slimness and gracefulness and soft-breathing youth were a refreshment to him. It was like the dew falling, like the morning breaking to the old man; and, besides the sense of freshness and new life, it was a perpetual amusement to him to watch the workings of her unaccustomed mind, and the thoughts that welled up in the creature's face. He had perhaps never watched the growth of a young soul before, and he had never got over his first surprise and amusement at the idea that such a little being, only the other day a baby, only the other day running after a ball like a kitten, should think or have opinions at all.

"Middle-aged," said Margaret, with her pretty head upon one side, and great gravity in her face. "Perhaps, papa, you will not have the same idea as I have. Would it be twenty-five? That is not old, of course; but then it is not young either. If you were going to have any sense, I think you would have it by that age."

"Do you think so, my Peggy? That is but a little way to travel to get sense. Where is sense to be found, and can you tell me the place of understanding? It would be easily learned if it could be got at twenty-five."

"Oh, but twenty-five is a very good age, papa. Me—I am only seventeen."

"And you think you have a good deal of sense already, and have found out whereabouts wisdom dwells?" said Sir Ludovic; "then, to be sure, in eight years more you will have gone a long way toward perfection."

"Papa, you are making a fool of me again."

"No, my dear, only admiring and wondering. It is such a long time since I was twenty-five; and I am not half so sure about a great many things as I was then. Perhaps you are right, my little Peggy; one changes one's opinions often after—but it may be that just then you are at the crown of the brae. Far be it from me to pronounce a judgment. Dante puts it ten years later."

"But what Dante means," said Margaret, boldly—for, ignorant as she was, she had read translations of many things, even of the Divine Comedy, not having, perhaps, anything more amusing to read, which was the origin of most of the better knowledge she possessed—"what Dante means was the half of life, when it was half done."

"Ay, ay, that was it," said the old man, "half done! yet you see here I am, at seventy-five, still in everybody's way."

"Oh, papa," she said, fixing upon him reproachful eyes which two tears flooded, brimming the crystal vessels over—"oh, papa!"

"Well, my Peggy; I wonder if it is the better for you that your old father should live on? Well, my dear, it's better for some things. The old nest is gray, but it's warm. Though Jean and Grace, you know—Jean and Grace, and even Mrs. Ludovic, my dear, all of them think it's very bad for you. You would be better, they tell me, in a fine boarding-school in London."

"Papa!"

"Oh, I'm not going to send you away, my little Peggy, not till the old man's gone—a selfish old man. You must be a good girl, and prove me right to everybody concerned. Now, good-night. and run away to your bed; and you can tell John."

"Good-night, papa. I will be a good girl," she said, half laughing, with the tears in her eyes, as she had done when she was a child; and she made a little pause when she kissed him, and asked herself whether she should speak to him about Rob Glen, and ask if he would like to see the pictures? Surely to see such pictures would be a pleasure to anybody. But something kept Margaret silent. She could not tell what it was; and in the end she went away to tell John, without a word about her old acquaintance. Down-stairs she could hear Bell already fastening the shutters, and Jeanie passed her on the stair, fresh and smiling, though sleepy, with a "Gude-nicht, Miss Margret."

"Good-night, Jeanie; and you'll call me early?" she said; upon which Jeanie shook her head with a soft smile.

"If you were aye as ready to rise as me to cry upon you!"

"I will rise to-morrow," said Margaret. How good she was going to be to-morrow! Light as a bird she ran down to the old couple down-stairs. "John, papa is ready. You are to go to him this very minute. I stopped on the stair to speak to Jeanie, and papa will be waiting."

John answered with a grunt and groan. "And me, I'm to pay for it because little miss tarries!" Bell pushed him out of the kitchen with a laugh. "Gae away with you," she said. "Miss Margret, my man John would stand steady and be cut in sma' pieces with a pair o' scissors sooner than that any harm should come to you. But his bark is aye waur than his bite. And what have you been doing all this night, my bonnie bird? I've neither seen your face nor heard your fit upon the stair."

"Oh, I was thinking," said Margaret, after a pause; "thinking—"

"Lord bless us and save us, when the like of you begin thinking! And what were you thinking upon, my bonnie dear?"

"Nothing," said Margaret, musing. She had fallen back into the strain of her usual fanciful thoughts.

"Naething? That's just the maist dangerous subject you can think upon," said Bell, shaking her head; "that's just what I dinna like. Think upon whatever you please, but never upon naething, Miss Margret. Will I come with you and see you to your bed? It's lang since I've put a brush upon your bonnie hair."

"Oh, my hair is quite right, Bell. I brush it myself every night."

"And think about naething all the time. Na, Miss Margret, you maunna do that. I've gathered the fire, and shut the shutters, and put a' thing ready for Sir Ludovic's tea in the morning. Is there onything mair? No, not a thing, not a thing. Now come, my lamb, and I'll put you to your bed."

Margaret made no objection. She could follow her own fancies just as easily while Bell was talking as when all was silent round her. They went together up the winding stair, Bell toiling along with a candle in her hand, which flickered picturesquely, now here, now there, upon the spiral steps. Margaret's room was on the upper story, and to reach it you had to traverse another long hall, running the whole length of the building, like the long room below. This room was scarcely furnished at all. It had some old tapestry hanging on the walls, an old harpsichord in a corner, and bits of invalided furniture which were beyond use.

"Eh, the bonnie dances and the grand ladies I've seen in this room!" Bell said, shaking her head, as she paused for breath. The light of the one little candle scarcely showed the long line of the wall, but displayed a quivering of the wind in the tapestry, as if the figures on it had been set in motion. "Lord bless us!" said Bell. "Oh, ay, I ken very well it's naething but the wind; but I've never got the better o' my first fright. The first time I was in this grand banqueting-hall—and oh, but it was a grand hall then! never onything so grand had the like of me a chance to see. I thought the Queen's Grace herself could not possess a mair beautiful place."

"If it was any use," said Margaret, with a sigh.

"Oh, whisht, my bonnie bird. It's use to show what great folk the Leslies were wance upon a time, and that's what makes us a' proud. There's none in the county that should go out o' the room or into the room afore you, Miss Margret. You've the auldest blood."

"But what good does that do if I am the youngest girl?" said Margaret, half piqued, half laughing.

She was proud of her race, but the empty halls were chill. She did not wait for any more remarks on Bell's part, but led the way into her room, which opened off this banqueting-hall, a turret room of a kind of octagon shape, panelled like all the rest. It looked out through its deepest window on entirely a different scene, on the moonlight rising pale on the eastern side, and the whitening of the sea, the *tremolar della marina*, was in the distance, the silvery glimmer and movement of the great broad line of unpeopled water.

The girl stood and looked out while the old woman lighted the candles on the table. How wide the world was, all full of infinite sky and sea, not to speak of the steady ground under foot, which was so much less great. Margaret looked out, her eyes straying far off to the horizon, the limit beyond which there was more and more water, more and more widening firmament. She was very reluctant to have it shut out. To draw down a blind, and retire within the little round of those walls, what a shrinking and lessening of everything ensued! "But it's more sheltered like; it's no so cold and so far," said Bell, with a little shiver. She was not so fond of the horizon. The thick walls that kept out the cold, the blind that shut out that blue opening into infinity, were prospect enough for Bell. She made her young lady sit down, and undid the loops of her silken hair. This hair was Bell's pride; so fine, so soft, so delicate in texture, not like the gold wire, all knotted and curly, on Jeanie's good-looking head, who was the other representative of youth in the house. "Eh, it is a pleasure to get my hands among it," said Bell, letting the long soft tresses ripple over her old fingers. How proud she was of its length and thickness! She stood and brushed and talked over Margaret's head, telling her a hundred stories, which the girl, half hearing, half replying, yet wholly absorbed in her own fancies, had yet a certain vague pleasure in as they floated over her.

It was good to have Bell there, to feel the touch of homely love about her, and the sound of the voice which was as familiar as her own soft breath. Bell was pleased too. She was not offended when she perceived that her nursling answered somewhat at random. "What is she but a bairn? and bairns' ways are wonderful when their bit noddles begin working," Bell said, with the heavenly tolerance of wise affection. She went out of the room afterward, with her Scotch delicacy, to give Margaret time to say her prayers, then came back and covered her carefully with her hard-working hand, softened miraculously by love. "And the Lord bless my white doo," the old woman said. There were no kisses or caresses exchanged, which was not the habit of the reserved Scotchwoman; but her hand lingered on the coverlet, "happing" her darling. Summer nights are sweet in Fife, but not overwarm. And thus ended the long midsummer day.

CHAPTER V.

ROBERT GLEN, whose reappearance had so interested and excited the innocent mind of Margaret Leslie, was no other than the farmer's son, in point of locality her nearest neighbor, but in every other respect, childhood being fairly over, as far removed from her as if she had been a princess, instead of the child of an impoverished country gentleman. In childhood it had not been so. Little Margaret had played with Rob in the hay-fields, and sat by him while he fished in the burn, and had rides upon the horses he was leading to the water, many a day in that innocent period. She had been as familiar about the farm "as if it had belonged to her," Mrs. Glen had said, and had shared the noonday "piece" of her little cavalier often enough, as well as his sports. Even Bell had found nothing to say against this intimacy.

The Glens were very decent folks, not on a level with the great farmers of Fife, yet well to do and well doing; and Rob's devoted care of the little lady had saved Bell, as she herself expressed it, "many a trail;" but in the ten years from seven to seventeen many changes occur. Rob, who was the youngest, had been the clever boy of the family at the farm. His mother, proud of his early achievements, had sent him to St. Andrews to the excellent schools there, with vague notions of advancement to come. That he should be a minister was, of course, her chief desire, and the highest hope of her ambition; but at this early period there was no absolute necessity for a decision. He might be a writer if he proved to have no "call" for the ministry; or he might be a doctor if his mind took that turn. However, when he had reached the age at which in Scotland the college supplants the school (too early, as everybody knows), Rob was quite of opinion that he had a call to be a minister; and he would have gone on naturally to his college career at St. Andrews, but for the arrival of an uncle, himself sonless, from Glasgow, whose family pride was much excited by Rob's prizes and honors. This was his mother's brother, like herself come of the most respectable folk, "a decent, honest man," which means everything in Scottish moral phraseology. He was

"a merchant" in Glasgow, meaning a shopkeeper, and had a good business and money in the bank, and only one little daughter—a fact which opened his heart to the handsome, bright boy who was likely to bring so much credit to his family. Whether Robert Hill (for the boy was his namesake) would have thought so highly of his nephew without these prizes is another question; but as it was, he took an immediate and most warm interest in him. Mr. Hill, however, felt the usual contempt of a member of a large trading community for every small and untrading place.

"St. An'rews!" he said; "send the boy to St. An'rews to sleep away his time in an auld hole where there's naething doing! Na, na, I'll no hear o' that. Send him to me, and I'll look after him. We know what we're about in Glasskie; nane o' your dreamin' and dozin' there. We ken the value o' time and the value o' brains, and how to make use o' them. There's a room that's never used at the tap o' the house, and I'll see till 'im," said the generous trader.

Mrs. Glen, though half offended at this depreciation of native learning, was pleased and proud of her brother's liberality.

"I'll no hear a word against St. An'rews," she said. "Mony a clever man's come out of it; but still I'm no blind to the advantages on the other side. The lad's at an age when it's a grand thing to have a man over him. No but what he's biddable: but laddies will be laddies, and a man in the house is aye an advantage. So if you're in earnest, Robert (and I'm much obliged to ye for your guid opinion of him), I'm no saying but what I'll take ye at your word."

"You may be sure I mean it, or I wadna say it," said her brother; and so the bargain was made.

Rob went to Glasgow, half eager, half reluctant, as is the manner of boys, and in due time went through his classes, and was entered at the Divinity Hall. A Scotch student of his condition has seldom luxurious or over-dainty life in his long vacations—six months long; and calculated for this purpose, that the student may be self-supporting, Rob did many things which kept him independent. He helped his uncle in the shop at first with the placidity of use and wont, thinking a good shop a fine thing, as who can doubt it is? But when Rob began to get on in his learning, and was able to take a tutorship, he discovered with a pang that a shop was not so fine a thing as he supposed.

Early, very early, the pangs of intellectual superiority came upon him. He was clever, and loved reading, and thus got himself, as it were, into society before he was aware of the process that was going on within him, making friends of very different social position from his own. Then the professors noticed him, found him what is easily called "cultivated"—for he had read much in his little room over the shop, with constantly growing ambition to escape from his lowly place and find a higher—and one of them recommended him to a lady in the country as tutor to her boys. This was a most anxious elevation at first, but it trained him to the habits of a class superior to his own; and after that the shop and its homely ways were anguish to Rob. Very soon he found out that it was inconvenient to go so far to college; then he found occupations in the evening, even during the college session, and thus felt justified in separating himself from his kind uncle, who accepted his excuses, though not without a shade of doubt. "Well, laddie, well, laddie, we're no the folk to keep you if you can do better for yourself," the good shopkeeper said, affronted yet placable. The process is not uncommon; and, indeed, the young man meant no great harm. He meant that his younger life was pushing out of the husk in which it had been confined, that he was no longer altogether the same as the people to whom he belonged. It was true enough, and if it was hard, who could help that? It gave him more pain to take his plentiful meal rudely in the room behind the shop than it could give them to take it without him.

So he reasoned, and was right and wrong, as we all are, in every revolutionary crisis. Had he been bred a shopkeeper or a farmer lad, no such thoughts would have distracted his mind, and probably he would have been happier; but then he had not been brought up either to the shop or to the farm, and how could he help the natural development which his circumstances and training brought with them? So by degrees he dropped the shop. There was no quarrel, and he went to see them sometimes on the wintry Sunday afternoons, and restrained all his feelings of dismay and humiliation, and bore their "ways" as best he could; but there is nobody so quick as a vulgar relation to find out when a rising young man begins to be ashamed of him. The Hills were sore and angry with the young man to whom they had been so kind. But the next incident in Rob's career was one that called all his relations round him, out of sheer curiosity and astonishment, to see a prodigy unprecedented in their lives.

After he had gone through all the Latin and Greek that Glasgow could furnish, and he had time for, and had roamed through all the philosophies and begun Hebrew, and passed two years at the Divinity Hall, this crisis came. Six months more and Rob would have been ready to begin his trials before the Presbytery for license as a probationer, when he suddenly petrified all his friends, and drove his mother half out of her senses, by the bewildering announcement that his conscience made it impossible for him to enter the Scotch Church. The shock was one which roused the entire family into life. Cousins unheard of before aroused themselves to behold this extraordinary spectacle. Such hesitations are not so common with the budding Scotch minister as with the predestined English parson, and they are so rare in Rob's class, that this announcement on his part seemed to his relations to upset the very balance of heaven and earth. Made up his mind not to be a minister! The first sensation in their minds was one of absolute incredulity, followed by angry astonishment when the "infatuated" young fellow repeated and stood by his determination. Not to be a minister! What would he be, then? what would satisfy him? Set him up! they all cried. It was like a fresh assertion of superiority, a swagger and flourish over the mall, unbounded presumption and arrogance. Doubts! he was a bonnie one to have doubts. As if many a better man had not signed the Confession before him, ay, and been glad to have the Confession to sign!

This at first was the only view which the kindred felt capable of taking. But by-and-by, when it became apparent that this general flutter of horror was to have no effect, and that Rob stood by his resolution, other features in his enormity began to strike the family. All the money spent upon him at the college, all the time he had lost; what trade could he go into now with any chance of getting on? Two-and-twenty, and all his time gone for nothing! His uncle, Robert Hill, who had been as indignant as any, here interposed. He sent for his sister, and begged her to compose herself. The lad's head was turned, he said. He had made friends that were not good for a lad in his class of life, that had led him away in other ways, and had made him neglectful of his real friends. But still the lad was a fine lad, and not beyond the reach of hope. This placable sentiment was thought by everybody to proceed from Uncle Robert's only daughter, Anne, who was supposed to regard her cousin with favorable eyes; but anyhow the suggestion of the Hills was that "the minister," their own minister, should be got to "speak to" Rob. Glad was the mother of this or any other suggestion, and the minister undertook the office with good-will.

"Perhaps I may be able to remove some of your difficulties," he said, and he called to himself a professor, one of those who had the young man's training in hand. Thus Rob became a hero once more among all belonging to him. Had the minister spoken? What had the minister said? Had he come to his right mind? the good people asked. And, indeed, the minister did speak, and so did the professor, both of whom thought Rob's a most interesting case. They were most anxious to remove his difficulties; nay, for that matter, to remove everything—doctrines and all—to free the young man from his scruples. They spoke, but they spoke with bated breath, scarcely able to express the full amount of the "respect and sympathy" with which they regarded these difficulties of his. "We too—" they said, in mysterious broken sentences, with imperfect utterance of things too profound for the common ear. And they did their best to show him how he might gulp down a great many things without hurting his conscience, which the robust digestion of the past had been able to assimilate, but which were not adapted for the modern mind. "There is more faith in honest doubt, believe me, than in half the creeds," these gentlemen said. But Rob held out. He would have been foolish, indeed, as well as rarely disinterested and unsusceptible to the most delicate of flatteries, had he not held out. He had never been of so much importance in the course of his life.

It may be doubtful, however, if it was his conscience alone which stopped him short in his career. Rob had learned in his tutorships, and among the acquaintances acquired at college, to know that a Scotch minister did not possess so elevated a position as in rural Fife he was thought to do. The young man had a large share of ambition in him, and he had read of society and of the great world, that abstraction which captivates inexperienced youth. A minister could no more reach this than, indeed, could the country laird who was the highest representative of greatness known to Rob; but literature could

(he thought), art could : and he could write (he
flattered himself), and he could draw. Why,
then, should he bind himself to the restraints
necessary for that profession, when other means
of success more easy and glorious were in his
power ?

This was a very strong supplementary argument to strengthen the resistance of his conscience. And he did not give in ; he preferred
to go home with his mother, to take, as all his
advisers entreated him, time to think everything
over. Rob had no objections to take a little time.
He wanted money to take him to London, to start
him in life, even to pay off the debts which he
said nothing of, but which weighed quite as heavily upon him as his troubles of conscience. This
was how he came to be, after such a long interval, once more living with his mother at Earl's-
hall farm. He had come home in all the importance of a sceptical hero, a position very dazzling to the simple mind, and very attractive to
many honest people. But it was not so pleasant
at home. Instead of being the centre of anxious solicitude, instead of being plied by concilia-
tory arguments, coaxed and persuaded, and respected and sympathized with, he found himself
the object of his mother's irony, and treated with
a contemptuous impatience which he fain would
have called bigotry and intolerance.

Mrs. Glen was not at all respectful of honest
doubt, and she had a thorough contempt for anything and everything that kept a man from making his way in the world. She was not indeed
a person of refinement at all. She had lived a
hard life, struggling to bring up her children and
to "push them forrit," as she said. The expression was homely, and the end to be obtained perhaps not very elevated. To "push forrit" your
son to be Lord Chancellor, or even a general of-
ficer, or a bishop, is a fine thing, which strikes
the spectator ; but when all you can do is to push
him "forrit" to a shop in Dundee, is the struggle less noble ? It is less imposing, at all events.
And the struggling mother who had done her
best to procure such rise in life and in comfort
as was within her reach for her children was not
a person of noble mind or generous understanding. When Rob came home, upon whom her
highest hopes had been set, not prosperous like
the others, but a failure and disappointment,
doing nothing, earning nothing, and with no
prospect before him of either occupation or gain,
her mortification made her bitter. Fury and
disappointment filled her heart. She kept silent
for the first day, only going about her household
affairs with angry energy, scolding her servants,
and as they said, "dinging everything about."
"So lang as she disna ding me!" said Jean the
dairy-maid ; but it was not to be expected that
any long time should pass before she began to
"ding" some one, and ere long the culprit himself began to feel the force of her trouble.

"What are you doing?" she cried ; "do you
call that doing onything—drawing a crookit line
with a pencil and filling it up with paint ? Paint !
ye might paint the auld cart if that's the trade
you mean to follow. It would aye be worth a
shilling or twa, which is mair than ever thae
scarts and splashes will be." Or when Rob escaped into the seclusion of a book : "Read, oh
ay, ye can read fast enough when it's for naething but diversion and to pass the time ; but ye'll

ne'er gather bawbees with your reading, nor be a
credit to them that belong to you." This was
the sting of the whole. He was no credit to
those who belonged to him, rather he was an
implied shame ; for who would believe, Mrs.
Glen asked, that this sudden return was by his
own will ? "Na, na," she said, "they'll think
it is for ill-doing, and that he's turned away out
of the college. It's what I would do mysel'.
And to think of all I've done, and all I've put up
with, and a' to come to naething ! Eh, man ! I
would soon, soon have put an end to your douts.
I would have made ye sure of ae thing, if it hadna
been your uncle Robert and his ministers, ye
should hae had nae douts about that : that no
idle lad should sit at my fireside and devour the
best o' everything. If ye had the heart of a
mouse ye couldna do it. Me, I would starve
first ; me, I would sweep the streets. I would
go down a coal-pit, or work in a gawley chain
afore I would sorn on my ain mother, a widow-
woman, and eat her out o' house and hame !"

Poor Rob ! he was not very sensitive, and he
had been used to his mother's ways and moods,
or these reproaches would have been hard upon
him. No doubt, had he been the innocent sufferer for conscience' sake which he half believed
himself to be, life would have been unendurable
in these circumstances ; but as it was, he only
shrugged his shoulders, or jibed in return and
paid her back in her own coin. They were both
made of the same rough material, and were able
to give and take, playing with the blows which
would have killed others. Rob was not driven
out of the house, out upon the world in despair,
as a more sensitive person might have been. He
stayed doggedly, not minding what was said, till
he should succeed in extracting the money which
would be necessary for his start ; and from this
steady purpose a few warm words were not likely to dissuade him. He, on his side, felt that he
was too much of a man for that. But it is not
pleasant to have your faults dinned into your
ears, however much you may scorn the infliction,
and Rob had gone out on the day he met Margaret very much cast down and discouraged. He
had almost made up his mind to confront fate
rather than his mother. Almost—but he was
not a rash young man, notwithstanding all that
had happened to him, and the discomfort of issuing forth upon the world penniless was greater
than putting up (he said to himself) with an old
wife's flyting ; but still the flyting was not pleasant to bear.

"Wha's that?" his mother said when he returned. "Oh, it's you! bless me, I thought it
was some person with something to do. There
was not the draigh in the foot that I'm getting
used to. Maybe something's happened! You've
gotten something to do, or you've ta'en another
thought! and well I wot it's time."

"No," he said, "nothing's happened. I'm
tired enough and ready enough to take anything
that offered, mother ; but, worse luck, nothing
has happened. I don't know what could happen here."

"No, nor me neither," said Mrs. Glen ; "when
a lad hangs on at hame looking for luck like
you, and never doing a hand's turn, it's far from
likely luck will ever come the side he's on. Oh,
pit away your trash, and dinna trouble me with
the sight o't ! Painting ! paint the auld cart, as

I tell ye, if you're that fond o' painting, or the byre door."

"Everybody is not of your mind," said Rob, stung by this assault. "There are some that think them worth looking at, and that not far off either: somebody better worth pleasing than—" you, he had almost said; but with better taste he added, "any one here."

"And wha may it be that has such guid taste?" said the mother, satirically; "a lass, I'll wager. Some poor silly thing or other that thinks Rob Glen's a gentleman, and is proud of a word from ane sae well put on. Eh, but it's easy to be well put on when it comes out of another person's pocket. It would be some lass out of the Kirkton. How dare ye stand there no saying a word, but smile-smiling at me?"

"Would you like it better if I cried?" he said; "smiling is not so easy always. I have little enough to smile at; but it is good sometimes to feel that all the world is not against me."

"And wha is't that's on your side? Some fool of a lass," repeated Mrs. Glen, contemptuously. "They're silly enough for onything when a young lad's in the case. Who was it?" she added, raising her voice; "eh, I would just like to gie her my opinion. It's muckle the like of them know."

"I doubt if your opinion would matter much," he said, with an air of superiority that drove her frantic. "I respect it deeply, of course; but she—a young lady, mother—may be allowed, perhaps, to think herself the best judge."

"Leddy!" said Mrs. Glen, surprised; and instinctively she searched around her to find out who this could be. "You'll be meaning Mary Fleming, the dress-maker lass; some call her Miss; or maybe the bit governess at Sir Claud's."

Rob laughed; in the midst of his troubles this one gleam of triumph was sweet. "I mean no stranger," he said, "but an old friend—one that was once my companion and playfellow; and now she's grown up into the prettiest fairy, and does not despise me even now."

Mrs. Glen was completely nonplussed. She looked at him with an air of imperious demand, which, gradually yielding to the force of her curiosity, fell, as he made no reply, into a quite softened interrogation. "An auld companion?" she said to herself, bewildered; then added, in a gentler tone than she had used since his return, a side remark to herself: "He's no that auld himsel'."

"No," he said, "but she is younger, mother, and as beautiful as an angel, I think; and she had not forgotten Rob Glen."

His mother looked at him more and more perplexed. But with her curiosity and with her perplexity her heart melted. Lives there a mother so hard, even when her anger is hottest, as to be indifferent to any one who cares for her boy? "I canna think who you're meaning," she said; "auld companions are scarce even to the like o' me—I mind upon nobody that you could name by that name, a callant like you. Auld playfellow! there's the minister's son, as great a credit to his family as you're a trial; but he's no a leddy—"

Again Rob laughed; he was indemnified for all his sufferings. "I will not keep you in doubt," he said, with a certain condescension. "It is little Margaret Leslie; you cannot have forgotten her, mother. If she is not a lady I don't know who is, and," he added, sinking his voice with genuine feeling, and a tender rush of childish recollection, "my little queen."

"Little Margaret Leslie!" said his mother, looking at him stupefied, "you're no meaning Miss Margret at Earl's-hall?" she cried, with a half shriek of astonishment, and gazed at him open-mouthed, like one in a dream.

CHAPTER VI.

MRS. GLEN was much more gentle with her son after this triumph of his. Margaret Leslie was but a girl, and her approbation did not mean very much; but it was astonishing how the farmer-woman calmed down, and what a different aspect things began to take to her, after she heard of this meeting. She said nothing more that night; but stared at her son, and let him go, with a half-reluctant relinquishment of her prey, for the moment. And many were the thoughts which crowded through her mind during the night. She had a respect for talent, like all her nation; but she did not admire the talent which was unpractical, and which did not serve a purpose. A young man who was clever enough to pass all his examinations with credit, to preach a good sermon, to get a living, that was what she could understand, and she had been proud by anticipation in her son's ability to do all this; but when it turned out that he did not mean to employ his talent so, and when his cleverness dwindled down into something impalpable, something that could neither be bought and sold, nor weighed and measured, something which only made a difference between him and other men, without being of any use to him or placing him in the way of any advantage—instead of respecting it, Mrs. Glen scorned the miserable distinction. "Clever! ay, and much good it did him. Tawlent! he would be better without it."

Such unprofitable gifts exasperated her much more than stupidity would have done. But when she heard of the interview with Margaret Leslie, and the renewal of friendship, and the girl's delight with those "scarts," of which she herself was so contemptuous, her practical mind stopped short to consider. Perhaps, after all, though they would never make a living for him, nor were of any earthly use that she could see, these talents might be so directed by a wise and guiding hand as yet to produce something, perhaps to bring him to fortune. A girl who was an heiress might be almost as good a thing for Rob as a kirk. To do Mrs. Glen justice, she did not put the heiress on a level with the kirk, or sceptically allow the one to be as good as the other. She only seized upon the idea as a *pis aller*, reflecting that, if the kirk was not to be had, a lass with a tocher might make some amends.

Here, then, was something to be done, something practical, with meaning and "an object" in it. Mrs. Glen dearly loved to have an object. It made all the difference to her. It was like going somewhere on business instead of merely taking a walk. The latter mode of exercise she could not abide; but put "an object" into it, and it changed the whole aspect of affairs. This was how her son Rob's hitherto useless accomplishments rose in her estimation now, when they began to appear no longer useless, but possibly capable of fulfilling some certain kind of end, if not a very exalted one. At once they acquired interest in her eyes. He himself and his presence at home ceased to be aimless, useless, almost disgraceful, as she had hitherto felt them to be. When she got up next morning, it was with a sense of comfort and encouragement greater than she had felt since the unhappy moment when he had declared to her that it was not possible for him to be a minister. Even now, she could not look back without exasperation on that sudden change and downfall of her pride and comfort. But here at least was a prospect for him, a something before him, a way in which his talents, unprofitable as they seemed, might yet be made of practical use. The change in her manner was instantly apparent to her household. "The mistress has gotten word of something," Jean, the dairy-maid, said, whose hope had been that she herself might not be "dinged" like everything else in the mistress's way. She did not "ding" anything on that blissful morning. She was even tolerant, though it cost her a struggle, when Rob was late for breakfast. Her whole being seemed softened and ameliorated, the world had opened out before her. Here was an object for exertion, an aim to which she could look forward; and with this life could never be quite without zest to the energetic disposition of Mrs. Glen.

The first sign of the improved condition of affairs that struck Rob occurred after breakfast, when his mother, instead of flinging a jibe at his uselessness, as she went off, bustling and hot-tempered, to her own occupations, addressed him mildly enough, yet with a hasty tone that sounded half shame and half offence. It was not to be expected, was it, that she should now encourage him in the habits she had despised and abused yesterday without some sense of embarrassment and a certain shamefacedness? A weaker woman would not have done it at all, but would have thought of her consistency, and kept silent at least. But Mrs. Glen was far too consistent to have any fears for her consistency. Her embarrassment only made her tone hasty, and made her postpone her speech till she had reached the door. When she had opened it, and was about to leave the room, she turned round to her son, though without looking at him. She said,

"If you will draw, if you ca' that drawing, there's a very bonnie view of the Kirkton from the west green. I'm no saying you're to waste your time on such nonsense, but if you will do't, there's the bonniest view."

With this she disappeared, leaving Rob in a state of wonder which almost reached the point of consternation. It made him superstitious. His mother—_his mother!_ to pause and recommend to him the bonniest view! Something must be going to happen. Never in his life had he been so surprised. He got up, half stupefied, as if under a mystic compulsion, and got his sketching-block and his colors, and went out to the west green. It was as if some voice had

come out of the sky above him, or from the soil beneath his feet, commanding this work. What was he that he should be disobedient to the heavenly vision? He went out like a man in a dream, his feet turning mechanically to the indicated spot.

It was a fresh yet sunny morning, the dew not yet off the grass, for everything was early at the farm. The hills, far off, lay clear in softest tints of blue, dark yet transparent, the very color of aerial distance, while all the hues of the landscape between, the brown ploughed land, the green corn, the faint yellowing of here and there a prosperous field, the darkness of the trees and hedges, the pale gleams of water, rose into fuller tones of color as they neared him, yet all so heavenly clear. The morning was so clear that Jean, in the byre, shook her head, and said there would be rain. The clearness of the atmosphere brought everything near; you might have stretched out your hands and touched the Sidlaws, and even the blue peaks of the Grampians beyond; and in the centre of the landscape the Kirkton, glorified, every red roof in it, every bit of gray-yellow thatch and dark brown wall telling against the background of fields; the trees scarcely ruffled by the light morning wind, the church rising like a citadel upon its mound of green, flecked with the burial-places of the past, the houses clustered round it, the smoke rising, a faint darkening, as of breath in the air, to mark where human living was. What a scene! yet nothing; the homeliest country, low hills, broad fields, a commonplace village. For a moment Rob, though he had no genius, fell into a trance, as of genius, before this wonderful, simple landscape. "A voice said unto me, Write; and I said, What shall I write?" How put it into words, into colors upon dull paper? His head was filled with a magical confusion. For once in his life he approached the brink of genius—in the sense of his incapacity. He sat down, gazed, and could do no more.

By-and-by Mrs. Glen came strolling out from the house, with that assumed air of ease and leisure which is always so comically transparent. She meant to assume that she had nothing to do, and was taking a walk for pleasure, which was about as unlikely a thing as could have happened, almost as unlikely as pure interest in Rob's work, which was her real motive. She wanted to see what he had done, whether he had taken that bonniest view, how he was getting on with it, and if it was a thing which could, by any possibility, dazzle and delight a young lady who was an heiress. Assuredly she had not sent out her son to dream over the landscape, to do anything but draw it there and then without delay, as if he had been sent to plough a field. She came up to him, elaborately unoccupied and at her ease, yet explanatory.

"I've just come out to look about me," she said, with fictitious jauntiness. "So you're at it again! Eh, laddie, what a waste o' time and good paper, no to speak of thae colors that cost money! And how far are you on by this time? are you near done?"

Rob had the presence of mind to shut his book hastily.

"I have just begun, mother; but I did not think you took any interest in my poor drawing."

"Me—take an interest? No! But if you're to waste my substance and your ain time taking pictures, I may as well see what there is to see as other folk."

"You shall see it when it is done," said Rob. "It is not in a condition to show now. It is not a thing that can be done in a minute. There is a great deal of thought necessary—the different harmonics of color, the relation of one part to another—"

Mrs. Glen was overawed.

"Ane would think it was some grand affair. A bit scart upon the paper, and a wheen greens and blues: and ye talk as if it was a battle to fight or a grand law-plea."

"My dear mother," said Rob, "many a man could fight a battle that could not draw the Kirkton, with all the hills behind it, and the clouds, and the air."

"Air! ye can paint air, ye clever lad!" cried Mrs. Glen, with a laugh. "Maybe you can paint the coos mowing and the sheeps baaing? I would not wonder. It's as easy as the air, which every bairn kens is no a thing you can see."

"I don't say I can do it myself," said Rob; "but I've seen pictures where you would think you heard the cows and the sheep—yes, and the skylarks up in the sky, and the hare plashing about in the wet woods."

"Just that," said his mother, "and the country gomerel that believes all you like to tell her. Among a' thae bonnie things there should be a place for the one that's to be imposed upon; but you'll no put me there, I'll warrant you," she cried, flouncing away in sudden wrath.

This interruption roused Rob and put him upon his mettle. If it was well to have thus dignified his work in her eyes so that she should be concerned in its progress, the result was not an unmitigated good. Hitherto he had worked as the spirit moved him, and when he was not sufficiently stirred had let his pencil alone. But this would not do, now that his labor had become a recognized industry. He betook himself to his task with a sigh.

Rob's artist-powers were not great. He drew like an amateur, not even an amateur of a high order, and would not have impressed any spectator who had much knowledge of art. But he had a certain amount of that indescribable quality which artists call "feeling," a quality which sometimes makes the most imperfect of sketches more attractive than the skilfullest piece of painting. This is a gift which is more dependent upon moods and passing impulses than upon knowledge and skill; and no doubt the subtlety of those flying shadows, the breadth of the infinite morning light, so pure, so delicate, yet brilliant, put them beyond the hand of the untrained craftsman. The consequence of this morning's work, the first undertaken with legitimate sanction and authority, was accordingly a failure. Rob put the Kirkton upon his paper very faithfully; he drew the church and the houses so that nobody could fail to recognize them; but as for the air of which he had boasted! alas, there was no air in it. He worked till the hour of the farm dinner; worked on, getting more eager over it as he felt every line to fail, and walked home, flushed and excited, when he heard his name called through the mid-day brightness. The broth was on the table when he went in, putting down his materials on a side-table; and Mrs. Glen was impatient of the moment he spent in washing his hands.

"You have as many fykes as a fine leddy," she said. It had not occurred to her to make this preparation for her meal. She drew her chair to the table, and said grace in the same breath with this reproach. "Bless these mercies," she said; and then, "Ye canna say but you've had a lang morning, and naebody to disturb you. I hope you have something to show for it now."

"Not much," said Rob.

"No much! It's a pretence, then, like a' the rest! Lord bless me, I couldna spend the whole blessed day without doing a hand's turn, no, if you would pay me for it. Eh, but we're deceived creatures," cried Mrs. Glen; "as glad when a bairn comes into the world as if it brought a fortune with it! A bonnie fortune! anxiety and care; and if there's a moment's pleasure, it's aye ransomed by days of trouble. Sup your broth; they're very good broth, far better than the like of you deserve; but maybe you think it's no a grand enough dinner for such a fine gentleman? Na, when I was just making up my mind to let you take your will and see what you could do your ain way—and you set up your face and tell me, no much! No much! if it's not enough to anger a saint!"

"There it is: you can judge for yourself," cried Rob, with sudden exasperation. He jumped up from the table so quickly that his mother had no time to point out his want of manners in getting up in the midst of his dinner. The words were stopped on her lips, when he suddenly placed the block on which he had been drawing before her. Mrs. Glen had not condescended to look at any of these performances before. It would have seemed a sort of acceptance of his excuse had she taken any notice of the "rubbitch" with which he "played himself," and she had really felt the contempt she expressed. Drawing pictures! it was a kind of childish occupation, an amusement to be pursued on a wet day, when nothing else was possible, or as a solace in the tedium of illness. But when Rob put down before her, relieved against the white table-cloth, the Kirkton itself in little, a very reproduction of the familiar scene she had beheld every day for years, the words were stopped upon his mother's lips.

"Eh!" she cried, in mere excess of emotion, able for nothing but a monosyllable. The very imperfection of it gave it weight in Mrs. Glen's unpractised eyes. "Losh me!" she cried, when she had recovered the first shock of admiration. "Rob, was it you that did that? are you sure it's your ain doing?" She could not trust her own eyes.

"And poor enough too," said Rob, but he liked the implied applause: who would not? Praise of what we have done well may satisfy our intellectual faculties, but praise of a failure, that is a thing which really goes to the heart.

"Poor! I would like to ken what you mean by poor?" Mrs. Glen pushed away the broth and took up the block in a rapture of surprise and delight. "It's the very Kirkton itself!" she said; "there's Robert Jamieson's house, and there's Hugh Macfarlane's, and there's the way

you go to the post, and there's the Kilnelly bury-
ing-ground, and the little road up to the kirk—
no a thing missed out. And do you mean to
tell me it's a' your own doing? Oh, laddie, laddie, the talents you've gotten frae Providence!
and the little use you make o' them," added his
mother, with a sudden recollection of the burden
of her prophecy against her son, which could not
be departed from even now.

Rob was so much encouraged that he ventured
to laugh. "There is nothing I wish so much as
to make more use of them," he said; "I ought
to study and have good teaching."

"Teaching! what do you want with teaching?
You were never one that was easy satisfied;
what mair would you have?" she cried. She
could not take her eyes from the drawing. She
touched it lightly with her finger to make sure
that it was flat, and did not owe its perspective
to mechanical causes. "To think it's naething
but a cedar pencil and a wheen paints! I never
saw the like! and you to do it, a laddie like you!
It beats me! Ay, there's Robert Jamieson's
house, and yon's Hugh Macfarlane's, and the wee
gate into the kirk-yard as natural! and Widow
Morrison's small shop joining the kirk. I can
'most see the things in the window. I would
like the Minister to see it," said Mrs. Glen.

"Not that one, it is not good enough; there
are others, mother."

She cast upon him a half-contemptuous
glance. He was "no judge," even though it
was he who had done it: how could he be a
judge, when he had so little appreciation of this
great work?

"It's a great deal you ken," she said; "I will
take it mysel' and let him see it. He would be
awfu' pleased. His ain kirk, and ye can just see
the Manse trees, though it's no in the picture.
And a' done in one forenoon! I suppose," she
added, suddenly, "the like of this brings in siller. It's a business, like any other trade?"

"When they are better than that, yes—pictures sell; but you should not speak of it as a
trade."

"I wish it was half as honest and straightfor-
ward as many a trade. Better than that! that's
aye your way. But you have not suppit your
broth. I would not say now," said Mrs. Glen,
in high good-humor "(sit down and finish your
dinner), but Miss Margret would like a look at
that."

"It is not half good enough."

"Hold your peace, you silly lad! I hope I
ken what I'm saying. She's but lonely, poor
thing—no a young person to speak to. It would
divert her to see it. I would not forbid you now
to give the young leddy the like o' that in a present. Sir Ludovic's our landlord, after a'. He's
no an ill landlord, though he's poor. It is aye
a fine thing to be civil, and ye never can tell but
what a kind action will meet with its reward. I
see no reason why you should not take that to
Miss Margret in a present," Mrs. Glen said.

CHAPTER VII.

Rob had not been so light of heart since he
made that momentous decision about his profession which had so strangely changed his life.

For the first time since then he felt himself an
allowed and authorized person, not in disgrace or
under disapprobation of all men, as he had hitherto been; and the permission to carry his drawing of the Kirkton to Miss Margaret "in a present" amused him, while it gave at the same
time a certain sanction to his engagement to
meet her, and show her the other productions of
his pencil. Rob had his wits about him more
than Margaret had, though not so much as his
mother. He was aware that to ask a young
lady to meet him at the burn, for what purpose
soever, was not exactly what was becoming, and
that the advantage he had taken of their childish
friendship was perhaps not quite so "like a gentleman" as he wished to be. He could not, indeed, persuade himself that his mother was any
authority in such a question; but still the fact
that she thought it quite natural that he should
carry on his old relations with Margaret, and
even encouraged him to make the young lady a
present, gave him a sort of fictitious satisfaction.
He would affect to take his mother's opinion as
his authority, if his conduct was called in question, and thus her ignorance was a bulwark to
him. He went out again after his broth, and
worked diligently all the afternoon, though Mrs.
Glen thought it very unnecessary.

"'Twill just spoil it," she said. "The like of
you never knows where to stop: either you do
nothing at all, or you do a hantle o'er much."

But on this point Rob took his own way.
Certainly, even when you despise the opinion of
those around, it is good to be thought well off.
The moral atmosphere was lighter round him,
and there was the pleasant prospect of meeting
Margaret in the evening, and receiving the delightful incense of her admiration; a more agreeable way of filling up this interval of leisure could
not have been devised, had his leisure been the
most legitimate, the most natural in the world.

While he sat at his drawing in the breezy afternoon, a further sign of the rehabilitation he
had undergone was accorded to him. Voices approaching him through the garden, which lay between the house and the west green, prepared him
for visitors, and these voices were too familiar to
leave him in doubt who the visitors were. It was
the Minister, whom Mrs. Glen was leading to the
spot where her son was at work on his drawing.
"I'll no say that I expected much," said Mrs.
Glen, "for I'm not one that thinks everything fine
that's done by my ain. I think I'm a' the mair
hard to please; but, Doctor, when I saw upon
the paper the very Kirkton itsel'! Losh me!
there wasn't a house but you would have kent it.
Robert Jamieson's and Hugh Macfarlane's, just
as like as if you had been standing afore them.
It clean beats me how a lad can do that, that
has had little time for anything but his studies;
for, Doctor, I never heard but that my Rob was a
good student. He hasna come to a good issue,
which is awfu' mysterious; but a good student
he aye was, and there's no a man that kens who
will say me nay."

"I am well aware of that," said Dr. Burnside.
"It makes it all the more mysterious, as you
well say; but let us hope that time and thought
will work a change. I'm not one to condemn a
young man because he has troubles of mind.
We've all had our experiences," the good man
said, as he came through the opening in the hedge

to the west green, which was nothing more imposing than the "green," technically so called, in which the farmer's household dried its clothes —a green, or, to speak more circumstantially, "a washing green," a square of grass on which the linen could be bleached if necessary, and with posts at each corner for the ropes on which it was suspended to dry, being a necessity of every house in Fife, and throughout Scotland. There was no linen hung out at present to share the breezy green with Rob. He sat on the grass on a three-legged stool he had brought with him ; a low hedge ran round the little enclosure, with a little burn purling under its shadow, and beyond were the green fields and the village, with all its reds and blues. Behind him an old ash-tree fluttered its branches and sheltered him from the sun.

"Well, Robert, and how do you do?" said Dr. Burnside. "I have come out to see you, at your mother's instance. She tells me you've developed a great genius for painting. I am very happy to hear of it, but I hope you will not let the siren art lead you away from better things."

"What are better things?" said Rob ; "I don't know any," and he got up to respond to the Minister's salutation. Dr. Burnside shook his head.

"That is what I feared," he said. "You must not give up for painting, or any other pleasure of this earth, the higher calling you were first bound to, my good lad. You've served your time to the Church, and what if you have passing clouds that trouble your spirit? Having put your hand to the plough, you must not turn back."

"Eh, that's what I tell him every day o' his life," said Mrs. Glen.

"I came on purpose to have a long conversation with you," said the Minister. "Yes, very pretty, very pretty. I am no judge of paintings myself, but I've no doubt it's very well done. I need not tell you I'm very sorry for all that's come and gone; but I cannot give up the hope, Robert, that you will see the error of your ways. I cannot think a promising lad like you will continue in a wrong road."

"If it is a wrong road," said Rob.

"Whisht, lad, and hearken what the Minister says ; but before I go in, Doctor, look at the picture. Is't no wonderful? There's your ain very trees, and the road we've ga'en to the kirk as long as I can mind, and a' the whigmaleeries of the auld steeple. Na, I put nae faith in it at first, no me! but when I saw it, just a bit senseless paper, good for nothin' in itsel'! Take a good look at it, Doctor. It's no like the kind of thing ye'll see every day."

"Yes, Mrs. Glen," said the Minister, "I do not doubt it is very pretty. I am no judge myself. I would like to hear what Sir Claude would say ; he is a great connoisseur. But it was not about pictures, however pretty, that I was wanting to speak to Robert. My good lad, put away your bonnie view and all your paints for a moment, and take a walk down to the Manse with me. I would like to satisfy myself how you stand, and perhaps a little conversation might be of use. There is nothing so good for clearing the cobwebs out of the mind, as just entering into the state of the case with a competent person, one that understands you, and knows what to advise."

"That is what I aye said when all thae professors in Glasgow was taighling at him ; the Doctor at hame would understand far better, that is what I aye said. Go with the Minister, Rob, and pay great attention. I'll carry in the things. But I wish ye would take a good look at the picture, Doctor ; and ye'll no keep him too long, for he has a friend to see, and two-three things to do. You'll mind that, Rob, my man."

Never since the fatal letter which disclosed his apostasy had his mother addressed him before as "my man." And Rob knew that the Doctor was not strong in argument. He went with him across the fields he had just been putting into his sketch, with an easy mind. He was fond of discussion, like every true-born Scotsman, and here at least he was pretty sure of having the victory. Mrs. Glen, for her part, carried in "the paints" with a certain reverence. She put the sketch against the wall of the parlor, and contemplated it with pride, which was a still warmer sentiment than her pleasure. It was "our Rob" that had done that ; nobody else in the country-side was so clever. It was true that Sir Claude was a connoisseur, as the Minister said, and was supposed to know a great deal about art, but nobody had ever seen a picture of his to be compared with this of "our Rob's." Mrs. Glen set the sketch against the wall, and got her knitting and sat down opposite to it, not to worship, but to build castles upon that foundation, which was not much more satisfactory than Alnascher's basket of eggs. The thought passed through her mind, indeed, that he who could do so much in this accidental and chance way, what might he not have done had he followed out his original vocation? which was a grievous thought. But then it never could have been in Rob's way to be Archbishop of Canterbury, or anything but a parish minister, like the Doctor himself ; whereas, perhaps, with this unsuspected new gift, and out of his very idleness and do-nothingness, who could tell what might come? Mrs. Glen's imagination was of a vulgar kind, but it enabled her to follow out a perfectly feasible and natural line of events, and to settle what her own line of conduct was to be with admirable good sense : not to press him, not to put herself forward as arranging anything, not to interfere with the young lady, but to wait and see how things would happen. Nothing could be more simple. The end was a mist of confusion before the farmer-woman's eyes. Perhaps she fell asleep, nodding over her half-knitted stocking in the drowsiness of the afternoon ; but if so, a vague vision of "our Rob" turned into Sir Robert, and reigning at Earl's-hall, glistened at the end of that vista. How he could be Sir Robert, by what crown matrimonial he could be invested with the title and the lands of which Ludovic Leslie, and not Margaret, was the heir, we need not try to explain. The dreamer herself could not have explained it, nor did she try ; and perhaps she had fallen asleep, and was not accountable for the fancies that had got into her drowsy brain.

As for Rob, he had a long conversation with the Minister, and posed him as he had intended and foreseen. Dr. Burnside's theology was ponderous, and his information a trifle out of date. Even in the ordinary way of reasoning, his arguments were more apt to unsettle the minds of good believers and make the adversary rejoice, than to produce any more satisfactory result; and it may be supposed that he was not very well prepared for the young sceptic, trained in new strongholds of learning which the good Doctor knew but by name. Dr. Burnside shook his puzzled head when he went into the Manse to tea. "Yon's a clever lad," he said to his wife. "I sometimes think the devil always gets the cleverest."

"Well, Doctor," said Mrs. Burnside, who was a very strong theologian, "have you forgotten that the foolish things of this earth are to confound the strong?"

But the Doctor only shook his head. He did not like to think of himself as one of the foolish things of this earth, even though by so doing he might have a better hope of confounding the audacious strength of Rob Glen. But he pondered much upon the subject, and polished up his weapons in private, going through many an argument in his own mind, which was more successful, and preparing snares and pitfalls for the young heretic. He had patronized Rob when Rob was orthodox, but he respected him now as he had never done before.

"I think I will preach my sermon on the fig-tree next Sabbath morning," he said to his wife after tea. "I think that will stagger him, if anything can."

"Well, Doctor," Mrs. Burnside replied, "it will always be a pleasure to hear it; but I fear Robert Glen is one of those whose ears are made heavy, that they cannot hear."

The Doctor shook his head again, out of respect to the Scriptures; but he was not so hopeless. Perhaps he believed in his sermon on the fig-tree more than his wife did, and he felt that to gain back the young man who had baffled him would be indeed a crown of glory. He spent an hour in his study that night looking up other sermons which specially suited the case. It gave him an interest in his sermons which he had not felt since Sir Claude gave up coming to the parish church, and seceded to the Episcopal chapel in St. Rule's. That had been a distressing event to the good Doctor, but he had got over it, and now providence had been kind enough to send him a young unbeliever to convince. Perhaps the good folks of the Kirkton and the parish generally would have heard of this looking up of the old discourses with some apprehension; but the Doctor wrote a new introduction to the sermon on the fig-tree, and that was some little gain at least.

Rob left his pastor with less respectfulness than the good Doctor felt for him. After running the gauntlet of the professors, and receiving all the attention he had received as the representative of honest doubt, it is not to be supposed that Dr. Burnside could impress him much, and he took up a great deal of time with his feeble argumentations. When, however, the Minister invited him to come to the Manse to tea, Rob made a very pretty speech about his mother. "She has been very kind to me, though I know I have disappointed her," he said, "and I must not leave her alone. I don't think I can leave her alone."

"That's the finest thing you've said, Robert," said the Doctor. "I see your heart is right, al-

though your head is all wrong;" and with this they parted, and the good man came in to look over his sermons. As for Rob, he hurried home to collect some sketch-books for Margaret's benefit, and would not share his mother's tea, notwithstanding his pretty speech. But it was astonishing how tolerant Mrs. Glen had grown. She shook her head, but she did not insist upon the bread-and-butter.

"I'll have something ready for your supper if you havena time now," she said; and entreated him to take the block with to-day's drawing, which she thought might be offered "in a present" to the young lady.

"Not that, mother," said Rob, "not till it is finished."

"Finished!" she said, with a disdain which was complimentary; "what would you have? You canna mend it. It's just the Kirkton itsel'."

And she would have liked him to put on his best black coat when he went to meet Miss Margaret, and the tall hat he wore on Sundays. "When you have good claes, why should ye no wear them? She should see that you ken the fashion and can keep the fashion with the best—as my poor purse will feel when the bill comes in," she added, with a sigh. But at last Rob managed to escape in his ordinary garments, and with the sketches he had chosen. After the events of the day, which had been a kind of crisis in his career, Rob's mind was full of a pleasant excitement; all things seemed once more to promise well for him—if only this little lady of romance would keep her promise. Would she come again? or had he been flattering himself, supposing a greater interest in her mind than really existed, or a greater freedom in her movements? He lingered about for some time, watching the sun as it lighted up the west, and began to paint the sky with crimson and purple; and as he watched it, Rob was natural enough and innocent enough to forget most other things. Who could attempt to put that sky upon paper? There was all the fervor of first love in his enthusiasm for art, and as he pondered what color could give some feeble idea of such a sky, he thought no more of Margaret. What impossible combination could do it? And if it was done, who would believe in it? He looked at the growing glory with that despair of the artist which is in itself a worship. Rob was not an artist to speak of, yet he had something of the "feeling" which makes one, and all the enthusiasm of a beginner just able to make some expression of his delight in the beauty round him; and there is no one who sees that beauty so clearly, and all the unimaginable glories of the atmosphere, the clouds and shadows, the wonderful varieties of color of which our northern heaven is capable, as the artist, however humble. He was absorbed in this consideration, wondering how to do it, wondering if he ever could succeed in catching that tone of visionary light, that touch of green amidst the blue—or whether he would not be condemned as an impostor if he tried, when suddenly his book of sketches was softly drawn out of his hand. Looking round with a start, he saw Margaret by his side. She had stolen upon him ere he was aware, and her laugh at having taken him by surprise changed into her habitual sudden blush as she caught his eye.

"You need not mind me," she said, confused. "I am very happy, looking at the pictures. Are you trying to make a picture out of that sky?"

"If I could," he said; "but I don't know how to do it; and if I did, it would not be believed, though people see the sunset every day. Did you ever see a Turner, Miss Margaret? Do you know he was the greatest artist—one of the greatest artists?"

"I have heard his name; but I never saw any pictures, never one except our own, and a few in other houses. I have heard, or rather I have read that name. Did he paint landscapes like you?"

"Like me!" Rob laughed. "You don't know what you are saying. I am a poor creature, a beginner, a fellow that knows nothing. But he! —and he is very fond of sunsets, and paints them; but he dared no more have done that—"

Margaret looked up curiously into the western heavens. It was "all aflame," and the glow of it threw a warm reflection upon her as she looked up wistfully, with a look of almost infantile, suddenly awakened wonder. Her face was very grave, startled, and full of awe, like one of Raphael's child-angels. The idea was new to her. She, who thought these sketches so much more interesting than the sunset, it gave her a new sensation to hear of the great artist who had never dared to represent that which the careless heavens accomplish every day. Some floating conception of the greatness of that great globe of sky and air which kept herself suspended a very atom in its vastness, and of the littleness of any man's attempt at representing it, came suddenly upon her, then floated away again, leaving her as eager as ever over Rob Glen's poor little sketches. She turned them over with hurried hands. Some were of scenes she did not know, the lochs and hills of the West Highlands, which filled her with delight, and now and then an old tumble-down house, which interested her less.

"Would you like to draw Earl's-hall?" she said. "I know you have it done in the distance. But it is grand in the distance, and close at hand it is not so grand, it is only funny. Perhaps you could make a picture, Mr.—Glen, of Earl's-hall?"

"I should very much like to try. Might I try? Perhaps Sir Ludovic might not like it."

"Papa likes what I like," said Margaret. But then she paused. "There is Bell. You know Bell, Mr.—Glen."

She made a little pause before his name, and he smiled. Perhaps it was hotter that she should not be so easily familiar and call him Rob. The touch of embarrassment was more attractive.

"Bell," she added, with a little furtive smile, avoiding his look, "is more troublesome than papa; and she will go and speak to papa when she takes it into her head."

"Then you do not like Bell? I am wrong, I am very wrong; I see it. You did not mean that!"

"Not like—Bell? What would happen if you did not care for those that belong to you?"

"But Bell is only your servant—only your house-keeper."

Margaret closed the sketch-book, and looked at him with indignant eyes.

"I cannot tell you what Bell is," she said. "She is just Bell. She took care of my mother, and she takes care of me. Who would be like Bell to me, if it were the Queen? But sometimes she scolds," she added, suddenly, coming down in a moment from her height of seriousness; "and if you come to Earl's-hall, you must make friends with Bell. I will tell her you want to draw the house. She would like to see a picture of the house, I am sure she would; and, Mr. Glen," said Margaret, timidly, looking up in his face, "you promised—but perhaps you have forgotten—you promised to learn me—"

(Learn, by one of the curious turns of meaning not uncommon over the Border, means teach in Scotch, just as to hire means to be hired.)

"Forgotten!" said Rob, his face, too, glowing with the sunset. "If you will only let me! The worst is that you will soon find out how little I know."

"Not when I look at these beautiful pictures," said Margaret, opening the sketch-book again. "Tell me where this is. It is a little dark loch, with hills rising and rising all round; here there is a point out into the water with a castle upon it, all dim and dark; but up on the hills the sun is shining. Oh, I would like, I would like to see it! What bonnie places there must be in the world!"

"It is in the Highlands. I wish I could show you the place," said Rob. "The colors on the hills are far beyond a poor sketch of mine. They are like a beautiful poem."

Margaret looked up at him again with a misty sweetness in her eyes, a recognition, earnest and happy, of another link of union.

"Do you like poetry too?" she said.

CHAPTER VIII.

MARGARET went home that evening with her head more full than ever of the new incident which had come into her life. More full of that, but not quite so much occupied, perhaps, by the thought of her new acquaintance. She had all the eagerness of a child to begin her studies, to learn how to make pictures as he did, and this for the moment took everything that was dangerous out of the new conjunction of young man and young woman which was quite unfamiliar to her, but which had vaguely impressed her on their first meeting. She came home this time no longer in a dream of roused and novel feeling, but with definite aims before her; and when she found Bell, as usual, seated outside the door in the little court, Margaret lost no time in opening the attack on the person whom she knew to be the most difficult and unlikely to be convinced.

"Bell!" she cried, running in, breathless with eagerness, "something is going to happen to me. Listen, Bell! I am going to learn to draw."

"Bless me, bairn!" cried Bell, drawing back her chair in semi-alarm. "Is that a'? I thought you were going to tell me the French were coming. No that the French have ony thought of coming nowadays, puir bodies; they've ower muckle to do with themselves."

"Bell, you don't take the trouble to think about me, and I am so happy about it. There never was a time that I did not care for pictures. And there's a view of Earl's-hall from the Kirkton, and I cannot tell how many more. You know I always was fond of pictures, Bell."

"No me! I never knew you had seen ony, Miss Margret," said Bell, placidly; "but for my part, I'm sure I've no objection. I would like it far better if it was the piany; but education's aye a grand thing, however it comes. Can do is easy carried about."

"And will you speak to papa?" said Margaret. "Bell, I wish you would speak to papa; for he jokes at me, and calls me little Peggy, and you know I am not little, but quite grown up."

"Oh, ay, as auld as him or me—in your ain conceit," said Bell; "but whisht, my bonnie doo—I wasna meaning to vex you. And what am I to speak to Sir Ludovic about?"

A slight embarrassment came over Margaret. She began to fidget from one foot to another, and a sudden wave of color flushed over her face. It did not mean anything. Was it not the trouble of her life that she blushed perpetually—blushed for nothing at all, with every fresh thought that rushed upon her, with every new impulse? It was her way of showing every emotion. Nevertheless this time it made her feel uncomfortable, as if it might mean something more.

"I told you," she said; "it is about learning to draw, and about letting him come here to show me the way."

"Letting *him* come! that's another story; and who's him?" said Bell. She made a rapid mental review of the county while she spoke—puzzled, yet not disconcerted; there was nobody of whom the severest duenna could be afraid. There was Sir Claude—known to be very fond of pictures—but Sir Claude was a douce married man, who was very unlikely to take the trouble, and, even if he did, would hurt nobody. "Na, I canna think. Young Randal Burnside he's away; that was the only lad in the countryside like to be evened to our Miss Margret, and him no half or quarter good enough. Na, ye maun tell me; there's no *him* in the country that may not come and go free for anything I care."

"Why should you care?" said Margaret. "But I will tell you who it is. It is Rob Glen—Mrs. Glen's son, at Earl's-lee. He used to play with me when I was little, and I saw him drawing a picture. And then he told me who he was, and then he said he would learn me to draw, if I liked to learn—and you may be sure I would like to learn, Bell. Fancy! to take a bit of paper out of a book, and put this house upon it or any other house, and all the woods, and the hills, and the sky. Look at that puff of cloud! it's all rosy and like a flower; but in a moment it will be gray, and next moment it will be gone; but if you draw it you have it forever. It's wonderful, wonderful, Bell!"

"Rob Glen," said Bell, musing. She paid no attention to Margaret's poetical outburst. "Rob Glen—that's him that was to be a minister; but something's happened to him; he's no conductit himself as he ought, or else he tired of the notion, and he's at hame doing naething." Bell paused after this historical sketch. "He wasna an ill laddie. He was very good to you, Miss

Margret, when you were but a little troublesome thing, greeting for drinks of water, and asking to be carried, and wanting this and wanting that, just what puts a body wild with bairns."

"Was I?" said Margaret, with wide-opened eyes. "No! Rob never thought me a trouble. You might do so," she added, with offence. "I cannot tell for you, but I am sure Rob—"

"I weel believe he never said a word. He was great friends with you, I mind well—oh, great friends. And so he wants to learn you to draw—or you want him? I see nae great objection," said Bell, doubtfully. "He's a young man, but then you're a leddy far above him; and you're old friends, as you say. I will not say but what I would rather he was marrit, Miss Margret; but I see nae great objection—"

"Married!" said Margaret, her eyes bigger than ever with wonder and amusement—"married!" She laughed, though she could scarcely have told why. The idea amused her beyond measure. There was something piquant in it, something altogether absurd. Rob! But why the idea was so ridiculous she could not say. Bell looked at her in her laughter with a certain doubt.

"Why should he no be married?" she said; "lads of that kind marry young—they've nae thing to wait for: the moment they get a kirk it's a' they can look for—very different from some. I dinna ken what Sir Ludovic may say," she added, doubtfully. "Sir Ludovic has awfu' high notions; a farmer's son to learn a Leslie. I canna tell how he'll take it."

"Bell!" cried Margaret, with indignation, "when you know it's you that have the high notions! Papa would never think of anything of the kind; but if you go and put them into his head, and tell him what to think—"

"Lord bless the bairn, me!" cried Bell, with the air of being deeply shocked; and then she got up and went back into her kitchen, which was her stronghold. Margaret, for her part, slightly discouraged, but still eager, stole upstairs. If Bell was against her, it did not matter very much who was on her side. She went softly into the long room where her father was reading. Would it ever happen to her, she wondered, to sit still in one place and read, whatever might be going on—never thinking what was happening outside, untroubled whether it rained or was fine, whether it was summer or winter? Though she came in and roamed about softly, in a kind of subdued restlessness, looking over the book-shelves, and flitting from window to window, Sir Ludovic took no notice. With her own life so warm in her, it was stranger and stranger to Margaret to see that image of the calm of age; how strange it was! He had not moved even, since she came into the room, while she was so restless, so eager, thinking nothing in the world so important as her present fancy. When she had fluttered about for some time without attracting his notice, she grew impatient. "Papa, I want to speak to you," she said.

"Eh? Who is that—?" Sir Ludovic roused up as if he had been asleep; "you, little Peggy?"

"Yes; were you sleeping? I wondered and wondered that you never saw me."

"I don't think I was asleep," he said, with a

little confusion. "To tell the truth, I do get drowsy sometimes lately, and I don't half like it," he added, in an undertone.

"You don't like it?" said Margaret: she was not uneasy, but she was sympathetic. "But then don't do it, papa; come and take a little walk with me"—(here she paused, remembering that to-night, for instance, Sir Ludovic would have been much out of place), "or a turn in the garden, like John."

Sir Ludovic paid not much attention to what she said: he rubbed his eyes, and raised his head, shaking himself with a determination to overcome the drowsiness, which was a trouble to him. "You must sit with me more, my little girl, and make a noise; a little sound is life-like. This stillness gets like"—(he made a pause; was the first word that occurred to him an unpleasant one, not such as was agreeable to pronounce?)—"like sleep," he added, after a moment, "and I have no wish to go to sleep."

"Sleeping is not pleasant in the daytime," said Margaret, unintentionally matter-of-fact. The old man gave a slight shiver, which she did not understand. It was no longer the daytime with him, and this was precisely why he disliked his unconscious doze; was it not a sign that night was near? He raised himself in his chair, and with the almost mechanical force of habit began to turn over the leaves of the book before him. It was evident he had not heard her appeal. She stood by for a moment not saying anything, then pulled his sleeve gently.

"Papa! it was something I had to say."

"Ay, to be sure. You wanted something, my little Peggy? what was it? There are not many things I can do, but if it is within my power—"

"Papa! how strange to speak to me so—you can do everything I want," said the girl. "And this is what it is: I want—don't be very much astonished—to learn to draw."

"To draw? I am afraid I am no good in that respect, and cannot teach you, my dear."

"You? Oh no! But there is one that would learn me."

"My little Peggy, you are too Scotch—say teach."

"Very well, teach if you like, papa; what does the word matter? But may he come to the house, and may I have lessons? I think it is the only thing that is wanted to make me perfectly happy."

Sir Ludovic smiled. "In that case you had better begin at once. Mr. Ruskin himself ought to teach you, after such a sentiment. At once, my Peggy! for I would have you perfectly happy if I could. Poor child, who knows what may happen after," he said, meditatively, putting his hand upon her arm and smoothing the sleeve caressingly. Margaret, occupied with her own thoughts, did not take in the meaning of this; but she was vaguely discouraged by the tone.

"You are not like yourself, papa; what has happened?" she said, almost impatiently. "You are not—ill? It is waking up, I suppose."

"Just that—or going to sleep—one or the other. No, no, I am not ill; yet—And let us be comfortable, my little girl. Draw? Yes, you shall learn to draw, and sit by me, quiet as a little mouse with bright eyes."

"You said just now I was to make a noise."

"To be sure, so I did. I say one thing one moment, and another the next; but, after all, they are much the same. So you sit by me, you may be quiet or make a noise—it will be all the same. Your noises are quiet, my Peggy. Your sleeve rustling, your hand moving, and a little impatience now and then, a start and a shake of your little head. These are noises an old man likes when Providence has given him a little girl."

"But really," said Margaret, with a crease in her forehead, "really! I am grown-up—I am not a little girl!"

"Well, my Peggy! it will be so much the better for you," he said, patting her sleeve. Margaret was vaguely chilled by this acquiescence, she could scarcely tell why; and the slight pain made her impatient, calling up a little anger, causeless and vague as itself.

"Don't, papa," she said. "You are not like yourself. I don't know what is the matter with you. Then, he may come?"

"Yes, yes, at once," said Sir Ludovic, with a dreamy smile; then he said, "But who is it?" as if this mattered little. Altogether, Margaret felt he was not like himself.

"Do you remember Rob Glen, papa, the son of Mrs. Glen at Earl's-lee? He used to play with me when I was a child; he was always very kind to me. Oh, don't shake your head; you *must* mind him. Robert Glen at the farm?"

"I *mind*, as you say—Scotch, Scotch, little Peggy; you should not be so Scotch—a Robert Glen who took the farm thirty or forty years ago. By-the-bye, the lease must be almost out; but how you are to get drawing or anything else out of a rough farmer—"

"Papa!"—Margaret put her hand upon his shoulder with impatience—"how could it be a Robert Glen of thirty or forty years ago? He is only a little older than me. He played with me when I was a little girl. He is perhaps the son, or he may be the grandson. He is a little older than me."

"Get your pronouns right, my little Peggy. Ah! the son; *va pour le fils,*" said Sir Ludovic, with a drowsy smile, and turned back to his book. Margaret stood for a moment with her hand on his shoulder, looking at him with that irritation which is the earliest form of pain. A vague uneasiness came into her mind, but it was so veiled in this impatience that she did not recognize it for what it was. The only conscious feeling she had was, how provoking of papa! not to take more interest, not to ask more, not to say anything. Then she dropped her hand from his shoulder and turned away, and went to sit in the window with the first chance book she could pick up. She was not thinking much about the book. She was half annoyed and disappointed to have got her own way so easily. Had he understood her? Margaret did not feel quite happy about this facile assent. It made of Rob Glen no wonder at all, no disturbing individuality. He was something more, after all, than Sir Ludovic thought. What was all her own tremor for, if it was to be lightly met with a *va pour le fils?* She was not satisfied; and indeed the little rustlings of her impatience, her subdued movements, as she sat behind, did all for her father that he wanted. They kept him awake. The drowsiness which comforted him, yet which he was afraid of, fled before this little thrill of movement. Even if she had been altogether quiet, is there not a thrill and reverberation in the air about a thinking creature? Sir Ludovic was kept awake and alive by the consciousness of another near him, living in every nerve, filling the silence with a little thrill of independent being. This kept him, not only from dozing, but even from active occupation with his book. After a little while he too began to be restless, turned the pages hastily, then himself turned half round toward her. "My Peggy!" he said. In a moment she was standing by his side.

"What is it? Did you want me, papa?"

"No, it is nothing, only to see that you were there. I heard you, that was all; and in the sound there was something strange, like a spirit behind me—or a little mouse, as I said before."

"Had I better go away? would you rather be without me?"

"No, my little girl; but sit in my sight, that I may not be puzzled. The thing is that I can feel you thinking, my Peggy."

"Papa! I was not thinking so much—not of anything in particular, not to disturb you."

"No, my dear, I am not complaining; they were very soft little thoughts, but I heard them. Sit now where I can see you, and all will go right."

"Yes, papa. And you are sure you have no objections?" Margaret said, after a moment's pause, standing by him still.

"To what? to the teaching of the drawing? Oh, no objections—not the least objection."

"And you don't mind him coming to the house—I mean—Mr. Glen?"

"Is there any reason why I should mind?" the old man asked, quickly, rousing into something like vigilance.

"Oh no, papa; but I thought perhaps because he was not—the same as us—because he was only—the farmer's son."

"This is wisdom; this is social science: this is worthy of Jean and Grace," said Sir Ludovic. "My little Peggy! I do not know, my child. Is this all out of your own head?"

At this Margaret drooped a little, with one of her usual overwhelming blushes. "It was Bell," she said; but was it indeed all Bell? Some instinct in her had made a more penetrating suggestion, but she could not tell this to her father. She waited with downcast eyes for his reply.

"Ah, it was Bell. I am glad my little Peggy was not so clever and so far-seeing; now run and play, my little girl, run away and play," he said, dismissing her in his usual tone. She had roused him at last to his ordinary mood, and neither he nor she thought more of his desire that she should stay in his sight. Margaret went away with her heart beating to the west chamber, which was her legitimate sitting-room. She was half ashamed of her own fears about Rob, which her father had treated so lightly. Was it entirely Bell that had put it into her head that this new visitor might be objected to? And was it entirely because he was the farmer's son? Margaret was too much puzzled and confused to be able to answer these questions. She was like a little ship setting out to sea without any pilot. An instinct in her whispered the necessity for guidance, whispered some faint doubts whether this step she was taking was a right

one; but what could the little ship do when the man at the helm was so tranquilly careless? At seventeen is one wiser than at seventy-five? It is not only presumptuous, it is irreligious to think so. And when her own faint doubt was laughed at by her father as being of the order of the ideas of Jean and Grace, what could Margaret do but be ashamed of it? Jean and Grace were emblems of the conventional and artificial to Sir Ludovic. He could not speak of them without a laugh, though they were his children; neither did they approve of their father—with some reason it may be thought.

Thus it was settled that Rob Glen should have access to Earl's-hall. Bell shook her head, but she did not interfere. "It will divert the bairn," she said to herself, "and I can aye keep my eye upon him." What was the need of disturbing Sir Ludovic, honest man? The Leslies had their faults, Bell reflected, but falling in love beneath them was not their weakness. They were very friendly, but very proud. "As sweet and as kind to the poorest body as if they were their own kith and kin; but it's hitherto mayst thou come, and no a step furder," said Bell; "that's the way o' them all. Even our Miss Margret, I would advise nobody to go too far with her. She's very young. She disna understand herself; but as for the canailye, I would not counsel them to come near by our young leddy, simple as she is; there's just an instinck; it's in the Leslie blood."

Thus all went smoothly in this first essay of wilfulness. Father and old duenna both consented that the risk should be run. But in Margaret's own mind there was one pause of hesitation. Had there been any opposition to her will she would have upheld Rob Glen to the utmost, and insisted upon her drawing-lessons; but as it was, there came a check to her eagerness which she did not understand, a subtle sort of hinderance in her path, a hesitation—because no one else hesitated. Was that all?

From this it will be seen that the ladies Jean and Grace were not so wrong as was supposed at Earl's-hall, when they shook their heads over their father's proceedings, and declared that he was not capable of being trusted with the charge of a young girl. Any young girl would have been rather unsafe in such hands, but a girl with money, a girl who was an heiress! As for Sir Ludovic, he went on serenely with his reading, or dozed over his book in the long room, and took no notice, or thought no more of the new teacher Margaret had got for herself. He was very glad she should do anything that pleased her. Now and then he was anxious, and his mind was occupied, by the drowsiness which came over him. He did not like this, it was not a good sign. It made his mind uneasy, for he was an old man, and knew he could not go on forever, and the idea of death was far from pleasant to him. This he was anxious about, but about his child he was not anxious. She was not going to die, or anything to happen to her. She had a long time before her, in which, no doubt, many things would happen; and why should her father begin so early to make himself uncomfortable about her? He did not see the use.

CHAPTER IX.

WHILE these events were going on in the long room, and up the spiral stairs, thoughts not less important to her than those that moved her young mistress were going on in the head of Jeanie, the young maid-servant at Earl's-hall. Jeanie had been chosen as her assistant by Bell on account of her excellent character and antecedents, and the credit and respectability of all belonging to her. "An honest man's daughter," Bell said, "a man just by-ordinary;" and the girl herself was so well spoken of, so pretty spoken in her own person, with such an artless modesty in the soft chant of her voice, true Fife and of the East Neuk, that there had been nothing to say against the wisdom of the choice. Jeanie was always smiling, always good-humored, fresh as a rose and as clean, singing softly about her work, with the natural freedom yet sweet respectfulness which makes a Scotch lass so ingratiating an attendant. Jeanie could not have waited even upon a stranger without a certain tender anxiety and affectionate interest— a desire not only to please, but to "pleasure" the object of her cares, i. e., to give them pleasure with sympathetic divining of all they wanted. Whether it was her "place" or not to do one thing or another, what did it matter? Her own genuine pleasure in the cleanness and neatness she spread round her, and in the comfort of those she served, reached the length of an emotion. It did her heart good to bring order out of chaos, to make dimness bright, and to clear away stain and spot out of her way. She had been two years at Earl's-hall, and before that had been away as far as the west country, where her mother's friends were. Jeanie was her father's only daughter, and great was his comfort and rejoicing when she came back to be so near him; for John Robertson was not well enough off to keep her with him at home, nor could he have thought it good for Jeanie to keep her in his little cottage "learning nae-thing," as he said. Perhaps there had risen upon Jeanie's bright countenance some cloud of uneasiness during these recent days; at least it had occurred to Bell, she could scarcely tell how, that something more than usual was in the girl's mind. "It'll do you good to go and have a crack with your father," she had said, the day after Margaret's second meeting with Rob Glen. Perhaps Bell wanted to have her young lady all to herself—perhaps it was only consideration for Jeanie.

"You can go as soon as the dinner is up," she said, "and take the old man a print o' our sweet butter and twa-three eggs. It'll please him to see you mind upon him."

"No me, but you," said Jeanie; "and I'm real obliged to you, Bell."

Perhaps a rigid moralist would have said it was not Bell, but Sir Ludovic, who had the right to send these twa-three eggs; but such a critic would have met with little charity at Earl's-hall, where, indeed, Bell's thrift and care, and notable management, as constant and diligent as if the house-keeping had been her own, kept plenty as well as order in the house; nor did it ever occur to the good woman that she was not free to give as well as to increase this simple kind of household wealth. Jeanie set out in the sum-

mer evening, after six o'clock, when she had delivered the last dish into John's hands. She went along the country road with neither so light a step nor so light a heart as those which had carried Margaret in dreamy pleasantness between the same hedges, all blossomed with the sweet flaunting of the wild rose.

Jeanie, as was natural, being three-and-twenty and a hard-working woman, was more solid and substantial than the Laird's daughter at seventeen; but it would have been difficult to imagine a more pleasant object, or one more entirely suiting and giving expression to the rural road along which she moved, than was Jeanie, a true daughter of the soil. She was not tall or slim, but of middle height, round and neat and well proportioned, with a beautiful complexion, impaired by nothing but a few freckles, and golden-brown hair, much more "in the fashion," with its crisp undulations and luxuriant growth, than the brown silky locks of her young mistress. Dark eyes and eyelashes gave a touch of higher beauty to the fair, fresh face, which had no particular features, but an air of modesty, honesty, sweet good temper, and kindness very delightful to behold. She was "a bonnie lass," no more, not the beauty or reigning princess of the neighborhood, or playing any fatal *rôle* in the country-side. Jeanie was too good, too simple and kind, for any such position : but she was a bonnie lass, and "weel respeckit," and had her suitors like another.

As she went along by herself in that perfect ease of solitude, unseen by any eye, which subdues all instincts of pride and self-command, a vague cloud became visible on her face. The smile with which she met her little world, true always, yet true sometimes rather in the sense of self-denial than of fact, faded away; her simple countenance grew serious, a curve of anxiety came into her forehead, not deadly anxiety, such as wrings the heart, but a wistfulness and longing for something unattained; for something, perhaps, which ought to be attained, and which might end in being a wrong if withheld from her. Nothing so abstruse as this could be read in Jeanie's face, which would besides have cleared up and awoke into the soft sunshine of friendly response, had any one met her; but as she went on alone, with nobody to see, there was a gravity in her eyes, a wistfulness in the look which she cast along the field-path which Margaret had followed so pleasantly, which was not like Jeanie. Was she looking for some one who ought to be coming along that green and flowery path? She breathed out a soft little sigh as she went on. "My faither will ken," Jeanie said to herself; and though there was this anxiety in her face, a certain languor was in her step, as of one by no means confident that the news she is going to seek will be comforting to hear.

The Kirkton, to which Jeanie was bound, and of which Rob Glen had made so many sketches, was, as already said, an irregular village surrounding the kirk from which it took its name, and built upon a mound, which stood eminent over the low rich fields of Stratheden. The greater portion of the church was new, and quite in accordance with the eighteenth-century idea of half-barn-half-meeting-house which, unfortunately, in so many cases represents the parish church in Scotland. But this was all the worse in the present case, from being added on to a beautiful relic of the past, the chancel of an old Norman church, still in perfect preservation, not resenting, but silently indicating with all the force of fact, the incredible difference between the work of the united and catholic past, and the expedient of a Scotch heritor to house at the smallest possible cost, the national worship which he himself is too fine to share. The little round apsis of the original church, with its twisted arches and toothed ornaments, brown with age and lichen, and graceful, natural decay, was the only part of it visible from the road along which our Jeanie was coming. Jeanie neither knew nor cared for the Norman arches, but the grassy mound that rose above her head, with its grave-stones, and the high steps which led up to it, upon which the children clustered, were dear and familiar to her eyes.

At the foot of the kirk steps was a road which led to "the laigh toun," a little square or *place* —semi-French, as are so many things in Scot-land—surrounded by cottages; while the road, which wound round the base of the elevation on which the church stood, took in "the laigh toun," in which was the post-office and the shop, and the "Leslie Arms," and two or three two-storied houses, vulgar and ugly in their blue slates, which were the most important dwellings in the Kirkton. Jeanie, however, had nothing to do with these respectable erections; her steps were turned toward the high town, where her father's cottage was. Everybody knew her on the familiar road. "Is that you, Jeanie?" the men said, going home from their work with long leisurely tread, which looked slow, yet devoured the way. The children on the kirk steps "cried upon her" with one voice, or rather with one chant, modulating the long-drawn vowels with the native sing-song of Fife. Even Dr. Burn-side, walking stately down the brae, shedding a wholesome awe about him, with hands under his coat-tails, stopped to speak to her.

"Your father is very well, honest man," the Doctor said. When she reached the little square beyond the church, where the women were sit-ting at their doors in the soft evening air, or standing in groups, each with her stocking, talk-ing across the open space like one family, a uni-versal greeting arose.

"Eh, Jeanie, lass, you're a sight for sair cen!" they cried. "Eh, but the auld man will be pleased to see you;" and "He's real weel, Jeanie, my woman," was added by various voices. This was evidently the point on which she was supposed to be anxious. The girl nod-ded to them all with friendly salutations. They had their little bickerings, no doubt, now and then; but were they not one family, each know-ing everything that concerned the others?

"I'm real pleased to see you a', neebors," Jeanie said; "but I maunna bide. I've come to see my faither."

"That's right, Jeanie, lass," the women said; "he's been a good faither to you, and weel he deserves it at your hand." "Faither and mither baith," said another commentator; and Jeanie went on with a warm light of pleasure and kind-ness in her face. Perhaps her name in the air had caught her father's ear, though no name was more common than Jeanie, or more often heard in "the laigh toun;" or perhaps it was that more subtle personal influence which her-alds a new-comer—magnetical, electrical, who can tell what? As she made her way to the end of the square, where "the laigh toun" below, he came out to his cottage door. He was a tall man, thin and stooping, and very pale, his face sicklied o'er with more than thought. He wore the sign of his trade, a shoemaker's apron, and looked along the line of houses with a wistful expression, like that which Jeanie had worn when she was alone. He was a man "above the common," everybody said, for long years a widower, who had been "faither and mither baith" to his children; and only some of them had repaid poor John. Those of the lads who were good lads had emigrated and gone far out of his neighborhood, and those who were within reach were not models of virtue. But Jeanie had always been his support and stay. His wistful inquiring look yielded to the tenderest pleasure as he perceived her; but there was no enthusiasm of greeting between the father and daughter. Few embracings are to be seen in Scotch peasant families. The cobbler's face lighted up; he said, "Is that you, Jeanie, my bonnie woman?" with a tone that had more than endearment in it. The sight of her brought a glow to his wan face. "You are as good as the blessed sunshine, my lass—and eh, but I'm glad to see you!"

"And me too, faither," said Jeanie. That was their greeting. "They tell me you're real well," she added, as they went in-doors.

"A great deal they ken," said John Robert-son, with that natural dislike to be pronounced well by the careless outside world which every invalid shares. "But I'm no that bad either," he added, "and muckle the better for seeing you. Come in and sit you down."

"I have but little time to stay," said Jeanie. As she went in before him the shade again re-turned to her face, though only for that moment during which it was unseen. The small window of the cottage gave but a dim greenish light, a sort of twilight after the full glow and gladness outside. But they were used to this partial gloom; and there seemed a consciousness on the father's part as well as the daughter's of some-thing serious that there might be to say. He looked at her closely, yet half stealthily, with his vivacious, dark eyes which lighted up his pale face; but he asked no question. And Jeanie, for her part, said nothing about herself. She asked when he had seen Willie, and if all was well with John, and he replied, shaking his head, "Oh, ay, weel enough, weel enough for such a ne'er-do-weel."

"No a ne'er-do-weel, faither. Poor laddie! he's so easy led away; but by-and-by he'll tak' a thought and mend."

"Like the de'il—at least, accordin' to Robert Burns. Ay, ay, Jeanie, by-and-by! But maybe he'll break our hearts afore then."

"And Willie, faither?"

"Since Willie 'listed, I try to think of him nae mair," said the cobbler, with a quiver in his lips; then he added, "But he'll be held weel un-der authority, as the centurion says in Scripture, and maybe it's the best thing that could have happened for himself."

"That's aye what Bell says—"

"Bell! and what does Bell ken about it—a woman that never had a son! If I were to have my family over again, I would pray for a' lasses, Jeanie, my woman, like you."

"Eh, faither! but you mustna forget Robin and Alick, though they're far away; and a' the lasses are no like me," said Jeanie, with a tear and a smile. "I might have been marrit, and far from hame; or I might have been licht-headed;" this she said, with a faith laugh at the idea, and rising blush; for to be anything different from her modest self was half incredible, half alarming. The cobbler shook his head.

"Another might, but no my Jean. But what is sent is the best, if we could but see it, nae doubt, nae doubt."

"And that minds me," she said, abruptly, with a little gasp of rising agitation. Then she stopped herself as quickly; "how is the work getting on? have ye aye plenty jobs to keep ye going, faither?" she added, as by an after-thought.

"No that bad," said the shoemaker. "Plenty wark—pay's no just the same thing. There was three pair last week for Merran Linsay, you ken she's aye to be trusted."

"Trusted!" said Jeanie, "ay, for kindness and a good heart, but for the siller—"

"My heart's wae for the poor decent woman," said John Robertson, "with aye the wolf at her door. The shoes thae bairns gang through! no to speak of other things. How could I bid her depart, and get something elsewhere to put on their feet when she came to me? Would you ca' that Christianity—no that I'm blaming them that can do it," he added, hastily. "Na, whiles I wish I could do it; but nature's mair strong than wishing—"

"You are aye the auld man," said Jeanie, tenderly; "it's real foolish, faither, but I canna blame ye. I like ye a' the better. You would make shoes for a' the parish, and never take a penny."

"Na, na, lass! there you're wrong," he said, briskly. "I charged a shilling mair than the price to auld Will Heriot, nae further gane than Friday last. He was in an awfu' hurry, and awfu' ill tempered. I put on a shilling," said the cobbler, with a low laugh. "In the abstract it wasna right, and I'll no say but I may gie it back; but the auld Adam is strong now and then."

"No half strong enough," said Jeanie. "I wouldna gie him back, no a brass farden." Then she paused, and her countenance changed again—that scarcely perceptible darkening, paling, came over it, and this time she spoke quickly, with a little almost impatient determination, as if resolved not to allow herself any more to be crushed and silenced by herself. "Faither," she said, "you'll ken he's come back. Have you heard anything of Rob Glen?"

"Not a word, Jeanie, no a word. I thought that was what you were coming to tell me."

There was a pause—Jeanie said nothing. She turned her face away, and made believe to look out at the dim little window, while the cobbler, with the delicacy of a prince, turned in the other direction that he might not seem to watch her.

"It's a long time since the lad has been hame," he said, with a slight tremor in his voice. "He will have many things to take him up; and his mother—his mother's a proud woman; he knows neither you nor me would welcome him against the will o' his ain folk."

"It's no that, faither," said Jeanie, with a low sound like a sob, which escaped her unawares. "It's no that. The like of that is nothing. Am I one that would judge a hard judgment? It's no that."

"You would never mean it, Jeanie, my bonnie woman; but when the heart is troubled the judgment's a' ajee. You maun possess your soul in patience; maist things come right one way or anither to them that will wait."

Jeanie gave a weary sigh, the light dying out of her face. She kept gazing out of the little window, in a strained attitude, with the tears unseen, blinding her eyes. "It was just that I came for," she said, "to see if you could tell me what to do. He has made great friends, I kenna how, with our Miss Margaret, and he's coming to Earl's-ha'; maybe I'll have to open the door till him, maybe I'll have to show him up the stair—to say Sir till him, and never let on he's onything to me." Here a sob once more broke the hurrying current of Jeanie's words. "What will I do, faither—what will I do?" she cried, with an intense undertone of pain, which made the words tragical in their simplicity—smiling Jeanie, so fair and friendly, turning all at once into a tragic representation (for the millionth time) of disappointed love, and that aching loss which by reason of some lingering possibility of redemption for it, is more hard to bear than despair.

"My bonnie woman!" said the cobbler; the same ring of pain was in his voice; but the very delicacy of his sympathy, and its acuteness, kept him silent. He made another pause: "Jeanie, my lass," he said, "in a' the trials o' this life I've found that true that was said to them that were first sent out to preach the Word. God's awfu' good, to give us the same for the common need as is for the divine. 'Tak' nae thought in that hour what ye will say.' That's aye the guide as long as you're innocent of harm. It will be put into your mouth what is best."

Jeanie turned upon him wistfully. "Is that a' you have to say to me?—is that a', faither? I want mair than that; will I take the thing just as it comes, or will I haud out o' the way? Will I let him see me, or will I no let him see me? Will I throw it on him to acknowledge me for—a friend: or will I take it on me? See how many things I have to ask! It's no just what to say."

"I maun turn that ower in my mind," said John; and there was a pause. Jeanie, after this little outburst, sat still with her head turned again toward the window, not looking at him, concealing the tears in her eyes, and the agitation of her face, which even to her father was not to be betrayed. As for John, he dropped naturally upon his familiar bench, and took up unconsciously a shoe at which he had been working. The little knock of the hammer was the natural accompaniment to his thinking. Outside, the voices of the neighbors, softened by the summer air, made a murmur of sound through which some word or two fell articulate now and then through the silence. "She kens my mind; but she will gang her ain gait," one woman said to another; and then there arose a cry of "Tak care o' the bairn—it'll fa' and break its neck," and a rush of feet. All these sounds and a great deal more fell into the silence of the dim cottage room, where nothing but the little tap of the cobbler's hammer disturbed the stillness. Jeanie sat very still, her hands clasped in her lap, the moisture in her eyes, turning over many thoughts in her mind. The time that had been! the day when they met in Glasgow, she a fresh country lass, half friend, half servant, in the house of her relation; he a student, half-gentleman, with his old red gown, the sign of learning, on his arm.

How glad then had Rob been to see Jeanie! And even when he began to have "grand friends," and to eschew his uncle's shop, her smiling looks, her soft sympathy, had kept him always faithful. And Jeanie had not thought very much of the two years of silence since she came back to Fife. They were both young, and she knew that Rob's mother was not likely to smile upon so humble a daughter-in-law. But his return had roused all the past, and the thought of meeting him again had stirred Jeanie's being to the depths. Even this visit had changed the aspect of affairs for her. For it had not seemed possible that Rob could have entirely neglected her father, whom everybody esteemed, and she had come to the Kirkton—honestly to ask counsel in her difficulty, yet not without hope of hearing something that might charm all difficulty away.

"Jeanie," said her father, at last, "whatever we meet with in this world there's aye but one path for right-minded folk. You maun neither flee from your duty nor gang beyond your duty. We've nae business to rin away from trouble because its trouble, but we've nae call to put oursels in its way. If it's clear that no person can let the lad in but you, open the door till him, take him up the stair—do it, my woman, and never think twice; but if it's no needfu', forbear. And as for leaving it on him to own you for a friend, you must not do that; it would be untruthful on your part, for I hope you're ower weel bred, my bonnie woman, to pass any person you ken without a smile or a pleasant word. You wouldna disown your friend if he turned poor, and why should he, when he's turned rich? or I should say grand in his ways, for rich Rob Glen will never be. Sae it will be but honest when you see the lad to say 'How is a' wi' you, Robin,' or 'I hope you're keeping your health,' or the like of that. Say nothing of other things. Let no lad think you are seeking him; but neither should any lad think you are feared to let it be seen you ken him. Na, I'll hear o' nae concealments; my Jeanie must be as clear as the running water, aye true, and scornin' to deceive. 'Ay,' you'll say, 'Miss Margaret, I ken Robert Glen.'"

"Ay," said the poor girl, with a wistful echo, "I ken Robert Glen!" she shook her head, and the tears with which her eyes were full, brimmed over. "Ay, that do I, faither; I wish I had never kent him, I wish I had never thought so weel of him. Eh, but it's strange—awful strange —to think ane ye ken can deceive! Them ye dinna ken are different. But to say a thing and no to mean it, faither—to give a promise and forget—to mak' a vow before the Lord and think nae mair o't! Can such things be?"

"Such things have been, Jeanie. I'm like you, I cannot believe in them; but they have been. And a' that you and me can do is to bear whatever comes, and be aye faithful and steady, and wait till you see the end."

"It's sae lang waiting," said Jeanie, with a smile in her wet eyes, as she rose from her seat; "and it's no as if it would be ony satisfaction to see them punished for't that do amiss. But fareyewell, faither; I'm muckle the better o' your good advice. Thinkna of me, I'll win through. It's no like a thing that would make a person useless, no fit to do their day's work or get their living. I'll win through."

And the tears were all clear out of her brown eyes, and her smile ready, to meet the world with, when she came out of the dimness of the cottage door. John Robertson stood there watching her as she went along by the neighbors' doors, and it was more from the shadow on his face than on hers that the women divined some trouble in the family.

"Is't about Willie?" they said. "You should speak to your faither, Jeanie, a sensible lass like you. Though he's listed, what's to hinder but he may do real well yet?"

"I had an uncle, as decent a man as ever was, that listed in his young days," said another.

Jeanie received those consolations with her habitual smile.

"I think that too," she said. "There wouldna be so muckle about good sodgers in the Bible if they were all bad men that listed; and so I've tellt him."

So close to her heart did she wear it, that nobody suspected Jeanie's own private cincture of care.

CHAPTER X.

"PAPA has no objections," said Margaret, demurely; "he says if you will come he will be —glad to see you." This, however, being an addition made on the spot, she faltered over it, not quite knowing how it was to be supported by fact; and she added, timidly, "Will you really take all that trouble for me?' Perhaps I am stupid. I think very likely I am stupid; for I cannot draw anything—I have been trying," she said, with a great blush.

"You have been trying! I should like to see what you have done. If you could have seen my stumbles and blunders, you would have had no respect for me at all," said Rob Glen; "and how I dare now to take upon me to teach you, who probably know more than I do—"

"Oh, I know nothing at all—just nothing at all! What shall we do, Mr.— Glen? I found a book and some pencils. I think there is everything in the world up in the old presses in the high room. What shall we do first? Might I begin with—the house? or a tree?"

"There are some preliminary exercises," said Rob, "that are thought necessary; very simple —drawing straight lines, and curves, and corners. I am sure you will do them all—by instinct."

"Oh!" said Margaret again. Her countenance fell. "But any child would draw straight lines; a straight line is nothing—it is just that," she added, tracing a line in the soft, brown, upturned earth of the ploughed field through which the path ran. But when Margaret looked at it, she reddened and furtively attempted another.

She had met Rob by the burn as before, and he was walking back with her toward home. The sky was overcast and lowering. The brief interval of lovely weather had for the moment come to an end. Clouds were gathering on all the hills, and the winds sighed about the hedges, heavy with coming rain.

"The furrow is straight," said Rob, "straight as an arrow; that is the ploughman's pride; but it is not so easy to draw a straight line as you think. I have known people who could never do it."

Margaret was crimson with the failure.

"It's me that am stupid!" she cried, in sudden rage with herself. "How do the ploughmen learn to do it? There's nobody to show them the way."

"It's their pride; and it's their trade, Miss Margaret."

"Oh!" cried Margaret, stamping her foot, "it shall be my pride, and my trade too. I will begin to-night when I go home. I will never, never rest till I can do it."

"But it will never be your trade—nor mine," said Rob Glen, with a sigh. "I wish I knew what mine was. You are rich and a lady; but I am a poor man, that must work for my living, and I don't know what I must do."

"If I were you—" said Margaret. As she spoke she blushed, but only because she always did, not with any special signification in it. Rob, however, did not understand this. He saw the glow of color, the sudden brightness, the droop and sensitive fall of the soft eyelids: all things telling of emotion, he thought, as though the supposition, "if I were you," had thrilled the girl's being; and his own heart gave a leap. Did she—was it possible—feel like this for him already? "If I were you," said Margaret, musingly, "I would be a farmer; but no, not, perhaps, if I were you. You could do other things; you could go into the world, you could do something great—"

"No, no," he said, shaking his head. "I? No, there is nothing great, nothing grand about me."

"How can you judge yourself?" said Margaret, with fine and flattering scorn; "it is other people that can judge best. No; if I were you, I would go away and paint and write, and be a great man; and then you could come home and visit the place where you used to live, and see your old friends; but just now I would go away. I would go to London, into the world. I would let people see what I could do—only first I would learn Margaret Leslie to draw," she said, with a little laugh; "that would be kind—for she never could find any one else to learn her about here."

"That would be the finest office of all," said Rob, inspired. "To go to London, every adventurer can do that; but to teach Miss Leslie is for few. I would rather have that privilege than—"

"Oh," cried Margaret, careless of the compliment, "and will you paint a picture, a great picture of Earl's-hall? I know we are poor. We are not great people, like the Bruces, or the Lindsays, or Sir Claude. We have not grand horses and carriages, and men in livery. That is just why I should like poor old mossy Earl's-hall to be in a bonnie picture, to make folks ask where is that? what beautiful old house is that? You see," she added, laughing, "it is not just a beautiful house. It is not what you would call comfortable, perhaps. Jean and Grace, that is, my old sisters, Miss Leslie and Mrs. Bellingham, are never tired of abusing it. It is quite true that we have not got a thing that can be called a drawing-room—not a real drawing-room," she said, shaking her head. "You will wonder, but it is true. There is the long room, and there is the high room; the one papa sits in; and we dine in it, and he lives in it; and the other is empty, and full of—oh, everything you can think of! But there is no drawing-room, only the little West Chamber, such a little place. They say it was Lady Jean's room, and Lady Jean—is the only ghost we have."

"Is she the lady with the silk gown?"

"She is the Rustle," said Margaret, not disposed to treat the family ghost lightly. "You never see her, you only hear as if a grand lady walked by with her train sweeping. I think there is that very train in the old aumrie, as Bell calls it. But what I was saying was, because it is so old, Mr. Glen, because it's not grand, nor even comfortable—oh, I would like a bonnie picture, a real beautiful picture, of poor old Earl's-hall!"

"You must make one," he said.

"Yes, if I can; but you must make one first. You must take a big sheet of paper and draw it all out; I will show you the best view; and you must paint in every bit of it, the tower and the view from the tower (but, perhaps, after all, it would be difficult to put in the view, you must make another picture of that); and you must put it up in a beautiful frame, and write upon it 'Old Earl's-hall.' Oh! that will make Jean and Grace jump. They will say, 'Who can have done it? Earl's-hall—papa's place—that horrid, tumble-down old Scotch crow's-nest!'" Margaret was a mimic, without knowing it, and mouthed this forth with the warmest relish in Mrs. Bellingham's very tone. But her own acting of her elder sister called forth lively indignation in the girl's warlike soul. "That's what they dare to call it," she cried, stopping to stamp her foot. "My Earl's-hall! But this is what you will do, Mr. Glen, if you want to please me. You will make a picture—not a common thing —a beautiful picture, that everybody will talk about; and send it to the biggest place in London, in the season when everybody is there, and hang it up for everybody to see."

"To please you," said Rob, "I would do a great deal—I would do—" he went on, sinking his voice, "as much as man can do." Margaret scarcely turned to him as he began to speak; but when his voice sank lower, her attention was caught. She raised her head with a little surprise, and, catching his eye, blushed: and paused, arrested, and wondering—What did he mean? Her frank girlish astonishment was very discomposing; he himself blushed and faltered, and stopped in the middle of his pretty speech—"as much as man can do!" but it was not so very much she asked him for. It seemed necessary to Margaret to say this to make things clear.

"Oh no," she said, with a shake of her head, "not that; though there are many men could not do what I want you to do, Mr. Glen; but you can do it easy—quite easy. What will I want to begin with?" she added, changing the subject abruptly, and with true Scotch disregard for the difference between shall and will. This gentle indifference to his protestations chilled Rob a little. She had been so sweet and gracious to him that her demand upon his services only as something that he could do "easy, quite easy," brought him to a sudden stand-still. He did not know how to reply.

"It may not be much," he said; "but it will be all I can do. Miss Margaret, I will begin to-morrow, to show that I want to please you; and if it is not a good drawing it will not be my fault, nor for want of trying."

"I am sure it will be beautiful," she said. "Oh, I would like to see Grace and Jean jump when they see all the people, all the fine folk in London, running to look at old Earl's-hall."

Alas! Rob knew the great London people were not very likely to run in crowds to any performance of his. But the idea was delightful, however unlikely. He suffered himself to laugh, too, though he shook his head. He had never seen any one so sweet, so enchanting, or felt so near to being transported and carried out of himself as by this gracious little lady. Never before, he thought, had he known what such enthusiasm was. He had not forgotten Jeanie, and perhaps others. He was a connoisseur indeed in these soft emotions, the excitement of love-making, the pleasure of pursuit, the flattering consciousness of being admired and loved. All these sensations he knew well enough, not in any guilty way, except in so far as multiplicity of affections implied guilt; but this was not only something new, it was something altogether novel. Margaret had much of the great lady in her, simple as she was. She was not like his previous loves. Even in the little foolishnesses she said, there were signs of a wider world, of something more than even Rob himself, heretofore the oracle of his friends and sweethearts, was acquainted with. All the Fife gentry, all the rural aristocracy, all the great world, so fine at a distance, seemed to glide toward him half caressingly, half mocking, in that girlish figure. It gave him a new sensation. He was dazzled, enchanted, drawn out of himself. Who could tell what this new influence might effect in a young man avowedly "clever," whose abilities everybody had acknowledged? Love had inspired men who had no such eminence to start from. Love had made the blacksmith a painter; why should it not make Rob Glen a painter. To please her! she had put it on that ground. She was not like any of those he had trifled with before. Love had done wonders in all ages, and why not now—if perhaps this new sentiment, so mingled, yet so strange, so dazzling, so bewildering, might be Love.

"If that is what will please you best," he said, faltering a little with something which felt to him like real emotion, "then it shall be done, Miss Margaret, you must let me say so, if man can do it—I mean, if my skill can do it. But perhaps the two things can be done together. I will begin to-morrow, and you can watch me. I will tell you all I know, and you will see how I do it; that will be better, perhaps, than the straight lines."

"Oh, a great deal better," cried Margaret, fervently. "Come early; be sure you come

early, Mr. Glen. I will be ready. I will be waiting. I will let you see the best place for the view. And perhaps you would like to see the house? And then I will go with you, and stand by you, and hold your colors and your pencils, and watch the way you do it. Oh!" cried Margaret, putting her hands together, and breathing forth an earnest invocation of all the good spirits of the elements. "Oh, that it may only be a fine day!"

This very prayer brought home to them both the too plain suggestion conveyed by these gathering clouds, that it might not be a fine day, and chilled their very souls within them. If it should rain! "I think," said Rob, but timidly, "that it is looking better. The sky is cloudy here, but it's clear in the quarter where the wind is, and a north wind is seldom rainy. I think it will be a fine day."

"Do you think so, Mr. Glen?" Margaret looked up at him very wistfully, and then at the sky. Then she cleared up all at once, though the sky did not. "Any way," she said, "you will come? If it's wet, I could let you see the house. I think you would like to see the house. And bring a great many pictures and sketchbooks to let papa see. Even if it is wet, it will be not so very bad," said Margaret, throwing a smile suddenly upon him like a light from a lantern. But then she recollected herself, and blushed wildly and grew serious—for he was a man and a stranger. Was he a stranger? No, she said to herself—and not even a gentleman, only Robert Glen. What fury would have been in poor Rob's heart had he known this last consoling sentiment which kept Margaret from feeling herself overbold. But she did not mean all the arrogance and impertinence that appeared in the thought. Not all of it, nor half of it. She meant no impertinence at all. She parted with him where the by-way came out upon the road, and went along the flowery hedge-row very demurely, thinking very kindly of Rob Glen. Margaret had not known before what it was to have a companion of her own age. Youth loves youth, all the more if youth has little experience of anything but age. Rob was a great deal more amusing (to Margaret) than Bell. This, perhaps, was a mistake, for Rob was not nearly so original as Bell was, nor so well worth knowing. But Margaret did not know that Bell was original. She knew all her stories, and was not too anxious to call forth that homely philosophy which so often (or so the girl thought) was subtly adapted for her own reproof and discouragement. Rob was a novelty to Margaret, even more than she was to him. The prospect of his visit made her feel that even a wet day would be endurable. He amused her more than any one had ever done before. And then she comforted herself that she could not be thought forward, or too bold, because, after all, he was not a gentleman or a stranger, but only Rob Glen!

Jeanie had got in before her young mistress, before the clouds had risen that threatened to cover the sky. What different thoughts were hers on the same subject! She listened to Margaret's voice talking to Bell, as she moved about putting everything in order for the night. What a sweet voice it was, Jeanie thought, speaking so softly, such bonnie English! no like us common folk. The tones which were so wofully Fifeish to Sir Ludovic, and which made Mrs. Belling-ham cry, seemed the very acme of refinement to Jeanie; and when a lady spoke to him so sweet-ly, looked at him with such lovely een, would it be wonderful if Rob forgot? And he was a gen-tleman himself, for what was it that made a gen-tleman but just education? and nobody could say but he had that. It gave Jeanie's heart a pang, but she was too just and candid not to see all this. How could he think of Jeanie Robert-son with Miss Margaret for a friend? Jeanie went away into the depths of those low vaulted rooms, which formed the under-story of Earl's-hall in order to escape the sweet sound of Mar-garet's voice. Here there was a maze of rooms and cellars one within another, among which you might escape very easily from sounds with-out. You might escape, even, which was more difficult, from pursuers, even from persecutors, as had been known, it was said, in the old times; but, ah me, in the very deepest of recesses, how could poor Jeanie escape from herself?

Next day, next morning, Margaret looked at the sky long before any one was up at Earl's-hall. She looked out over the tree-tops to the sea, which swept round in a semicircle as far as the eye carried. From the Eden to the Tay the silvery line swept the horizon one dazzling curve of light. St. Andrews lay on her right hand, with all its towers and its ruins, and the glim-mer of water beyond the headland on which it stood. Not a trace of smoke or human breath came from the brown old city, which stood there silent, with a homely majesty, in the profound stillness of the early morning. Not a human creature was awake between Margaret's window and the old town of St. Rule, except, indeed, in the fishing-boat, with its brown sail, out upon the dazzling line of sea, which was bearing slow-ly toward the bar after a night's fishing, with scarce wind enough to move it. The birds were all up and awake, but nothing else — not the ploughmen and laborers, so early was it, the sun still low over the sea. The girl's heart leaped at the beauty of the sight, but sank again so far as her own interests were concerned. Is it not a bad sign when it is so bright so early? And the light which thus lavished itself upon the world with none to see it, had a certain pale gleam which frightened the young observer, too much used to atmospheric effects not to know something about them. "Oh, what a lovely morning!" she said to herself; but even san-guine Margaret shook her head, thinking it doubtful if the day would be as fine. And oh, if she had but learned, if she could but make a picture of that old town upon the headland, ly-ing voiceless in the morning light, with the great silver bow of the sea flashing round the vast horizon, all round to the vague shores of Forfar-shire, and the dazzling breadth of Tay! If Rob were but here with his pencil and his colors! Margaret was in the enthusiast stage of ignorant faith, believing all things possible to Rob. He was to her the young Raphael, the Michael An-gelo of the future. Or perhaps it would be bet-ter to say (but Margaret at that stage knew no difference) the Claude, the Turner of the new generation. She seemed to see all that scene transferred to canvas—nay, not even to canvas, to paper (but she knew no difference), dazzling,

shining with early dew and freshness, with the chirp of the birds in it, and the silence of nature, fixed there never to die. Poor Rob and his box of water-colors! He would himself, fortunately, at least when unintoxicated by the firmness of her faith in him, have had sense enough not to try.

But when the common world was awake, and when the working day had begun, the brilliancy did not last. First, mists crept over the sun, then the silver bow of the sea paled and whitened, the old brown tower turned gray, the blue sky disappeared. By eight o'clock everything was the hue of mud—sky, sea, and land together, with blurred shades of green and brown upon the last, but not an honest color; and lastly, it began to rain, softly, slowly, persistently, at first scarcely audible upon the leaves, then pattering with con-tinuous sound, which filled all the air. Nothing but rain! The very air was rain, not disagreea-ble, not cruel, but constant.

"Well, it's aye good for the turnips," said Bell; "and I'll get my stocking done that's been so long in hand."

"And what do you say till the hay?" asked John, who was a pessimist, "and a' the low land about Eden in flood already."

But he, too, comforted himself by getting out the oldest plate, and giving it "a guid clean," which was an occupation he kept for this kind of weather; it is easier to endure a wet day when you are old than when you are young. Jennie was less well off. When her work was done, she was not happy enough to take out the stocking, with which every woman in Fife is provided against a moment's leisure. To sit down tran-quilly and turn the heel was not in Jeanie's pow-er. She went up to her little turret room, and began to turn over her little possessions, and there found a keepsake or two from Rob, poor Jeanie! which filled her already dewy eyes with tears. But even that was an occupation, and Margaret, who had no occupation, was worst off of all. She flitted all over the house, up-stairs and down, sometimes disturbing Sir Ludovic with restless movements, taking down books and putting them up again, then flying down-stairs to warm her hands by the fire and tease the long-suffering Bell.

"Eh, Miss Margaret, if you would but try something to do! To see you aye coming and going makes my head gang round and round."

"How can you sit there with your stocking?" cried Margaret, "as if you were a part of the day? Will nothing happen—will nothing ever happen? Will it go on till dinner-time, and then till bed-time, and nobody come?"

"Wha would come, or what should happen?" said Bell, startled. It was a new idea to her that succor should come from without. "I ken no-body that is such a fool as to come out of their ain house on such a day. But, bless me! what is that?" And lo! in a moment as they listened, making Bell wonder and Margaret clap her hands, there came—blessed sound—a knock at the door!

<hr />

CHAPTER XI.

"PAPA," cried Margaret, rushing in, her face bright with excitement and pleasure. Some one stood behind her on a lower step of the winding stair. They filled up that narrow ascent altogether with their youth and the importance of their presence, and of all they had to say and do. She went in lightly, her eyes dancing, her light figure full of eagerness, a large portfolio in her hands. She had no doubt either that this advent of something to break the tedium would be agreeable to her father too, or that he must feel, as she did, the influence of the falling rain and heaviness of the monotonous sky. She went in, taking him amusement, variety, all that she would herself have rejoiced to see coming. It was the best of introductions, she felt, for the new-comer. As for Rob, he stood behind, ready to follow, with a little tremor in him, wondering how he would be received. He had never been in the company of any one so dignified as Sir Ludovic before, never had addressed a titled personage, upon terms of anything like equality; and this of itself was enough to make him nervous.

It seemed like an introduction into a new world to Rob. Then Sir Ludovic had the name of being a great scholar, a man of learning as well as a man of rank and position, and in every way above the range of a farmer's son; and, last of all, he was Margaret's father, and much might depend on the way in which he allowed the new visitor, who felt himself out of place at Earl's-hall, even while he felt himself "as good as" any one whom he might meet anywhere. Altogether it was an exciting moment. Rob was moved by the joyful welcome Margaret had given him, perhaps, to a higher idea of himself than he had ever entertained before. He had felt the flattery of it penetrate to his very heart. She had rushed out of the lower room, where she had been with Bell, almost meeting him at the door. She had spoken before he had time to say anything, exclaiming how glad she was to see him.

Rob had forgotten the rain. Notwithstanding that his mother had brought forth that very argument, bidding him "Go away with you; they would be glad to see you the day, if they never let you in again;" yet in the pleasure of being so received he had forgotten the very chiefest cause of his welcome. The brightened looks, the eager greeting, were too pleasant, too flattering, to be taken unmoved. It was not possible to believe that it was not for himself; and all these things had worked upon Rob to an extent he was scarcely aware of. He who had at first approached the young lady so respectfully, and with so little ulterior motive, and who had been half shocked, half amused at his mother's treatment of the renewed acquaintance between them, came almost with a bound to his mother's conclusion when he saw the brightness of Margaret's eyes this particular rainy morning. There could be no doubt that she was glad to see him; he was here by her own invitation. She was eager to associate him with herself in the interests of the old house, and anxious to accept the lessons he offered, and to "put herself under an obligation" to him in this way.

Margaret, entirely unacquainted with money and the value of things, never thought of any "obligation;" but he did, who was accustomed to consider the price of lessons, and to whom money's-worth would never be without importance. He was very willing, very anxious to confer this favor; but he could not help attaching a certain significance to her acceptance of it, a significance entirely unjustified by any idea in Margaret's innocent mind. She was willing to accept the obligation; therefore, was it not at least permissible to think that some other way of clearing it, making up to him for his kindness, was in her mind? If she had any dawning thought of bestowing all she had upon him, of giving him herself and her money, her heiress-ship altogether, that would indeed be a very good reason for laying herself "under an obligation" to him. Thus Rob had come to think with a beating heart that there was meaning in the innocent girl's happy reception of him, in her eagerness to introduce him to her father, and warm desire that he should please him. And thus the moment was very serious to him, like nothing he had experienced before.

But Sir Ludovic did not stir. He had dropped asleep again, and did not wake even at his daughter's call. As he lay back in his chair, with his old ivory hands spread out upon its arms, and his white hair falling back, Rob thought he had never seen a more venerable appearance. If it were possible that things should so come about as that he should be familiar here, one of themselves, perhaps, calling this old man father (such things had been—and his mother thought were likely to be again—and what else could be the meaning in Margaret's eyes?), Rob felt that he would have reason to be proud. Even the very idea swelled his heart. The room, upon the threshold of which he stood, was unlike anything else he had seen before. He had been in wealthy Glasgow houses where luxury abounded—he had seen dwellings much more wealthy, costly, and splendid than Earl's-hall; but there was something in the aspect of the place, its gray noble stateliness outside, so poor, yet so dignified, its antique old-world grace within, the walls lined with books, the air of old establishment and duration that was in everything, which exercised the strongest influence over him. It was like a scene in a fairy tale—an old magician, and his fresh, fair young daughter, so liberal, so gentle, receiving him like a princess, opening wide the doors to him. He stood, as we have said, in a kind of enchantment. He was on the borders—was it of Paradise? certainly of some unknown country, more noble, more stately than anything he had known before.

This train of thought was interrupted by Margaret, who came back to him walking softly, and putting her finger to her lips. "Papa has fallen asleep again," she said, half annoyed, half anxious, and she pushed open softly the door of the little west chamber. "Here, come here!" she said, and went in before him, pointing to a chair and clearing Lady Jean's work and other obstacles with her own hands from the table. "Now let me see them," she cried. How eager she was, how full of interest and admiration! She spread the portfolio open before him which she had herself snatched from his hands and carried to her father. In it was the drawing of the Kirkton which his mother had suggested he should give "in a present" to Margaret. She was not aware yet of this happiness; but she was as simple as Mrs. Glen in ready admiration, and it seemed to her that nothing ever was more beautiful. "Oh!" she cried, struck dumb with wonder and delight. She said nothing more at first, then suddenly burst into ecstasy. "Did you ever see it from the tower, Mr. Glen? Oh, it does not look like that, you are so high above it. But I know that look just as well; that might be from the wood. It would be in the morning when the dew was on the grass. It would be when everything was quiet, the men away to their work, the children in the school, the women in their houses — and the church standing against the sky: oh, how can you paint things that are not things?" cried Margaret— "the air, and the light, and the wind, and the shadows flying, and the clouds floating! Oh, how can you do it? how can you do it?"

Rob was carried away by this flood of delicious praise; he stood modest and blushing, deprecating, yet happy. He knew at the bottom of his heart that his drawing was not a poem like this, but only very ordinary water-color. He did not know what to say.

"You make me ashamed of my poor work. It ought to be a great deal better to deserve to be looked at at all. The beauty is in your eyes," he said. But Margaret took no notice of this speech. She put that portfolio aside, and opened the other, and plunged into a world of amusement. These were his more finished works, the larger drawings which he had done from his sketches; and, indeed, Rob had spent a great deal of time and trouble upon them; they had occupied him when he was going through the squabbles and controversies of the last few months. They had been his refuge and shelter from a great deal of annoyance; and sometimes, when he looked at them, he had thought they might be worthy of exhibition, and perhaps might help to make his fortune—at least might open the door to him and put him in the way of making his fortune. But at other times he fell into gulfs of despair, and saw the truth, which was that they were only very tolerable studies of an amateur. He shook his head now while Margaret praised them. "Only daubs," he said, "only scratches. Ah, you should see real artist work. I am only an amateur."

"And so you ought to be," said Margaret. "An amateur means a lover, a true lover, doesn't it? I mean of pictures, you know," she added, with her usual blush. "And if you do anything for love, it is sure to be better than what you do for—any other reason—for money. Could anybody paint a real beautiful picture for money? No," cried the daring young theorist, "it must be for love."

"I think so too," said Rob. He reddened also, but with more conscious sentiment. "I think so too! and if I paint Earl's-hall, it will be so."

"Will you?" said Margaret, grateful and happy. Love of her was not what the girl was thinking of; nothing was farther from her mind, nor did it ever occur to her that the word had other meanings than that she gave it. Then she pushed the portfolio away from her, and changed the subject in a moment. "You cannot begin to make the picture, Mr. Glen; what shall we do now? Will I show you the house?" said Margaret, with her Scotch imperfection of grammar, "or will you begin me with the straight lines, or will you (that would be the best) draw something and let me watch. Draw papa! I will open the door, look, like this; and he never stirs, I know

he will never stir for an hour at a time. Oh, that is the thing I should like you to do. Draw papa!"

Her voice sank into a softer cadence, not to disturb Sir Ludovic; but her face was more eager than ever. She put the door open, showing like a picture the other room within: the background of books in many tones of subdued color, with gleams of old gilding, giving a russet edge of light here and there. In the midst of the scene thus disclosed sat Sir Ludovic, his head, with its silver locks, leaning back upon his high chair.

"I cannot draw the figure," Rob had said, with anxiety and alarm, feeling the task too much for him; but, after all, when he looked again there was not much of the figure visible. The wide old velvet coat was folded over the old student-sleepers' knees; only his cheek was visible, still perfect in its fine oval, and the outline of his noble old head against the dark leather of the chair. It was a study of still life, not a portrait, that was wanted. Rob looked at the "subject" thus proposed to him, and Margaret looked at him with great anxiety, to see in his face what he was going to do. Would he consent? Would he refuse to her this thing, which, now that she had proposed it, she felt that she wanted more than anything else in the world? Recklessly Margaret threw herself "under obligations" to the young man.

"Oh, if you please, do it!" she cried, in a half whisper, putting her two pretty hands together in a pretty, spontaneous gesture of supplication. How could Rob resist, whose first desire was to please her, and to whom in pleasing her so many soft brightnesses of pleasure to himself opened up? Even without that motive, to do him justice, he would have been melted by her entreaty —he would have been proud to do anything for her.

"I don't think I can do it; but if it will please you, Miss Margaret, I will try."

"Oh, I know you can do it," Margaret cried. "Oh, tell me what to bring for you—water? You have left your big book down-stairs, but I will run and fetch it, and the pencils, and—"

"Miss Margaret, I cannot let you wait upon me."

"Oh, but I will, though; I like it. Fancy! when you are going to paint papa for me," cried Margaret, flying down-stairs. She came up again, breathless, laughing and glowing, before he could think what was the right thing to do. "There it is," she said, putting down the sketching-block before him, "and I will bring the water in a moment. You are not to stir. Oh, Mr. Glen, think what it will be to have a picture of papa!"

"But I cannot, indeed, make a picture of him. I cannot draw the figure; it is quite difficult. I am not so clever as you think," cried Rob, with sudden fright. Margaret, carried away by the flutter of haste and pleasure, and half-childish familiar acquaintance, put up her hand as if to stop his mouth.

What wonder if Rob almost forgot himself. He half put out his hand to take hers, and he raised his eyes to hers with a look which somehow stopped the girl. She did not understand it, but it frightened her. She drew a little farther away, and her usual blush rushed over her face in a flood of color. "That will be the best place to sit," she said, half abashed, she could not tell why. And Rob remembered himself, and took his place as she indicated. She stood by him, the most eager, watchful attendant. When she had got everything he could want, she put herself behind him, watching over his shoulder every line he drew. This was bad for the drawing; but it was wonderfully enchanting and inspiring for the young man thus elevated into an artist, a genius, a creator. He felt her hand upon his chair, he felt her breath as she bent over him, a kind of perfumed atmosphere of her enveloped him. Her eagerness grew as lines began to come on the paper, he hardly knew how, her voice ran on close by his ear with exclamations and broken notes of soft, subdued sound, half a whisper, half a cry. "Oh, is that how you begin?" Margaret cried; "me, I would have thought the chair first. Oh! that is his face and the line of the hair—yes; but what do you make that dot for in the middle? there is no spot there."

"You know we must measure the lines, and see that one is in proportion with the other," said Rob, holding up his pencil as a level; "it would not do to make one part larger than the other. I might take all my paper for one arm if I did not measure; and that is what beginners often do."

"Oh!" said Margaret. She watched him with her head a little on one side, her lips just parted with eagerness and interest, her brown eyes all aglow. Sometimes her hand would touch his shoulder as she leaned more and more over him; her breath moved the hair on his temples, and went through and through the young man. And he was very open to this kind of influence. It did not require any mercenary hopes, any dazzling realization of an heiress, to send him into all the seductive beguilements of the love-dream. Jennie had done it with her simple rural attractions—how much more her young mistress, with a whole romance about her, and so many charms, both visionary and real!

Rob was not a fortune-hunter, bent on an heiress. This was what his mother would have had him to be; but his nature was too susceptible for such a cold-blooded pursuit. He did what was far better, infinitely more likely to succeed, a greater stroke of genius than any skill of fortune-hunting—he fell simply over head and ears in love. He had done it before many times; it was not the intense and real passion which now and then carries a man out of himself, the love that has no room in its heart for more than one image. But still it was what he knew as that sentiment; and it was quite genuine. A little mist came into Rob's eyes, through which he saw Sir Ludovic in his chair, the task he had set before him; his heart beat in his ears, a soft confusion and excitement seized him. He did not know what he was doing, as he sat there with Margaret looking over his shoulder. His experiences before of this same kind had been pleasant enough, but none of them had possessed the charm, the sweetness of this. Not only was she more charming than any of his former loves, but he himself was vaguely raised and elevated as to another sphere of being. In the dazzlement and tremor of the new crisis, the gratification of his vanity and self-regard, he seemed to himself only now to have attained his true sphere.

"Oh, how wonderful it is!" said Margaret;

"two or three strokes with a lead-pencil, and there is papa! This is more wonderful than the views. Now his hand, Mr. Glen. How sleeping it is on the chair! You could tell he was sleeping only from the look of his hand. Hasn't he a beautiful hand? I never saw one like it. My sister Jean's is white, with dimples in it; they say she has a pretty hand; but then she has so many rings, and she never forgets them. But papa's hand is beautiful, I think. Did you ever see one so fine? It has bones in it, but Jean's has no bones. It is like himself in little. Don't you think so, Mr. Glen?"

"You forget how little I know Sir Ludovic. I have not seen him since I was a boy. But very often the hand is like the owner of it, in little, as you say. Your own is, I have noticed that."

"Mine?" Margaret raised the hand referred to, and looked at it, then laughed softly. "Mine is a brown thin thing, all fingers."

"May I stop to look at it?" said Rob.

She laughed still more, and blushed, and held it out with a little tremor.

"It is nothing to look at—unless you know about the lines or can tell any one's fortune. Can you tell any one's fortune by their hand, Mr. Glen? Mine is as brown as a toad, and not soft and round like Jean's, nor like papa's. Oh, there is nothing to look at in my hand. It is so brown. I think shame when I see a lady's; but then I always lose my gloves, or at least one of them," said Margaret, half penitent, half laughing. While this dialogue was going on, a change had begun; Sir Ludovic had not stirred when she went to call him, but the subdued sound of the voices, and that sense of being looked at which is so sure a spell against sleep, began at last to affect him; he stirred slightly, then made a little change of position; then he said, drowsily, "Little Peggy! are you there, my little girl?"

She sprang away from Rob in a moment, leaving him somehow dazzled, disappointed, and impoverished, he could scarcely tell how. He would have caught at her dress to detain her, but dared not. He tried one whisper, however, very earnest and urgent.

"Stay, stay, Miss Margaret! He must not move till I have done. Do not answer, and he will doze again."

She only shook her head in reply, and went to her father's side lightly and rapidly like a bird. "Yes," she said, "I am here, papa; but keep still, you are not to move;" and she put her arms round him, standing behind, her pretty hands—still pretty, though they were brown—upon his breast. "Now, quick, quick, Mr. Glen," she cried, not thinking how she had changed the group and the entire sentiment of the scene. All at once it became dramatic, and utterly beyond Rob, who had no gifts that way. He sat for a few moments vaguely gazing at her, lost in admiration and pleasure; but he shook his head. He could do no more.

"Eh, my Peggy? what has happened?" said Sir Ludovic, faintly struggling to wake himself. "Not to—move?—why am I not to move? I am—living, I think, still."

"He is drawing you, papa. Oh, you will spoil it—you will spoil my picture!" cried Margaret. She took away her arms from his shoulders, provoked and ready to cry. "If you only would have stayed still two minutes longer—oh, papa! and if you only would have been quick—quick, Mr. Glen! But now my picture's all spoiled," cried the girl.

Sir Ludovic came to himself in a moment at the name.

"Where is your—Mr. Glen?" he said, and sat upright and looked round. Then Rob rose, very much embarrassed, and came forward slowly, feeling more and more awkward. He felt like a country lout when he was in presence of this fine old gentleman. He did not seem able even to walk as he ought with Sir Ludovic's eyes upon him, and grew very red and very uncomfortable; he had not so much as a hat to occupy his uncultivated hands, and all his self-possession and powers of speech seemed to go from him. Margaret, too, now that the moment had come, felt a little afraid.

"We came while you were sleeping, papa," she said, unconscious that she was thus identifying herself with her visitor; "and as it was wet, and nothing else was to be done, and you were sleeping, and I could not disturb you, I asked Mr. Glen to draw you; and he has been making a beautiful picture—just you, your very self, in your big chair—when you wakened. Why did you waken just at that moment to stop Mr. Glen's beautiful picture, papa?"

CHAPTER XII.

SIR LUDOVIC was not quite sure that he liked the sudden interposition between his child and himself of this Rob Glen. He half forgot the permission he had given that Rob Glen might come and teach drawing to Margaret—that was how he put it to himself. He was altogether cross and annoyed by the circumstances generally. The name of Rob Glen, and the description of him as Mrs. Glen's son at Earl's-lee, had sounded quite innocent, but the apparition of a good-looking young man had quite a different effect upon Sir Ludovic. Perhaps he did not look altogether a gentleman, but then he looked quite as much a gentleman as various Fife potentates whom Sir Ludovic readily recalled to mind, and whose claims to gentility were unquestionable. For that matter, young Fallow of Greenshaw, with the best blood of the county in his veins, looked a much greater lout than Rob Glen; so that was no safeguard. And then he was half, or more than half, affronted by the advantage they had taken of his doze. It might be Margaret's fault, but then he had no desire to blame his Peggy, and a great desire to find the young fellow pushing and disagreeable. He ought not to have permitted himself to take such a liberty as to make a drawing of a gentleman when he was asleep, notwithstanding any request that a foolish girl might make to him.

By-and-by Sir Ludovic was mollified toward Margaret by her delight in having what she called "a picture" of him at any cost, and he would not forbid that it should be finished sometime or other; but he did not for that fully forgive the artist, nor, indeed, did it make much difference that it was really a clever drawing, slight as it was. He was determined to give no further facilities for its completion—not to fall

asleep again when Rob Glen was in the way. Perhaps if Sir Ludovic had wanted amusement as much as his daughter did, Rob and his portfolios would have afforded him so much relief on this wet day as to earn forgiveness; but unfortunately Sir Ludovic did not care for the rain. He was not depressed by it, nor were his other occupations interfered with. Rain or shine, he sat in the same chair and read over the same books, of which he was never tired. And what was a new little event to him? if it were innocent, a bore and interruption, and if it were not innocent, an annoyance and trouble.

Margaret would have been grateful to anybody—a peddler, if no better could be had; but Sir Ludovic felt no want, and therefore knew no gratitude. He was civil. He looked at the portfolios and gave to their contents a faint praise. He did not deny that the outline of himself, just put in to be finished another time, was a clever drawing; but at the same time he made Margaret a little sign with his eyebrows to take the young man away. And though Sir Ludovic had been startled into alarm on Margaret's account at the sight of Rob Glen, it did not occur to him that he was increasing all the dangers by thus requiring of her that she should get him away. He threw his child farther and more intimately into the young man's society, though he felt it was not society for her; but what then? he was too fine a gentleman to be rude even to the farmer's son, but was he to take the trouble to talk to him, making conversation for a youth who did not amuse him, who bored him, who kept him from his books? This was a thing which Sir Ludovic did not understand. He gave Margaret that silent intimation of his will, and he opened his book, which was another hint to the intruder. If the young man would take the hint and go, so much the better—if not, then for this once it was better that Margaret should entertain him, and leave her father in peace.

"Perhaps we might go on with our lesson now, Mr. Glen," said Margaret, with one of her sudden suffusions of color. There was some meaning in it this time, for she felt that her father was wanting in courtesy, and was terrified lest Mr. Glen should think he was cavalierly treated. She took up the great portfolio herself to carry it away, and would not let Rob take it from her.

"Why should not I carry it?" she said. "You came to give us pleasure, not to please yourself, Mr. Glen—and of course I will carry the book. It is not at all heavy," she said, lugging it along. Perhaps she intended to convince Sir Ludovic of his own indifference to his visitor and failure in the politeness necessary; and some idea of this kind did cross the old man's mind, but too lightly to make the impression his daughter intended. It was not much to him to see her carrying big books, and he was glad to get rid of the visitor. He drew a long breath of relief when the young pair disappeared in the West Chamber. He could not be troubled with Rob Glen. He had been civil enough. Sir Ludovic was not capable of being uncivil under his own roof; but why should he take more trouble? As for Margaret, the idea of any danger to her, or impropriety in this companionship for her, died out of his mind when put in comparison with his risk of being disturbed in his own person. He was glad to get rid of the two. Had Margaret even been alone, he would have said, "Run away, my little Peggy, run and play," in those habitual words which wounded Margaret's pride of young womanhood so much. He opened his book, and set it straight before him, and placed himself at a more comfortable angle: and then—his eyelids began to come together once more, his head drooped on his breast, then settled on the back of his chair.

It was afternoon, and all was drowsy and still; very still was the long room, now those younger creatures were gone. The rain streamed down outside with a soft, continuous patter upon the trees. The skies were all gray, the earth all silent. The faintest hum, no more than might come from a beehive, might sometimes be audible from the West Chamber, but the walls were thick and the doors fitted closely. If he heard the voices at all, they fell into the subdued patter of the rain, the general stillness. Afternoon—and seventy-five. What reason had he to keep himself awake, to insist upon living instead of sleeping through that heavy, silent, drowsy afternoon? And yet he did not like to think he had been sleeping. When John came in behind the screen and began to prepare for dinner, Sir Ludovic sat upright with very wide-open eyes. He was always erect, but now he sat bolt-upright in his chair.

"Is that you, John?" he said, with unusual suavity, so that the old man might entertain no doubt of his perfectly wide-awake condition.

"Ay, it's just me, Sir Ludovic," said John. No one could have been more indifferent on this subject than John was. He knew very well that his master was apt to doze the afternoon through—but what of that? It was a privilege of his position, not a misfortune. Old John would gladly have dozed too, and found it entirely natural. He himself took a nap whenever he could get it, and though he would cling with natural vehemence to the fact that he had "not slept a wink," there was neither shame nor annoyance in his mind at being caught in the act. The signs of old age were not alarming nor troublesome to John; he had a distinct pleasure in perceiving them in his master, and no objection to put them forth for himself, to boast a little of what he still could do "at my age," and to claim all manner of little exemptions on this score. The old master sat up very erect in his chair, with a great pretence of interest and absorption in his book, to cheat the other's observations, but the old servant was not to be cheated. He said to himself quite calmly, and to Bell when he went down-stairs, "Sir Ludovic's getting an auld man."

"No so much aulder than yoursel'," Bell retorted, promptly.

"Was I saying he was much aulder than mysel'? He's nearer ten years than five—and that makes a great difference; but you women are aye for comparisons," said John. "I said he was getting an auld man."

How differently the same sentiment mingled with the great stillness in the long room! Sir Ludovic did not want any change; he was well enough, willing to last just as he was, hoping nothing different, satisfied if he could only go on

so. But here, creeping about him, irresistible, not even to be kept at arm's-length or regarded as something outside of himself, were the symptoms of change coming. How erect he sat, how wide-awake he forced himself to look! he would not own to the weakness, and perhaps, who could tell, by mere ignoring, might vanquish—or, at least, appear to vanquish it. But it was not to be forgotten, nor even resisted very effectively. Even John's movements, the passing of himself or his shadow across the light, the sound of his heavy old leisurely footsteps, the slight clang of the silver and tinkle of the glass as it was put on the table, began to take a certain rhythm, and to lull the listener once more. "There must be something the matter with me," Sir Ludovic said, as he roused himself once more with an effort, and got up to shake himself free, by movement, from the spell. Movement, that must be what he wanted—a little exercise, which he was aware he had neglected sadly. But now, perhaps, it might be of use. He had to go to prepare for dinner, which was always of use in charming the drowsiness away.

Margaret came in a few minutes after with a little flutter and rustle of roused life about her, which was very different from the slumbrous atmosphere of old age, in which Sir Ludovic had discovered himself to be sinking. She was very eager, and at the same time doubtful, as to what he would say to her; she had not found her visitor so delightful as she had done, she felt. To Margaret the afternoon had been full of pleasure. The wet day, which in the morning had filled her with despair, had become more attractive than the finest of weather: Rob's society, the novelty of talking to him, of pouring forth her own ideas upon subjects with which Bell, for instance, had little sympathy, and of hearing from him a great deal which, if not very new in itself, was profoundly intellectual, brilliantly original to the little country girl—had transported Margaret. How clever he was, how well he could talk! She had never met with anybody like him. What worlds of books he had read! not, perhaps, such learned books (but of this she was not quite sure) as papa. But then papa did not talk of them; and Mr. Glen was so willing to talk of them, mingling his own impressions and ideas with hers, quoting his favorite poets and leading Margaret herself, shyly, with glowing eyes and flaming cheeks, to quote hers, and "say" verses out loud which she had said to herself with all the sweet enthusiasm of youth in many a solitary place, but had never found anybody to care for. Even Jeannie, Jeannie who was young, and full of natural poetry too, when Margaret had tried to "say" her beloved "pieces" to her, had dropped asleep, which had been one of the girl's great disappointments in life.

When she was younger, Bell, indeed, had listened with great complacency to these "pieces," as proving how clever the child was; but from that time to this, when she suddenly found that Rob Glen knew them too, and would 'say half, asking if she remembered the next—most delightful of suggestions—she had found nobody who cared, nobody who would listen and respond. Margaret's eyes grew brighter and brighter, the ready flush of feeling went and came over her face like the flying shadows on a sunshiny landscape, as quick as those shadows fly upon the hills; and a soft excitement got possession of her. She talked as she had never talked in her life before, and impressed him as he impressed her by that easy poetry of youth which can look almost like genius in its early outpouring. A mutual admiration, a mutual interest, thus sprang up between them: and how much your admiration of the superiority of another is increased by the certainty that the other shows his superiority by admiring *you*, who can doubt? Rob, too, felt all this. He was dazzled himself by the pretty, simple strains of thinking and feeling which Margaret showed unawares, and he dazzled her (wittingly and of purpose) by his own eloquence, his theories, his deep thoughts, his lofty fancies. How delightful it all was, and how the hours of wetness out-of-doors, of slow-falling rain, and heavy clouds, and drippings and patterings and overflowings, tedious to everybody else, flew over the two young people in the little panelled room!

The drawing-lesson was not so happy: spite of all the master's efforts, it had been impossible to get Margaret's wavering pencil to execute the necessary straight line. This had been humbling; but it had been partially sweetened by Rob's assurance that many who could not overcome such a commonplace difficulty became excellent in color, and in a sense of the harmonies of Nature. What a lovely phrase this was, "the harmonies of Nature!" Margaret felt instinctively that she would understand them, though she could not make a straight line. Then she took him over the house, showing him "the high room," which was over the long room, the vaulted gallery with its tapestries, which filled him with wonder and admiration. Neither of them perceived another figure, which retreated before them, getting out of their way as they lingered at every point of interest, and which was poor Jeanie, who finally took refuge behind the tapestry, with a forlorn wish to see and hear again the faithless "freend" who had forgotten her. The two stood close to that tapestry for some time, he talking, smiling upon the young lady, giving her a great deal of information (of dubious accuracy) about tapestry and art manufactures, while Jeanie, in great terror of discovery, and still greater shame and horror of herself for so mean an action as "listening," lurked behind, scarlet with anxiety, confusion, and wretchedness. Jeanie, however, it is needless to deny, was a little comforted by what she heard.

Courtship goes quickly on the lower levels of society, and how Rob should occupy the time in talking of the old hangings which were just "an awfu' place for dust," if he really wished to make himself agreeable to Miss Margaret, Jeanie could not understand. "No a word but that the hale world might hear," she said to herself, puzzled but soothed, as she escaped to her little room in the top of the turret, after the others had gone away. She could hear their voices, with little breaks of laughter still going on, as they went down-stairs—the same sound which was as the humming of bees to Sir Ludovic in his great chair. Not so, Jeanie knew, had Rob made his advances to herself. These approaches were much less abstract, far more rapid. Perhaps "he wasna meaning onything," perhaps it was but a polite visit, for abstract reasons, occupied by abstract subjects. This thought consoled Jeanie, and made her heart swell with a secret

pride in Rob's education and capability to hold his place with the best.

But, after all this, Margaret, it may be supposed, did not present herself quite so calmly as usual at the dinner-table. She had a little rose-tint, which was very seldom permanent, upon her pretty cheek, and her eyes glowed with unusual brightness. She was more resigned than usual to the ceremony of being handed to her seat, and did not think the two old men were making a fool of her, as she was apt to do; and she did not say anything, but awaited her father's questioning with much suppressed excitement. Sir Ludovic for some time disappointed her by saying nothing on the subject—which, when you expect to be questioned, and, indeed, to be found fault with, and stand on the defensive, is the most trying of all treatment. However, after a time, Margaret's pulses woke again to liveliest beating.

"Did your artist stay long, my Peggy?" she heard Sir Ludovic saying, without any warning at all.

"Oh! n-not very long, papa," said Margaret, slightly faltering. 'Then—for she suddenly remembered that John, who knew everything that went on, did by no means hesitate to contradict her when he thought proper—she added, hastily, "But first he learned me to draw."

"That was very clever of him," said Sir Ludovic; "and did you learn, as you say, to draw —all in one lesson, my little Peggy? That was very clever of you, too."

"Why should you always make a fool of me?" said Margaret, pathetically. "You know I did not mean that, papa. But we tried; and then I let him see the house, and the high room, and the tapestry. We could not go up to the tower, because it was raining. He is to come another day," said Margaret, with the extreme of simple candor, "to see the view from the tower. And he thought the tapestry was very fine, papa."

"Did he, my little Peggy? Then I fear he cannot know very much about it," said Sir Ludovic. "He is rather a clumsy imitation of a hero, very rustic and Fifish, your Mr. Glen."

"You call *me* Fifish too," said Margaret, with a little laugh which expressed a good deal of irritation. The finest and most significant satire was implied in Margaret's tone. "If *me*, then anybody!" it seemed to say, with a mixture of wounded pride and sense of absurdity. Sir Ludovic forgot the moral he had meant to draw in his amusement. He laughed, with that tender laugh which is called from us by the dear follies of our children.

"Did I call you Fifish too, my Peggy?—which shows I am a very ignorant, ridiculous old man. But he should not have begun that drawing of your old father while I—dozed. It is not often I doze," said Sir Ludovic, with the same uneasy feeling which Margaret had felt, that old John behind his chair was quite capable of contradicting him; "and if he had been a gentleman, I don't think he would have done it."

"Oh!" cried Margaret, clasping her hands, "it was all my fault—I assure you it was all my fault, papa."

"Well, my little girl; but a gentleman would not have done it. He would not have taken an advantage of a man he did not know. Friends may do that kind of thing, but not a stranger, my little Peggy."

"Oh, papa!" cried Margaret, the tears coming to her eyes, "why will you always blame other people for what was my fault? He did not want to do it (this was a fib, but perhaps a pardonable one); it was me that wanted it, papa; and when I said to him, 'Oh, Mr. Glen, I have not got any picture of papa, not even a poor photograph — oh, draw me a picture of papa!' he did it; but it was me that wanted it—and how could he refuse me?"

"He would have been a brute if he had," said the old man, melted; "but still it is true, my Peggy, your stranger should not have done that, without my knowledge, the first time he ever saw me."

"As if he had not known you all his life!" cried Margaret. "He knew you as well as I did when we were little—when you used to walk about. He wondered why you never walked about now; he asked me if you were ill, and I told him you were not ill, only—"

"Only what, my little girl?—old and useless?" said Sir Ludovic, with a pathetic undertone of protest, yet acquiescence, a wistful desire to be contradicted in his faltering voice.

"No—oh, I beg your pardon, papa. I did not mean to be so—impudent. It sounds so, but I did not mean it. I said you were only—lazy."

Sir Ludovic laughed. What relief was in the laugh! what ease from the pang which had struck him! His little girl, at least, did not see the true state of affairs, and why should he not be able to look at this, at least, through her eyes?

"Perhaps there is some truth in it," he said. "You were always saucy, my Peggy. If I were not so lazy, but moved about a little more, it might be better for me. What have you to say against that?" he cried, turning round half angrily to old John, who had given a significant "Humph!" behind his chair.

"Oh, just nothing at all, Sir Ludovic. I wasna speaking. But exercise is good for man and beast—when they're no ower auld or ower frail."

Sir Ludovic laughed again, though less pleasantly.

"I will defy the cleverest talker in the world," he cried, "old John, you old grumbler, to make anything of you."

"I just aye say what I think, Sir Ludovic," said the old man, without a smile; but he chuckled when he went down-stairs and recounted the incident to Bell. "Would he hev me say he was as souple as a laud o' twenty?" said old John.

"Ye auld grumbler, as Sir Ludovic weel says. What for could you no say a pleasant word to pleasure the maister?" cried the more sympathetic Bell.

CHAPTER XIII.

SIR LUDOVIC was reading a book which was of the greatest interest to him, connected with a branch of study in which he was strong, and in which he himself meant to leave his mark for other students; but he could not fix his attention to it. Was it that he was drowsy again this fresh morning? The rain and all the clouds had cleared away. The whole earth was freshened and sweetened by the deluge of the previous day, and everything was rejoicing in the return of the sun. The birds chirped more loudly than usual, and a playful little wind, a kind of baby-breeze, an elemental urchin, full of fun and mischief, was in the wood, shaking the trees, and sending showers of glittering drops at any moment upon the soaked and humid soil. The fragrance of the grass, and "goodly smell" of the turned-up rich brown earth, that genial mother soil out of which was not man made, and unto which he goes back when the world is done with him? was in the air. Summer is so wide in her common blessings; for everybody something; to those who have, the joyful fruits of the earth, to those who have not, at least this goodly smell.

The window was open; the wind came in fresh and sweet, ruffling such papers as it could find about, and singing airy songs to Margaret as she went and came. But it was an air of a different kind that it breathed about Sir Ludovic in his chair. Drowsy? — no, he was not drowsy, in the softness of the morning, but his mind was full of thoughts which were not cheerful. He had lived for so long a time in one steady, endless, unchanging routine, that it had seemed as if it never would end. The more active pleasures and toils of life must end, it is certain; but why should the gentle routine of a recluse life ever be disturbed? Five years ago, when he had been seventy, thoughts of the age he had attained and the crisis he had reached had been in his mind. The full score of years had been accomplished, and what reason had he to expect that they should be prolonged! But they had been prolonged, and the old man had been lulled into absolute calm. He had good health; nothing except

"Those locks in silvery slips,
This drooping gait, this altered size,"

to remind him how near he must be to the end. He had risen up cheerfully in the morning, and gone to bed cheerfully at night; and what was to hinder that it should be so forever? But now all at once the old man seemed to hear the messenger knocking at the door. He was knocking very softly as yet, only a confused, faint tapping, which might be some chance passer-by, and not the emissary of the Great King — tapping very softly, and the door had not yet been opened to him; but how if it was he? This was the thought that assailed Sir Ludovic with something like the same fretting, disturbing influence as actual knocking at the old door, faintly persistent, though never violent, might have had. He was impatient of it, but he had not been able to get rid of it. After all, it was not wonderful that an old man should get tired and be drowsy in the afternoon. He had not for a long time acknowledged to himself that this was the case; but lately it had been difficult to deny it, and the little event of yesterday had forced it, with a deepened touch of the disagreeable, on his notice.

Rob Glen's sketch, though it was so slight, had conveyed a stronger impression to his own mind of his own agedness and feebleness than all his other experiences of himself. The old figure reclining back in the easy-chair, thin, with meagre limbs following the angles of the chair, and languid, helpless hands stretched out upon its supports: the sight of it had given Sir Ludovic a shock. He had been partially soothed afterward by the natural desire of Margaret to have "a picture" of him, as she said. "Not like the grand gentleman over the mantel-piece," the girl had said, "but in your chair, sitting there with your book, as you have always, always been to me." This "always, always," had been a comfort to him. It had breathed the very essence of that continuance which had seemed to become the one quality of life that mattered much; but notwithstanding Margaret's "always," the sketch had given him a shock. He thought of it again this morning as he sat in the same spot and felt now and then the soft puff of the fresh summer air. Was it, perhaps, that even Margaret, his little Peggy, was already conscious of that "afterward," when it would be something for her to have even so slight a sketch of her father? That bit of paper would last longer than he should. When his chair had been set back against the wall, and his books all dispersed to the ends of the earth, how well he could fancy his little girl taking it out, crying, perhaps—then smiling, saying, "This is the one I like best of poor papa; that was how he used to be at the last." She would cry at first, poor little girl—it would make a great difference to his little Peggy; but after a while she would smile, and be able to tell how like it was to poor papa.

So vivid was this imagination that Sir Ludovic almost seemed to see and hear already all that he imagined; and the fancy gave him no pang. It was only part of a confused discomfort of which he could not get rid. This is so different from most of our disquietudes. In other matters it is almost certain that the future which alarms us will come with a difference at least. Our apprehensions will change, if no more, and we will be able to persuade ourselves either that the evil we fear may not come, or that it will not be so great an evil as we thought. But the case is otherwise when it is death that is coming, when to another or to ourselves. That is the one thing which is not to be got rid of. Poor human nature, so shifty, so clever at eluding its burdens, so sanguine that to-morrow will not be as to-day, is brought to a stand before this one approach which cannot be eluded. No use attempting to escape from this, to say that something unforeseen may happen, that things may turn out better. Better or worse than we think, it may be; but there is no eluding it. Sir Ludovic could not steal past on one side or the other to avoid the sight of Him who was approaching. This was the inevitable in actual presence. If not to-day, then to-morrow, next day; in any case, coming always nearer and more near.

These thoughts had been forced upon him by the progress of events, chiefly by that drowsiness which he did not like, but could not ignore nor yet resist. Why should he be so ready to sleep? it had never been his way; and the thoughts it roused within him now, when it had forced itself on his attention, were very confusing. He was rather religious than otherwise, not a man of profane mind. True, he had not of late, in the languor that had crept over him, been very regular in his attendance at church; but he was not undevout—rather, on the whole,

disposed toward pious observances; and without going into any minuteness of faith, a sound believer. The effect of these new thoughts upon him in this respect was strange. He said to himself that it was his duty to think of his latter end, to consider the things that concerned his peace before they were forever hid from his eyes. Anyhow, even if he was not going to die, this would be right. To think of his latter end, to consider the things that concerned his everlasting peace. Yes, yes, this was, there could be no doubt, the right thing as well as the most expedient; but as soon as he had repeated this suggestion to himself, the most trivial fancy would seize upon him, the merest nothing would take possession of his mind, till, with a little start as of awaking, he would come back to the recollection that he had something else to do with his thoughts, that he must consider his latter end. So easy it was to conclude that much, if that would do—but so difficult to go farther! And all was so strange before him, far more confusing than the thought of any other change in life. To go to India, to go to China, would be troublesome for an old man—if such a thing had been suggested to him, no doubt he would have said that he would much prefer to die quietly at home—yet dying quietly, when you come to think of it, is far more bewildering than going to China. It was not that he felt afraid; judgment was not the thing that appalled him.

No doubt there were many things in his life that he might have done better, that he would gladly have altered altogether, but these were not the things that oppressed him. Nothing could be farther from the old man's mind than that thought of "an angry God" which is supposed in so much simple-minded theology to be the great terror of death. It was not an angry God that Sir Ludovic feared. He had that sort of dumb confidence in God which perhaps would not satisfy any stern religionist, but which is more like the sentiment of the relation which God himself has chosen to express his position toward men than any other—a kind of unquestioning certainty that what God would do with him would be the right thing, the most just, the most kind; but then he had no notion what kind of thing that would be, which made it very confusing, very depressing to him.

An old man, by the time he has got to be seventy-five, has given over theorizing about life; he has no longer courage enough to confront the unknown—quiet continuance, without any break or interruption, is the thing that seems best for him; but here was an ending about to come, a breaking off—and only the unknown beyond; and no escaping from it, no staving it off, no postponement. All so familiar here, so natural, the well-known chair, the old cosy coat: and beyond —what? he could not tell what: an end; that was all that was certain and clear. He believed everything that a Christian should believe, not to say such primary principles as the immortality of the soul; but imagination was no longer lively nor hope strong in the old man, and what he believed had not much to do with what he felt. This was not an elevated state of mind, but it was true enough. He himself felt guilty, that he could not realize something better, that he could not rise to some height of contemplation which would make him glad of his removal into realms

4

above. This was how he ought to think of it, ought to realize it, he knew.

But he could not be clear of anything except the step which was coming. To sit in his old chair with his old book, the fresh morning air breathing in upon him, his little girl coming and going, these were not much to have, of all the good things of which the world is full; but they were enough for him. And to think that one of these mornings he should no longer be there, the chair pushed away against the wall, the books packed up on its shelf, or worse, sent off to some dusty auction-room to be sold; and himself—himself: where would old Sir Ludovic be? shivering, unclothed in some unknown being, perhaps seeing wistfully, unable to help it, the dismantling of everything here, and his little girl crying in a corner, but unable to console her. He knew he ought to be thinking of high spiritual communion, of the music of the spheres. But he could not; even of his little Peggy crying for her old father and missing him, he did not think much: but most of the dull, strange fact that he would be gone away, a thing so strange and yet so certain that it gave him a vertigo and bewildering giddiness—and sometimes, too, a kind of dreary impatience, a desire to get it over and know the worst that could happen; though he was not afraid of any worst. There was no Inferno in that vague world before him, nothing but dimness; though, perhaps, that was almost worse than an Inferno—a wide, vague, confusing desert of the unknown.

These thoughts were present with him even while he held playful conversations with Margaret and talked to old John and Bell, always with a certain kindly mockery in all he said to them. He laughed at Bell, though she was so important a personage, just as he laughed at his little Peggy: yet all the while, as he laughed, he remembered that to-morrow, perhaps, he might laugh no more. One thing, however, that he did not think it necessary to do was to send for the doctor, to try what medical skill might be able to suggest toward a little postponement of the end. What could the doctor do for him? there was nothing the matter with him. He was only drowsy, falling asleep without knowing why. Even now, while Sir Ludovic sat upright in his chair and defied it, he felt his eyelids coming together, his head drooping in spite of himself; and he felt a wondering curiosity in his mind, after a momentary absence of this kind, whether other people noticed it, or if it was only himself who knew.

"Do you want anything, papa?" said Margaret, at the door. She had her hat in her hand, and stood at the door looking in, with little more than her head visible and the outline of her light summer frock.

"Going out, my little Peggy?" He raised his head with a start, and the young, fresh apparition seemed to float upon him through some door in the visionary darkness about, as well as through that actual opening at which she stood.

"I think so, papa: unless you want me. It is such a bonnie morning, and Mr. Glen is going to begin his sketch. He thinks," said Margaret, with a little hesitation, "that it will be a better lesson for me to see him drawing than doing the straight lines; they were not very straight," she added, with blushing candor. "I was not clever at them, though I tried—"

"Mr. Glen," he said, with a little annoyance. "Mr. Glen again; did you not have enough of him yesterday?"

"Oh!" cried Margaret, half alarmed; "but yesterday it was to let you see the pictures, and to-day it is to learn me—"

"I hope he will not learn you—as you call it —too much," said the old man. "I wish somebody would learn you English. I have a great mind—" But here he stopped and looked at her, and seeing the alarm on Margaret's face, was melted by the effect which ought to have made him stern. Perhaps it might be so short a time that she would have any one to indulge her. "Well, my little Peggy! run, run away, since you wish it, and learn."

He ought to have been all the more determined because she wanted it so much. This was a lesson which his daughters Jean and Grace could both have taught him; but an old man with a young girl is proverbially weak. It just crossed his mind, though, that he ought to write to Jean and Grace, and invite them to hasten their usual visit. On the whole, they would take more trouble about his little Peggy than Ludovic could, to whom the old house would go. Sir Ludovic had no particular feeling one way or another about these middle-aged people. They were people whom he knew very well, of course, belonging to the family; but there was no special sympathy between them and himself. Ludovic had a large family, and "a good deal to do." It was all he could manage to make his ends meet, to keep up his position, to do the best he could for his own children. And Jean and Grace would be very fussy, they would worry his little girl out of her life; but still they would be kind to her, too kind—no more of her own way for poor little Peggy. He could not but smile as this aspect of the future rose before him; they would watch her so that she would be unable to put in a pin that they did not know of. And perhaps, in a way, it would be better for her; perhaps she had done too much as seemed right in her own eyes. This Rob Glen, for instance—Sir Ludovic was by no means sure that he was doing exactly as was right about Rob Glen. He would see to it, he would speak to Bell about it; and with this he floated away again on his own vague stream of thought, which was not thought.

Margaret came in, however, late in the afternoon, all aglow with enthusiasm and delight. "Oh, papa!" she cried, "it will make the most beautiful picture; he has taken it from the east, where you can see the house best, how it is built. I never knew it was so fine before. The tower all round, with that great ivy-tree, and then the side of the house all in shade with the big windows that are shut up, the windows *there*, you know, papa, that would look out upon the court if you could see through them; and then the gable, and the round turret with the stair in it, and all the little openings. But the sun would not stay in one place," said Margaret, laughing; "first it sent the shadows one way and then another, and gave Mr. Glen a great deal of trouble. I understand now about shadows," she added, with a serious air of importance. Sir Ludovic had been getting drowsy again. Her coming woke him entirely, with a little pleased sensation of liveliness which roused his spirits.

"Have you been about your picture all this time?" he said.

"Yes, papa, out there among the potatoes. You could have seen us from the east window if you had liked to look. And Bell gave us 'a piece' at one o'clock, just as she used to do when I was little. Often she would give Rob a piece too—I mean Mr. Glen," said Margaret, blushing wildly; "I forgot he was not a boy now."

"My little Peggy," said Sir Ludovic, looking grave, "there are some things which you ought to be very careful not to forget."

"I did not mean to be rude, papa," said Margaret, half alarmed; "indeed it was not that: I don't think I ever could be rude and hurt people's feelings; indeed he said it himself; he said to Bell, 'You often gave me my lunch when I was a boy,' and she said, 'Ay, Rob Glen, many's the piece I've given you.' I was rather shocked to hear her," Margaret acknowledged, "but he only laughed, he was not offended; and so—"

"And so you did the same? that was not like my little girl," said Sir Ludovic; "whatever happens, you must always be civil. So it is a beautiful picture, is it—as good a picture of the old house as of the old man it belongs to? Two old things, my Peggy, that you will miss, that you will like to have pictures of when you go away."

"Papa!"—Margaret looked at him with suddenly dilated eyes—"I am not going away."

"Not till I go first," he said, with a sigh and a smile. "But that will not be long, that will come sometime; and then, my little Peggy, then —why, you must go too."

Margaret came behind his chair and put her arm round him, and laid down her head on his shoulder. The old man could have cried too. He too was sorry for what was going to happen —very sorry; but he could not help it. He patted the arm that had been thrown round him. "Poor little Peggy, you will miss the old man and the old house. It is well you should have pictures of them," he said.

"I want no pictures now," cried Margaret, weeping. "Oh, are you ill—are you ill, papa?"

"No, I am just as usual. Don't cry, my little girl. Whisht, now whisht, you must not cry; I did not mean to vex you. But we must not have too much of Rob Glen or Mr. Glen, whichever is his name. It might be bad for him, my darling, as well as for you."

"I don't care anything about him or them, or anything," cried Margaret; "all the pleasure is gone out of it. Will I send for the doctor? will I cry upon Bell? You must be feeling ill, papa."

"Will you speak decent English?" said her father, with a smile; her anxiety somehow restored himself to himself. "Cry upon Bell! what does that mean, my little Peggy? You are too Fifish; you will not find anything like that in books, not in Shakspeare, or in—"

"It is in the Bible, papa," said Margaret, roused to a little irritation in the midst of her emotion. "I am quite sure it is in the Bible; and is not that the best rule."

Sir Ludovic was a little puzzled. "Oh yes, certainly the best rule for everything, my little girl; but the language, the English is perhaps a little old-fashioned, a little out of use, a little—"

"Papa! is it not the Word of God?"

Sir Ludovic laughed in spite of himself.

"It was not first delivered in English, you know. It was not written here; but still there is something to be said for your view. Now, my Peggy, run away."

But when she left him reluctantly, unwinding her arms from his shoulders slowly, looking at him anxiously, with a new awakening of feeling in her anxiety and terror, Sir Ludovic shook his head, looking after her. He was not capable of crossing his little girl; but he had his doubts that her position was dangerous, though she was far too innocent to know it. Unless what he had said were to disgust her altogether, how could he interfere to prevent the execution of this picture which it would be so pleasant for her to have afterward? "Decidedly," he said to himself— "decidedly! I must write to Jean and Grace."

CHAPTER XIV.

As there was, however, no more said on this subject, and Sir Ludovic was—probably having shaken off something of the heaviness of his mind by putting it in words—as gay as usual at dinner and during the evening, the impression on Margaret's mind wore off. She had been very unhappy for half an hour or so, then less wretched, then not wretched at all; deciding that it was nothing particular, that it was only some passing cloud or other, or a letter from her brother, or something which had vexed him about "business," that grand, mysterious source of trouble. Instead of going out that evening, she went down-stairs to where Bell sat in her chair "outside the door," breathing the quiet of the evening. Bell was full of the excitement of "the view." "It will be equal to ony picture in a museeum," said Bell. "To think a creature like that, that I mind just a little callant about the doors, should have such a power." Margaret, however, did not respond at first. Her mind was still occupied with her father, notwithstanding that his demeanor since had wiped much of the alarming impression away.

"Do you think papa is quite well?" she said. "Bell, will you tell me true? Do you think anything is the matter with papa?"

"The matter with your papa? is he complaining?" said Bell, hastily rising from her chair. "Na, no me, I've heard nothing; that's just the way in this world, the one that ought to ken never kens. Miss Margret, what ails your papa?"

"It was me that was asking you, Bell: it was not him that complained; he spoke of—going away: that some day I would leave Earl's-hall, and some day he—would be gone," said Margaret, faltering, large tears coming to her eyes.

"Was that a'?" said Bell, sitting down again on her chair. "Dyin' is a thing we a' think of whiles. Sir Ludovic is just in his ordinary so far as I ken, just as particular about his dinner. No, no, my bonnie dear, you need not fash yoursel' about what the like of us old folk says. We say whiles mair than we mean; and other times it will come to us to think without any particular occasion (as we aye ought to be thinking) of our latter end."

"Would that be all, Bell?'"

"That would just be all. I havena heard a word of ony complaints. He takes his meals aye in a way that's maist satisfactory, and John he would be the first to see if onything was wrang. Na, na, my bonnie doo, you need not fash your head about Sir Ludovic. He's hale and strong for his age, and runs nae risks: and the Leslies are long-living folk. We mustna count upon that for ourselves," said Bell, seriously. "I would not say sae to him; for to think of our latter end is what we should a' be doing, even the like of yoursel', young and bonnie, far mair auld folk; but auld Sir Paitrick lived to be ninety. I mind him as weel as I mind my ain faither; and every Sabbath in the kirk, rain or shine, a grand-looking auld man with an ee like a hawk. Na, na, my bonnie dear, troubles aye sune enough when it comes; we needna gang out to look for it; but wait till it chaps at the ha' door."

This gave Margaret great comfort; the tension of her mind relaxed, and even before Bell had done speaking her young mistress had done thinking. She went back with a bound to the more agreeable subject. "You are to be sitting here, Bell," she said, "just here, when the picture is done."

"Bless my heart!" said Bell; the change was so sudden that she scarcely could follow it; "the picture? I thought you had forgotten all about the picture; but, Miss Margret, what would ye hae an auld wife for, sitting here on her auld chair? Something young and bonnie, like yoursel' now—or even Jeanie—would be mair to the purpose in a picture than an auld wife like me."

"But it is you I want," said Margaret, with pretty obstinacy. "What should I care about myself? And Jeanie is very good, but not like you. It must be you, Bell, or nobody. It would not be natural not to see you with your stocking outside the door."

"Weel, weel!" said Bell, with the air of yielding, half against her will, "you were aye a wilfu' miss, and would have your way, and few, few have ever crossed you. If a' your life be like the past, and ye win to heaven at the end, ye may say you were never out of it; for you've aye had your ain way."

"Do they get their own way in heaven?" said Margaret, half laughing; "but I wish you would not speak of the past like that, and my life. Nothing's past. It has always been just as it is now. Papa is only seventy-five—that makes fifteen years before he can be as old as grandpapa; and by that time I will be old myself. Why should there be any change? I like things to be as they are: you at the door, and John taking a look at the potatoes, and papa reading in the long room. And the summer nights so long, so long, as if they would never end."

"But this ane is ending, and you must go to your bed," said Bell. "The dew's no so heavy io-night after the rain; but it's time to go inbye and go to all our beds; it's near upon ten o'clock."

Margaret lingered to look at the soft brightness of the skies, those skies which never seemed to darken. And now that her mind was relieved, there was something else she wished to look at and pass a final judgment upon. Though it was ten o'clock and bedtime, she could still see all there was to see in the little sketch-book which Rob had given her to draw in. She had made a few scratches in the intervals of her careful attendance upon the chief artist; and Rob had looked with satisfaction upon these scraps, and said that this was good and that better. Margaret, for her part, surveyed them now with mingled hope and shame. They were not like the picture at all, though they were intended to represent the same thing; but perhaps if she worked very hard, if she gave her mind to it! Bell did not think very much of them, as she came and looked over the young lady's shoulder. She shook her head. "He's a clever lad, yon," said old Bell, "but I wish he could learn you the piany instead of drawing pictures. I canna think but you would come more speed." Margaret shut up her book hastily, with some petulance, not liking the criticism, and this time she did not resist the repeated call to go "inbye." She could not but feel that a great deal was wanting before she could draw like Rob; but as for the piano which Bell brought up upon all occasions, what could Margaret do? She had tried to puzzle out "a tune" upon the old spinnet in the high room with indifferent success, and this had given Bell real pleasure. But then that was apt to disturb papa; whereas these scratches of uneven lines in the sketch-book disturbed nothing except her own self-esteem and ease of mind.

Margaret said nothing about it next morning, learning prudence by dint of experience, but was out among the potatoes arranging the artist's seat, and the little table to hold all his requirements, and the water for his colors, in readiness for his appearance. The whole house indeed, except Sir Ludovic among his books, who had fallen back into his ordinary calm, externally at least, and asked no questions, was in agitation about this picture. Jeanie, poor girl, kept in the background altogether. She would not even come to look at the picture, though Bell adjured her to do so.

"What makes you blate, you silly thing?" Bell said. "It's no a gentleman; it's naebody but Rob Glen, Mrs. Glen's son, at Earl's-lee—a neebor lad, you to speak. You must have been at the school with him. Gang forward and see what's doing, like the rest." But nothing would make Jeanie gang forward. She felt sure by this time that he did not know she was here, and had begun to think that there was some mistake, and that perhaps he was not to blame. It wrung her heart a little, peeping from her turret-window, to see Miss Margaret hovering about him, looking over his shoulder, waiting on him, a more graceful handmaid than Jeanie; but at the same time a little forlorn pride was in her mind. Miss Margaret understood about his painting, no doubt, and could talk about things that were above her own range; but it was not in that stiff polite way that Rob would have conducted his intercourse with Jeanie. She watched them, herself unseen, with pain, yet with consolation. Not like that; not with so many commonplace witnesses—Bell lingering about looking on, even old John marching heavily across the lines of potatoes to take a look—would Rob have been content to pass the hours if she had been by, instead of Margaret. But it was well for Rob to have such grand friends. She would not put herself in the way to shame him or make him uncomfortable. Jeanie went to her work magnanimously, and with a lightened heart. She would not even sing as she put the rooms in order, lest her voice should reach him through the open window, and he should ask who it was. She hid herself in the depths of the old house that he might not see her; but yet his presence made a difference in the atmosphere. She could not blame him now that she had seen him. And she had waited long already, and had not lost heart. After all, Jeanie reflected, nothing was changed; and insensibly a little confidence and hope came back to her; for it was very evident, for one thing, that he did not know she was here.

As for Margaret, she was very happy in the fresh exhilaration of the morning air, in the excitement of what was going on, and in the society of her new friend. Nobody had so much amused her, occupied her, filled her mind with novel thoughts as Rob Glen. To watch him as he worked was an unceasing delight. He had chosen his place on the edge of the little belt of wood which encircled Earl's-hall. Had the Leslies been well-to-do this would have been a mere flower-garden for beauty and pleasure; but as the Leslies were poor, it was potatoes, a more profitable if less lovely crop. The fir-trees, of which the wood was chiefly composed—for that corner of Fife is not favorable to foliage—sheltered them from the sun, which streamed full upon the old house, with all its picturesque irregularities. The little court, with its well and its old thorn-tree, which lay so deep in shadow in the evening, was now full of light. The door standing open let in a mass of sunshine into the little vaulted passage which led to the lower story, and touched the winding stair with an edge of whiteness; and the huge old "ivy-tree," as Margaret called it, the branches of which, against the wall which shut in the court on the west side, were like architecture, great ribs of wood, dark, mossy, and ancient, as if they had been carved out of stone—shone and glowed, and sent back reflections from the heavy masses of blunt-leaved foliage, which clad the tower completely from head to foot. Bell's chair was placed in front of this open door to show where the figure was to be.

"But to pit me there in the forenoon with the sun in my een, and a' the work of the house lyin' neglectit!" said Bell. "Well, I wat you'll never see me sae."

"It might be Sunday," suggested Rob, "the day of rest."

"The Sabbath's more than a day of rest," said Bell, reprovingly. "In the morning all right-minded folk are at the kirk, the only place for them; and to gie a stranger to suppose that me, I was letting ony idle lad draw my picture on the Lord's-day!"

"Bell, Bell!" cried Margaret, horrified.

But Rob could afford to laugh.

"Never mind," he said; "I am not offended. Bell can call me an idle lad if she likes—so does my mother, for that matter. She thinks I might as well swing on a gate all day, as do what I am doing now."

"Poor body!" said Bell, with a deep sigh of sympathy. "I feel for her with a' my heart. But you'll be wanting a piece," she added, turning to go in, "and, Miss Margret, there's a cold air about. If I was you I would slip on a bit of a jacket or something. The earth's damp amang the pitawties. I'll send you out your piece."

"I feel as if I were a boy again, fishing in the burn, when Bell speaks of a piece," said Rob, in an undertone.

"I hope you are not angry," said Margaret, humbly. "Bell always says whatever she pleases. She does not stand in awe of anybody —even my sister Jean, who is a grand lady— at least, I am sure she thinks she is very grand; but Bell never minds. You must not be angry, Mr. Glen."

"Angry! I am pleased. I like to feel myself a boy again; then too, if you will recollect, I had a beautiful little lady beside me, Miss Margaret, who would hold the rod sometimes and watch for a nibble."

"Don't call me that," said Margaret, with momentary gravity. "Yes—a funny little girl in a sun-bonnet. How glad I used to be when you caught anything! It was not very often, Mr. Glen."

"Not at all often, Miss Margaret; and sometimes you would take off your little shoes, and dabble your little white feet in the water—how white they were! I remember thinking the fishes would bite just to get nearer, just to have a sight of them."

"Indeed the fishes were not so silly," cried the girl, blushing, and half affronted, but too shy to venture on showing her offence. In such matters as this Rob's gentleman-breeding failed him. He did not know in what he had gone wrong. "The sun is changing already," she said, hurriedly; "have you got your shadows right, Mr. Glen? I think you will soon want the umbrella."

"Not yet," he said; "I can work for another hour; but here is old John interfering with my foreground. Is this the 'piece?' It is not so simple as that you used to share with me on the burn-side."

"It is a picnic," said Margaret, with a little awe, as John appeared, slowly progressing among the potatoes, with a white-covered tray. John's approach was a solemnity under any circumstances, but across the long lines of potatoes it was still more imposing.

"You're to pit that on, Miss Margaret," he said, after he had set down his burden, with a sigh of relief, handing to her the little gray jacket which he carried over his arm.

"But it is not cold. I don't want it, the sun is shining; and, John, will you bring the big umbrella, the great big one with the heavy handle, to shelter Mr. Glen?"

"She said you were to pit it on. I maun finish one errant afore I begin anither," said the old man. "She said there was a cauld air, and that you were to pit it on."

"I will when I am cold. Oh, tell Bell she has sent us a great deal too much. Chicken and cake, and white bread and cheese—and jam!" The last pleased the critic, and subdued her remonstrance. "But it is too much. I would like a little milk instead of the wine."

"She said the wine was better for ye," said the old man; "and she said you were to pit that on."

"Oh, John! you are worse, you are a great deal worse than Bell is. You never will hear any reason. She, if one speaks to her, one can make her see what is sense," cried Margaret, half crying; "but you, you are a great deal worse—you are tyrannical!"

"I am doing what I'm bid," said John. "It's no me. Do I ken when you should pit on your jaicket and when you should pit it off? But *she* said you were to pit that on."

"And Bell is a very sensible woman," said Rob. "It is cold this morning after the rain; and, John, I hope you will tell her that her provision is noble. I never saw such a 'piece' before."

John made no reply. He gave a glance of surly disdain at the interloper. What had Rob Glen to do here, beside "our young leddy?" "And me to wait upon him—set him up!" the old man grumbled to himself as he went back grimly to the house, having seen one, at least, of his orders fulfilled. There were points upon which John was proud to think he himself was "maister and mair;" but on ordinary domestic occasions he was content to accept the *rôle* of executor, and see that his wife's behests were carried out.

Margaret, in her gray jacket (which was not unacceptable, after all), went away from Rob's side and opened her sketch-book. She did not choose to be laughed at, which she felt to be possible, and it was time for her to try that gable again, which had eluded her so often. To jump at the outline of a rugged Scotch gable, after having proved your incapacity to draw a straight line, was, perhaps, a bold proceeding; and there was a perplexing little round of masonry penetrated by slits of little windows, and giving light, as Margaret knew, to the second little spiral staircase, the one at the east end of the house, which tried her ignorance dreadfully, but which she returned to notwithstanding, again and again. Margaret was gazing up against the sky, intently studying this, when her eyes were caught by a face at the high window looking down as intently upon the group in the sunshine.

"Ah, Jeanie!" she said, with a nod and a smile; but Jeanie took no notice of the little salutation.

"Did yon speak, Miss Margaret?" said Rob Glen, busy over his drawing, and not looking up.

"I was only nodding to Jeanie," said the girl. Jeanie! Rob did not budge. It was the commonest of names; there was nothing in it to rouse his special attention. And even if he had known that it was the one Jeanie with whom he had some concern, would that have made any difference? He worked on quite calmly. But Jeanie withdrew in haste, with a pang for which she could not account. She had seen and heard, by the sound of the voices, that something was said between them; but Rob never looked up to see who it was of whom Miss Margaret spoke. When Jeanie came back to peep again, they were sitting together at the little luncheon Bell had sent them, with much talking and soft laughter, sharing the same meal, and reminding each of humbler picnic meals eaten together in other years. As they grew more at ease with each other, the doubtful taste of Rob's compliments ceased to offend Margaret; or perhaps in the greater intimacy of this odd conjunction, so absolutely free, yet so entirely under restraint, public to all the watchful eyes that guarded her, there was something that made him avoid compliments. There is always much that is suggestive in a meal thus shared by two, with no intrusive third to break its completeness. A certain romance infolds the laughing pair; the very matter-of-fact character of the conjunction, the domesticity, the homeliness, increase their sense of union. It suggests everything that is in life. The boy and girl over their "piece," the youth and the maiden over their impromptu repast: what was it but playing at honey-mooning, a pleasant mockery, or essay at, or caricature of, the most serious conjunction? Even Margaret felt a certain half delightful shyness of her companion in this odd union, free as her mind was of all embarrassing thoughts; and as for Rob, the suggestion gave him a thrill of pride and pleasure not to be put into words. Jeanie stole to the window to look at them again, while they were thus engaged, and the sight went to her heart.

"If I were you, I wouldna let them bide ower lang philandering, they twa," said John. "I'm no that sure that I would have left them there ava'. Like twa young marrit folk, the ane forenenst the ither—"

"Haud your tongue, you ill-thinking man!" cried Bell, with a half-shriek. "How dare ye! But be a lassie the maist innocent that ever was born, ye'll aye put it upon her that she kens as muckle as yoursel'."

"It's no what she kens I'm thinking o': it's a' instinck," said John. "A lad and a lass—they're drawn to ane anither; it's nature. I wish it was a gentleman that had come this gate instead o' that laud. Plenty gentlemen waste their time drawing pictures. There's Sir Claude; he's auld and a married man? I kent you would say that. Was I meaning Sir Claude? but he aye has his house fu' o' his ain kind; or even if it had been Randal Burnside—yon's a lad that will rise in the world; but whatever evil spirit sent us Rob Glen—"

"John, my man, you're no an ill man, and if you'll haud to the things ye understand—"

"I wuss there was one of ye a' that understood that poor bairn's living, and what's to come o' her," said John. "Sir Ludovic, he's no lang for this world."

"He's just in his ordinar, and his faither lived to ninety."

"He's no just in his ordinar. I havena likit the looks of him this month past; and now he sees it himsel'."

"Lord bless us, man!" cried Bell, in alarm; "and ye never said a word to me!"

"What good would that have done if I had said a word to ye? You canna keep out Death. If he's coming, he'll come, and no be hindered by you or me. But now he's found it out himsel'. Will I tell ye what he said to me no an hour ago? But I'll not tell you; maybe ye would think it was just naething, and pit your jokes on me."

"You may do just what you like," said Bell: "speak or no speak, he seems just in his ordinar to me."

"Is this like his ordinar?" says John, indignantly. "He says to me no an hour ago, 'Are the horses busy, John?' he said; and I says (for it doesna do to let on when wark's slack; you never ken what folk may take into their head), 'Oh ay, Sir Ludovic,' I says, 'they're aye busy.' 'Could we have them for the carriage on Sunday?' he says. 'Weel, Sir Ludovic,' says I, 'it might be sae; but what would it be for? Miss Margret, she aye walks, and wouldna thank ye for ony carriage; and the ither leddies, they're no here.' Then he strikes his stick on the floor. 'Can I have the carriage on Sunday?' he cries, him that's aye so quiet. Aweel! that's a'; and if that doesna prove that he's been turning many a thing ower in his mind."

"Was it to gang to the kirk?" said Bell, somewhat struck by awe; "he hasna been at the kirk this year or more."

"I tell ye sae," said John; "and Sir Ludovic, he's no man to make a careless end. He'll do all decently and in order. He'll no let the minister think he's neglectit. Ye'll give me out my best claes, as if it was a funeral. I ken what he means, if naebody else does; and syne what is to become of that bairn?"

"Oh, man, haud your tongue, haud your tongue," cried Bell. "Sir Ludovic! that has aye been so steady and so weel in health. I canna credit what you say. Your best claes! Put on your bonnet, mair like, and gang and bid the doctor come this way, canny, the morn's morning, without saying a word to anybody. That's the thing for you to do. And now I'll send that laud away," she added, briskly. This was a little outlet to her feelings; and to do Bell justice, she was glad to have a moment alone after hearing this alarming news.

———

CHAPTER XV.

THE doctor came, very careful to explain that he had come to call out of friendship only, because it was so long since he had seen Sir Ludovic. But he could perceive nothing to justify John's alarm. Sir Ludovic was glad to see the neighbor who was more intelligent than most of his neighbors, and with whom he could have a little talk. The doctor was a plain man of homely Scotch manners and speech; but he knew all about the county and everybody in it, and was not unacquainted with books. Sir Ludovic, who was glad to be delivered from himself, and who found it easier to escape from the prospect which oppressed him, by means of society than in any other way, detained the doctor as long as he could, and listened with much more patience than usual to the gossip of the parish, and smiled at the jokes which Dr. Hume carried about from patient to patient to "give the poor bodies a laugh," he said.

"Come back again soon," the old man said, accompanying his visitor to the door. The doctor was pleased, for he had seen Sir Ludovic much less complaisant. He stepped into the vaulted kitchen before he left the house, to tell Bell what he thought.

"I see no difference in him," said Dr. Hume; "he's an old man. We are none of us so young as we once were, Bell; and an old man cannot live forever. He's bound to get an attack of bronchitis or something else before long, and to slip through our fingers. But I see nothing to be alarmed at to-day. There's a little bit of a vacant look in his eyes; but, Lord bless us! many of us have that all our lives, and never die a day the sooner. He tells me the ladies are expected—"

"Na, but that's news, doctor!" said Bell; "the ladies! it's no their time for three months yet, the Lord be thanked, and I've never heard a word."

"Well," said the doctor, "now you're warned, and you can take your measures accordingly. He certainly said they were coming. They're no the wisest women on the face of the earth; but still, if you are anxious, it would be a comfort, do you not think so, to have some of the family in the house?"

"Ye dinna ken our ladies, doctor—ye dinna ken our ladies," said Bell.

"Atweel, I ken a heap of ladies," said the doctor, with a laugh. He liked a joke at women when it was to be heard. "One's very like another; but if it was only for his little Peggy, as he calls her, I should think he would be glad to have his daughters here."

"He's no a bit glad, no more nor the rest of us—nor Miss Margaret either," said Bell; and it was with a clouded countenance that she saw the doctor mount his horse at the door of the court. And when John came in to ask what Dr. Hume thought, she gave him an answer which was full of sorrowful impatience. "He said nothing it was any pleasure to hear," said Bell, and it was only later that she unbosomed herself of her vexation. "He says there's nothing wrong; and syne he goes away telling me that the ladies are coming, and that it will be a comfort to have some of the family in the house. That means that a's wrong, so far as I'm equal to judging. Sir Ludovic in his bed wi' a long illness and the ladies here!"

Bell flung up her hands with a groan; the very idea was too much for her; but John was obstinate in his preconceived certainty.

"Na," he said, "Sir Ludovic will no have a long illness. He'll just fail, just in a moment; that's what he'll do. If I dinna ken him better than a dizzen doctors, it would be a wonder—me that have been his body-servant these twenty years."

"I maun gang up the stair and see for mysel'," said Bell. She tied on her clean apron with decision, and could not quite banish from her countenance the look of a person who would stand no nonsense, who was not to be taken in —but whose inspection would be final. And Sir Ludovic was pleased to see Bell too. He was not annoyed to be disturbed. He turned toward her with a vague smile, and gave his book a scarcely perceptible push away from him. This little action made Bell's heart sink, as she confessed afterward. She would much rather have seen him impatient, and been requested to cut her errand short. On the contrary, her master was not displeased to talk. He let her tell him about the drawing which was still going on, and her own wonder that one who had been the other day "a callant about the doors" should possess such a wonderful gift.

"Callants about the doors are very apt to surprise us as they grow up," Sir Ludovic said, "and Rob Glen is certainly clever; but you must not let him lose his time here. It is certain that I cannot afford to buy his picture, Bell."

"But maybe the ladies would do it, Sir Ludovic," said Bell, seeing an opening; "maybe the ladies would like a picture of the auld house

—though me at the door (as Miss Margret will have me) would be a drawback. I hear from the doctor, Sir Ludovic, that you're expecting the ladies? I didna think it was near their time."

"To be sure," said Sir Ludovic, "I wrote, but the letter has never been posted. If you had not spoken I should have forgotten all about it. Bell, I thought they might come a little sooner."

"It's very true," said Bell, with a grave countenance, "that it's bonnie weather; and when they were here last, in September, we had nothing but wind and rain; but for a' that, when ladies have made their plans, it's a great deal of trouble to change them, and it's aye in September they come. Do you no think, Sir Ludovic, they would like it better if you let them come at their ain time?"

"Do you suppose they would think it a trouble, Bell?" Sir Ludovic had written his letter as a matter of duty for his little Peggy's sake; but he was not disinclined to get out of it, to allow a feasible reason for not sending it, if such a one should present itself; for he did not anticipate the arrival of his daughters with any pleasure.

"Weel, Sir Ludovic, you see they've all their plans made. They're awfu' leddies for plans. You ken yoursel' it's a' laid out every day what they're to do; and Mrs. Bellingham, she canna bide being put out o' her way."

"That's true, Bell, that's very true," said Sir Ludovic, suddenly remembering how his eldest daughter received any interference with her projects. "I am very glad you reminded me," said the old man; "after all, perhaps, I had better let things take their course. I thought it might be better, whatever happened, to have them here; but, as you say, Jean does not like any interference with—I think I will keep my letter to myself, after all."

"And nothing's going to happen that I ken of, Sir Ludovic. We are all in our ordinar."

"That is very true, too," he said, with a smile; "and now you can go away and tell John to bring me my wine and my biscuit. The doctor and you together have wasted my morning." He drew his book toward him again as he dismissed her. This was the only "good sign" that Bell saw in her master; and her face was so grave when she went down-stairs that John paused in his preparation for his master's simple luncheon with a sombre triumph.

"Aweel? You'll not tell me I'm an auld fule again," John said.

"Then I'll tell you you're an auld raven, a prophet o' evil," said his wife, with vehemence. "Gang up the stairs this moment and gie the maister his drop o' wine; he's crying for that and his biscuit, and there he might sit, and you never take the trouble to gang near him. Oh ay!" said Bell, dreamily—"oh ay! The bairn divined it, and the auld man saw it, and the doctor sees it too, though he winna say sae; and Bell's the last to ken! In our ordinar, just in our ordinar! but them that has een can see the end."

However, though this foreboding gathered force by the adhesion of one after another, it was not as yet any more than a foreboding, and the days went on very quietly without any new event. The next Sunday, on which Sir Ludovic had intended to go to church, was very wet, and it was not until a fortnight after his first announcement of his intention, that the old carriage was at last got out, and the horses, which had been making themselves useful in the farm, harnessed. They were not a very splendid or high-spirited pair, as may be conceived, but they answered the purpose well enough. It was a true summer Sunday, the sunshine more warm, the air more still, than on any other day. The roses were fading off the hedge-rows, the green corn was beginning to wave and rustle in the fields; the country groups that came from afar on every visible road, not all to the kirk on the hill (for there was a Free Church in the "laigh toun," not to speak of "the chapel," which was Baptist, and had a dozen members, like the Apostles), were sprinkled with light dresses in honor of the season, and all was still in the villages save for this gathering and animated crowd. The big old coach, with its old occupant, called forth much excitement in the Kirkton. Carriages and fine people had failed to the parish church.

Perhaps it is one of the penalties which Scotland has paid for being no longer unanimous, and dividing herself into different camps, that her gentry should have deserted that old centre of local life, and left the National Church which has played so large a part in Scotch history. It is one of the least sensible as well as the least lovely features of modern Scotland. Of all the squires in this division of Fife, not one but old Sir Ludovic united in the national worship. The others drove miles away to the "English Chapel" at the county town, which was gay with their carriages and finery, like the corresponding "English Chapel" in Florence or Rome; very like it, indeed, in more ways than it is necessary to mention. Gentility poured thither, even the rich shopkeepers, or at least the manufacturers of the second generation; for to belong to the English Church gave a kind of brevet rank. Sir Ludovic, perhaps, was too indifferent to change his ways in his old age; and then neither he nor the world required any outward proof that he was a very superior person. Why it was that he had set his mind on going to church at all after this long gap in his attendance it would be hard to tell. He could not have told himself. It was like a last visit to court, a last parade to an old soldier, a thing to be done as long as he could calculate upon his time, before the days had arrived, which he could see advancing, when he would no longer have command of his own movements.

Sir Ludovic felt a sensation of relief when he had fairly set out. Of this thing, then, which he had determined to do, he was not to be balked. He was to have power and time to accomplish this last duty. The burial-place of the Leslies was close to the east end of the church, the head of the vault touching the old chancel, a relic of the times when to be near that sacred spot in the morning quarter, "toward the sunrising," was to be doubly safe. Here Sir Ludovic stood for a moment, looking less at the familiar grave than at the still more familiar landscape, the low hills round the horizon on three sides, the glimmer of the sea that filled up the circle, the broad amphitheatre of fertile fields that swept around. He did not care to turn from that wide and liberal prospect, all sweet with summer air and warm with sunshine, to the heavy mass of stone that shut in the remains of his kindred. He gave one glance at it only, as he walked past, though it was that spot he had chosen to view the landscape from. A faint smile came upon his face as he looked at it. There was his place waiting and ready, and soon to be filled. He asked himself, with a little thrill of strange sensation, whether he would feel the breezes, such as were always rife in Stratheden, or have any consciousness of the landscape, when he lay there, as, by-and-by, he should be lying. He walked very steadily, yet with a nervous tremor, of which he himself was conscious, if nobody else, and kept his hand upon Margaret's shoulder, scarcely to support him—that was not necessary—but yet to give him a little prop. Some of the people, the elders and the farmers who felt themselves sufficiently important, threw themselves in his way, and took off their hats with kindly respect.

"I'm real glad to see you out, Sir Ludovic," and, "I hope you're well this fine morning, Sir Ludovic," they said. The old man took off his hat and made them all a sweeping bow.

"Good-morning to you all, my friends," he said, and, with a little additional tremor, hurried into church, to be safe from all these greetings. The church, as we have already said, was a monstrous compound, such as perhaps only Scotland could produce nowadays. The old door opened into a noble but gloomy old Norman church, very small, but lofty and symmetrical, in the corners of which some old monuments, brass denuded of their metal (if that is not a bull), rude in Northern art, but ancient, and looking, by dint of their imperfections, more ancient than they were—were piled together. In the little round basement of the tower, where there had been a tiny chapel behind the altar in the old days, a man in his shirt-sleeves stood pulling the rope, which moved a cracked and jingling bell; and the vast chancel arch opposite was blocked up with a wooden partition, through which, by means of a little door, you entered the new painted and varnished pews of the modern building, which Sir Claude Morton had built for the parish. The parish was quite contented, be it allowed, and Sir Claude went to the English Chapel, and did not have his sins brought home to him every Sunday; and among the higher classes you may be sure that it was the old Reformers and John Knox who were supposed to be in fault, and not an enlightened connoisseur like Sir Claude, who did so much for the art-instruction of the world away from home. Sir Claude was the chief "heritor" of the parish, for the lands of the Leslies had dwindled almost to nothing.

We will not affirm that Sir Ludovic would have done much better, but then, at least, he was not a connoisseur. He, for his part, made no reflections upon this as he went in, and placed himself in the great square pew, the only one of the kind in the new church, all lined with red cloth, and filled with chairs instead of benches, which marked his own importance in the parish. He thought of the difference between the old and the new without troubling himself about art, and with a little shiver acknowledged that the light and air and brightness of the wooden

barn were more comfortable than the stately grace and dampness of the old building, which was, like himself, chilled and colorless with age. But how many generations of old men like himself had passed under the great gray arch that "swore," as the French say, at the vulgar new walls! A lifetime of threescore and fifteen years was as nothing in the history of that ancient place. And there it would stand for generations more, watching them come and go— It, and he with it, lying so close under the old stones. Would it be anything to Ludovic Leslie, once placed there, who came and who might go? This thought gave him, as it always did, a kind of vertigo and swimming of the brain. To fancy one's self—one's self, not another, as insensible to everything in life—

"Whirled round in earth's diurnal course,
With rocks, and stones, and trees."

Is that possible? Sir Ludovic tried, but could not do it. It made his head swim round and round.

All the time the people were taking their places, clattering in with much noise, and perhaps not much reverence. Ordinarily they waited about, the men at least, until the bell stopped and the hour had struck. But perhaps out of respect to old Sir Ludovic, who had not been there for so long, and who might never—who could tell?—be there again, for he was an old man, they came in after him, making a great noise, shutting and fastening after them the doors of their pews. And then Dr. Burnside walked into the pulpit, solemnly preceded by the beadle with the big Bible, and the service began. Neither Sir Ludovic nor his daughter paid any attention to the fact that the singing of the old metrical psalms was very rough and tuneless. Margaret did not know much better, having had no training, and heard no music; and Sir Ludovic, it must be confessed, was full of his own thoughts, and paid but little attention. He was scarcely caught even by the words of that Psalm, known from their cradles to all Scots, which Dr. Burnside hastily, and with some perturbation, on hearing of Sir Ludovic's presence, had changed for the one before chosen.

Dr. Burnside had not had it in his power for a long time now to set Sir Ludovic's duty before him. And when his wife brought him the news that the old carriage from Earl's-hall had passed, with the Leslies in it, the minister had a moment of great excitement. His sermon had not been at all adapted for such an occasion, but had been addressed very generally to the parish world about its commonplace sins of gossip and fibbing, and such-like. Dr. Burnside ran to his writing-table and hastily chose a sermon of a different complexion. He had preached it before, but he had a great and consoling consciousness that nobody paid much attention, and certainly Sir Ludovic had never heard it. It was about the conclusion of life. He did not think of it as touching himself, and never had known the tremulous attempt to realize that conclusion which made Sir Ludovic's head turn round; but he knew that an old man ought to think of his latter end, and that it was of great importance not to neglect an opportunity that might not occur again.

"Will you tell the precentor, my dear, to wait

a moment. I have some changes to make," the Doctor said, hastily; and thus it was that the Psalm was altered, and the one now chosen sung to an unusual tune, which had been intended for the former one, and which put the rude singers out—

"Yea, though I walk in death's dark vale,
　Yet will I fear none ill ;
For Thou art with me, and Thy rod
　And staff me comfort still,"

sang the rough, rural voices. They sang as if the object of their worship was far away at sea, and required a hearty shout to catch his ear. And Sir Ludovic did not pay much attention. He had known the words by heart ever since he knew anything, which made them less striking to him. Besides, he had no trouble on that point; he did not doubt the rod and staff that would support him; he wanted rather dimly to know what sort of place that dark valley was, and what—not whether it was bliss or despair, but what—lay beyond.

Dr. Burnside preached his sermon with great feeling and great meaning, so that everybody in church felt that it had a bearing upon Sir Ludovic; but Sir Ludovic himself did not see it. He propped himself in the corner and listened respectfully, sometimes asking himself, however, how Burnside could keep on so long, and why the fact of being in the pulpit should bring twaddle to the lips of a reasonable man. Once when the good Doctor was moved by his own eloquence almost to weeping, Sir Ludovic was quite roused too, and sat more upright, and gave his whole attention to the speaker; but it was rather with an amazed desire to know what could have so much moved his old friend than from any mere personal motive. Even then he could not make it out. He said to himself that what you say yourself may possibly seem more striking than what another says; but still he could not see what Burnside had to cry about. Notwithstanding those thoughts, which were not visible, Sir Ludovic was a most respectful and devout worshipper. Though prayer is supposed to be extempore in the Church of Scotland, and the idea of reading their devotions out of a book would have shocked the people beyond measure, yet Sir Ludovic having gone to church regularly for a great many years, knew Dr. Burnside's prayers by heart, and was able to follow them as closely as if they had been in a prayer-book. He knew where and how the habitual supplications would come. He knew in what words the good minister would embody his ascriptions of praise. All was familiar to him, as if it had been going on forever, as if it would never come to an end.

By-and-by it was over, and the people all streamed out with equal noise and no more reverence, putting on their hats before they were out of church, and beginning to talk in loud whispers. It was over like everything else—another thing ended—another something removed between him and the end. This was the thought that came involuntarily to the old man. He smiled to himself, but not with pleasure, with a kind of amused pain or painful amusement, as the little roll of things to be done was worked out. Here was another over and done with, though it had begun only a moment since. Just so the philosopher might have watched the hours

stealing away that lay between him and that slave with the hemlock, just so noticed the gradual development of the symptoms afterward —the beginning of the death-cold, the rising gasp in the throat. Sir Ludovic was like Socrates, yet with a curious sense that it was somebody else he was watching, not, it could not be, himself. He felt half inclined to laugh as the things to be got through lessened in number; and now this church-going was over, which was one of the last incidents of all.

"Even though I walk in death's dark vale,
　Yet will I fear none ill."

No, no, not any ill; but what? That was the question; and in the mean time this was ended too.

"I think we may go now, the crowd is gone, papa," whispered Margaret; and he assented with a smile. They came out again, once more through the fine Norman arch, which had been there from time immemorial.

"Just there, my little Peggy, is where my place will be," he said, still smiling, pointing to the wall of the apse, and came out, with his hand upon her shoulder, into the sunshine, his erect, delicate head, with its white hair, held up with unconscious, gentle stateliness, leaning upon the young creature in her white frock—leaning only a very little, rather for love than for support. A great many people had lingered about the church-yard, scattered among the graves, to look at them. The parish that day had listened to the sermon much less drowsily than usual. They had recognized by instinct that it was not themselves, but Sir Ludovic, who was addressed, and they had all been interested to hear what the Doctor had to say to Sir Ludovic. They stood with friendly and shy curiosity, pretending to study the tombstones, to look at him as he came out. It was a long time since he had been there before, and who could tell if he would ever be there again?

And the sight of the pair touched the people. An old man leaning upon his child is always a touching sight, and Margaret's pretty, slim figure, in her white frock, her head raised to him, a look of wistful half-anxiety in her eyes, mixed with her pleasure in having him by her, made a great impression upon the kindly neighbors. Some of the women unfolded the handkerchiefs which they carried with their Bibles and put them to their eyes. He was "sore failed" since he had been last seen at the kirk—failed and frail, and no long for this world. And ah, how well the Doctor had set his duty before him ! The father and daughter went softly round the east end of the old church ; and it was when they were passing the Leslie vault again, that Sir Ludovic suddenly stumbled. It was not "a stroke," nor any fainting on his part, as at first the trembling yet eager spectators thought, but only a projecting stone in his way, against which his foot caught. Margaret gave a cry of distress.

"It is nothing, my Peggy, nothing," said the old man. But the shock and the shake affected him, and he turned very pale, and tottered as he went on.

"Will he take my arm ?—ask him to take my arm," said some one close by. Sir Ludovic did not wait to be entreated ; he put forth his hand eagerly and grasped the strong young arm, which he felt, without knowing whom it belonged to, to be sustaining and steady.

"That is right, that is all I want," he said, and walked along the rest of the path to the carriage, leaning upon Rob Glen. Margaret was at his other side. He smiled at her, and bade her not be frightened. "This is all I want," he said, leaning upon the young man. As for Margaret, she, in her fright and anxiety, thought nothing of the words he was saying; but who can describe with what a thrill the repeated assurance went through the ambitious heart and glowing imagination of Rob Glen?

CHAPTER XVI.

THERE were a great many spectators of this scene in the church-yard. Mrs. Burnside, the minister's wife, had been detained most unwillingly by some importunate "poor bodies" from the "laigh toun," and was hurrying round from the other end of the church, with her son Randal, to speak to "the Earl's-hall family," when Rob Glen thus made himself conspicuous. There were various people who held the opinion that he had made himself conspicuous, and none more than Mrs. Burnside, who thought the group very incongruous. Margaret on one side, and a young country lad, Janet Glen's son, on the other! It was quite out of the question. But an old man was an ill guide for a young girl. She hastened round, calling Randal to follow, and reached the gate just as John was putting up the carriage steps.

"Margaret, my dear Margaret, will you not come to the Manse and get a glass of wine? And, Sir Ludovic, I hope you're not hurt. The Doctor will be quite disappointed if he does not see you."

Rob Glen stood at the carriage-door, but Mrs. Burnside took no notice of him.

"Thank you," said Sir Ludovic. "I'm not hurt; but I've got a shake, and the best thing I can do is to get home. Tell the Doctor I will be glad to see him, very glad to see him, whenever he will come so far—with my thanks for a very good sermon." He smiled, but he was still very pale, and old John stood upon little ceremony. He took his seat beside the coachman, and bade him in low tones "no to bide a moment if it was the Queen, but to get hame, to get hame." The consequence of this was that the carriage was already in motion when Mrs. Burnside resumed.

"A glass of wine will do you good, Sir Ludovic; and here's my son Randal. Margaret, my dear, you're not going like this, without a word!" cried the Minister's wife; but Margaret only waved her hand, and said something that was inaudible in the rush of the carriage-wheels.

"I don't call this civil," said Mrs. Burnside, growing red. "I cannot think it civil, Randal, either to you or to me."

"It was not intended for incivility," said Rob Glen. "But Sir Ludovic was shaken. He was more shaken than you would have thought possible. It was the best thing he could do to get home, and I think I will go and tell the doctor. He has certainly grown much weaker within the last month."

How did Rob Glen know how Sir Ludovic had been for the last month? Mrs. Burnside looked upon him with a disapproving countenance. He had made himself a great deal too conspicuous. Janet Glen's son, a lad of no consideration! what right had he to put himself in the way?

"Sir Ludovic shows himself so little that there's very few can be able to judge," she said, meaning to snub the forward young man. And what should Randal do but neutralize all her dignity by making a step forward with friendly hand outstretched?

"Why this," he said, "must be Rob Glen?"

"Oh yes, it is Rob Glen," said his annoyed mother; while Rob accepted the overture graciously. Randal was a year or two older than Rob, and had begun life in the company of the whole juvenile family at the parish school; an early association which made all his father's parishioners his friends. He was a handsome young fellow, full of high spirits and kindness, but so shy that the paths of society were pain and grief to him. He had been absent for a long time, studying in Germany, and had but lately returned, and taken his place in Edinburgh, with every prospect of success at the bar; for he had a family firm of Writers to the Signet behind him. Though Randal had an old boyish kindness for little Margaret, her grown-up looks had somewhat disconcerted him, and it was with more relief than regret that he had seen the carriage turn away. But Randal's shyness did not affect him in respect to the people of the parish, to most of whom his notice was a favor; and, indeed, at this moment he had no idea that it was anything else than an honor to Rob Glen.

"You may as well tell your father, Randal, that Sir Ludovic has gone," said Mrs. Burnside, with a little nod to the intruder. "Good-morning, Rob; I saw your mother, worthy woman, was out this morning. I am glad her cold is better;" and, so saying, she went slowly away toward the Manse in anything but a' tranquil state of mind. She was not mercenary, nor had she really engaged in any matrimonial speculations for her son. But he was a young man, she well knew, who would be a credit to everybody belonging to him; and if Margaret and he had met, and if they had taken a fancy to each other, why then— They had both a little money; indeed, it was generally known that Margaret had more than a little; but upon this point the minister's wife assured herself that she had no information; and they were both well-born (for the Burnsides were as old as anything in the county), and it would have been very suitable: he a rising young lawyer, with a good profession and a good head, and the best of prospects before him. There was no unworthy scheming in her desire to bring these two perfectly matched young people together. The question in her eyes was not, was Randal good enough for Margaret? but, was Margaret good enough for Randal? But they had played together when they were children, and there was nobody far or near so like Margaret as Randal, so like Randal as Margaret. This was what Mrs. Burnside was thinking, as she walked very gently toward the Manse. The children and the old women did not courtesy when they met her, for such are not the habits of rural Scotland; but the little things looked at her with shy smiles, and the women wished her good-day, and were blithe to see Mr. Randal back. "And so am I, Jenny," she said; "more glad than words can say."

"Eh, mem, ye hae nae need to say it; a' the kirk," said the old woman, sympathetic, "could see it in your face." And why should she not ask herself, what was the very best thing to be had—the fairest and the sweetest to get for her boy? But that intrusive Rob Glen making himself so conspicuous! what was he, a country lad, nobody at all, not a gentleman, to put himself in Randal's way?

"And what have you been doing, Rob, all these years? I've heard of you from time to time; but I've been wandering, as you know, and for some time back I know nothing. Little Margaret Leslie, I thought her a child, and lo! she's a lovely lady. I thought I should have found you in the pulpit preaching for my father; but here you are, without so much as a black coat. What has happened to you?"

"Not much," said Rob. He paused rather nervously, and looked at his gray coat, wondering, perhaps, was it the proper dress to come to church in, even when you have ceased to think of being a minister. Randal's coat was black, and he seemed to Rob a young man of fashion. This thought made him very uncomfortable. "Indeed nothing at all has happened to me. I am a failure, Mr. Burnside. Your father tries to set me right; but I am afraid we don't even agree as to the meaning of words."

"A failure?" said Randal, puzzled.

"Yes; the church is too exacting for me. I can't sign a creed because my great-grandfather believed it."

"Ah! oh!" said the other young man. It meant that he had nothing to say on the subject, and did not care to enter into it; but it meant at the same time the slightest tone of disapproval, a gravity which would not smile. Randal thought a man should stick to his colors, whatever they were. "And what are you doing now?"

"Nothing; idling, drawing, dreaming, losing my time; absolutely nothing;" then he added, for he did not want to conceal his privileges, "I have been busy for the last fortnight with a picture of Earl's-hall."

"Are you turning artist, then? I did not think the parish had any such possession. I hope I may come and see it," said young Burnside, wondering whether he might venture to ask his old school-fellow to dinner. He would have done it instantly had he been alone. But his mother was not to be trifled with. As he hesitated, however, his father joined him, coming from the church.

"So Sir Ludovic has gone," said the doctor; "I expected he would have waited to see you, Randal, and perhaps gone on to the Manse; but he is looking frail, and perhaps he was wearied. It's an unusual exertion for him, a very unusual exertion. Good-day, Rob; I am glad to see you have resumed church-going; I hope it's a good sign."

"I don't think it means much," said Rob; "but perhaps it would be a good thing if I were to go on to the doctor, and tell him of Sir Ludo-

vic's stumble. It might be well that he should know at once."

"What's about Sir Ludovic's stumble?" said the Minister; while Randal called after the other as he went away, "I will come and see you to-morrow."

Rob Glen replied with an acquiescing nod and wave of his hand. But he said within himself, "if you find me," and went along with a jubilant step and all kinds of dreams in his head. Sir Ludovic had not received Rob with enthusiasm when he had gone to Earl's-hall. He had not applauded his drawings as Margaret did, who knew nothing about it, though he allowed them to be clever. But at the same time he had always tolerated Rob, never objected to his visits, nor to the hours which Margaret had spent flitting about his encampment among the potatoes. If he had disapproved of this association, surely he would have prevented it; and what could those words mean, as the old man grasped at his offered arm, "This is all I want?" Wonderful words! meaning all, and more than all, that the brightest hopes could look for. "This is all I want." Margaret had taken no notice, but it did not seem possible to Rob that she could have heard such words unmoved. It is astonishing how easy it is to believe miracles on our own behalf. In any other case, Rob Glen would have had enough of the shrewd good-sense of his class to know how very unlikely it was that Sir Ludovic Leslie should choose for his young daughter, who was an heiress, in addition to every other advantage she possessed, an alliance with the son of a small farmer in the neighborhood, a "stickit minister," not at all successful or satisfactory even to his own humble kith and kin. But the fact that it was he himself, Rob Glen, who was the hero, dazzled him, and threw a fictitious air of probability upon things the most unlikely. "This is all I want." What could the fond father, who has selected an Admirable Crichton to insure his child's happiness, say more?

"Oh ay," said Mrs. Glen, on her way home from church. "The Earl's-hall family makes a great work with our Rob. He's there morning, noon, and nicht. I never see him, for my part. Either he's drawing pictures of the house, or he's learning Miss Margret to draw them, or he's doin' something for Sir Ludovic. They take up a' his time that he never does a hand's turn for his ain affairs. It's an awfu' waste of time; but when there are young folk concerned, really you never can ken what's the maist profitable occupation; just nonsense, in that kind of way, is sometimes mair for their advantage in the long-run; but that's no my way of judging in the general, far enough from my way."

"That is just what I was thinking," said Mrs. Cupar, of the Longriggs, a neighboring farm, but a much more important one. If Mrs. Cupar walked, it was because she chose to do so, not from any need to employ this vulgar natural mode of locomotion; for, besides her husband's gig, there was a pony-chaise at her orders, and her dress was made by one of the best artistes in Edinburgh, and her daughters, who came behind, were young ladies who might have walked through the Park without remark, infinitely better dressed than Margaret Leslie. They were better than Margaret in a great many ways; they could play on the piano; and it was their mother's determination to keep them clear of Rob Glen, or any other suitor of his class, that made her so "neighbor-like" with Rob Glen's mother. If he had finished his studies in an orthodox way, and become a "placed minister," then, indeed, she might have relaxed her vigilance; but as matters were, no fox could have been more dangerous to the hen-roost than this idle young man of education, who was only a sma' farmer's son. Small farmers, who cannot be denied as part of the profession, yet who sink it down among the ranks of the commonalty, are not liked by their larger neighbors in the kingdom of Fife.

"That is just what I was thinking," said Mrs. Cupar. "I did not imagine you were one who would give in to idleness under any excuse."

"No me," said Mrs. Glen; "if my lad had taken up his head with foreign travel, and wanderings about the world like that son of the minister's, Randal—no that it's our place to judge our neighbors; but there is a time for everything, as is said in Scripture, and I've confidence in my Rob that it's no just for nothing his stopping here so long. They make a great work with him at Earl's-hall. Sir Ludovic, you see for yourself, is very frail. How he grippit to Rob's arm! It's a grand thing for an auld man to find a young arm to lean upon, and a kind person to be good to him."

Mrs. Glen could not help bragging a little. She was as much elated as Rob was, and as entirely blind to all the difficulties, though in any other case, who would have seen more clearly? She had kept herself in the background, having sense enough to see that Rob's mother could not further his pursuits; but she could not hold her tongue, or refrain from waving her flag of triumph before her neighbors—these neighbors who were themselves "upsetting," and gave themselves airs much beyond any possible at Earl's-lee. Mrs. Glen was not by any means sure that "the Misses" at Longriggs, and their mother had not designs of their own upon her son, and, to tell the truth, either Bessie or Jessie Cupar would have been an excellent match for Rob. If he had fulfilled his fate and become "a placed minister," what could have been better? But Margaret Leslie and her fortune had intoxicated Mrs. Glen. She could not help flourishing this sublime hope before her neighbors' eyes.

"Then we need not be surprised if we hear of an engagement," said Mrs. Cupar, "in that quarter." She thought the woman was daft, as she said to the girls afterward. Miss Leslie! a beauty, and an heiress, and one of the proudest families in Fife. Surely the woman was out of her wits! But it was as well to give her her own way, and hear all that there was to hear.

"Na, it's no for me to say," said Mrs. Glen. "I'm no saying just that. I'm saying nothing, it's no my part, and Rob, he's no a lad to brag; but I keep my een open, and I form my ain opinions for all that. My son's not just a common lad. Till something opens him up, he's real hard to divine. He's more than ordinar clever, for one thing, and when he gets with folk that can enter into his ways—I'm free to confess I'm no one of that kind mysel'. I've nae education to put me on a par with him. There's his pictures. You've no seen his pictures? I'm told, and I can well believe it," said the proud mother, "that there's many a warse in the National

Gallery, though that's considered the best collection in a' the world."

"Dear me, now, to think of that!" said the other farmer's wife. "Jessie and Bessie are both very good at drawing. They were considered to have a great taste for it; but for my part I've always thought for a man that it was a great wastery of time."

"No when it's the best kind," said Mrs. Glen, in her superior knowledge. "I wouldna say for the young ladies' bits of drawings; but when it's the right kind, there's nothing I ken that brings in more money." Rob's mother felt justly that this was the true test. "There's thousands on thousands o' pounds to be made by it; but it wants a real genius, and that's just what Rob has shown."

"Dear me," said her listener again. Notwithstanding a natural undercurrent of scorn, she could not help being impressed by so positive an assertion. Had Jessie and Bessie shown real genius? There was something deeply impressive, even though she scarcely believed in it, in a thing by which thousands and thousands could be made.

"I must look out the girls' sketches to-morrow," she said, "and see what your son thinks of them. It must be a great comfort for you, Mrs. Glen, when he has made up his mind not to follow one thing, to find he has a good prospect in another. It's not often a young man has that luck when he gives up what he's been brought up to. But now I must bid you good-day, for this is our nearest road; and I hope you'll let me hear when anything happens." "The woman's daft," Mrs. Cupar said, as she went on. "She thinks because Sir Ludovic, poor old frail gentleman, gripped Rob's arm, finding him the foremost, that he's going to give her son his daughter Margaret Leslie!—that thinks herself of a different kind of flesh and blood from the like of you; and I would think myself sore brought down in the world if I had to give one o' you to Rob Glen!"

"Well, mamma," said one of the girls, "he is what the maids call a bonnie lad." "And very like a gentleman," said the other. They both gave a glance behind them as they spoke, not at all unwilling, if truth were told, to be overtaken by Rob Glen.

"Jessie, Jessie, how often must I tell you not to be vulgar? There is nothing so vulgar as that broad Scotch," cried the genteel farmer's wife. She was more horrified than Sir Ludovic was with Margaret's idioms and Fifish confusion of grammar; but the girls were not nearly so decided as to the folly of Mrs. Glen. They thought there was something to say on the other side. Margaret Leslie had no education; she had never been out of that old crow's-nest of a house. She had never had masters for anything, or seen the world. Family was not everything, nor money either; and if there was a nice-looking, handsome, well-educated young man who did not mind her want of education— Mrs. Cupar thought her own girls were almost as daft as Mrs. Glen.

But there was another humble pedestrian coming after them, who was of the same opinion as the girls. Jeanie had seen Mrs. Glen and her son from a distance, but had not been seen by Rob, who had eyes only for Margaret, and, under the shade of her book, the poor girl had watched him, all unconscious of her observation. He had not been at church before since he returned to his mother's house, and all his thoughts were bent, it seemed to Jeanie, upon the large, square, red-lined pew which held her master and Miss Margaret. Even if Margaret were not there, was it likely that he would have greeted her in the face of day—he, a gentleman, and she but a servant-lass? Jeanie felt the impossibility of the connection more than she had ever done before. She had seen nothing, indeed, that was impossible in it when she had gone to his uncle's shop, or taken a Sunday walk with Rob out by Glasgow Green and upon the waterside. But here the reality of the matter burst upon her. She saw him walk past with Sir Ludovic leaning on his arm, while she hung back while "the kirk skaaled." She saw him shake hands with Randal Burnside. And she was nothing but Bell's helper, a servant-lass. Her father had been one of the elders who stood at the plate on this eventful day, and John Robertson understood the wistful look his daughter gave him when the service was over.

"Ay, ay, he saw me weel enough—he could not help seeing me. He gave me a little nod as he passed, quite civil: but—I would think na mair of such a whillie-wha," said John.

"You must not ca' names, faither," said gentle Jeanie; but it was a heavy heart which she carried along that same road, keeping far behind Mrs. Glen and Mrs. Cupar and the young ladies. It was no wonder to Jeanie, nor had she any doubt about Sir Ludovic. Who would not be glad of such a lad as Rob? She was not angry with Margaret, nor even with Rob himself, for that matter. It was her own fault ever to think that she was his equal. What was he but a laddie, that did not know his own mind, when he had pledged himself to her that ought to have known better? She was younger than he was, yet she ought to have known better. He was not a whillie-wha, as her father said, but only too tender-hearted, liking to please those he was with. Only this could ever have made him waste so much of his time and kindness upon John Robertson's daughter—a servant-lass—he that, at the least, would be "a placed minister!" At last Jeanie saw clearly the absurdity of the thought.

CHAPTER XVII.

Sir Ludovic was "none the worse" of his stumble, and next day all things went on as before. Rob Glen was one of the first who came to inquire, and he was asked to go up-stairs, and was thanked for his aid with all ceremony, yet kindness, Margaret standing by, beaming upon him, beaming with pleasure and gratitude. Rob, she felt, was her friend much more than her father's, and she was grateful to him for his succor for her father, and grateful to Sir Ludovic for accepting the service. She stood by and smiled upon the young man. "I am very thankful too," she said, "Mr. Glen," and the look in Rob's eyes made her blush. She had always been given to blushing; but Margaret blushed more than ever now, in the vague excitement of thought and feeling which these last weeks had revived in her. They had been spent almost in Rob's constant companionship, so long had the sketching lasted; and the two had been for hours together, alone, in close proximity, with unlimited opportunities of conversation. He had told her a great deal about himself, and she had revealed to him all the corners of her innocent memory. They had become again as closely united as when little Margaret sat by the big boy, with her little feet dabbling in the water, spoiling his fishing, but filling him with vague delight.

He had indulged in various other loves since then; but, after all, when you came to look back upon it, was not little Margaret his first love? He got her to go with him one day to the burn, which they had haunted as children, and told her he meant to make a picture of it. This was just the spot, he said. It was nothing but a bit of grassy bank, a ragged willow dipping into the brook, a great old hawthorn-bush upon the slope. "You used to be so fond of the white hawthorn" ("And so I am still," Margaret said), "and here was where you sat with the clear water running over your little feet. I think I can see them now." Margaret grew crimson, but that was an effect so easily produced; and she too thought she could remember sitting on these summer afternoons, with the soft ripple, like warm silk, playing over her feet, and the scent of the hawthorn (we do not call it May in Fife) filling the air, and flies and little fishes dimpling the surface of the pool. "I will paint a picture of it," said Rob; and the idea pleased her. Thus the days went on; they were shorter than any days had ever been before to Margaret, full of interest, full of pleasure. An atmosphere of soft flattery, praise, too delicate to be put into words, a kind of unspoken worship, surrounded her. She was amused, she was occupied, she was made happy. And it did not occur to her to ask herself the reason of this vague but delightful exhilaration. She felt it like an atmosphere all round her, but did not ask herself, and did not know what it was.

And perhaps with this round of pleasant occupation going on outside, she was not quite so much with her father, or so ready to note his ways as she had been. On the Monday evening, Rob, by special invitation, dined with them, and exerted himself to his utmost to amuse Sir Ludovic; and after this beginning he came often. He did amuse Sir Ludovic, sometimes by his knowledge, sometimes by his ignorance; by the clever things he would say, and the foolish things he would say—the one as much as the other. "Let your friend come to dinner," the old man would say, with a smile. "John, you will put a plate for Mr. Glen." And so it came about that for a whole week Rob shared their meal every evening. When Sir Ludovic got drowsy (as it is so natural to do after dinner, for every one, not only for old men), the two young people would steal away into the West Chamber and watch the sun setting, which also was a dangerous amusement. Thus it will be seen poor little unprotected Margaret was in a bad way.

During all this time, the old servants of the house watched their master very closely. Even Bell had to give up the consideration of Margaret and devote herself to Sir Ludovic. And they saw many signs and tokens that they did not like, and had many consultations whether Mr. Leslie or "the ladies" should be sent for. The ladies seemed the most natural, for the young master was known to have his business to attend to, and his family; but Bell "could not bide" calling for the ladies before their time. And Sir Ludovic was just in his ordinar; there was nothing more to be said; failing, but that was natural: nothing that anybody could take notice of. It was well to have Rob Glen at night, for that amused him; and when the Minister called, bringing his son to be re-presented to his old friend, they were glad, for Sir Ludovic was interested. When Dr. Burnside went away, he stopped at the door expressly to tell Bell how glad he was to see the old gentleman look so well.

"He's taking out a new lease," said the Doctor.

"Eh me," Bell said, looking after him, "how little sense it takes to make a minister!" But this was an utterance of hasty temper, for she had in reality an exalted respect for Dr. Burnside, both as minister and as man.

But it fell upon the house like a bomb-shell, when suddenly one morning, after being unusually well the night before, Sir Ludovic declined to get out of bed. No, he said, he was not ill, he was quite comfortable; but he did not feel disposed to get up. Old John, upon whose imagination this had an effect quite out of proportion to its apparent importance as an incident, begged and entreated almost with tears, and, finding his own remonstrances ineffectual, went to get Bell.

"I canna stand it," the old man said. "Get you him out of his bed, Bell. Pit it to me ony other way, and I'll bear it; but to see him lie yonder smiling, and think of a' that's to come!"

Bell put on a clean apron and went up-stairs.

"Sir Ludovic," she said, "you're no going to bide there as if you were ill, and frighten my auld man out of his wits. Ye ken, John, he's a dour body on the outside, but within there's no a baby has a softer heart; and he canna bide to see you in your bed—nor me either!" cried the old woman, suddenly, putting up her hands to her face.

Sir Ludovic lay quite placid, with his white head upon the white pillows, his fine dark eyes full of light, and smiling. It was enough, Bell thought, to break the heart of a stone.

"And why should I get up when I am comfortable here?" said Sir Ludovic, "my good Bell. You've ruled over me so long that you think I am never to have a will of my own; and, indeed, if I do not show a spark of resolution now, when am I to show it?" he said, with a soft laugh. "There is but little time."

On this John made an inarticulate outburst, something between a sob and a groan—a roar of grief and impatience such as an animal in extremity might have uttered. He had stolen up behind his wife, not able to keep away from his old master. Bell had long been her husband's interpreter when words failed him. She dried her eyes with her apron, and turned again to the bedside.

"Sir Ludovic," she said, solemnly, "he says you'll break his heart."

"My good friend," said the old man, with a humorous twitch about his mouth, "let us be honest. It must come some time, why shouldn't it come now? I've been trying, like the rest of you, to push it off, and pretend I did not know. Come, you are not so young yourself, to be frightened. It must come, sooner or later. What is the use of being uncomfortable, trying to keep it at arm's-length? I'm very well here. I am quite at my ease. Let us go through with it," said Sir Ludovic, with a sparkle in his eye.

"You're speaking Hebrew-Greek to me, Sir Ludovic. I canna tell no more than the babe unborn what you're going through with," cried Bell; and when she had said this she threw her apron over her head and sobbed aloud.

"Well, this is a cheerful beginning," said Sir Ludovic. "Call ye this backing of your friends? Go away, you two old fools, and send me my little Peggy; and none of your wailing to her, Bell. Leave the little thing at peace as long as that may be."

"I hope I ken my duty to Miss Margret," said Bell, with an air of offence, which was the easiest to put on in the circumstances. She hurried out of the room with hasty steps, keeping up this little fiction, and met Margaret coming down-stairs, fresh as the morning, in her light dress, with her shining hair. "You're to go to your papa, Miss Margret," said Bell, "in his ain room: where you'll find him in his bed—"

"He's not ill, Bell?" cried Margaret, with quick anxiety.

"Ill! He's just as obstinate and as ill-willy as the mule in the Scriptures," cried Bell, darting down the winding stair. She could not bear it any more than John. Margaret, standing on the spiral steps, an apparition of brightness, everything about her

"Drawn
From morning and the cheerful dawn;"

her countenance all smiling, her eyes as soft and as happy as the morning light—Bell could not see her for tears. She seemed to see the crape and blackness which so soon would envelop them all, and the deeper darkness of the world, in which this young creature would soon have no natural home. "No another moment to think upon it," Bell said to herself; "no a moment. The ladies maun come now."

Margaret, surprised, went through the long room in which, by this hour, her father's chair was always occupied, but felt no superstitious presentiment at seeing it desolate. Sir Ludovic's rooms—there were two of them, a larger and a smaller—opened off from the long room. He had taken, quite lately, as his bedchamber, the smaller room of the two, an octagon-shaped and panelled room, as being the warmest and most bright; and there he was lying, smiling as when Bell saw him first, with the morning light upon his face.

"You sent for me, papa," said Margaret. "Are you ill that you are in bed? I have never seen you in bed before."

"Remember that, then, my Peggy, as a proof of the comfortable life I have had, though I am so old. No, not ill, but very comfortable. Why should I get up and give myself a great deal of trouble, when I am so comfortable here?"

"Indeed, if you are so very comfortable—" said Margaret, a little bewildered: "it must be only laziness, papa;" and she laughed, but stopped in the middle of her laugh, and grew serious, she could not tell why. "But it is very lazy of you," she said. "I never heard of any one who was quite well staying in bed because it was comfortable."

"No? But then there are things in heaven and earth, my Peggy, and I want you to do something for me. I want you to write a letter for me. Bring your writing things here, and I will tell you what to say."

She met John in the long room, coming in with various articles, as if to provision a place which was about to be besieged. He had some wood under his arm to light a fire, and a tray with cups and glasses, and a hot-water bottle (called in Scotland a "pig"); and there was an air of excitement about him, suppressed and sombre, which struck Margaret with vague alarm. "Why are you taking in all these things?" she said; "he did not say he was cold."

"If he doesn't want them the day, he may want them the morn," said John.

"The morn! he is not going to lie in bed always because it is comfortable; that would be too absurd," said Margaret. "What is it? There is not going to be—anything done to papa?—any—operation? What is it? You look as if there was—something coming—"

"I have my work to do," said John, hastily turning away. "I've nae time to say ay and no to little misses that canna understand."

"Oh, John, what an old bear you are!" said Margaret. He made her uneasy. It seemed as if something must have happened during the night. Was her father, perhaps, going to have a leg off, or an arm? She knew this was nonsense; but John's paraphernalia and his face both looked so. She went to the West Chamber, where all her special possessions were, and got her little writing-case, which one of her sisters had given her. Last night before she went to bed she had set up a little drawing she had done, and which she thought was more successful than any hitherto attempted. She had set it up so that she might see it the first thing in the morning, to judge how it bore the light of day. And on the table was Rob's block with the sketch he had made of Sir Ludovic in his chair. He was to come again that very day, with her father's consent, to go on with it. All this looked somehow, she could not tell how, a long way off to Margaret, as if something had happened to set these simple plans aside. She felt, in the jargon of her new art, as if the foreground had suddenly grown into such importance that all that was behind it was thrown miles back. It was very strange; and yet nothing had happened, only her father was lazy, and had not got out of bed.

"Who is it for? And am I to write from myself, papa, or am I to write for you?" she said, sitting down at the bedside and opening her writing-case. He paused, and looked at her for a moment before he spoke.

"It is to your sisters, to Jean and Grace, my little Peggy."

"To Jean and Grace!"

"To ask them, if it is quite convenient, to come here now, instead of waiting till September, according to their general custom—"

"Oh, papa!" cried Margaret, suddenly realizing the change that was coming in her life; the sketches and the drawing-lessons, and the talks, and the confidences, and Rob Glen himself— What would Jean and Grace say to Rob? She felt as if in a moment all her little structure of amusement and pleasure was falling to pieces. She closed her writing-case again with a gesture of despair. "Oh, papa, is not September soon enough? I don't want them here now. In—the summer," said Margaret, hastily, blushing for herself at the little subtle subterfuge to which she was resorting to conceal her real terror—"in the summer there is always something—I mean so many things to do."

"Yes," her father said, with a smile; "and for some of us, my little girl, things we shall never do again."

She did not realize the meaning of this, and perhaps may be pardoned if, not knowing the sadder circumstances involved, her mind was for the moment absorbed in her own disappointment and confusion; the sudden sense of arrest and stoppage in all her pleasant ways which overwhelmed her. "Why do you want them, papa?" she went on; "am I not enough? You used to say you liked me best. You used to say, just you and me, you and me, got on best in the old house."

"And so I would say still," said the old man, "my little Peggy, my bonnie Peggy! Yes, it is enough to have you and me. (I forgive you the grammar.) But however selfish I might be were there only myself to think of, I must think now of you, my little girl."

"And what is about me?" cried Margaret; "if you think I want Jean and Grace, papa, what will they do but find fault? They are never satisfied with anything we do. They find fault with everybody. They say John is stupid—"

"And so he is, a doited old body—and, my Peggy, sometimes very far from civil to you."

"Old John, papa? To me? He is as fond of me as if I were his own. When he scolds, I don't pay any attention, any more than when you scold."

Sir Ludovic laughed.

"That is a pretty way of telling me how little authority I have," he said.

"Papa!" cried Margaret, impatiently, "you know very well that is not what I mean. I would not vex you, not for the world—never you —and not even John. I cannot bear him to be called names, and everything found fault with. There's not this and there's not that; no drawing-room; and the bedrooms are not big enough, and me not well enough dressed."

"Perhaps they are right there, my Peggy. I fear you are dressed anyhow, though I see nobody that looks so well."

"Then why must they come before September?" said Margaret. "Let them come, papa, at their own time."

He laughed a little, lying there upon the white pillow, with a delicate hue of life in his old cheek, and all the vigor of twenty in his dark eyes. He did not look as if there was anything the matter with him. He only looked comfortable, luxuriously comfortable, that was all. She laughed, too, as she looked at him. "How lazy you are, papa!" she said; "do you think it is right? What would Bell say to me if I did not get up? You look so comfortable—and so happy."

"Yes, very comfortable," he said; but the laugh went off his face. "My Peggy," he went on, with sudden gravity, "don't ask any questions, but write to your sisters. Say I wish them to come, and to come now. No more, my dear, no more. I am not joking. Say I will look for them as soon as they can get here."

She opened her writing-book again, and got her paper, and began to write. When he took this tone, there was nothing to be done but to obey. But when she had written a few lines, Margaret stopped suddenly with a little start, as if all at once overtaken by a sense of the meaning of what she was doing. "Papa," she cried, the color leaving her face, two big tears starting into her eyes, "you are hiding something from me: you are ill!"

"No, no," he said—"no, I am not at all ill; but, my Peggy, one never knows what may be going to happen, and I want to have your sisters here."

"Oh," cried Margaret, throwing away her book, "let them stay away—let them stay away! I want you all to myself. I can take care of you better than they can. Papa, I know you are ill, though you will not own it."

"No, no," he said, more feebly. "Run away and play, my little girl. I am—tired, just a trifle tired: and come back in half an hour, in half an hour, before post-time."

"Here's a cordial to ye, Sir Ludovic," said John, and he made an imperative sign to his young mistress. "Let him be—let him be! he's no weel enough to be teased about anything," he whispered in her ear.

Margaret stood gazing at her father for a moment thunderstruck. Then she snatched up the letter she had begun, and rushed rapidly, yet on noiseless feet, out of the room. Oh, old John was cruel! Would she do anything to tease her father? And, oh! *he* was cruel not to tell her—to wish for Jean and Grace, and to hide it from her. She went down-stairs like the wind, her feet scarcely touching the steps, making a brightness in the dim light of the stair, and a movement in the stillness, to go to Bell, her referee in everything, and to ask what it meant. "Oh, Bell, what does it mean?" was on her lips; when suddenly, through the open door, Margaret saw two figures approaching, and stopped short. They were young men both, both pleasant to behold; but even at that agitated moment, and in the suddenness of the apparition, the girl observed the difference between them without knowing that she observed it. The difference was to the disadvantage of Rob, on whose behalf all her prepossessions were engaged; and this gave her a faint pang, the cause of which she was at the moment quite unconscious of. "Oh!" she cried, not able to restrain her little outcry of trouble, as she met their surprised and questioning looks—"oh, papa is ill; I think he is very ill; and I don't know what to do."

The second of the visitors was Randal Burnside, who had met Rob Glen at the door; and it was he who answered first, eagerly, "I passed Dr. Hume's carriage on the road, at a cottage door. Shall I go back and tell him to come here?"

"Oh, will you?" cried Margaret, two big tears trembling out with a great plash, like big raindrops, from her anxious eyes. "Oh, will you? That is what I want most."

He did not stop to tell his errand, or to receive any greeting or acknowledgment, but turned, with his hat in his hand, and sped away. Rob had said nothing; he only stood gazing at her wistfully, and took her hand when the other was gone. "I see what is the matter," he said, tenderly; "is there anything new? is there any cause for fear?"

In her excitement, Margaret was not like herself. The touch and the tone of tenderness seemed to go through her with a strange, almost guilty, sense of consolation; and yet she was angry that it was not he who had gone to serve her practically. She drew her hand away, frightened, angry, yet not displeased. "Why did you let him go?" she cried, with a reproach that said more than confession.

Rob's face brightened and glowed all over. "I wanted to stay with you and comfort you," he said; "I can think of no one else when you are in trouble. Come in and rest, and tell me what it is. You must not overdo yourself. *You* must not suffer. I want to take care of *you!*"

"Oh, what is about me?" said Margaret. But she suffered herself to be persuaded, and went with him up to the West Chamber to tell him how it all was.

CHAPTER XVIII.

MRS. BELLINGHAM and Miss Leslie arrived as soon as convenient trains could bring them. The summons which Margaret wrote later that day, taking down her father's message from his lips, was not instant, though as decided as he could make it without too much alarming the girl, whose nerves were shaken, and who sat and gazed at him with a wistful countenance, large-eyed and dismal, watching every look. When he spoke to her, her eyes filled, and she did not seem able to keep that anxious gaze from his face. But the doctor, when he came, was more consoling than alarming. There was nothing to be frightened about, he said, scolding Margaret, paternally. And by degrees the household calmed down and accepted the new state of affairs, and began to think it natural that Sir Ludovic should have taken to his bed. His son came and paid him a visit from Edinburgh, staying a single night, and sitting for a solemn hour or two by his father's bedside, though he did not say much. "Is there anything I can do for you, sir?" he asked, and begged that he might be written to daily with news of his father's state, though he could find so little to say to him. But the visit of Mr. Leslie was not nearly so important as that of "the ladies," to which everybody looked forward with excitement. They arrived in the afternoon, having slept in Edinburgh the previous night. Just at the right moment they arrived, at the hour which is most proper for the arrival of a visitor at a country house, leaving just time enough to dress for dinner. And they came in with a rustle of silk into Sir Ludovic's octagon room, where there was scarcely room for them, and gave him each a delicate kiss, filling the place with delicate odors.

"I hope you are a little better, dear papa," Grace said; and Mrs. Jean, who was large and round, and scarcely could pass between the bed and the wall, cried out cheerily that it was a relief to her mind to see him looking so well.

"I never should have found out he was ill at all, if I had not been told," Mrs. Bellingham said, whose voice was pitched higher than that of the others. Sir Ludovic greeted them kindly, and allowed them to put their faces against his for a moment without disturbing himself.

"Yes, I told you—I am very comfortable," he said to Margaret, who stood behind, very eager to see what impression her father's appearance would make on her sisters. She was very happy, poor child, to hear those cheerful words from Mrs. Bellingham's high-pitched voice.

"Well, papa, now we have seen you, and I feel quite happy about you, we will go and make ourselves comfortable too," said Mrs. Bellingham. "I hope you have a cup of tea for us, Margaret, after our journey? and you must come and pour it out, for I want to look at you. Papa will spare you a little. John is waiting in the next room, I see."

"John will do very well," said Sir Ludovic; "don't derange yourselves, my dears, from your usual habits for me."

"I assure you, dear papa," said Grace, "I do not care at all for being put out of my usual habits. I will stay with you. What is there in comparison with a dear father's wishes? You go, dearest Jean; I am sure you want some tea, and I will stay with dear papa. I can see in his eyes," she added, in an audible undertone, pushing her sister gently toward the door, "that he wishes me to stay."

"My dear," said Sir Ludovic, "you must not begin your self-sacrifices as soon as you enter the house. I am looking quite well, as you both say. There is no reason why you shouldn't have your tea in peace. My eyes are very deceitful if they say anything about it except what I have said. Go, and make yourselves quite comfortable."

"Come, come," said Mrs. Bellingham. "This is just your usual nonsense; of course papa likes his old John, whom he can order about as he pleases, better than you in that old silk that makes such a noise. We shall come and sit with papa after dinner; good-bye for the moment," she said, kissing the tips of her fingers. Sir Ludovic laughed to himself softly as they disappeared. They came back every year with all their little peculiarities unchanged, all their little vanities and *minauderies*—Grace self-sacrificing, Jean sensible. They were so little like his children that he could laugh at their foibles without any harshness, but without any pain. The constant reappearance of these two ladies, always falling into their little genteel comedy as they entered the room, exactly at the point where, on the previous year, they left it off, made the interval of time appear as if it had never been. John, who was coming in with one of the many additional adjuncts to comfort which he was always bringing, caught the sound of the laugh. John did not know if he approved of a laugh from a dying man, but he could not help joining in with a faint chuckle.

"The ladies, Sir Ludovic, are aye just the same, a' their little ways," he said.

Meanwhile Margaret followed them in a little flutter of excitement. She had not wanted them to come; but now that they were here, the novelty was always agreeable, and she had been grateful to them for thinking so well of Sir Ludovic's looks, which by dint of anxiety and watching she had ceased to be satisfied with. Bell, who knew the ways and the wants of the ladies, had sent up tea to the West Chamber, whither they went, giving a sensation of company and fulness to the quiet old house. The other voices in Earl's-hall had a different sound; they were lower, softer, with a little of the chant and modulation which belongs to Fife, and did not make the air tingle as Mrs. Bellingham did. Even down-stairs the women-servants could trace the movements of the new-comers by the flow of what was chiefly a monologue on the part of the elder lady. Miss Leslie had no objection to take her share; but Mrs. Bellingham had most boldness and most perseverance, and left little room for any one else. "Hear to her lang tongue," Bell said; "high English, and as sharp as the clipping of a pair of shears." It ran on from Sir Ludovic's dressing-room, through the long room, which was so vacant, and which Margaret could scarcely go through without tears.

"I wish papa would have been advised about this room, it might have been made so much more comfortable. A partition where that screen is would have given a real dining-room and library, instead of this ridiculous long wilderness. Oh, Margaret, why do you leave that huge old chair standing out there, to break one's legs against? It should be put back out of the way," said Mrs. Bellingham, advancing her hand to put aside the chair.

"Oh, stop, stop! It is papa's chair; it must not be moved!"

"Ah, to be sure, it is papa's chair," said Mrs. Bellingham. She stood and looked at it for a moment, with her head on one side. "Well, do you know it *is* touching, this? Poor papa! I remember he always sat here. It is affecting, like a soldier's sword and his horse. But, my dear little Margaret, my poor child, you cannot leave it always here blocking up the way."

"Dear papa's chair!" said Miss Grace, putting her hand caressingly upon it; and then she touched the back with her cheek, as she had touched Sir Ludovic's face. "Poor dear old chair! never again to be what it has been, never again—"

"Yes, poor old thing, I should not like to see it sent away to a lumber-room," said Mrs. Bellingham. "But there will be so many changes, that it is sad to contemplate! Now, Margaret, tell me all about it: how was he seized? You did not say anything about a fit, and he does not look as if there had been any fit. No sugar for me, dear. Were you with him when it happened? or how did it come on? We must know all this, you know, before we see the doctor. I shall make it a point of going fully over the case with the doctor. One knows then what we have to expect, and how long a course it is likely to run."

"Jean!" cried Margaret, aghast with grief and horror; "I thought you thought he was looking well! You said you would not have known there was anything the matter. You said—"

"My dear child, did you expect me to tell *him* that I saw death in his face? Is that the sort of thing, do you think, to let the patient know? Do you expect me to say to him—Good gracious, child! what is the matter? What are you going to do?"

"You must pour out your tea for yourselves," said Margaret; "I am going to papa. Oh, if you think he is so ill, how can you sit and take your tea? How can you sit down and talk, and tell him you will come after dinner, as if it was nothing? You cannot mean it!" said the poor girl, "you cannot mean it! Oh! how can you tell, that have seen him only once? The doctor thinks he will soon be well again; and Ludovic—Ludovic is as old as you are—he never said a word to me."

"Ludovic thought you were too young to be told; he thought it was best for us to come first; and there are some doctors that will never tell you the truth. I don't hold with that. I would not blurt it out to the patient to affect his spirits, but I would tell the family always. Now, Margaret, you must not go to papa with that crying face. Sit down and compose yourself. He is very well; he has got old John. You don't suppose that I am looking for anything immediate—"

"Take this; it will do you good," said Miss Leslie, forcing upon Margaret her own cup of tea. "I will pour out another for myself."

Margaret put it away from her with outstretched hands. She turned from them with an anguish of disgust and impatience which Jean and Grace had done nothing to deserve, feeling only the justice of that one advice not to go to her father with her countenance convulsed with weeping. But where could she go? She had been frightened, and had recovered from her fright; had taken comfort from what the doctor said, and joyful consolation from the comments of her sisters on the old man's appearance: but where was she to seek any comfort now? With her heart sick, and fluttering, tingling, with the stroke she had received so unexpectedly, the girl turned to the window, where at least she could conceal her "crying face," and stood there gazing out, seeing nothing, stunned with sudden misery, and not knowing what to do. But the intolerable pain into which she had been plunged all at once did not deaden her faculties. Though her mind was in such commotion, she could not help hearing all that went on behind her. Jean and Grace were quite free from any bewilderment of pain. They were glad to have their tea after their journey, and they discussed everything with a little excitement and expectation, just touched by solemnity. To be thus summoned to their father's death-bed, to be placed in the foremost places at this tragic act which was about to be accomplished, themselves sharing in the importance of it, and with a claim upon the sympathy and respect of the world in consequence, gave Jean and Grace a sense of solemn dignity. When the heart is not deeply affected, and when, indeed, your connection with the dying is, as it were, an official one, it is difficult not to feel thus advanced in moral importance by attendance on a death-bed. It was Miss Leslie who felt this most.

"How sad to think of poor dearest papa on that bed from which he will never rise!" she said, shaking her head; "and when one remembers how active he used to be! But we

have nothing to murmur at. He has been spared to us for so many years—"

"What are you thinking of, Grace?" said Mrs. Bellingham. "I am older than you are, but I never can remember a time when papa was active; and, to be sure, he is an old man, but not half so old as grandpapa, whom I recollect quite distinctly. He was active, if you like."

"At such a time, dearest Jean, why should we dispute about words? Of course, you are right; I am always making mistakes," said Miss Grace; "but all the same, we have no right to complain. Many, many years we have had him longer than numbers of people I could mention. Indeed, to have a father living is rare at our time of life."

"That's true, at least," said Mrs. Bellingham. "I hope you are not going to keep on that dress. I told you in Edinburgh that a silk gown with a train was preposterous to travel in, and it is quite impossible for a sick-room. I shall p on a soft merino, that does not make any noise. Merino is never too warm, even in the height of summer, at Earl's-hall."

"I have nothing but black, and I could not put on black to hurt poor papa's feelings," said Grace. "He would think we were getting our mourning already. Indeed, when you think how long we will have to wear it without putting it on a day too soon—"

"As if he would remark what you are wearing! But I must go and see that Steward has unpacked. It is true there will be black enough before we are done with it, and once in mourning, I always say you never can tell when you may take it off," said Mrs. Bellingham; "but I will not let you come into the sick-room in that rustling dress. He was always particular about the best of times. He would not put up with it. There's your muslins, if you are not afraid of taking cold; but I won't have silk," said the elder sister, peremptory and decided.

Miss Leslie came to Margaret, and put an arm round her where she stood at the window, as the other went away.

"Dearest child, you must not cry so," she said. "He is not suffering, you know. What a blessing that there is no pain, that he is comfortable, as he says. Dear Jean seems to be a little hard, but she means it very well; and now that we are here, you will be able to rest; you will not have so much responsibility."

"Oh, do you think I want to rest? am I thinking of myself? It is because you are all wrong—you are mistaken. The doctor did not say so. It is not true!"

Miss Leslie shook her head, and gave a little moan.

"Dearest child!" she said, putting her cheek against Margaret's wet and tear-stained cheek. "But I must go and see about my things too," she said. "Steward never thinks of me till she has done everything for Jean. I am very glad of that, of course; it is just what I like; but it gives me a little more to do. Come with me, dear, and tell me what to put on. It will amuse you a little to see my things, though I haven't got anything new—not a thing all this year. You see, dear Ludie told us of dearest papa's uncertain state of health, and what was the good? There is nothing more provoking than having got a supply of colored things just before a long mourning. Alas! it is bad enough without that," said Grace, with a deep sigh.

After they had made their toilet, the ladies dined, and not without appetite, while Margaret sat unable to swallow a morsel, unable to escape to her father's room for the tears which she could not suppress. In the mean time it was Bell that had taken the place of watcher. Bell's heart was heavy too; but she exerted herself to amuse her patient, to tell him all the circumstances of his daughters' arrival.

"They've but a box apiece," said Bell, "and that's wonderful for our ladies. But they've minded this time that it's not that easy to get trunks up our stairs. They've minded and they've no minded, Sir Ludovic: for Mrs. Bellin'am's is that big that no mortal, let alone John, could get it up the stair. Her woman has had a' the things to carry up in armfu's. And oh, the heap o' things a leddy wants when she gangs about! It's just a bondage—gowns for the mornin' and gowns for the evenin', and gowns to put on when she's dressing hersel', and as mony fykes of laces and collars, and caps for her head—if they ca' thae vanities caps."

Sir Ludovic laughed.

"Poor Jean and poor Grace!" he said. "I hope they think mourning is becoming to them, Bell, for they will not stint me of a ribbon; I know my daughters too well for that. They will give me everything that is due to me, to the very last scrap of crape."

"They'll do that, Sir Ludovic," said Bell, divided between her desire to humor him and her wish to keep off painful subjects; "the ladies have never shown any want o' respect. But Miss Grace was aye fond of bright colors. They're no so young as I mind them, but they're weel-fa'ured women still. The Leslies were aye a handsome family. They take it from yourself, Sir Ludovic, if I may make so bold."

"Not entirely from me," said Sir Ludovic, with a smile. He did not dislike the allusion to his good looks, even though he was dying. "Their mother, whom you scarcely remember, was a handsome woman. We were not a bad-looking couple, people said. Ah! that's a long time ago, Bell."

"Deed and it's a long time, Sir Ludovic;" but Bell did not know what to say on this subject, for the interpolation of a third Lady Leslie no doubt made the matter somewhat more difficult. Probably this struck Sir Ludovic too, and he was in the condition when human nature is glad to seek a little help from another, or sympathy at least, no help being possible. This time he sighed—which was a thing much more befitting than laughter on a dying bed.

"That's a strange subject altogether," he said; "any meeting after so long a time would be strange. If she had been at one end of the world and I at the other, there would be many changes even then. Would we understand each other?" Sir Ludovic had ceased to speak to Bell. He was musing alone, talking with himself. "And the difference must be greater than any mortal separation. Know each other? Of course we must know each other, she and I; but the question is, will we understand each other?"

"Eh, Sir Ludovic," said Bell, "it was God's will that parted you, not your ain. There would be fault on one side or the other, if my lady had

been in, say America, a' this time, and you at hame; but she's been in—heaven; that makes a' the difference."

"Does it?" he said; "that's just what I want to be sure of, Bell. Time has made great changes on me. If I find her just where she was when she left me, I have gone long beyond that; and if she has gone on too, where is she? and how shall we meet, each with our new experiences which the other does not know?"

Bell was very much perplexed by this inquiry. It had not occurred to her own mind. "Eh, Sir Ludovic," she said, "I am no the one, the like o' me, to clear up sic mysteries. But what new things can the lady meet with in heaven, but just the praise o' God and the love o' God? and that doesna distract the mind."

"Ah, Bell! but I've met with a great many more things since I parted with her; and then," he said, with a gleam in his eyes which might have been half comic in its embarrassment had the circumstances been different, "there is—my little Peggy's mother, poor thing."

Bell sat down, in her confusion and bewilderment, by the bedside, and pondered. "I'm thinking," she said, "that my late leddy, Miss Margret's mother, will be the one that will maist cling to ye when a's done."

"Poor little thing!" he said, softly, with a smile on his face — "poor little thing! She should have seen me safe out of the world, and then had a life of her own. That would have made a balance; but how are we to know what my wife thinks? You see, we know nothing—we know nothing. And it is very hard to tell, when people have been parted so long, and things have happened, how they are to get on when they meet again."

(Sir Ludovic, perhaps, was a little confused in his mind as to which of the Ladies Leslie he meant when he said "my wife;" but at all events it was not the last one, the "poor little thing," Margaret's mother, who was to him as a child.)

"Sir Ludovic, there's neither marrying nor giving in marriage there," said Bell, solemnly. It had never occurred to herself certainly that old John would not form part of her paradise; but then there was no complication in their relations. "And you maunna think of things like that," she added, reverently, "eh, Sir Ludovic? There's One we should a' think of. And if He's pleased, what does it matter for anything else in the wide world?"

"Ay, Bell; that's very true, Bell," he said, acquiescing, though scarcely remarking what she said. But the dying will rarely see things with the solemnity which the living feel to be appropriate to their circumstances, neither does the approach of death concentrate our thoughts on our most important concerns, as we all fondly hope it may, without difficulty or struggle. "I would like to know—what my wife thinks," he said,

"What are you talking so much about?" said Mrs. Bellingham, coming in. "I heard your tongues going all the time of dinner. Is that you, Bell? How are you, Bell? I was wondering not to have seen you before; but I don't think you should let papa talk so much when he is so weak. Indeed, I don't think you should talk, papa. It is always exhausting your strength. Just lie quiet and keep quite still, till you get your strength back."

Sir Ludovic turned round and looked at Bell with a glimmer of fun, about which this time there could be no mistake, in his eyes. Bell did not know what it meant. She did not see any fun in Mrs. Bellingham's orders, nor in the way in which she herself was speedily, noiselessly displaced from the position she had taken. But so it was. Bell was put out of the way very innocently and naturally, and, with a soft flood of unrustling merino about her, Mrs. Bellingham took possession. She made no sound; she was quite fresh in dress, in looks, in spirits.

"I have made Margaret tell me all about how it came on, and cheered her up, the silly little thing. She has never seen any illness; she is like to cry if you only look at her. But we must make her more practical," said the elder sister. Grace was in a blue gown with rose-colored ribbons. She came in, stealing with noiseless feet, a much slimmer shadow than her sister, and bent over the bed, and put her cheek to Sir Ludovic's again, and kissed his hand and murmured, "Dearest papa!" If he had been in the article of death Sir Ludovic must have laughed.

But Margaret did not appear. She could not present herself with her swollen eyes and pale cheeks. Oh! if Jean and Grace had but stayed away—had they but left him to herself, to Bell, and John, who loved him! But she could not creep into her corner in her father's room while the ladies were there, filling it up, taking possession of him. Her heart was as heavy as lead in her bosom; it lay there like a stone. People will sometimes speak of the heart as if it were a figure of speech. Margaret felt hers lying, broken, bleeding, heavy—a weight that bent her to the ground.

CHAPTER XIX.

MARGARET roamed about the house, unable to take any comfort or find any. Jeanie found her crying in the long room when she went to remove the remains of the dinner; for John had a hundred things to do, and showed his excitement by an inability to keep to his ordinary work.

"Oh, Miss Margret, dinna be so cast down!" Jeanie said, with tender sympathy, brushing the tears from her own eyes.

"What can I be but cast down," she cried, "when papa is— Oh, Jeanie, what does Bell say? Does Bell think he is—" Dying, the girl meant to say, but to pronounce the word was impossible to her.

"Oh, Miss Margret," said Jeanie; "what does it matter what Bell says; how can she ken? and the doctor he says quite different—"

This was a betrayal of all that Margaret had feared; Bell, too, was then of the same opinion. The poor girl stole to the door of her father's room, and stood there for a moment listening to the easy flow of Mrs. Bellingham's dogmas, and Grace's sigh of "Dearest papa!" and she heard him laugh, and say something in his own natural tone. Would he laugh if he were—dying?

"Come in, Miss Margret," said John, coming through the dressing-room, this time with some extra pillows (for he might want to have his head higher, John thought).

"Oh, I cannot—I cannot bear it!" cried Margaret, turning away. He put his large old hand softly upon her arm.

"My bonnie leddy!" he said. He would not have said it, Margaret felt, if there had been any hope. Then she went out in her despair, restless, not knowing where to seek relief from the pain in her heart, which was so sore, and which could not be shaken off. She said to herself that she could not bear it. It was her first experience of the intolerable. The fine weather had broken which had so favored the drawing, and the wind was moaning about the old house, prophesying rain. With another pang in her heart—not that she was thinking of Rob, but only of the contrast between that light-heartedness and her present despair, she stumbled through the potato furrows, past the place where she had spent so many pleasant hours, thinking no evil—though the evil she remembered must have been in existence all the same—and made her way into the wood. There was shelter there, and no one would see her. The trees were all vocal with those sighings of melancholy cadence that are never long absent from the Scotch fir-woods. The wind came sweeping over them, with one great sigh after another, like the waves of the sea: and she sighed, too, in heaviness. Oh, if she could but sigh deep enough, like the wind, to get that burden off her breast! Margaret sat down on a damp knoll, with all the firs rising up round her like a congregation of shadows, and the wind sweeping with long complaint, sadder and sadder over their melancholy branches: and gazed at the gray old house through her tears. How different it had looked in the morning sunshine, with her father sitting among his books, and no evil near! All the color and light had gone out of it now; it was gray as death, pale, solemn—the old tower and gables rising against a sky scarcely less gray than they were, the trees swaying wildly about, the clouds rolling together in masses across the colorless sky.

It was not a time or a place to cheer any one. All the severity of aspect, which melts so completely out of a Scotch landscape with the shining of the sun, had come out in fullest force. The trees looked darker in their leafage, the house paler in its grayness, than houses and trees are anywhere else. But Margaret did not make any comparisons. She knew no landscape half so well. She was not disposed to find fault with it, or wish it more lovely. And for this moment she was not thinking of the landscape, but of what was going on in that room, where she could see a little glimmer of fire-light at the window. Both John and Bell thought it natural and seemly, when there was illness in the house, that there should be a fire. Dying! oh, the chill and mysterious terror of the word; lying there smiling, but soon, perhaps at any moment, Margaret thought, in her inexperience, to be gone out of reach, out of sight! he who had always been at hand to be appealed to in every difficulty, to be greeted morning and evening! he who was always smiling at her, "making a fool of her," as she had so often complained. Perhaps there is no desolation so complete as the shrinking and gasp of the young soul when it first comes thus within sight, within realization, of death. If it had been she who had to die, Margaret would not have found it so hard. She would have been ineffably, childishly, consoled by the thought of the flowers with which she would be covered, and the weeping of "all the house," and the broken hearts of those whom she would leave behind; but nothing of this comforted her now. For the first time in her life, misery took hold upon her—a thing that would not be shaken off, could not be staved aside. She sat at the foot of the big fir-tree, gazing with wide eyes at the gray old house which was like her father, who was dying. The tears gathered and fell, minute by minute, from her eyes, blinding her, then showing clearer than ever, as they fell, the old pale outline, the ruddy glimmer in that window where he was lying. Why did she not rush to him, to be with him every moment that remained? But she could not bear it. She could not go and watch for *that* coming. To have it over, to get through the unimaginable anguish anyhow, at any cost, seemed the best thing, the only thing that remained for her. She had not heard any one coming, being too much rapt in her own thoughts to pay attention to what was going on around her; and indeed the moaning of the trees and the sweep of the wind were enough to silence all other sounds.

Thus Margaret was taken entirely by surprise, when a well-known voice over her head suddenly addressed her.

"Miss Margaret!" Rob Glen said. He was greatly surprised and very glad, having heard of the arrival, which he feared would put a stop to the possibility of his visits. But then he added, in anxious tones, "What is the matter? you are crying. What has happened?" He thought, so miserable were her looks, that Sir Ludovic was dead, and it was with a natural impulse of tenderness and pity that the young man suddenly knelt down beside her and took her hand quietly between his own.

"Oh no," said Margaret, with a sob; "not that, not yet! but they tell me—they tell me—" She could not go any farther for tears.

Rob did not say anything, but he put his lips to her hand, and looked anxiously in her face. Margaret could not look at him again—could not speak. She was blind and inarticulate with tears. She only knew that he wept too, and that seemed to make them one.

"Did *you* hear *that?*" she said: "is that what everybody says? I think it will kill me too!"

Rob Glen had no premeditated plan. His heart ached for her, so desolate, so young, under the moaning firs. He put his arm round her unconsciously, holding her fast.

"Oh, my poor darling!" he said, "my love! I would die to keep any trouble from *you!*"

Margaret was entirely overpowered with the sorrow and the sympathy. She leaned her head upon him unawares; she felt his arm support her, and that there was a vague comfort in it. She cried and sobbed without any attempt to restrain herself. No criticism was here, no formal consolations, nothing to make her remember that now she was a woman, and must not abandon herself like a child to her misery. He only wept with her, and after a while began to kiss her hair and her pale cheeks, murmuring over her, "My Margaret, my poor darling!" She did not

hear or heed what he said. She was conscious of nothing but anguish, with a vague, faint relief in it, a lessening of the burden, a giving way of the iron band that had seemed to be about her heart.

When this passion of weeping was spent, the evening had fallen into dusk. The house had become grayer, paler than ever; the glimmer of the window more red; the trees about were like ghosts, looming indistinctly through the gloom: and Rob was kneeling by her with his arms round her, her head pillowed against him, his face close to hers. There did not seem anything strange in it to poor Margaret. He was very, very kind; he had wept, too, breaking his heart like her; it seemed all so natural, so simple. And she was a little relieved, a little consoled.

"Darling," he was saying, "I don't think it can be quite true. The doctor would not deceive me, and he did not say so. Who should know best—they who have just come, or we who have been here all the time? Oh, my sweet, don't break your dear heart!—that would break mine too. I don't think it can be so bad as they say."

"Oh, do you think so? do you think there is any hope?" said Margaret.

This gave her strength to stir a little, to move from the warm shelter in which she found herself. But he kept her close to him with a gentle pressure of his arm.

"Yes, let us hope," he said; "he is not so old, and he is not very ill. You told me he was not suffering—"

"No—he ought to know better than they do; he said he was not ill. Oh, I do not think it can be so bad," said Margaret, raising herself up, "and you—don't think so, Mr. Glen?"

"Do you call me Mr. Glen *still?*" he said, with his lips close to her ear. "Oh, my darling, don't tempt me to wish harm to Sir Ludovic. If I may only comfort you when you are in trouble—if I am to be nothing to you when you are happy—"

"Oh!" said Margaret, with a deep sigh, "do you think I am happy yet? I am not quite so wretched, perhaps; but I shall never be happy till papa is out of danger, till he is well again, sitting in his chair with his books. Oh, you do not say anything now! You think that will never be—"

"And I working at my drawing," he said. He did not want to deceive her, and his voice was husky; but he could not do other than humor her, whatever shape her fancy might take. "I finishing my drawing, and making it more like him; and my sweet Margaret sitting by me, not trying to escape from me: and her kind father giving us his blessing—"

"Oh," Margaret cried, starting away from him, "it is quite dark, it is quite late, Mr. Glen."

"Yes, darling," he said, rising reluctantly, "I must take you in now; it is too cold and too late for you, though it has been better than the brightest day to me."

"I thought you were sorry for me," said Margaret. "I thought you were unhappy too. Oh, were you only glad because I was in trouble, Mr. Glen?"

There was a poignant tone of pain in the question which encouraged Rob. He caught her hand in his, and drew it through his arm and held her fast.

"You don't know," he said, "because you are so young, and love is new to you. You don't know that a man can be happy in his worst misery if it brings him close, close to the girl he loves."

Margaret did not say a word. She did not understand : but yet did not she feel, too, a vague bliss that overwhelmed her in the midst of her sorrow? The relief that had stolen over her, was it real hope, or only a vague sense that all must be well because something had come into her life which made her happy? She was willing to go with Rob, when he led her, the long way round, through the wood, and by the other side of the house. He did not want to be circumscribed in his good-night by the possible inspection of old John or Bell. "This is the best way for you," he said, leading her very tenderly along the margin of the wood. All the way he talked to her in a whisper, saying, Margaret could not tell what, caressing words that were sweet, though she did not realize the meaning of them ; nor did she in the least resist his "kindness." She suffered him to hold her hand and kiss it, and call her all the tender names he could think of. It seemed all quite natural. She was half stunned by her sorrow, half intoxicated by this strange sweet opiate of tender reassurances and impassioned love. It did not occur to her to make any response, but neither did she repulse him. She trembled with the strangeness and the naturalness, the consolation, the tremor ; but her mind was so much confused between pain and relief that she could not realize what this new thing was.

They had come round to the door in the court-yard wall, which was the chief entrance to the house, and here Rob reluctantly parted with her, saying a hundred good-byes, and venturing again, ere he let her go, to kiss her cheek. Margaret was much more startled now than she had been before, and made haste to draw her hands from his. Then she heard him utter a little sharp, short exclamation, and he tried to hold her back. But she was not thinking of spectators. She stepped on through the doorway, which was open, and came straight upon some one who was coming out. It did not occur to her to think that he had seen this parting, or what he had seen. She did not look at the stranger at all, but went on hurriedly into the court-yard. Rob had dropped her hand as if it had been a stone. This surprised her a little, but nothing else. Any necessity for concealment, any fear of being seen, had not entered into Margaret's confused and troubled mind, troubled with more than grief now, with a kind of bewilderment, caused by this something new which had come upon her unawares, and which she did not understand.

The two young men stood together outside. There was no possibility of mistake, or chance that they might be unable to recognize each other. There had been a moment's intense suspense, and then Randal Burnside, coming out from his evening inquiries after Sir Ludovic, had discovered, in spite of himself, the discomfited and abashed lover. Randal's surprise was mingled with a momentary pang of disappointment and pain to think so young a creature as Margaret,

and so sweet a creature, should have thus been found returning from a walk with, evidently, her lover, and capable of dalliance at such a moment, when her father was dying. It hurt his ideal sense of what was fit. He had scarcely renewed his childish acquaintance with her, and had no right to be disappointed. What did it matter to him whom she walked with, or what was the fashion of her wooing? But it wounded him to class this delicate Margaret with the village lasses and their "lads." He tried not to look at the fellow, not to surprise her secret. Heaven knows, he had no desire to surprise anybody's secret, much less such a vulgar one as this. But his eyes were quicker than his will, and he had seen Rob Glen before he was aware. This gave him a greater shock still. He stared with a kind of consternation, then gave his old acquaintance a hasty nod, and went on much disturbed, though why he should be disturbed he could not tell. She was nothing to him—why should he mind? Poor girl, she had been neglected ; there had been no one to train her, to tell what a lady should do. But Randal felt vexed as if she had been his sister, that Margaret had not known by instinct how a lady should behave. He went on more quickly than usual to drive it out of his mind.

But Rob had the consciousness of guilt in him, and could not take it so lightly. He thought Randal would betray him ; no doubt Randal had it in his power to betray him ; and, on the whole, it might be better to guard the discovered secret by a confidence. He went hastily after the other, making his way among the trees ; but he had called him two or three times before Randal could be got to stop. When at last he did so, he turned round with a half-angry "Well!" Randal did not want the confidence ; he did not care to play the part of convenient friend to such a hero ; he was angry to find himself in circumstances which obliged him to listen to an explanation. Rob came panting after him through the gathering dark.

"Mr. Burnside," he said, breathless, "I must speak to you. I am sure you could not help seeing who it was that went in as you came out, or what was between her and me." Rob could not help a movement of pride, a little dilation and expansion of his breast.

"I had no wish to notice anything, or any one," Randal said ; "pray believe me that I never pry into things which are no business of mine."

"I am sure you are the soul of honor," said Rob, "but it is better you should know the circumstances. Don't think she had come out to meet me. She had been driven out by despair about her father, and I was in the wood by chance—I declare to you, by chance. I might have gone there to see the light in her window, that was all. But she did not come with any idea of meeting me."

"This is quite unnecessary," said Randal ; "I expressed no opinion, and have no right to form one. I didn't want to see, and I don't want to know—"

"I perceive, however," said Rob, "that you do not approve of me, and won't approve of me ; that you think I had no right to do what I have done, to speak to Mar—"

"Hold your tongue," said Randal, savagely ;

"what do you mean by bringing in a lady's name?"

Rob blushed to his very shoes; that he should have done a thing which evidently some private rule in that troublesome unwritten code of a gentleman, which it was so difficult to master in all its details, forbade, was worse to him than a crime. The annoyance with which he felt this took away his resentment at Randal's tone.

"Of course you are right," he said; "I made a mistake; but, Mr. Burnside, you must not judge us too harshly. We have been thrown in each other's way all day long, and almost every day. They have allowed us to be together so much, that we were encouraged to go a little farther. And she was very unhappy," he added, with a little tremor in his voice; "not to console her was beyond the strength of man."

How Randal would have liked to pitch him over the hedge-row into a flourishing bed of nettles which he knew to be thereabout! But he restrained himself, and made a stiff bow instead.

"This is very interesting," he said, "no doubt; but I fail to see what I have to do with it. It was not my fault that my coming was at so indiscreet a moment."

"Then I may ask you not to betray us," said Rob; "the circumstances are peculiar, as you will easily perceive. I should not wish—"

"Really this is doubly unnecessary," said Randal, angrily; "I am not a gossip, nor would it occur to me to betray any one. Is not this enough?"

"I should have liked to take you into my confidence," said Rob, "to ask your advice—"

"My advice? It could not be of much use." But why should he be angry? Other love affairs had been confided to him, and he had not rejected the confidence; but this fellow was not his friend, and it was a dastardly thing to take advantage of a poor little girl in her trouble. "I am no more a judge than I am a gossip," he said; "take my assurance that what I saw shall be precisely as if I had not seen it. Good-night." he added, abruptly, turning on his heel. Rob found himself alone in the middle of the road, feeling somehow shrunken and small, he could not tell why. But presently there burst upon him the recollection, the realization of all that had happened, and Randal Burnside's implied contempt (if it was not rather envy) ceased to affect him. He turned down the path across the fields where he had first met Margaret, in a kind of half-delirious triumph. He was "in love" too, and had that delight quite honestly, if also superficially, to fill up the measure of his happiness. To be in love with the girl who can make your fortune, who can set you above all slights and scorns, and give you all the good things the world contains—is not that the most astounding piece of good-fortune to a poor man? A mercenary courtship is always despicable; but to woo the girl whom you love, notwithstanding that she has the advantage of you in worldly goods, is permissible, nay, laudable, since it shows you to have a mind far above prejudice. Rob felt, too, that he had got this crowning gift of fortune in the most innocent and disinterested way. Had it been Jeanie whom he had met in trouble—Jeanie, who was but a poor servant-lass, and no heiress, and with whom he had been once in love, as he was now in love with Margaret—his tenderness would all have come back to him, and he would have exerted himself to console her in the self-same way. He would have done it by instinct, by nature, out of pure pity and affectionateness, and warm desire to make her happy, if he had not done so out of love. The weeping girl would have been irresistible to him. "And thus I won my Genevieve," he said to himself, as he turned homeward in an intoxication of happiness. His success went to his head like wine. He could have danced, he could have sung, as he went along the darkling path through the fields. He had won his Margaret, the prettiest, the sweetest of all his loves. His heart was all aglow with the thought of her, and melting with tenderness over her tears and her grief. His beautiful little lady, Margaret! The others had been but essays in love. He did not forget them; not one of them but Rob had a kind thought for, and would have been kind to had occasion served, Jennie among the rest. He did not suppose for a moment that it had ever occurred to him to marry Jeanie. She would have been as unsuitable a wife for a minister as for a prince. He had not meant very much one way or other; but he had been very fond of Jeanie, and she of him. He was very fond of her still; and if he had seen her cry would have been as ready to comfort her as if Margaret did not exist. But Margaret! Margaret was the queen of all. That white, soft, lady's hand! Never any like it had lingered in Rob's before. He was as happy as kings very seldom are, if all tales be true, and was no more ashamed of himself than if he had been a young monarch giving a throne to his chosen, as soon as he had got clear of Randal Burnside.

CHAPTER XX.

RANDAL returned to the Manse preoccupied and abstracted, his mother could not tell why. He brought her word that Sir Ludovic was in the same condition as before, neither better nor worse, and that the ladies had arrived; but he told no more.

"Did you see nobody?" Mrs. Burnside asked. Perhaps in her heart she had hoped that her son might occupy some such post of comforter as Rob Glen had assumed, if not quite in the same way.

"I saw old John," said Randal; "the ladies were with their father, and John was so gruff that I fear things must be looking badly. He grumbled behind his hand, 'What change could they expect in a day?' as if your inquiries irritated him. I don't wonder if they do. I think I should be worried too by constant questions, if any one was ill who belonged to me."

"Oh, don't say that, Randal," said Mrs. Burnside; "we must always pay proper respect. You may depend upon it, Jean and Grace are capable of saying that we paid no attention at all if we did not send twice a day. One must be upon one's p's and q's with such people. And Margaret—you saw nothing of poor little Margaret? It is for her my heart bleeds. It is more a ploy than anything else for Jean and Grace."

The same remark had been made by Bell in

the vaulted kitchen the very same night. "It's just a ploy for the leddies," Bell said; "I heard them say they were going to look out all the old things in the high room. You'll see they'll have a' out, and make their regulations, wha's to have this, and wha's to have that; but I say it should all go to Miss Margret. She'll have little enough else on the Leslie side of the house. I'll speak to Mr. Leslie about it. He has not muckle to say, but he's a just man."

"A wheen auld duds and rubbitsh," said John, who was busy preparing still another tray-ful of provisions for his beleaguered city up-stairs.

"Ay; but leddies think muckle o' them," said Bell. They had not surmounted their sorrow, but already it had ceased to affect them as a novelty, and all the inevitable arrangements had been brought nearer by the arrival of the visit-ors. These arrangements, are they not the sav-ing of humanity, which without them must have suffered so much more from the perpetual falling out of one after another familiar figure on the way? Even now it occupied Bell a little, and the ladies a great deal, to think of these stores, which must be arranged and disposed of some-how, in the high room. Margaret's wild grief and terror were not within the range of any such consolation; but those who felt less keenly found in them a great relief.

The day after their arrival, Mrs. Bellingham and her sister went up-stairs with much solem-nity of aspect, but great internal satisfaction, to do their duty. Sir Ludovic was still "very com-fortable," he said; but dozed a great deal, and even when he was not dozing kept his eyes shut, while they were with him. They had remained by his bedside all the previous evening with the most conscientious discharge of duty, and Jean had done everything a woman could do to keep up his spirits, assuring him that he would soon feel himself again, and planning a hundred things which were to be done "as soon as you are about." To say that this never deceived Sir Ludovic, is little. He listened to it all with a smile, knowing that she was as little deceived as he was. If he had not been in bed and so fee-ble, he would have shrugged his shoulders and said it was Jean's way. Miss Grace had not the opportunity to talk, had she wished it; but she did not take the same line in any case. She stood by him on the other side, and from time to time put down her face to touch his, and said, "Dearest papa!" When he wanted anything, she was so anxious to be of use that she would almost choke him by putting his drink to his lips as if he had been a baby.

Poor Sir Ludovic was very patient; they amused him as if they had been a scene in a comedy; but he was very tired when night came, and this was one of the reasons why he kept his eyes closed next morning. He woke up, however, when Margaret stole in—a pale lit-tle ghost, large-eyed and trembling. She looked at him so piteously, scarcely able to speak, that the old man was moved to the very heart, not-withstanding the all-absorbing languor of his condition. "Are you better to-day, papa?" she said, in a scarcely audible whisper. When he put out his hand to her, she took it in both hers, and laid down her pretty head upon it, and cried silently, her shoulders heaving with suppressed sobs, though she tried her best, poor child, not to betray them.

"My little Peggy!" said her father, "why is this? Have I not told you I am very comforta-ble? And by-and-by I shall be more than com-fortable—happy; so everybody says; and so I believe, too, though it troubles me not to know a little better. And you will be—like all of us who have lost our parents. It is a loss that must come, my little girl."

"Oh no, no, papa!" her voice was muffled and hoarse with crying. She could not consent to her own desolation.

"Ah yes, my little girl, it must come; and so we go on to have children of our own, and then to leave them à la grace de Dieu. My Peggy, listen! If you were old like Jean and Grace, you would not care; and then think this wonder to yourself: I am glad that my little girl is so young and breaks her heart. Glad! think of that, my little Peggy. It is good to see that your little heart is broken. It will mend, but it warms my old one."

"Oh, papa!" she cried, kissing his pale hand, "oh, papa!" but could not lift her head or look him in the face.

"So now, my little girl," he said, "we will not make believe, you and I, but acknowledge that we are going to part for a long, long time, my Peggy. I hope for a very long time; but probably," he said, with a smile, "if all is true that we fancy and believe, it will not be so long for me as for you. I shall have the best of it. You would like your old father to have the best of it, my little girl?"

At this she lifted her face and gave him a look which said Yes, yes, a hundred times! but could not speak.

"I knew you would," he said. "I, you see, will find myself among old friends; and we will have our talks about what's come and gone since we parted, and there will be a great many peo-ple to make acquaintance with that I have known only—in the spirit, as the Bible says;—and there will be the One, you know, that you say your prayers to, my Peggy. When you say your prayers, you can fancy (the best of life is fancy," said Sir Ludovic, with a faint smile,) "that I'm there somewhere, about what the Bible calls His footstool, and that He, perhaps, being so tender-hearted, may call to me and say, 'Ludovic! here is your little girl.'"

"Oh, papa! will you say something more, something more?"

"I would if I could, my Peggy; but I am tired again. I'll have a little doze now; but sit still and stay by me, my own little girl."

And there Margaret sat almost all the day. Excessive weeping brought its own cure, and she could not weep any more, but sat like a snow statue, except that her eyes were swollen; and by-and-by fell into a kind of torpor, a doze of the spirit, sitting in the warm stillness, with no sound but the soft stir of the fire, and sometimes the appearance of old John, who would open the door stealthily, and look in with his long, grave, serious face to see if anything was wanted. Mar-garet sat holding her father's hand, stilled by ex-haustion and warmth, and quiet and grief: and Sir Ludovic dozed, opening his eyes now and then, smiling, dozing again. So the long, still morning went by.

A very different scene was going on in the high room, which was over the long room, and as long and large, running the whole width of the house. It had a vaulted roof, curiously painted with old coats of arms, and was hung with old tapestry, gradually falling to pieces by process of time. Several of the windows, which had originally lighted it, had been built up in the days of the window-tax, and stretching across the place where two of them had been was a great oak "aumory" or press, full of those riches which John called "old rubbitsh," but which were prized by ladies, Bell knew. There were old clothes enough to have set up several theatres, costumes of all kinds, sacques and pelisses, brocade and velvets, feathers and lace. Mrs. Bellingham remembered specially that there was a drawer full of lace; but Sir Ludovic had never permitted these treasures to be ransacked when his elder daughters were at Earl's-hall. He would not tolerate any commotion over his head, and accordingly they had been shut out from these delightful hoards. It was with corresponding excitement now that they opened the doors, their fingers trembling with eagerness. Mrs. Bellingham had interpreted something he said into a desire that they should make this investigation, and had immediately declared that his wish was a law to her.

"Certainly, Grace," she had said; "we will do it at whatever cost, since papa wishes it."

"Oh yes, if dearest papa wishes it," said Grace. And Sir Ludovic smiled, as usual, seeing the whole, with an amused toleration of their weakness. Jean got out the drawer of lace with nervous anxiety. "It may be nothing, it may be nothing," she said, meaning to save herself from disappointment. She took out the drawer altogether, and carried it to the window where there was a good light, with her heart beating.

"Don't be excited, Grace," she said, "perhaps it is only modern; most likely mere babies' caps, Valenciennes and common stuff." Then she made a little pause, gave one hurried glance, and produced the one word "Point!" with an almost shriek.

"Point?" said Miss Grace, pressing forward with the point of her nose; she was short-sighted, and only thus could she inspect the treasure. Mrs. Bellingham held her off with one hand, while with the other she dived among the delicate yellow rags; the excitement grew to a height when she brought out her hand garlanded with wreaths as of a fairy web. There was a moment of silent adoration while the two ladies gazed at it. Some sea-fairy, with curious knowledge of all the starry fishes and twisted shells, and filmy fronds of weed at the bottom of the ocean, must have woven this. "Venice! and I never saw finer; and not a thread broken!" cried the finder, almost faint with delight.

"And enough to trim you from top to toe," said Grace, solemnly. Bell coming in jealously on some pretence, saw them, with their hands uplifted and eyes gleaming, and approached to see what the cause of so much emotion might be.

"Eh!" said Bell, "the heap o' things that us poor folk miss for want o' kennin'. Is that something awfu' grand now, leddies, that makes you look so fain?"

"It is a most lovely piece of lace," cried Mrs.

Jean. "Venice point; though I fear, Bell, you will not know what that means. Every little bit done by the needle—you will understand that. Look at all those little sprays."

"Eh, leddies," said Bell. "Ye ken what the fishwife says in ane o' Sir Walter's novels—'It's no fish you're buyin', but men's lives.' Eh, what heaps o' poor women's een must be workit into that auld rag. But it was my late lady's a' the same. I've seen her wear it, and many a time she's told me the same story. So it will be Miss Margret's part o' her fortune," said the old house-keeper, with malicious demureness. This discouraged the investigators considerably.

"I never saw it before," said Mrs. Bellingham; "but then I knew but little of the late Lady Leslie; of course, if it was her mother's it must be Margaret's. Fold it up and put it aside, Grace. Was this Lady Leslie's too?"

"Na, I canna say; I never saw that before," said Bell, overwhelmed. "Eh, that was never made by woman's fingers. It must be shaped out o' the gossamer in the autumn mornings, or the foam of the sea."

But Bell's presence disturbed the inquiry; it was not until she was called away to see to Sir Ludovic's beef-tea that they fully rallied to their work.

"I don't believe a word of what that old woman says. Lady Leslie, indeed! Lady Leslie was not five-and-twenty when she died, poor thing. Stand out of the way, Grace, don't come so close. You may be sure you shall see it all—and no girl understands lace. It might be her mother's? Dear me, what a memory you have got, Grace! She had no mother. She would never have married poor papa if there had been a mother to look after her. Thank Providence, Margaret will be better off. This affliction," said Mrs. Bellingham, with solemnity, "which is so sad for all of us, will not be without its good side for poor little neglected Margaret. Though whether it is not too late to make any change in her—"

"She is very nice-looking," said Miss Grace, "and being pretty covers a great deal—at least as long as you are young."

"Pretty! None of the Leslies were ever ugly," said her sister; "but it breaks my heart to look at her. Neither education nor manners. She might be a country lass at the meanest farm; she might be a fisher-girl mending nets—Grace, I wish you would sometimes let me get in a word! It's melancholy to see her running about in those cotton frocks, and think that she is my father's daughter. We will have our hands full with that girl. Now this is old Flanders—there is not very much of it. I remember it as well as if I had seen it yesterday, on old Aunt Jean."

"Then that should be yours, for you were her name-daughter—"

"Grace, how can you be so Scotch! Say godchild—you can always say godchild—it sounds a great deal better!"

"But we were not English Church people when we were born, and there's no godmo—"

"I think there never was such a clatter in this world!" cried Mrs. Bellingham. "Talk—talk—one cannot get in a word! I know papa's old-fashioned ways as well as you do, but why should we publish them? What would anybody think at the Court if it was known that we were Presbyterians—not that I ever was a Presbyterian after I was old enough to think for myself."

"It was being at school," said Grace; "and a great trouble it was to have to drive all the way to Fifetown on Sundays, instead of going to Dr. Burnside. You were married, it didn't matter for you; but—do you mean to have Aubrey down, Jean, after all?"

"Of course I mean to have Aubrey," said Mrs. Bellingham. She had been carefully measuring on her finger and marking the lengths of the lace, which was the reason Miss Leslie had been allowed to deliver herself of so long a speech. "He will perhaps join us somewhere after this sad time is over. It is not to be supposed that we will be able for much company at first," she said, with a sigh. "There are three yards of the Flanders—too much for a bodice and too little for anything else, and it would be wicked to cut it. After all we have gone through, of course there will be a time when we will have no spirits for company; but Aubrey is not like a stranger. Being my nephew, he will be a kind of cousin to Margaret. Dear me, I wish I could think there was a good chance that he would be something more; for the responsibility on you and me of a young girl—"

"Oh, he will be very willing to be something more," cried Miss Grace, with alacrity; "a pretty young creature like Margaret, and a good income."

"Her income is but a small one to tempt a Bellingham; but I suppose because he is my nephew you must have a fling at him. I have often noticed that inclination in you, Grace. I am sure my family, by marriage, have never but shown you the greatest attention, and Aubrey never makes any difference between us. He calls you Aunt Grace, though you are no more his Aunt Grace— Here is a very nice piece, I don't know what it is. It is English, or perhaps it might be Argentan, or one of the less known kinds. Would you like to have it? It is very pretty. So here are three pieces to commence with: the Venice point for Margaret, if it really was her mother's—but I don't believe it—and the Flanders for me."

Grace lifted the piece allotted to her now with but scant satisfaction. It was Jean who had always the lion's share; it was she who took the management of everything, and put herself forward. Though Miss Leslie was very willing to sacrifice herself when occasion offered, she did not like to be sacrificed calmly by others, without deriving any glory from it. But she said nothing. There was a great deal more still to be looked over, and Jean could not always have so good an excuse for appropriating the best, as she had when she secured Aunt Jean's old piece of Flanders lace.

While these very different scenes were going on within the walls of Earl's-hall, the old gray house in which so soon the last act of a life was to be accomplished was the centre of many thoughts and discussions outside. At the breakfast-table at the Manse Mrs. Burnside read aloud a letter from Mrs. Ludovic in Edinburgh, asking whether the Minister's wife could receive her husband, who was uneasy about his father, and anxious "to be on the spot," whatever happened.

"I thought of sending my Effie with Ludovic,

if you would take her in," Mrs. Leslie wrote. "Of course, Earl's-hall, so little bedroom accommodation as they have, is quite full with Jean and Grace and their maid. It is very provoking that it should be such a fine old house, and one that we would be very unwilling to let go out of the family, and yet so little use. Ludovic has always such confidence in your kindness, dear Mrs. Burnside, that I thought I might ask you. Of course, you will say No at once, if it is not convenient. Effie is not very strong, and I would like her to have a change; and we thought it might be something for poor little Margaret, if anything happens, to have some one near her of her own age. She is the one to be pitied; and yet she has been sadly neglected, poor child— and I don't doubt but in this, as in other matters, all things will work together for good."

"That's a sorely misused text," said the Minister, shaking his head.

"Is this better?" said Randal: "'Wheresoever the carcass is, there will the eagles be gathered together.' They seem all rushing upon their prey."

"No, no, you must not say that. Their own father—who should come to his death-bed but his children? I'll write and say, 'Certainly, let Ludovic come;' and if you can do without that green room for your old portmanteaux, Randal, I'll find a place for them among the other boxes; and we might take little Effie too. I am always glad to give a town-child the advantage of good country air."

"She cannot be such a child if she is the same age as Margaret—"

"And what is Margaret but a child? Poor thing, poor thing! Yes, she has been neglected; she has not had the up-bringing a lady of her family should have; but, dear me," said Mrs. Burnside, who was of the old school, "I've seen such things before, and what harm did it do them? She cannot play the piano, or speak French, or draw, or even dance, so far as I can tell; but she cannot be a lady—it was born with her—and the questions she asks are just extraordinary. I would not make a stipulation for the piano myself everywhere; but still there's no doubt she has been neglected. Jean and Grace are far from being ill women; but I don't think I would like to change old Sir Ludovic, that never said a harsh word to her, for the like of them."

"Yes, mother, Margaret can draw. The young fellow who put Sir Ludovic into his carriage last Sunday, whom you were so impatient of—"

"Me impatient! Randal, you take the very strangest ideas. Why should I be disturbed, one way or other, by Rob Glen? What about Rob Glen?"

"Not much, except that he is giving her—lessons. It seems he is an artist—"

"An artist—Rob Glen! But oh, did I not say Mrs. Ludovic was right? She has been sorely neglected! Not that old Sir Ludovic meant any harm. He was an old man and she a child; and he forgot she was growing up, and that a girl is not a child so long as a boy. After all, perhaps, she will be better in the hands of Grace and Jean."

"And so the text is not misused, after all," said the Minister, once more shaking his head.

CHAPTER XXI.

LUDOVIC came accordingly, with his little daughter Effie — a sentimental little maiden, with a likeness to her aunt Grace, and very anxious to be "of use" to Margaret, who, though only six months older than herself, was her aunt also. Ludovic himself was a serious, silent man —not like the Leslies, everybody said, taking after his mother, who had been a Montgomery, and of a more steady-going race. While Mrs. Bellingham sat by her father's side and talked to him about what was to be done when he was better, saying, "Oh yes, you are mending —slowly, making a little progress every day, though you will not believe it;" and Grace stood, eager, too, to "be of use," touching his cheek—most generally, poor lady, with her nose, which was cold, and not agreeable to the patient —and saying, "Dearest papa!" Ludovic, for his part, would come and sit at the foot of the bed for an hour at a time, not saying anything, but keeping his serious eyes upon the old man, who was more glad than ever to doze, and keep his eyes shut, now that so many affectionate watchers were round him. Now and then Sir Ludovic would rouse up when they were all taking a rest from their anxious duties, as Grace expressed it, and "was just his ain man again," Bell would say.

"Oh, if my children would but neglect me!" he said, when one of these blessed intervals came.

"There is nobody but me here now, papa," said Margaret, like a little shadow in the corner, with her red eyes.

"And that is just as it ought to be, my little Peggy; but who," he said, with that faint little laugh, which scarcely sounded now at all, but abode in his eyes with all its old humor—"who will look after your pronouns when I am away, my little girl?" But sometimes he moaned a little, and complained that it was long. "Could you not give me a jog, John?" he would say; "I'm keeping everybody waiting. Jean and Grace will lose their usual holiday, and Ludovic has his business to think of."

"They're paying you every respect, Sir Ludovic," said John, not feeling that his master was fully alive to the domestic virtue exhibited by his children. Perhaps John, too, felt that to keep up all the forms of anxious solicitude was hard for such a lengthened period, which made the "respect" of the group around Sir Ludovic's death-bed more striking still. Sir Ludovic smiled, and repeated the sentiment with which he began the conversation—"I wish my children would but neglect me." But he was always patient and grateful and polite. He never said anything to Grace about her cold nose; he did not tell Ludovic that his steady stare fretted him beyond measure; he let Jean prattle on as she would, though he knew that what she said was all a fiction. Sir Ludovic was never a more high-bred gentleman than in this last chapter of his life. He was bored beyond measure, but he never showed it. Only when he was alone with his little daughter, with the old servants who loved him, who always understood him more or less, and always amused him, which was, perhaps, as important, he would rouse up by moments and be his old self.

As for Margaret, she led the strangest double life—a life which no one suspected, which she did not herself realize. They made her go to bed every night, though she came and went, a white apparition, all the night through, to her father's door to listen, lest anything should happen while she was away from him ; and in the evenings after dinner, when the family were all about Sir Ludovic's bed, she would steal out, half reluctant, half eager, half guilty, half happy ; guilty because of the strange flutter of sick and troubled happiness that would come upon her.

"Yes, my bonnie lamb, ye'll get a moment to yoursel' ; gang your ways and get a breath of air," Bell would say, all unwitting that something else was waiting for Margaret besides the fresh air and soft soothing of the night.

"I will be in the wood, Bell, where you can cry upon me. You will be sure to cry upon me if there's any need."

"My bonnie doo! I'll cry soon enough ; but there will be no need," said the old woman, patting her shoulder as she dismissed her.

And Margaret would flit along the broken ground where the potatoes had been, where her feet had made a path, and disappear into the sighing of the firs, which swept round and hid her amidst the perplexing crowd of their straight columns. There was one tree, beneath the sweeping branches of which some one was always waiting for her. It was a silver-fir, with great angular limbs, the biggest in the wood, and the little mossy knoll between its great roots was soft and green as velvet. There Rob Glen was always waiting, looking out anxiously through the clear evenings, and with a great gray plaid ready to wrap her in when it was cold or wet. They did not feel the rain under the great horizontal branches of the firs, and the soft pattering it made was more soothing than the wild sweep of the wind coming strong from the sea. There the two would sit sheltered, and look out upon the gray mass of Earl's-hall, with that one ruddy lighted window.

Margaret leaned upon her lover, whom, in her trouble, she did not think of as her lover, and cried and was comforted. He was the only one, she felt, except, perhaps, Bell, who was really good to her, who understood her, and did not want her to be composed and calm. He never said she should not cry, but kissed her hands and her cheek, and said soft caressing words : "My darling! my Margaret!" His heart was beating much more loudly than she could understand ; but Rob, if he was not all good, had a certain tenderness of nature in him, and poetry of feeling which kept him from anything which could shock or startle her. At these moments, as the long summer day darkened and the soft gloaming spread over them, he was as nearly her true and innocent and generous lover as a man could be who was not always generous and true. He was betraying her, but to what?—only to accept his love, the best thing a man had to give ; a gift, if you come to that, to give to a queen. He was not feigning nor deceiving, but loved her as warmly as if he had never loved any one before, nor meant to love any other again. And then he would go toward the house with her, not so far as he went that first night in over-boldness, when they were caught — an accident he always remembered with shame and self-reproach, yet a certain pride, as having proved to Randal Burnside, once for all, his own inferiority, and that he, Rob Glen, had hopelessly distanced all competitors, however they might build upon being gentlemen. He led her along the edge of the wood always under cover, and stole with her, under shadow of the garden-wall, to the corner, beyond which he did not venture. Then he would take her into his arms unresisted, and they would linger for a moment, while he lavished upon Margaret every tender name he could think of—

"Remember that I am always thinking of you, always longing to be by you, to support you, to comfort you, my darling."

"Yes, I will remember," Margaret said, meekly, and there fluttered a little forlorn warmth and sweetness about her heart; and then he would release her, and, more like a shadow than ever, would stand and watch while she flitted along the wall to the great door.

And what thoughts were in Rob's mind when she was gone! That almost innocence, and nobleness and truth, which had existed in the emotion of their meeting, disappeared with Margaret, leaving him in a tumult of other and less noble thoughts. He knew very well that he had beguiled her, though he meant nothing but love and devotion to her. He had betrayed her, in the moment of her sorrow, into a tacit acceptance of him, and committal of herself from which there was no escape. Rob knew very well—no one better—that there were girls who took such love passages lightly enough; but to a delicate little maiden, "a lady," like Margaret, he knew there could be but one meaning in this. Though she had scarcely responded at all, she had accepted his tenderness, and committed herself forever. And he knew he had betrayed her into this, and was glad with a bounding sense of delight and triumph such as made him almost spurn the earth. This occurrence gave him, not only Margaret, whom he was in love with, and whose society was for the time sweeter to him than anything in the world, but with her such a dazzling flood of advantages as might well have turned any young man's head: a position such as he might toil all his life for, and never be able to reach: money, such as would make him admired and looked up to by everybody he knew: a life of intoxicating happiness and advancement, with no need to do anything he did not care to do, or take any further trouble about his living, one way or another. Rob's organization was not so fine as to make him unwilling to accept all these advantages from his wife; in practical life there are indeed very few men who are thus delicately organized; neither were his principles so high or so honorable as to give him very much trouble about the manner in which he had won all this, by surprise. He just felt it, just had a sense that there was something here to be slurred over as much as possible—but it did not spoil his pleasure. It was, however, terribly difficult to know what it would be best to do in the circumstances, what step he should next take: whether he should boldly face the family, on the chance that Sir Ludovic would be glad before he died to see his daughter with a protector and companion of her own, or whether it was wise to keep in the background, and watch the progress of events, keeping that sure hold

upon Margaret herself, which he felt he could now trust to. He had done her good; he had been more to her than any one else, and had helped her to bear her burden; and he had thus woven himself in with every association of her life, at its, as yet, most important period, and made himself inseparable from her.

He had no fear of losing his hold of Margaret. But from the family, the brother and sisters who were like uncle and aunts to the young creature, Rob knew very well he should find little mercy. They would all want to make their own out of her, he felt sure; for it is hard, even when escaping from all sensation of vulgarity in one's person, to get rid of that deeply-rooted principle of vulgarity which shows itself in attributing mean motives to other people. This birth-stain of the meaner sort, not always confined to the lower classes, was strong in him. He did not feel that it was her fortune and her importance which made Margaret valuable in his own eyes (for was he not in love?), but he had no hesitation in deciding that her family and all about her must look at her in this mercenary light. They certainly would not let her fortune slip through their fingers if they could help it. There might be some hope of a legitimate sanction from Sir Ludovic, who was beyond the reach of any advantage from his daughter's money, and might like to feel that she was "settled" and safe; but there could be no hope from the others. They would have plans of their own for her. The Leslies were known not to be rich, and an heiress was not a thing to be lightly parted with. They would keep her to themselves; of that he was sure. And at such a moment as this, what chance was there of reaching Sir Ludovic's bedside, and gaining his consent? It would be impossible to do so without running the gauntlet of all the family; it would make a scene, and probably hurt the old man or kill him.

Thus he was musing, as after an interval he followed Margaret's course under the shadow of the garden-wall, meaning to make his way out by what was called the avenue, though it was merely a path opened through the belt of wood, which was thin on that side, to the gate in the high-road. But this spot was evidently unlucky to Rob. When he was about to pass the door of Earl's-hall, he met Mr. Leslie coming out. Mr. Leslie was one of the men who are always more or less suspicious, and he had just seen Margaret, with her hat in her hand and the fresh night air still about her, going up the winding stair. Ludovic looked at the man walking along under the wall with instinctive mistrust.

"Did you want anything?" he asked, hastily. "This path is private, I think."

"I think not," said Rob; "at least everybody has been free to pass as long as I can remember; but I was on my way," he added, thinking it good to try any means of conciliation, "to ask for Sir Ludovic."

"There is no change," said Mr. Leslie, stiffly. He was himself, to tell the truth, very weary of this invariable answer, but there was nothing else to be said; and he tried to see who the inquirer was, but was unable to make him out in the late dusk. He had never seen him before, for one thing. "You are from—"

"I am from nowhere," said Rob. "I don't suppose you know me at all, Mr. Leslie, or even my name. I am Robert Glen; but Sir Ludovic has been very kind to me. He has allowed me to come and sketch the house, and latterly I have seen a great deal of him. His illness has grieved me as much—as if I had a right to be grieved. He was very kind. Latterly I saw a great deal of him."

"Ah!" said Mr. Leslie. He had heard the people at the Manse talking of Rob Glen, and he had seen Margaret's return a minute before. What connection there might be between these two things he did not very clearly perceive; but there seemed to be something, and he was suspicious, as indeed he had a right to be.

"Is he too ill—to ask to see him?" said Rob, with a sense that a refusal would take all the responsibility off his shoulders. If he could see Sir Ludovic it might be honorable to explain everything; but if not—

"See him!" said Mr. Leslie; "I don't know what your acquaintance may be with my father, Mr. Glen, but he is much too ill to see anybody—scarcely even his own children. I am leaving early, as you perceive, because I feel that it is too much for him to have even all of ourselves there."

"I am very sorry to hear it," said Rob, with the proper expression in his voice; but in reality he was relieved; no need now to say anything to the family. He had Margaret only to deal with, and in her he could fully trust, he thought. "I began a sketch of Sir Ludovic," he said, "for which he had promised me a second sitting; will you kindly ask Miss Margaret Leslie to send it back to me, that I may finish it for her as well as I can? Poor though my drawing was, it will have its value now."

"I will tell my sister," said Mr. Leslie, and he swung open the gate and waited till Rob passed through. "Good-night," said the young man. It was better in any case to be courteous and friendly, if they would permit it, with "the family." But Mr. Leslie only made an indistinct murmur in the darkness. He gave no articulate response; there was no cordiality on his side; and why, indeed, should he be cordial to the farmer's son? Rob went quickly homeward, forcing a smile of contempt, though there was nobody to see. This haughty and distant personage would yet learn to respond to any salutation his sister's husband might make; he would have to be civil, if nothing more, Rob said within himself. What was he that he should be so high and mighty? An Edinburgh advocate working for his living, a poor laird at the best, with a ramshackle old house for all his inheritance. Thus the vulgar came uppermost again in Rob's heart; he scorned for his poverty the man with whom he was indignant for scorning him, because he was unknown and poor. He hurried home with this little fillip of additional energy given to all his schemes. His mother was standing at the door as he approached, looking out for him, or perhaps only looking to see the last of the cows looming through the dusk coming in from the fields. He was absent every night, and Mrs. Glen wanted to know where he went. She was getting impatient on all points, and had determined to wait no longer for any information he might have to give.

"Where have you been?" she asked, as he came in sight.

"To Earl's-hall."

"To Earl's-hall! And what have you been doing at Earl's-hall? No drawing and fiddling while the poor auld man lies dying? Ye're ill enough, but surely you have not the heart for that?"

"I have neither been drawing nor fiddling—indeed I did not know that I could fiddle; but, all the same, I have come from Earl's-hall," he said. "Let me in, mother; I've been sitting in the wood, and the night has got cold."

"What have you been doing—sitting in the wood? There's no light to take your views—tell me," said Mrs. Glen, with determination, "what have you been doing, once for all."

"I may as well tell you," he said; "I have been sitting in the wood with Margaret."

"With—Margaret? you're no blate to speak o' a young lady like that. Rob, my bonnie man, I aye thought you were to be the lucky bairn of my family. Have ye naething mair to tell me about—Margaret? I would like weel, real weel, to hear."

"Can you keep a secret, mother?" he said. "I will tell you something if you will swear to me never to repeat it, never to hint at it, never to brag of what is coming, or to give the slightest ground for suspicion: if you will promise me this—"

"I was never a tale-pyet," said Mrs. Glen, offended, "nobody ever laid tittle-tattle, or bragging of any kind, to my door. But if you canna trust your mother without promises, I see not why you should trust her at all."

"It is not that I doubt you, mother; but you know how difficult it is not to mention a thing that is much in your mind. Margaret Leslie is my own; it is all settled and fixed between us. She came out to me in her trouble when she found her father was dying, and what could I do but comfort her, and support her, and show my feeling—"

"Oh, ay, Rob," his mother interpolated, "you were aye grand at that!"

"What could a man do else?—a sweet young creature like Margaret Leslie crying by his side! I told her, what I suppose she knew very well before, for I never hide my feelings, mother, as you say. And the issue is, she's mine. However it was done, you will not say but what it was well done. I have been fond of her since ever I can remember."

"And of twa-three mair," said Mrs. Glen, "but no a word o' that, Rob my man. Eh, but I'm weel pleased! That's what I've been thinking of since the very week you came hame. 'Now if Rob, with all his cleverness, could get that bonnie Miss Margret,' I said to mysel'. The Lord bless ye, my man! I aye thought you were born to be the lucky one of my family. Is it a' in her ain disposition, or have the family ony power over it, Rob? Eh, my bonnie man, what a down-sitting! and the bonniest leddy in Fife of her years. You're a lucky lad, if ever there was one."

"Let me in, mother; I don't want to tell this to any ears but yours."

"Ay, ay, my man, I'll let you in," said his mother, standing aside from the door. "Come in and welcome, my lucky lad. Is there anything you would like for your supper? Naething in a' the house is ower good for such good news. We'll take a bottle o' wine out of the press, or maybe ye would like a drap toddy just as well, which is mair wholesome. Come in, come in, my bonnie man. A bonnie lass, and plenty wi' her; and a real auld family an honor to anybody to be connected with. My word, Rob Glen, you're a lucky lad! Wha will look down upon you now? Wha will say a word about your opinions? I've never upbraided you mysel'; I saw your talents, and felt ye could bide your time. Eh," cried Mrs. Glen, exultant, "wha will say now but that marriages are made in heaven? And Rob, my bonnie man, when is it to be?"

"We are not so far as that, mother," he said; "do you think she has the heart to think of marrying, and poor old Sir Ludovic lying on his death-bed? We must wait for all that. I'm too happy in the mean time to think of more. She's mine; and that is more than I could have hoped."

"That's very true, my man: but still something settled would have been a grand stand-by," said Mrs. Glen, slightly disappointed; "I would have thought now it would have been a great comfort to Sir Ludovic to see his daughter married and settled before he slips away. But the gentry's ways are not our ways. I'm doubting you'll have some trouble with the family, if nothing's settled afore the auld gentleman dies."

"I doubt I will, mother," said Rob; "but whatever trouble I may have, Margaret's mine, and she will never go back from her word."

CHAPTER XXII.

At last the time came when old Sir Ludovic's dozing and drowsiness, his speculations, and the gleam of humor with which they were all accompanied, and which most of those around him thought so inappropriate to his circumstances, came to an end. All his affairs were in order, his will made, though he had not much to leave, and Dr. Burnside (which was a great satisfaction to the family) paid him a daily visit for the last week of his life; so that everything was done decently and in order. Dr. Burnside had not so very much to say to the old man. He had no answer to give to his questions. He bade Sir Ludovic believe. "And so I do," he said; he could not be got to be frightened; and now that he had got over the shock of it, and into that dreamy slumbrous valley of the shadow, he did not even wish to avoid what was coming. "It is not so bad as one thinks," he said to old John, his faithful servant, and to the good minister, who was approaching old age too, though not so near as either of these old men. Dr. Burnside was a little disturbed by the smile on his patient's face, and hoped it did not show any inclination toward levity; but he was glad to hear, having that journey in view, that it was not so bad as one thought. "He is a man of a very steady faith," the Minister said, and he himself was wise enough to let Sir Ludovic glide away out of the world with that smile upon his face.

As for Jean and Grace, they did their best to disturb their father and to unsettle him, and insinuated that Dr. Burnside's instructions were of an unsatisfactory kind. Even Bell held it unorthodox that, except in cases of religious triumph and ecstasy, which no doubt were on record, a human creature should leave this earth smiling, to appear in the presence of his Maker, as she said. Mrs. Bellingham did all she could to question her father on the subject, but was not successful. "Leave him in peace," his son said; but neither was Mr. Leslie satisfied. It was very strange to them all. The old man did not even seem to feel that anxiety for Margaret's future which they expected, and never made that solemn appeal to them to take care of her, to which both the sisters were prepared to respond, and which even Ludovic expected, though he felt that, with such a large family of his own, nothing much could be looked for from him. But Sir Ludovic made no appeal. He said "My little Peggy," when all other words had failed him; and on the very last day of his life a gleam as of laughter crossed his face, and he shook his head faintly at her when she said "me" instead of "I," and thus faded quite gently and pleasantly away.

There was silence in Earl's-hall that night, silence and quiet, scarcely a whisper even between the sisters, who generally had a meeting in Mrs. Bellingham's room for a last discussion of everything that had passed, notwithstanding that they were all the day together. But on this evening nobody talked. Ludovic went away with the Minister and ate a solemn late meal, having, as everybody said, eaten nothing all day (but that was a mistake, for he had not been called to the last ceremonial till after luncheon). And in Earl's-hall everybody went to bed. They had been keeping irregular hours, had sometimes sat late, and sometimes been called early; and John and Bell, in particular, had not for a week past kept any count which was night and which was day. A few broken phrases about "him yonder," a groan from John, a few tears rubbed off, till her eyes were red, by Bell's apron, and the sound of "greeting" from Jeanie's little turret-room, was almost all that could be heard in the silent house. Margaret, for her part, could not "greet" as Jeanie did. She was stunned, and did not know what had happened to her. For the moment it was over; the worst had come, and a blank of utter exhaustion came over the girl. She allowed herself to be put to bed, and did nothing but sigh, long sighs which went to Bell's heart, sighs which seemed almost a physical necessity to the young bosom oppressed with such an unknown burden. Mrs. Bellingham (though she was not quite satisfied in her mind) said a few words to her maid that it was a most peaceful end, that it was beautiful to see him lying there at rest just as if he were asleep; and Miss Leslie cried copiously, and said "Dearest papa!" They were all in bed by ten o'clock, and the old gray house shut up and silent. A dark night, the wind sweeping through the firs, everything silent and hushed in earth and heaven, and all dark except the one window in which a faint watch-light burned palely, but no longer the warm, inconstant glimmer of any cheerful fire.

But with the morning, what a flood of pent-up energy and activity was let loose. They were all anxious to keep quiet in Margaret's part of the house, that she might sleep as long as possible and be kept out of every one's way. The arrangements into which everybody else plunged were not for her. The first thing to be thought of, of course, Mrs. Bellingham said, was the mourning, and there was not a moment's time to lose. Telegraphs were not universally prevalent in those days, and one of the men from the farm had to be sent on horseback to Fifeton to send a message to Edinburgh about the bombazine and the crape.

As Sir Ludovic had anticipated, his daughter Jean did not stint him of a single fold ; she meant to show "every respect." Fortunately Steward, their maid, was quite equal to the occasion, both the ladies congratulated themselves. "Of course, we shall want no evening dresses, nothing beyond the more necessary here," Mrs. Bellingham said. "One for the morning and another to go out with, a little more trimmed, that will be all." But even for this little outfit a good deal of trouble had to be taken. That very evening a man arrived from Edinburgh with mountains of crape and boxes full of hemstitched cambric for the collars and cuffs. There was crape all over the house—even Bell and Jeanie had their share— no stint. When a man has been so much thought of as Sir Ludovic, and has a respectable family whose credit is involved in showing him every respect, a good deal of quiet bustle becomes inevitable ; the house was full of whispers, of consultations, of measurements, and a great hurry and pressure to get done in time for the funeral ; though the funeral was delayed long, according to use and wont in the country.

Mr. Leslie, on his part, went over all the house, and walked diligently about the farm and inspected everything, though, being a silent man, he said little about it. It was too early to say anything. When his sisters put questions to him about what he was going to do, he said he had not made up his mind ; and it was only when the funeral was over, and the shutters opened, and old Sir Ludovic's chair put against the wall, that he at all opened his mind. Nearly a week passed in this melancholy interval ; he had become Sir Ludovic himself, but nobody in Earl's-hall could give him the familiar title ; old John ground his teeth together (though he had not many left) and tried to get it out, but the conclusion was a hurried exclamation,

"I canna do it! Pit me away, sir. Bell and me, we're ready to gang whenever ye please ; but I canna ca' ye your right name."

The new Sir Ludovic, though he said little, had a kind heart. He said, "Never mind, John ; tell Bell never to mind ;" but Mrs. Bellingham had no such feeling. She said it was ridiculous in servants, when the family themselves had to do it. "I hope I know what is due to the living as well as to the dead," she cried ; "and if I can say it, why should not John ?"

But at first, no doubt, it was difficult enough. After the funeral, however, the new Sir Ludovic went "home" to Earl's-hall, where his wife came and joined him. The eldest boy, too, arrived for the ceremony itself, and walked with his father to the church-yard as one of the chief mourners. The house was filled to overflowing with the family as soon as the last act of old Sir Ludovic's earthly history was accomplished. Beds were put in the high room to accommodate the boys. It was all novelty to them, who had not known very much of their grandfather, and their mother liked being my lady. It was natural. She

had not known much of the old man any more than her children had, and he was only her father - in - law — not a very tender relationship. Thus the new tide rose at once, and new life came in. Had there been only the elders in the house, no doubt they would have kept up a drowsy appearance of gravity ; but that was not to be done with young people in the house.

As for Margaret, this period passed over her like a dream. While the house was shut up, and everything went on in a pale twilight, she wandered about like a ghost, not knowing what to do or say, unable to take up any of her occupations. It seemed years to her, centuries since the careless time when she went and came so lightly, fearing no evil ; trying to draw straight lines with an ineffectual pencil ; flitting out and in of her father's room ; getting out books for him ; searching for something she might read herself ; taking up for half an hour Lady Jean's old work ; knitting a bit of Bell's stocking ; roaming everywhere about as light as the wind. All that, Margaret thought, was over forever ; but she did not "break her heart" altogether, as she supposed she would. Sometimes, indeed, an aching sense of loss, a horrible void about her would make her heart sick, and her whole being giddy with pain ; but in the intervals life went on, and she found that it was possible to sit at table, to talk to the others, to have her dresses fitted on. And when the children came, there were moments when she felt inclined to smile at their curious little ways, even (was that possible ?) to laugh at little Loodie, who was the youngest of the boys, and never, Heaven forbid! would be Sir Ludovic. Bell, too, found little Loodie "a real diverting bairn." "Eh, if his grandpapaw had but been here to see him !" she said, with tears and smiles.

But Margaret, naturally, was more unwilling to be "diverted" than Bell was. When she was beguiled into a smile at little Loodie, it was very unwillingly, and she would recover herself with a sense of guilt ; for it was a terrible revelation to Margaret, a most painful discovery to feel that a smile was possible even within a week of her father's death, and that her heart was not altogether broken. She wept for her own heartlessness as well as for her dear father, of whom she had thought beforehand that all she wished for would be to be buried in his grave.

But she went out of the house only once between the death and the funeral. Rob, for his part, roamed round about it, and stayed for hours in the woods, looking for her ; but it seemed to Margaret that for the moment she shrank from Rob. Oh, how could she have thought of Rob, or any one, while he lay dying ? How could she have gone out and spent those hours in the wood with him, which might have been spent with Sir Ludovic ? What would she give now, she said to herself, to be able to steal up-stairs to him, to sit by his bedside, to hold his hand, to hear him say "My little Peggy" again. Now that this was no longer possible, she felt a kind of resentment against Rob, who had occupied her at times when it was still possible. And the state of his mind during this interval was not pleasant to contemplate. When he had asked once or twice for the ladies, he had no further excuse for returning openly, and he was afraid to be seen lest he should again meet some one—perhaps the new

Sir Ludovic himself—who had not been delighted by his previous appearance, or some jealous spectator like Randal Burnside.

Rob stood for hours behind the big fir-tree looking toward the house in which there were more lights now, but no glimmer in that window which had been his beacon for so long, and more voices audible—never Margaret's soft notes, like a bird. He was very fond of Margaret. Those dreary evenings when she was kept from him, or kept herself from him, Rob was wild with love, and fear, and disappointment. Could *they* have found it out? could *they* be keeping her away? He stood under the fir-tree scarcely daring to move, and watched with his heart beating in his ears. Sometimes John would loom heavily across the vacant space, coming out again, according to his old habit, to "take a look at the potatoes." Sometimes Bell would appear at the opening of the little court-yard to "cry upon" her husband when something was wanted. "There's aye something wanting now," John would say, as he turned back. Or Rob would see some one at the wall, drawing water, under the shade of the thorn-tree, without knowing who it was, or that there were any thoughts of himself, except those which might be in Margaret's bosom, within the gray shadow of those old walls. How breathlessly he watched John's lumbering steps about the potatoes, and the whiteness of Bell's aprons, and the clang of the water-pails!

But no one came. Had she accepted his consolations only because there was no one else to comfort her, without caring for him who breathed them in her ear? Were all his lofty hopes to end in nothing, and his love to be rejected? Terror and anxiety thrilled through Rob as he stood and watched, tantalized by all those sounds and half-seen sights. Once only she came, and then she would say little or nothing to him: she had never said much; but she shrank from his outstretched arms now, crying, "Don't, don't!" in tones half of terror. That one meeting was a greater disappointment than when she did not come at all. Had she but been taking advantage of him, as great people, Rob knew, were so ready to take advantage of small people? And now that she needed him no longer, was she about to cast him off? In that case, all his fine anticipations, all his triumph, would be like Alnascher's hopes in the story. His very heart quailed in terror. The disappointment, the downfall, the decay of hopes and prospects would be more than he could bear.

The truth was that Margaret, left all alone suddenly in the midst of what to her was a crowd of people, all more or less strangers, seemed to have lost the power of doing so much for herself as to go anywhere. Though they amused her sometimes in spite of herself, they kept her in a kind of subjugation which was very confusing and very novel.

"Where are you going, Margaret?" Mrs. Bellingham would say, if she went across the room. "Darling Margaret, don't leave us," Grace would add, next time she moved. Even Effie, who was so anxious to be "of use," would interfere, throwing her arms about her youthful aunt, whispering, "You are not to go to your own room and cry. Oh, come with me to the tower, and look at the sunset."

"Yes, my dear Margaret, go with Effie; it

will take off your thoughts a little," said the new Lady Leslie.

Thus Margaret had weights of kindness hung round her on every side, and was changed in every particular of her life from the light-hearted creature who flitted about like the wind, in and out a hundred times a day. Even Bell approved of this thraldom.

"Ah, my bonnie dear, keep wi' Miss Effie. She's your ain flesh and blood. What would you do out your lane when you have sic company?"

"I always went out alone before," Margaret said, mechanically turning up-stairs again.

"Yes, my bonnie doo; but you hadna a bonnie young Miss, a cousin of your ain (for niece is but a jest), to keep ye company."

Thus Margaret was held fast. And by-and-by her habit of wandering out would probably have been broken, and she might have been carried away by her sisters safe out of all contact or reach of her lover. For the lover, as will be seen, was not violently in Margaret's mind. If she missed him, there were so many other things that she missed more! He was but part of the general privation, impoverishment of her life. She had lost everything, she thought—her father, her careless sweetness of living, her light heart, the sunshine of her morning. All these other happinesses being gone, how could Margaret make an effort for Rob only? She was not strong enough to do this. She was not even unwilling to let him go with all the rest. Perhaps there was ingratitude in the feeling. He had been very "kind" to her, had given her a little comfort of sweet sympathy in her trouble. It was ungrateful to forget that now; and she did not forget it, but was too languid, too weary, and had lost too much already to be able to make any effort for this. Meanwhile, while she sat in a kind of lethargy within, and followed the directions of all about her, and let him drop from her, Rob roamed about outside, gnashing his teeth, sometimes almost cursing her, sometimes almost praying for her, watching every door and window, holding the post of a most impatient sentinel under the great fir-tree.

It happened to Margaret, however, one evening to find herself alone. Mrs. Bellingham had a headache, a thing which was not generally regarded as a great calamity in places where Mrs. Bellingham paid visits. It confined her to her room, and it was, on the whole, not a disagreeable change for her friends. Her sister, who in weal and woe was inseparable from her, though she would have been glad enough to escape too, was, under Jean's orders, writing letters for her in her room. And the new proprietors of Earl's-hall were glad enough for once to be by themselves. They took a conjugal walk about the place, examining into everything—the ruined part to see if anything could be done to it; the stables, which had been made out of part of the ruin; even the pigsty, which was John's favorite spot in the demesne. The subject of consideration in the mind of the pair was whether the old place, with all its associations, should be sold, or whether anything could be done with it, cheaply, to adapt it for the country residence of the family. In its present state, certainly, it did not take much to "keep up;" but, on the other hand, the rental of the little scraps of estate which old Sir Ludovic had left scarcely justified the new Sir Ludovic, with his large family, in "keeping up" any country place at all. To decide upon this subject was the reason of Lady Leslie's presence here.

And Effie, whose mourning was less deep, and her mind less affected by "the family loss" than Margaret, had gone to visit Mrs. Burnside. Even little Loodie was being put to bed. Margaret, for the first time since her father's death, was alone. She had found that day, among a collection of papers into which it had been shuffled heedlessly amidst the confusion of the moment, the drawing of her father which Rob Glen had begun on his first appearance at Earl's-hall; and this had plunged her back into all that fresh agitation of loss and loneliness which is, in its way, a kind of pleasure to the mind, instead of the dull stupor of habitual grief which follows upon the immediate passion of an event. She had wept till her eyes and her strength were exhausted, but her heart relieved a little; and then that heart yearned momentarily for some one to comfort her. Where was *he*? She had not thought of him in this aspect before—perhaps looking for her, perhaps waiting for her, he who had been so "kind." She put on her hat with the heavy gauze veil which Jean had thought necessary. She was all hung and garlanded with crape, the hat itself wrapped in a cloud of it, her dress covered with it, so that Margaret's very movements were hampered. The grass always damp, more or less, the mossy underground beneath the firs, the moist brown earth of the potato-ground, were all alike unsuitable for this heavy and elaborate robe of mourning. Margaret gathered it about her and put on her hat, with its thick black gauze veil—she did not know herself in all this panoply of woe—and went out. There was nobody about. John was showing the new Baronet his pigsty, and Bell, more comforted and cheerful than she had yet felt, stood in the door of the byre and talked to Lady Leslie about her favorite, her bonnie brown cow. The old people were amused and pleased; they were more near "getting over it" than they had felt yet; and even John began to feel that it might be possible, after a while, to say Sir Ludovic again.

Margaret went out, hearing their voices, though she did not see them. She had no feeling of bitterness toward her brother, though he was assuming possession of her old home. He had not much to say, but he was kind; and good Lady Leslie was a good mother, and could not but speak softly and think gently of everybody. They were, perhaps, a humdrum and somewhat care-worn couple, but no unkindness was in them. It gave Margaret no pang to hear them talking about Bell's beloved Brownie or what they were to do with the stables, neither did it occur to her to take any pains not to be seen by them. It was still light, but the evening was waning, the sky glowing in the west, the shadows gathering under the fir-trees in the woods which lay to eastward of the house. She made her way to her usual haunt, her feet making no sound on the soft path. Would he be there, waiting for her as in that dreadful time? or would he have gone away? Margaret had not enough animation left to feel that she would be disappointed if he were not there, but yet

her heart was a little lighter, for the first time relieved from the dull burden of sorrow which is so intolerable to youth. And who can say with what transport Rob Glen saw this slim black-clad figure detach itself from the shadow of the house? He had come here, as he said to himself, half indignantly, half sullenly, for the last time, to wait for her—the last time he would come and wait—but not on that account would he give up the pursuit of her. She was his—that he would maintain with all his force. He would write to her next day, and ask why she did not come. He would let her feel that he had a claim upon her, that she could not cast him off when she pleased. But in his very vehemence there was a tremor of fear, and it is impossible to describe with what feelings of anxiety he had come, putting his fortune to the touch, meaning that this vigil should be final before he proceeded to "other steps." And how had fortune, nay, providence, rewarded him! Not John this time, not Bell smoothing down her apron, nor Jennie with her pitcher at the well; but slim and fair as a lily in her envelope of gloom, pale with grief and exhaustion, with wet eyes and a pitiful lip, that quivered as she tried to smile at him, at last Margaret was here.

CHAPTER XXIII.

"At last!" He came out from the shadow of the firs and took her hands, and drew her toward him. "At last! my Margaret, my own Margaret! Such a weary time it has been waiting, but this repays all. Say that it is not your doing, darling. You have been kept back; you have not forgotten me, or that I was waiting here?"

"No," she said; "but I did not know you were waiting here. I did not know, even, if I would find you to-night."

"It would have been strange, indeed, if you had not found me. Every evening, as sure as the gloaming came, I have been here waiting for you, Margaret. I did not think you would have kept me so long. But it is not as it used to be between us, when I thought, perhaps, you might cast me off at any moment. I a poor farmer's son, you the young lady of Earl's-hall; but that could not be now; for you are mine, and I am yours."

"It would not have been at any time—for that reason," said Margaret. She was uneasy about the very close proximity he wished for, and avoided his arm. In her great trouble she had not thought of this, but now it troubled and partially shocked her, though she could scarcely tell why. She was roused, however, by the idea that she could have slighted him for any ignoble reason. "It is you that have always been kind to me," she said. "I, who am only a country-girl, and know nothing at all."

"You are a princess," said Rob; "you are a queen to me. *My* queen and my Margaret; but you will not keep me so long hungering and thirsting out here, far from the light of your sweet countenance? you will not leave me so long again?"

"Oh, Mr. Glen!" said Margaret, "I ought to let you know at once, we are going away."

"Do not, for Heaven's sake, call me Mr. Glen! Do you want to make me very unhappy, to take away all pleasures from me? Surely the time is over in which you should call me Mr. Glen. You cannot want to play with me and make me wretched, Margaret?"

"No," she said, with a tremor in her voice; "I will call you by your name, as I used to do when I was little. But it is quite true that I said—we are going away."

"Going away? Where are you going, and who are we? Oh yes, I knew it was not likely they would stay here," cried Rob, with mingled irritation and despair. "Where are they going to take you, my Margaret?—nowhere that I cannot come and see you, nowhere that I will not follow you, my darling. I would go after you to the world's-end."

"I am going with my sisters, Jean and Grace. They are my guardians now. I am to live with them till—for three years at least, till I am twenty-one; then they say I can do what I like. What does it matter now about doing what I like? I do not think I care what becomes of me, now that I have no one, no one that has a right to me! and they will not even let me cry."

She began to weep, and he did not stop her, though his mind was full of impatience. He drew her to him close, and this time she did not resist him.

"Cry there," he said, "Margaret—my Margaret! I will never try to keep you from crying. Oh! he deserved it well. He loved you better than all the earth. You were the light of his eyes, as you are of mine. They! what does it matter to them? They will bother you; they will make you do what they like; they will not worship you as he did, and as I do. But, Margaret, there is still one that has a right to you. Had he known, had I but had the courage to go and tell him everything, he would have given you to me; I am certain he would. He would have thought, like you, that it was better, far better for you, to have some one of your very own. The others! what are you to them? But to him you were everything, and to me you are everything. Margaret! say this, darling! Say, Rob, I am yours; I will always be yours, as you are mine!"

Margaret looked in his face with her wet eyes. But she did not say the words he dictated to her. Her heart was full of emotion of another kind. She was thankful to Rob for his kindness, and he was not like—any one else; he had a special standing-ground of his own with her. To nobody else could she talk as she was talking, on nobody else would she lean; but still it did not occur to her to obey him, to say what he asked her to say.

"I found that picture you made," she said, "only to-day. It is him, just himself. I took it away to my own room that nobody might see it. It must have been some angel that put it into your mind to do that."

"Yes, Margaret," he said, "it was an angel, for it was you. And it was not I that did it, but love that did it; but if you will give it to me, I will make it still more like him. I will never forget how he looked, and how you looked —and my heart all full, and running over with love, which I dared not say."

Alas! there was this peculiarity in the conver-sation, that while Rob was eager to speak of himself and his love, Margaret, in the most innocent and unwitting way, made it apparent that this was not the subject that interested her most. She was too polite not to listen to him, too grateful and sensitively affected by the curious link between them to show any opposition; but when she could, she turned aside from this subject, which to him was the most interesting subject in heaven or earth; and it is impossible to say how this fact moved Rob, who had never met with anything of the kind before. It piqued him, and it made him more eager. He watched her with an anxiety and impatience which he could scarcely keep in check, while she, with downcast eyes full of tears, pursued that part of the subject which interested her most.

"I should not like it touched," she said; "I would not give it for all the pictures in the world! If I gave it to you, it would be only that it might be put into some case that would preserve it. I have folded it in paper, but that is not enough. I would not give it for all the pictures in the world!"

"Thank you, my darling," he said. "It is something to have done a thing that so pleases you. If you will bring it to me, I will get it put in a case for you. Indeed, it was an angel that put that scene before me; for now when you look at that, and think of him, you will think of me too."

"Oh no, Mr. Glen," said Margaret—then she stopped, confused: "I mean, Rob—I am very, very thankful to you. But when I look at that, all the world goes away, and there is only papa leaning back, sleeping. I am glad he was sleeping. He slept a great deal, do you know, before he died. But it was better to see him in his chair, as he used always to be, than in his bed. I don't want any one to see it hut myself—other people do not understand it. They would hand it about from one to another, and say, 'Is it not like?' and talk. I could not bear that; I prefer to keep it to myself."

"But you don't mind me seeing it?" he said. "I should not be so unfeeling. Many a time when we are together—when we are married, darling—we will look at it together; and I will make a picture from it, a real picture, with you at my elbow, and it shall be hung in the best place in our house."

At this Margaret winced slightly, but made no remark. She had not the courage to contradict him, to say anything against this strange view; but it disturbed her all the same. Probably it would have to be some time. There seemed a necessity for it, though she could not quite tell why; but as it could not be now, nor for a long time, why should it be spoken of, or brought in to disturb everything? She said, not knowing how to put aside this subject gently, yet to say something all the same: "Jean and Grace are going to take me to the Grange—to my house."

"To your house!" Rob felt the blood flush to his face with the excitement of this thought. "I did not know you had a house of your own, Margaret."

"Oh yes; it was my mother's. It is away in England, where I never was. I have seen a picture of it. They say it is very English, with creepers hanging about the walls, roses and honeysuckle, and beautiful great trees. Jean thinks everything in England is better than anything in Scotland. However pretty it may be, it will never, never be like old gray Earl's-hall."

Rob dropped his arm from her, and hung his head. "What am I thinking of?" he said; "you a great lady, with beautiful houses and lands, and I a poor man, with nothing. I must be mad to think that you could care for me—that you would even think of me at all."

"Mr.—Rob! oh, what must you think of me that you say so? Do I care for money or for a house? Are you going away? Are you going to—leave me? oh!" cried Margaret, penitent, clasping her hands; "did you not know I had a fortune? But what does that matter? You have been kind, very kind to me, thinking I was poor— Rob! are you going to cry, you!—no, don't, don't; you will break my heart! I am calling you by your name now," she said, anxiously, with one hand upon his arm, and with the other pulling down the hand which covered his face. She put her own face close to his in her generous, foolish earnestness—"I am calling you by your name now, Rob; don't hide your face from me, don't go away and leave me. If I am rich, is it not all the better? There will be plenty for us both."

"It makes a difference," he said; and indeed he was able to play his part very well, for never before in his life had Rob been so entirely ashamed of himself. Her very earnestness, she who had been so cool and calm before, her generous trouble and importunity humbled him to the very depths. A man may do a great many things that will not bear examination before he finds himself out; but to act such a falsehood as this—to pretend that he did not know what he knew so much more definitely than she did—to pretend to resist her generous anxiety—to avert his face, and let her woo him, she who had taken his hot wooing with such shy coldness! This made Rob feel himself the most wretched creature, the most despicable, miserable, mercenary wretch. He could not endure himself. Well might he hide his face for a poor swindler and cheat, worse, far worse than he had ever known himself before! To breathe deceitful vows, to say more than he meant, to promise more than he intended to perform, all this was not a thousandth part so bad; for indeed he had always been "in love," when he made love; and a promise more or less, what is that? The common coin of young deceivers. Hitherto Rob had not been bad, only fickle and false. But what was he now? A cheat, a liar, a traitor, unfit to breathe where such innocent creatures were. Thus he played his part very well; his misery was not dissembled; and when he allowed himself to yield to her entreaties, to be moved by the eager eloquence of that soft lip which was so ready to quiver, what vows he made in his heart to be to Margaret something more than ever man had been before!

After this their intercourse was more easy, and by-and-by Rob came to feel that perhaps the momentary fear of losing him (which was how, in his native vulgarity and self-importance, he put it, after a while, to himself) had been a good thing. More than ever now she had committed herself. They wandered about among the trees and talked. They talked of her departure, and

of how he could write to her—which Margaret was half shy again to think of, yet half happy too, a novelty as it was. But she could not tell him how this was to be managed, or how he could come to see her; all was strange, and Jean and Grace were very different from anything she had known in all her previous life.

"They tell me to sit down when I am standing, and to stand up when I am sitting down; they will always have me doing something different," she avowed, though gently, and with a faint sense of humor. But this made it very evident that the life before her would be quite unlike the past. And it did not occur to Margaret that Jean and Grace ought perhaps to be informed of Rob, and the understanding between him and herself. Rob naturally said nothing about this, and to Margaret the thought did not occur. She had no idea of concealment, but simply did not think of her sisters in connection with this "secret," which was something too strange and confusing to herself to be capable of explanation to others, who could not know how it had come about.

"Will you come up to the tower?" said Effie Leslie to Randal Burnside, who had walked home with her from the Manse. Randal had been much about Earl's-hall since Sir Ludovic's death. He had been ready to do anything for the family, and the family had been very willing to employ him. It was a kindness to give him something to do, his mother said, who was glad to throw him in Margaret's way; and the decorousness of the grief which made Mrs. Bellingham and Miss Leslie quite unable to see anybody was put aside on his behalf as well as on his father's. And Margaret and he had grown friends, though she was almost the only one in the house who never gave him any commissions in that moment of bustle. She had never ceased to be grateful to him for calling the doctor when her father's illness began, but she was too independent to have any personal wants to which he could minister, and too shy to have asked his aid if she had. Effie was much more disposed to make use of the young man. She was not unhappy—why should she be, having seen so little of grandpapa? She was a little elated, indeed, to think that mamma was now my lady, and she herself entitled to precedence as a baronet's daughter, and she was very glad to have some one to speak to who did not melt into tears in the middle of the conversation, or say, "Hush, child! remember that this is a house of mourning." The Manse was not a house of mourning, and she liked to go there, and she liked Randal to walk home with her and talk. Lady Leslie was still looking at the brown cow and John's pigsty, and Mrs. Bellingham, as has been said, had a headache. Effie peeped into the West Chamber and the long room, and saw nobody. And then she said, "Have you ever been on the tower, Mr. Burnside? Oh, do come up to the tower."

Randal had climbed the tower a hundred times in former days. He went up the winding stair very willingly, thinking he would have all the better chance of seeing "the others," when the falling night drove them in from their walks. Perhaps "the others" meant only the new Sir Ludovic; perhaps it had another significance. He was interested about Margaret, he allowed to himself—more interested than he dared let any one know; for had he not almost seen a lover's parting between her and Rob Glen ?—a secret knowledge which made him very uneasy. Randal felt that he could not betray them; it would be a base thing in their contemporary — or so, at least, he thought; but he was uneasy. Many thoughts had gone through his mind on this subject. He did not know what to do. The only thing that seemed to him possible was to speak to Rob Glen himself, to represent to him that it was not manly or honorable to engage a girl in Margaret's position, without the knowledge and consent of her friends. But to make such a statement to a young man of your own age, with whom you have not the warrant of friendship for your interference, nor even the warrant of equality, is a difficult thing to do. If Rob, resenting it, could have called him out, there would have been less harm; but that was ridiculous, and what could be done to expiate such an affront? There was nothing to be done, unless he permitted Rob to knock him down, and he did not feel that his forbearance was equal to that. So that Randal remained very uneasy on this subject, and did not know what to do. To let Margaret fall into the hands of a—of Rob Glen, seemed desolation and sacrilege; but what could Randal—who had known them both from his cradle—what could he do between them. Was it his part to *tell*—most despicable of all offices in the opinion of youth? This train of uneasy thought was brought back when Effie looked into the little white-panelled sitting-room, the West Chamber, where Margaret, he knew, spent most of her time. She liked it better than the long room, every nook of which was so full of her father's memory; and the ladies humored her, and, small as it was, made the West Chamber their centre. Where was she, if she was not there? Possibly out-of-doors in the soft evening, confiding all her griefs to Rob Glen. Possibly it was the thought that Randal himself would have liked to have those griefs confided to him, and to act the part of comforter, that made his blood burn at this imagination. So soon after her father's death! He felt disposed to despise Margaret too.

"Go softly just here," said Effie, whispering; "for there is Aunt Jean's room, and we must not do anything to disturb her headache. It is a very good thing, you know, that she has a headache sometimes; even Aunt Grace says so —for otherwise she would wear herself out. Perhaps it is a little too late for the view, but the sky was still full of glow when we came in. Ah! it is very dark up here; but now there is only another flight. Oh no, it is not too late for the view," Effie cried, her young voice coming out soft yet ringing, as they emerged into the open air. "Nobody can hear us here," she said, with a laugh; "for at seventeen it is not easy to be serious all day, especially when it is only a grandfather, nothing more, who is dead."

It was not too late for the view, and the view was not a view to be despised. There does not seem much beauty to spare in the east of Fife. Low hills, great breadths of level fields: the sea a great expanse of blue or leaden gray, fringed with low reefs of dark rocks, like the teeth of some hungry monster, dangerous and grim without being picturesque, without a ship to break

its monotony. But yet, with those limitless breadths of sky and cloud, the wistful clearness and golden after-glow, and all the varying blueness of the hills, it would have been difficult to surpass the effect of the great amphitheatre of sea and land of which this solitary gray old house formed the centre. The hill, behind which the sun had set, is scarcely considerable enough to have a name; but it threw up its outline against the wonderful greenness, blueness, goldenness of the sky with a grandeur which would not have misbecome an Alp. Underneath its shelter, gray and sweet, lay the soft levels of Stratheden in all their varying hues of color—green corn, and brown earth, and red fields of clover, and dark belts of wood. Behind were the two paps of the Lomonds, rising green against the clear serene, and on the other side entwining lines of hills, with gleams of golden light breaking through the mists, clearing here and there as far as the mysterious Grampians, far off under Highland skies.

This was one side of the circle; and the other was the sea, a sea still blue under the faint evening skies, in which the young moon was rising: the yellow sands of Forfarshire on one hand, stretching downward from the mouth of the Tay—the low brown cliffs and green headlands bending away on the other toward Fifeness—and the great bow of water reaching to the horizon between. Nearer the eye, showing half against the slope of the coast and half against the water, rose St. Andrews on its cliff, the fine dark tower of the College Church poised over the little city, the jagged ruins of the Castle marking the outline, the Cathedral rising majestic in naked pathos; and old St. Rule, homely and weather-beaten, oldest venerable pilgrim of all, standing strong and steady, at watch upon the younger centuries. This was the view at that time from Earl's-hall. It is a little less noble now, because of the fine, vulgar, comfortable gray stone houses which have got themselves built everywhere since, and spoiled one part of the picture; but all the rest will remain forever, Heaven be praised. The little wood of Earlshall, pinched and ragged with the wind, lay immediately below, and the flat Eden, with its homely green lines of bank on either side, lighted up by here and there a sand-bank; but the tide was out, and the Eden meandered in a desert of wet brown sand, and was not lovely. The two young people did not speak for a moment. They were moved, in spite of themselves, by all this perfect vault of sky, and perfect round of earth and sea. It is not often that you can see the great world in little, field and mountain, sunset and moonrise, land and sea, at one glance. They were silenced for sixty seconds; and then Effie Leslie drew a long breath and began to chatter again.

"Well!" she said, with as much expression as the simple word was capable of bearing, "I don't think I should like to sell this old house when the family has been so long, if I were papa !"

"I would not sell it, if it were mine, for anything that could be offered me!" cried Randal, in the enthusiasm of the moment. Effie shook her head.

"Perhaps not, Mr. Burnside; but then you would not have ten children—or nine at least; for now Gracie is married she does not count.

But oh, I wish we could keep Earl's-hall! It must be very pleasant to live where everybody knows you, and knows exactly what you are—that is, if you are anybody. Poor Margaret will not like leaving, but then she is a lucky girl; she is an heiress; she has a house of her own; and I dare say she will get very fond of that when she knows it. Do you think I ought to call her *Aunt* Margaret, Mr. Burnside?"

Effie's laugh rang out so merrily as she said this, that she checked herself with a little alarm. "Suppose Aunt Jean should hear me!" she said; and then, after a pause, "Oh! look straight down, straight down under the fir-trees, Mr. Burnside. Oh, this is more interesting than the view! A pair of—"

"Do you think it is quite honorable to look at them?" said Randal. He had a presentiment who it must be.

"Oh, it can't be anybody we know," said light-hearted Effie.

Far down in the wood, under the firs, no doubt the lovers felt themselves perfectly safe; but there were treacherous groups of trees, whose branches had been swept in one direction by the wind, laying bare the two who stood beneath. They were standing close together, holding each other's hands.

"The girl is crying, I think," said Effie, "and leaning against the man. What can be the matter? can they have quarrelled? and she is all in black, with a thick veil—"

"Come to this side," said Randal, hastily, "there is a break in the mist. I think I can show you Schehallion."

"I like this better than Schehallion," said Effie; and then she started and cried, "O-oh!" with a long breath; and suddenly blushing all over, looked Randal in the face.

"I think Schehallion is much the most interesting to look at," he said, and, touching her elbow with his hand, endeavored to lead her away. But Effie was too much startled to conceal her wonder and alarm.

"Oh, Mr. Burnside! you are not thinking of Schehallion, you only want to get me away. I believe you know who *he* is."

"I don't know who either is, and I don't want to know," cried Randal; "and I think, Miss Leslie, I must bid you good-night."

That was easy enough; but Effie did not budge, though Randal went away.

CHAPTER XXIV.

EFFIE was not a tell-tale, and she was fond of her young aunt; but still this was such a revelation as made the blood stand still in her veins. She was deeply, profoundly interested, and strained her eyes to make out "the gentleman." Who could he be? Effie felt almost certain Mr. Burnside knew, and almost certain Mr. Burnside had seen them before, and was their confidant, or he would not have been so anxious to call her attention to Schehallion. Schehallion! nothing but a hill—whereas this was a romance! She leaned over the parapet of the tower till the night grew so dark that she took fright and felt disposed to cry for help, never thinking, unaccustomed to it as she was,

that she could grope her way in safety down the spiral stair. But she did manage it, partly fortified by a generous determination not to make any noise near Aunt Jean's room, which might end in a betrayal of the lovers. Effie would have gone to the stake rather than betray the lovers to Aunt Jean. But her mother was a different matter. She knew she could not go to bed with a secret from her mother; and perhaps it was not right, was it quite right, of Margaret? Effie reflected, however, as she stumbled down in the dark to the West Chamber, where John had just placed candles (the inspection of the pigsty being over), that perhaps grandpapa had known all about it; most likely Margaret had told him—and she had no need to tell any one else. But to meet a—gentleman, in the wood! It was the most strange, and most exciting, and most wonderful thing in real life which Effie had ever seen with her own eyes. She crept in to the West Chamber, where Miss Leslie had just come, relieved of her attendance on her sister.

"Your dear Aunt Jean is a little better," she said, "dear Effie; and where is dearest Margaret, and your dear papa and mamma? Dear Jean has gone to bed, she will not come down to-night. And had you a pleasant walk, my love? And how is dear Mrs. Burnside?"

All these dears put Effie out of breath; and she had been out of breath before, with the shock she had got, and with her progress downstairs: for a very narrow spiral stair which you are not familiar with is rather alarming, when it is quite dark. Effie, however, made what breathless answer she could, and sat down in a corner, getting some work to conceal her burning cheeks from Aunt Grace's gaze, and forgetting altogether that Aunt Grace was short-sighted, and saw nothing when she had not her spectacles on, which she did not wear when she was knitting. Miss Leslie, however, very glad to have a listener, and to have *la parole* in the absence of her sister, talked, without requiring any answer, straight on, flowing in a gentle stream, and gave Effie no trouble; and the girl sat turning her back to the light, and watching very keenly who should come in next. The first was her mother, placid and fresh from the cool air, saying it was very pleasant out-of-doors after having been in the house all day; and then, after an interval, Margaret followed, very pale, with her eyes red, and her hat, with its heavy veil, in her hand.

"Have you been out too, my dear?" said Lady Leslie. "I wonder we did not see you; your brother and I have been taking a walk."

"Yes," said Margaret, "I saw you; I was in the wood. I always go to the wood."

"I don't think it is at all a good place," said Aunt Grace, "a damp place; and no doubt you will have been standing about, or even sitting down upon the moss and grass. Your dear Aunt Jean—no, I forgot, she is not your dear aunt, darling Margaret, but your dear sister—it is so strange to have a dear sister so young— She is better, but she has gone to bed; that is why you see me here alone. Dear Effie has been a good child; she has been sitting, talking to me, while you have been out, dear Mary, with dearest Ludovic, and while dear Margaret has been out. But about the wood, darling Margaret; you must go and change your shoes di-

THE PRIMROSE PATH.

rectly. Dear Jean would never forgive me if I did not make you go and change your shoes."

"They are not wet," cried Margaret, going to the other corner opposite to Effie, who gazed at her with the eagerest curiosity; but Effie was much more like the heroine of a love-story than Margaret, and the little girl's heart was sore for her young aunt. She had no mother to go to and tell, and how could she tell Aunt Jean? As for Aunt Grace, that might be possible, perhaps; but then Aunt Jean would be told directly, and there would be no fun. These were Effie's thoughts, sitting with her back to the light, so that nobody might see the excitement in her scarlet cheeks; but Margaret did not seem excited at all. She was quite quiet and still, though she was obstinate about changing her shoes. Oh, Effie thought, if I could only lend her mamma! but then you cannot lend a mother. There was nothing to be done but to pity the poor girl, who had nobody to breathe the secret of her heart to, except Aunt Jean and Aunt Grace.

That night, however, after all the ladies had gone up-stairs, Lady Leslie appeared again in her dressing-gown in the long room, where her husband was sitting at his father's table. The room was dark, except in the small space lighted by his lamp; and if the good man, though he had not much imagination, was startled by the sight of the white figure coming toward him through the dimness, he may be forgiven, so soon after a death in the family. When he saw who it was, he recovered his calm, and drew a chair for her to the table.

"Is it you, my dear?" he said; "you gave me a fright for the moment." He thought she had some new light on the subject of the house; and as it was a matter of great thought to him, and they had not been able to come to any decision on the subject, he was very glad to see her. "I hope you have thought of some other expedient," he said, "I can make neither head nor tail of it." How was it likely he could think of anything but this very troublesome and knotty problem of their own?

"No indeed, Ludovic," said Lady Leslie, "I have no new light; and what I came to speak about is a new fash for you. No, nothing about the children, they are all right, thank God! But when I went to say good-night to Effie, I found her with red cheeks and such bright eyes, that I felt sure something was the matter."

"Not fever?" he said. "It was all quite right, in a sanitary point of view—far better than most old houses, the surveyor told me."

"No, no, not fever: when I told you it was nothing about the children! But I don't know what to do about it, Ludovic. It is poor little Margaret. Effie told me—the monkey to know anything about such things! that standing by accident on the tower, looking down upon the wood, she saw—"

"You and me, my dear, taking our walk; that was simple enough."

"No, not you and me; but two people under the big silver fir—Margaret and—a gentleman; there is no use mincing the matter. By what Effie saw, a lover, Ludovic! Well, you need not get up in a passion, it may be no harm. It may be somebody your father knew of. We are all strangers to her, poor little thing. There may

be nothing to blame in it. Only I don't know what gentleman it can be near this, for it was not Randal Burnside."

"How do you know it was not Randal Burnside?" said Sir Ludovic, rising and pacing about the room, in much fuss and fret, as his wife had feared. "No, but it could not be. He is too honorable a fellow."

"Mind, Ludovic, we don't know it is not as honorable as anything can be; your father might have sanctioned it. I would lay my life upon Margaret that she is a good girl. It cannot be more than imprudent at the worst, if it is that."

"She should be whipped," said her brother; "a little light-headed thing! not a fortnight since my father died!"

Sir Ludovic, though his blood was as good as any king's, was a homely Scotsman, and the dialect of his childhood returned to him when his mind was disturbed, as happens sometimes even in this cosmopolitan age.

"Whisht, whisht, Loodie!" said his wife. "She is a poor little motherless girl, and my heart bleeds for her—and I cannot bear to say anything to Jean. Jean would interfere with a strong hand, and make everything worse. If we only knew who it was! for I can think of no gentleman of these parts, unless it was one of the young men that are always staying with Sir Claude."

At this her husband started and gave a long whew-w! of suspicion and consternation. "I know who it is," he said—"I know who it is!" and began to walk about the room more than ever. Then he told his wife of his encounter with Rob Glen; and the circumstances seemed to fit so exactly that Lady Leslie could but hold up her hands in pain and horror.

"No doubt my father was foolish about it," said Sir Ludovic. "It is true that he used to have him here to dinner; it is true that he made a sketch of the house, spending days upon it. John says he always disapproved, but my father had taken a fancy to the young man. Rob Glen—I know all about him—the widow's son that has the little farm at Earl's-lee: a stickit minister, John says, an artist—a forward, confident fellow, as I saw from the way he addressed me; and, by-the-way, I met Margaret coming in just before I met him. That makes it certain. It is just Rob Glen, and no gentleman of these parts: not even an artist of the better sort from Sir Claude's—a clodpole, a lout, a common lad—"

"Oh, Ludovic!" Lady Leslie shivered, and covered her face with her hands; "but if your father took him up and had him about the house, Margaret was not to blame. If he is, as you say, 'a stickit minister,' he must have some education; and if he could draw your poor father, he must be clever. And probably he has the air of a gentleman—"

"I took him for a pushing forward fellow."

"And how was the child to know? Good-looking, very likely, and plenty of confidence, as you say; and she a poor little innocent girl knowing nothing, with nobody to look after her! Oh, Ludovic, you will not deserve to have so many sweet daughters of your own, if you are not very tender to poor Margaret; and if you can, oh, say nothing to Jean!"

"It is Jean's business," said Ludovic; but he

was pleased that his wife should think him more capable than his sister. "Jean thinks she can do everything better than anybody else," he said; "but what is to be done? I will speak to *him*. I will tell him he has taken a most unfair advantage of an ignorant girl. I will tell him it's a most dishonorable action—"

"Oh, Ludovic, listen to me a little! How do you know that it is dishonorable? I incline to think your father sanctioned it. But speak to Margaret first. You are her brother, though you might be her father; and remember, poor thing, she has never had a mother. Speak to her gently; you have too kind a heart to be harsh. Tell her how unsuitable it is, and how young she is, not able to judge for herself. But don't abuse him, or she will take his part. Tell her—"

"I wish you would tell her yourself, Mary. You could manage that part of the matter much better than I."

"But she is not my flesh and blood," said Lady Leslie. "She might not think I had any right to interfere."

And the decision they came to, after a lengthened consultation, was that Sir Ludovic should have a conversation with Margaret next morning, and ascertain how far things had gone, and persuade her to give up so unsuitable a connection; but that if she were obdurate, he should try his powers upon Rob, who might, perhaps, be brought to see that the transaction was not to his credit; and in any case the affair was to be kept, if possible, from the knowledge of the aunts, who henceforward would have the charge of Margaret. Sir Ludovic's calculations were all put out, however, by this troublesome piece of business, and Lady Leslie shook her head as she went away through the long room and up the dark stair, a white figure, with her candle in her hand.

"Papa will speak to Margaret to-morrow," she said, going into her daughter's room as she passed, "and we hope she will see what is right. But you must take great care never to breathe a word of this, Effie, for I am most anxious to keep it all from Aunt Jean."

"But oh, mamma, what will happen if she will not give him up? and who can it be?" said Effie. Lady Leslie did not think it necessary to make any further revelations to her daughter. She said, "Go to sleep, dear," and gave her a kiss, and took away the light. And shortly after, Ludovic, disturbed in all his thoughts (though they were much more important, he could not but feel, than any nonsense about a lassie and her sweetheart), tramped heavily up-stairs, also with his candle, shedding glimmers of light through all the window-slits as he passed; and silence and darkness fell once more over the house.

But Sir Ludovic had a face of care when he made his appearance next day. The sense of what he had got to do hung heavy on his soul. Though his wife had entreated him not to be harsh, it was not of cruelty, but of weak indulgence, that the good man felt himself most capable. He almost hoped the girl would be saucy and impertinent, to put him on his mettle; but one glance at Margaret's pale, subdued child's face, which had been so happy and bright a little while ago, made this appear impossible. If only his wife could have done it! But he supposed Mary was right, and that it was "his place" to do it. How many disagreeable things, he re-

flected, it is a man's "place" to do when he is the head of a family! He did not feel that the dignity of the place made up for its troubles. If Mary would only do it herself! And Mrs. Bellingham had emerged as fresh as ever after the little retirement of yesterday. Her headache was quite gone, she was glad to say. It was so much better just to give in at once, and go to bed, and then you were as right as possible next day. She was able for anything now, Jean said. Sir Ludovic gave his wife an appealing glance across the table. Jean would enjoy doing this, she would do it a great deal better than he should; but Lady Leslie paid no attention to these covert appeals. Mrs. Bellingham was in better spirits, she allowed, than she had been since papa's death. "Indeed, it would be wicked for us to grieve over that very bitterly, though great allowance must be made for Margaret; for he was an old man, and life had ceased to be any pleasure to him."

"Dearest papa!" said Miss Leslie, putting her handkerchief to her eyes.

"But here is a letter from my nephew, Aubrey Bellingham," said Jean. "I think you have met him, Ludovic—a very fine young fellow, and one I put the greatest trust in. He is to be at Edinburgh to-day, and to-morrow he is coming on here. I am sure good Mrs. Burnside will not mind giving him a bed. He has come to take us home, or to go anywhere with us, if we prefer that. It is such a comfort on a long, troublesome journey, with a languid party, to have a gentleman."

"I should have thought you were very well used to the journey," said Lady Leslie.

"So I am; and it is nothing with only Grace and myself; but three ladies, and one a very inexperienced traveller—I am too glad to have Aubrey's help. My spirits might not be equal to it, and my strength is not what it once was—"

"No, indeed, dear Jean," said Miss Grace; "those who knew you a few years ago would scarcely recog—"

"And Aubrey is invaluable about travelling. I never saw a man so good; for one thing I have very much trained him myself; he has gone about with me since he was quite a little fellow. I used to make him take the tickets, and then he got advanced to looking after the luggage. To be sure, he once made us a present of his beautiful new umbrella, letting the guard put it into our carriage; but that was a trifle. I think, as he has come, we must settle to go in a day or two, Mary. This just gives me the courage to go. I should have lingered on, not able to make up my mind to tear ourselves away from a spot—"

"Where we have been so unhappy." Miss Leslie took advantage of the moment when Mrs. Bellingham took up her cup of coffee. A mouthful of anything, especially when it is hot, is an interruption perforce of the most eloquent speech.

"It will be better for us all, and better for Margaret, not to linger here," said Jean. "Poor child! she will never do any good till we get her away. Yes, you will suffer, Margaret, but believe me, it is real consideration for your good—real anxiety for you. Ask Mary; she will tell you the same thing. Earl's-hall will never be the same to you again. You must begin your new life sometime or other, and the sooner the better, Margaret. Would you like to go to the Highlands and see a little of the country? or shall we go straight to the Grange at once? Now that Aubrey is to be with us, it is quite the same for my comfort; and we will do, my love, what you like best."

"Oh, I do not care about anything," said Margaret, "whatever you please."

"That is very natural, my dear," said Lady Leslie, "and Jean is right, though perhaps it sounds hard. Effie and I will miss you dreadfully, Margaret, but the change is the best thing for you. If you go to the Highlands, would you like Effie to go too, for company?" said the kind woman. But Margaret could not speak for crying, and Jean and Grace did not seem delighted with the suggestion.

"It will be best for her to make the break at once," said Mrs. Bellingham. "Effie can come after; we shall be most happy to see her when we are settled at the Grange."

"I dare say you are right," said Effie's mother; but this rejection of the offer, which she knew to be so kind on her own part, of her daughter's company made her heart colder to poor Margaret than all the story about Rob Glen.

Ludovic put his hand on his little sister's shoulder as she was leaving the breakfast-table.

"Will you come out with me and take a little walk about the place, Margaret? I want to say something to you," he said.

"What is that?" said Mrs. Bellingham. "I suppose, Ludovic, you would like me to come too? I will get on my hat in a moment; indeed Margaret can fetch it when she brings her own. A turn in the morning is always pleasant. Run away, my dear, and bring our hats; the air will do us both good."

"But I wanted your advice," said Lady Leslie—"yours and Grace's; there are still some things to settle. These laces, for instance, which we were to look over."

"That is true," said Mrs. Bellingham. "But I am afraid it will be a disappointment to Ludovic; and then, of course, it is necessary I should be there if he has really something to say to Margaret."

"Let me go, dear Jean," said Grace; "I will not mind, indeed I will not mind *much*, being away, and the lace could never be settled without you. I am not so clever about knowing the kinds, and I am sure you will not forget that I am fond of it *too*."

"Does Margaret want a chaperon when she goes out with me?" said Ludovic. "It is only to put a little color in her cheeks." But he was not clever at these little social artifices, and looked once more at his wife.

"Leave him alone with his girls," said Lady Leslie; "a man is always fond of a walk with girls. Get your hat, Margaret, my dear, and you too, Effie, and take a run with him. He will like that a great deal better than you and me, Jean. We are very well in our way, but he likes the young things, and who will blame him? and we will settle about the lace before they come in."

"There is no accounting for tastes," Mrs. Bellingham said; "but if there is anything particular, it will be better to wait till I can be with you, Ludovic; and, Margaret, put on your galoches, for it rained last night."

"You can take mine, dear," whispered Grace, who knew that Margaret did not possess these necessary articles. And thus, at last, the party got under way. Effie, warned by her mother, deserted them as soon as her aunts were safe in the high room, and Margaret, without any foreboding of evil, went out with her brother peacefully into the morning. It was very damp after the rain, as Mrs. Bellingham had divined, and cost her some trouble to keep her crape unsoiled. But except for that care, and that there was some excitement in her mind to hear of the speedy departure from Earl's-hall, Margaret went out with Ludovic, with great confidence in his kindness and without any fear.

CHAPTER XXV.

"I SAID to Jean it was nothing, for I did not care to mix her up with it; but I have something very serious to say to you, Margaret," said Sir Ludovic.

She looked up at him with eyes wistful, yet candid, fearing nothing still. The character of Margaret's face seemed to have changed within the last month. What she was in June was not like what she was in July. The trouble she had gone through had not seemed to develop, but to subdue her. She had been full of variety, animation, and energy before. Now the life seemed to have sunk to so low an ebb in her paled being, exhausted with tears, that there was little remaining but simple consciousness and intelligence. She did not seem able to originate anything on her own side, not even a question. A half smile, the reflection of a smile, came to her face, and she looked up, without any alarm, for what her brother had to say.

"Margaret," he said (how hard it was! harder even than he thought. He cleared his throat, and a rush of uncomfortable color came to his middle-aged countenance, though she took it so calmly, and did not blush at all)—"Margaret, I have found out something, my dear, that gives me a great deal of pain—something about you."

But even this solemn preamble seemed to convey no thrill of conscious guilt to Margaret's mind. She only looked at him again a little more earnestly. "Have I lost my—money?" she said.

"No, it is not that. What made you think of losing your money?"

"It often happens, does it not?" she said. "I am sure I should not care."

"Oh yes, you would care—we should all care; but your money is safe enough. I wish you yourself were as safe. Margaret, my dear, give me your full attention; you were seen last night in the wood."

"Yes!" she said, a little alarmed.

"With a—gentleman; or at least, let us hope he was a gentleman," said Ludovic. "You know that it is not—usual, nor perhaps—right. I want you to tell me all about it: and first of all, who was the man?"

Margaret was taken entirely by surprise. It had not occurred to her to think of Rob Glen as one about whom she could be questioned. He had grown so familiar while her father lived, and he had been so kind. There was no sort of novelty about it—nothing to be thus solemnly questioned about. But she looked up at her brother with startled eyes.

"Oh, Ludovic, the gentleman—"

"Yes; don't be frightened for me, my poor little sister, I will not be unkind; but tell me truly, everything. You must not keep back anything, Margaret."

"I don't know, perhaps, if—you would call him a gentleman," said Margaret, the color beginning to rise in her pale face. Keep back nothing! Would she have to tell him all they had said? Her heart began to beat faster. "It is Rob Glen, Ludovic; perhaps you remember him long ago, when he was a boy. I used to go fishing with him; he was very kind to me. Bell always says—"

"Yes—yes; it does not matter about children; but you are not a child now, Margaret. Have you always kept on such—intimate terms with Rob Glen?"

Margaret winced, and her face began to burn. He seemed to himself to be speaking brutally to her; but what else could he say?

"I did not see him at all for a long time," she said; "and then he came back. He always said he was not—as good as we were. But do you think it all depends upon where you are born? You can't help where you are born."

"No; but you must be content with it, and keep to your own place," said Ludovic, an argument which did not make much impression on his own mind.

"But he is very clever; he can draw most beautifully," said Margaret. "The first time he came— It was—papa that said he might come."

The name brought with it, as was natural, a sob; and Ludovic, horribly compunctious, patted his little sister on the shoulder with a kind and lingering hand.

"He made a picture of *him*," cried Margaret, half inarticulate, struggling with the "climbing sorrow." "Oh, Loodie! I found it just yesterday; it is *him*, his very self."

"My poor little Margaret! don't think me cruel," said the good man, with a break in his voice. "I *must* hear."

"Yes, Ludovic. He used to come often, and sometimes would cheer him up and make him laugh. And he grew—a great friend. Then, when *he* was ill, when I went out to cry—I could not cry when everybody was there."

"My poor child!"

"That was the first time I met him in the wood. He was very, very kind. I—could do nothing but cry."

Ludovic took her hand into his, and held it between his own. He was beginning to understand.

"I see how it was," he said, his voice not so steady as at first. "I see exactly how it was; and I don't blame you, my dear. But, Margaret, has he taken advantage of this? Has he got you to promise—to marry him? Is that what he talks to you about? Forget I am an old man, old to the like of you—or rather think that I am your father, Margaret."

"No, no," she said, "you are not that; no one will ever be that again; but you are very

kind. My father—would have been pleased to see how kind you are."

"God knows—and my poor father too, if he knows anything of what he's left behind him—that I want to be kind to you, as kind as he could have been, my poor little Margaret. Tell me then, dear, has this young man spoken of marriage to you, and love?"

"Of love? oh yes!" said Margaret, drooping her head. "I am not sure about the other. He was for going away yesterday when I told him I had a fortune; and I had to tell him myself that was no reason for going away, that there would be plenty for us both."

"Does that mean that you promised to marry him, Margaret?"

"I do not know," she said, slowly; "I did not think of that. I suppose, when you come to think of it"— the color had all gone out of her face, and she was quite pale again, and letting the words fall more and more slowly— "when you come to think of it, though I never did stop to think—that is what it would mean."

There was a touch of regret in her tone, a weary acknowledgment of necessity, but no blushing pride or fervor. It had not occurred to her before; but being put to her, it must, no doubt, mean that. She did not look at her brother, but at the ground; but not to hide any happy flush of consciousness. Ludovic was half bewildered, half irritated by her calm.

"But, Margaret," he cried, "you cannot think what you are saying. This must be put a stop to; it must be brought to an end! it is monstrous; it is impossible! My dear, you cannot really have the least idea what you are doing. Giving yourself up to the first fortune-hunter that appears—a vulgar fellow without a penny, without even the position of a gentleman. He has taken a base advantage of your youth and your trouble. It must be put a stop to," he said. He had dropped her hand and withdrawn from her side, and was crushing the damp grass under his feet with all those frettings and fidgetings of embarrassment and irritation of which his wife was afraid.

Margaret had looked up at him again. She was quite quiet, but as steady as a statue.

"How can it be put a stop to?" she said. "He is not what you say, Ludovic; he is very kind."

"Margaret! are you in love with him?" cried her brother; "is that what you mean?"

A slight color wavered over Margaret's face.

"It is he that is—*that*," she said, softly.

This gave Ludovic, ignorant man, courage.

"Heaven be praised if it is only he! I would make short work with him. The only difficulty would be to make you unhappy. My dear, I will see him this very day, and you shall never be troubled with him any more."

"He has not been a trouble at all, Ludovic. I cannot tell you how kind he was; and yesterday again he was very kind. He would have gone away if I had let him, but I would not let him."

"Now that you see how serious it is, my dear," said Ludovic, "you will let him now? I will go and see him at once. I will lose no time. Go you back to the house, and don't say anything to Jean. Speak to Mary, if you like, but not to Jean; and don't give yourself any more trouble about it, my dear; I will manage it all."

But Margaret did not move; she stood very steadily, all the trembling gone away from her, the tears dried from her cheeks, and her eyes shining. These eyes were still fixed on the ground, and her head was drooping, but she showed no other signs of emotion.

"Ludovic," she said, slowly, "it is a mistake you are making; it cannot be settled so easily. Indeed, it would be better just to let it alone," she added, after a pause.

"Let it alone!" cried Sir Ludovic; "that is just the thing that cannot be done."

Margaret put out her hand and touched his arm. She raised her head with a slight, proud elevation, unlike anything that had been seen in it before.

"You must not meddle with me," she said, with a wistful look, half warning, half entreating.

"But I must meddle with you, my dear. You must not go to your ruin; you cannot be allowed to go."

"Don't meddle with me, Ludovic! I have never been meddled with. You need not think I will do anything wrong."

"I must act according to my judgment, Margaret. You are too young to know what you are doing. I must save you from this adventurer. You do not even care about him. I know how a girl looks when she is in love: not as you do, Margaret, thank God for it; and that is the one thing of any importance. I must interfere."

"I do not want to be disobedient," she said; "but, Ludovic, you know there must be some things that are my own. You cannot judge for me always, nor Jean either. And whatever you may say about this, I will not do it; anything else! but about this I will not do it. It is very, very difficult to say so, when you are so kind; but I cannot, and do not bid me, Ludovic; oh, do not bid me, for I will not!" she said.

"But if I tell you you must!" He was entirely out of patience. What fantastic piece of folly was this that had made her set herself against him like a rock? He was beyond his own control with impatience and irritation. "I hope you will not drive me to say something I will be sorry for," he said. "You, Margaret, who have always been a good girl, and you don't even care for this young man!"

"He cares," said Margaret, under her breath.

"Is that why you resist me?" cried her brother. "He cares! yes, for your money, you foolish girl—for what you have got; because he will be able to live and think himself a gentleman!"

"Ludovic!" she cried, her face growing crimson; "but you are only angry; you don't mean to be so unkind."

And then he stopped short, touched, in the midst of his anger, by the simplicity of her confidence.

"Do you mean to tell me—that you are really going to marry—Rob Glen, Margaret?"

"Oh! but not for such a long, long time!" she said.

What was he to say to her—a girl so simple, so almost childish, so unyielding? If Mary had only done it herself! probably she would have had some means of insight into this strange, subtle girl's mechanism which was out of his way. What was reason, argument, common-sense, to

a creature like this, who refused to abandon her lover, and yet drew a long breath of relief at the thought that it must be "a long, long time" before he could claim her? Sir Ludovic was at his wit's end. They had been walking up and down in front of the house, where, out of reach of all the windows, their conversation was quite safe. The grassy path was damp, but it was noiseless, affording no interruption to their talk. On the ruined gable the tall wall-flowers were nodding, and the ivy threw a little shower of rain-drops over them whenever the wind blew. Looking up at that ruined gable reminded him of all his own cares, so much more important than this love nonsense. Should he ever be able to rebuild it? But in the mean time he must not think of this question at all, but address himself to the still more difficult subject of Rob Glen.

When the conversation, however, had come to this pass, beyond which it seemed so difficult to carry it, an interruption occurred. A lumbering old hackney-carriage, well known in the country, which carried everybody to and from the station, of the few who wanted any other means of conveyance but their own legs or their own carriage—and there were not many people of this intermediate class in Stratheden—suddenly swung in heavily at the gate, and sinking deep in the rut, which it went to Ludovic's heart to see, disfiguring the muddy road through the scanty trees, which called itself the avenue—came laboring toward them. There was a portmanteau on the outside of this vehicle, and somebody within, who thrust out his head as he approached, reconnoitring the curious old gray house. When he saw the two figures advancing from the other side, he called to the driver and leaped out. It was a young man, fair and fashionable, and spotless in apparel, with a beardless but not boyish face, an eyeglass in his eye and a great-coat on his arm.

"Excuse me," he said, "I am sure that I am speaking to—"

While at the same time Ludovic Leslie, leaving Margaret, upon whom the stranger had already fixed a very decided gaze, went forward, saying,

"Aubrey Bellingham—how do you do? My sister told us she expected you to-day."

"Yes," said the young man, "here I am. I came up as soon as I got her summons. It is a fine thing to have nothing to do, for then one is always at the call of one's friends. May I be presented to—Miss Leslie? whom I have heard of so often. As I am about to enter her service, don't you think I should know her at once when good-fortune throws me in her way?"

"Only Miss Margaret Leslie, Bellingham. You understand, Margaret, that this is Jean's nephew, whom she was speaking of this morning. I don't know what he means by entering your service, but perhaps he can explain that himself."

The stranger gave Margaret a very keen look of examination—not the chance glance of an ordinary meeting, nor yet the complimentary surprise of sudden admiration of a pretty face. The look meant a great deal more than this, and might have confused Margaret if she had not been far beyond noticing anything of the kind. He seemed to look, try, judge all in a moment, and the keen, sudden inspection struck Sir Ludovic, though he was not very swift to mark such undercurrents of meaning. It seemed to take a long time, so searching and thorough was it: and yet almost before Ludovic's voice had ceased to vibrate, Bellingham replied,

"I believe I am to be the courier of the party, which is the same as entering Miss Leslie's service. My aunts are used to me. Miss Leslie, it is a very quaint relationship this of yours to my aunts. I call both your sisters by that endearing title."

"I hope you don't mean to make my little sister into Aunt Margaret," said Sir Ludovic. "Perhaps, my dear, you had better go and tell Jean of Mr. Bellingham's arrival. I don't know what you will think," he added, escaping with some relief, into the more habitual current of his thoughts, "of my tumble-down old house."

"It is a most curious old house," said the stranger; "I can see that already. I have been studying it all the time; fifteenth century, do you suppose? Domestic architecture is always a little bewildering. I know there are people who can read it like a church, but I don't pretend to be clever about it. It always puzzles me."

"No doubt it is puzzling, when you know only a little about it," said Ludovic, who knew nothing at all.

"That is just my case," said the other, cheerfully. "I have been taught just a little of most things. It is very unsatisfactory. Indeed, to have the reputation of a handy man in a large family party is ruin to everything. You can neither work nor study: and when you are cursed, in addition, with a little good-nature—"

"A large share of that," Sir Ludovic said, chiefly because it seemed to him the only thing to say; and it was very good-natured, indeed, for a young man, a man so entirely *comme il faut*, and looking more like Pall Mall than Earl's-hall, to come when his aunt called him so readily. Ludovic knew he himself would not have done it for any number of old ladies, but then he had always had his profession to think of; and how many things he had at this moment to think of! Thank Heaven, at least he had got rid of Margaret's affairs for the moment. Let Mary put her own brains to work and see what she could make of it. For himself, there was a certain relief in the sight of a new face. In the mean time, while Sir Ludovic's mind was thus condoling with itself, the new arrival had paid his cab, and seen his portmanteau handed over to John, who had made his appearance at the sound of the wheels.

"For some things, sir," said young Bellingham, peering at John through his eyeglass, "this is a delightful country. Fancy your old butler, who looks an archbishop at least, meekly carrying off my portmanteau! If he had been on the other side of the Tweed, he would have looked at it helplessly, and requested to know what he was supposed to have to do with such an article."

"John is not used to much grandeur," said Sir Ludovic, not knowing whether this was compliment or depreciation; "a man-of-all-work about a homely Scotch country-house is not like one of your pampered menials in the South. Did you have a good crossing at the Ferry?"

There are times when the Ferry at Burntisland is not much more agreeable than the worse ferry at Dover, and it was always a civil question —though privately he thought that a little tossing, or even a little sea-sickness, would not have done any harm to this spruce gentleman. Ludovic felt plainer, rustier, in his old black coat, which had seen much service at his office, since this carefully dressed young hero had dawned upon the horizon. He felt instinctively that he did not like him; though nothing could be more cheerful or friendly than Mr. Aubrey Bellingham. He was good enough to explain the house to its master as they went in, and told him why the screen wall between the two blocks of building existed, and all about it. Ludovic was so startled that he found nothing to reply; he had even a little heraldic lecture upon his own coat-of-arms over the door.

CHAPTER XXVI.

THERE was quite a cheerful flutter of talk at the luncheon-table in the long room. Sir Ludovic had never much to say, and his wife was very anxious to know the result of his interview with Margaret, and Effie was shy, and Margaret herself perfectly silent. But the rapid interchange of question and answer between Mrs. Bellingham and her nephew made the most lively commotion, and stirred all the echoes in the quiet place, where nobody as yet had ventured upon a laugh. It was not to be supposed that Aubrey Bellingham, who was a stranger and had never seen the old Sir Ludovic, could be much subdued in his tone by "what had happened"—and Jean had already begun to feel that there was really no reason to regret such a happy release.

"I am just beginning to be able to look people in the face again," she said. "I need not tell you, Aubrey, it has been a dreadful time. My sister and I have had a great deal to do, and naturally, though it may not tell at the time, one feels it afterward. I did not leave my room yesterday at all. Grace will tell you I had one of my bad headaches. But what with seeing you to-day, and being obliged to bestir myself in the morning about some business, a piece of work quite after your own heart, Aubrey, arranging some lace."

"If it is fine, I quite understand the improvement in your health," he said. "What kind? and who is the happy possessor? I hope some of it has fallen to your share."

"Oh, a little," said Mrs. Bellingham; and Grace echoed "a little" with some dolefulness.

This division of the stores of the house into three portions had not been so successful as was hoped; and when it was again gone over, the scraps naturally fell to Lady Leslie and her daughters. It was Miss Leslie upon whom the loss chiefly fell, and there was accordingly in her tone a tinge of melancholy. She was not sorry that dear Mary and the dear girls should have it, but still it was notorious that she was generally the sufferer when any one had to suffer.

"Margaret is the most fortunate; Margaret has a piece of point de Venise. I never saw such a lovely piece. It will go to your very heart. After lunch you shall see it all, and I know you will think Margaret a lucky girl—too lucky! She will not appreciate it for a dozen years, and by that time she will have grown familiar with it, and it will not impress her," said Mrs. Bellingham, regretfully. "You don't think half so much of things you have had since you were a girl. But tell me, Aubrey, how is everybody? Had you heard from the Court before you left? What were they all doing? I declare it seems about a year since we came here in such a hurry. I dare say you have heard all about us, and the sad way in which we have been spending our time? I have had a great deal of flying neuralgia, and yesterday it quite settled in my head. Scotland does not suit me, I always say. It does very well for Grace, who is as strong as a pony, though she does not look it—"

"Dearest Jean!" said Miss Leslie, touched to the quick, and this time insisting upon a hearing. "I strong? Dear Aubrey knows better than to believe—"

"Oh yes, we all know, my dear, you are strong at bottom, though you have your little ailments; and with me it is just the other way. I am kept up by my spirit. Now, Aubrey, you have not given us one single piece of news. Tell us something about the Court."

"I appeal to your candor, Aunt Jean; what can I tell you about the Court when I am fresh from town?—unless you mean the other kind of a court, the royal one, or the Club. You shall hear, if you please, about the Club. You know about that trial that was so much talked of? It is to be all hushed up, I believe. *She* is to be condoned, and *he* is to have his debts paid, and they are all to live happy ever after. You should hear Mountfort on the subject. He says it will not be six months before it is all on again, and the detectives at work."

"Is it possible?" cried Mrs. Bellingham. "I thought Lady Arabella had really taken the last step and run off, you know, in the yacht; and that Lord Fred—"

"No names, my dear aunt, I entreat. Of course, everybody knows who is meant, but it is better not to bandy names about. Oh no; my lady would have done it, I don't doubt for a moment, but Fred is a fellow who knows very well how far the world will permit you to go, and he wouldn't hear of it; so it is all hushed up. There is something very piquant, however, going on in another quarter, where you would never suspect it. It sounds just like a romance. A couple that have always been one of the most devoted couples, and a friend who has been the most devoted friend — husband's school-fellow, you know, and saved his life in India, or something—and there they are, the three of them; everybody sees it, except the silly fellow himself. It's as good as a play to watch them; you know whom I mean. They have a place not a hundred miles from us; wife the most innocent, smiling creature—"

"Ah!" cried Miss Leslie, holding up her hands, "I can see who you me—"

"Of course, anybody can see," said Mrs. Bellingham. "The A.'s, of course, of A. C. Do you really mean it, Aubrey? and the man? Goodness gracious! why, of course it must be! —no—not that, don't say so—Algy—? I never heard of such a complication in all my life."

"Exactly," said the new-comer; "that is what everybody says. Algy, of all men in the world, with a character to lose! But in this sort of affair you never can trust any one; and still waters run deep, you know. It is the woman that puzzles me, smiling and looking so innocent. Happily Sir Cresswell Cresswell does not want a jury, for no jury would ever go against such an innocent-looking little woman."

Effie had been taking all this mysterious talk in with the most rapt attention. She did not understand a word of it, but still a lively discussion of other people, even when you don't know who they are, and don't know what they are accused of, has a certain interest. But Sir Cresswell Cresswell's well-known name roused Lady Leslie, who had been longing to interfere before, and woke up even Ludovic, who had been eating his luncheon steadily, and thinking how the avenue could be put in order at the least expense. What did he care for their chatter? But this name woke the good man up.

"You will think me very stupid," said Lady Leslie, "but we are only plain Scotch people, you know, and very seldom go to England, and don't know about your friends. I dare say Mr. Aubrey would be so kind as to tell us something about the Court, as he said—not Bellingham Court, but the Queen's Court. Effie would like to hear about the princes and princesses, and so would Margaret. They say we are going to have one of them up here."

"Oh, surely," said Aubrey, "there is always plenty of talk on that subject. Most of them are going a frightful pace. I am not posted up in the very last scandals, for, you know, I have never been a favorite. But there is a very pretty story current about a pretty Galician or Wallachian, or some of those savage tribes. The lady, of course, was quite civilized enough to know all about the proprieties—or perhaps it would be better to say the improprieties—of our princely society, and she thought, I suppose, that an English Royalty—"

"Oh!" said Lady Leslie; "but I feel sure half these stories are nonsense, or worse than nonsense. I know you gentlemen are fond of a little gossip at your club, and I suppose you don't mean the half of what you say. Were the pictures fine this year, Mr. Bellingham? That is one thing I regret never going to London for; one sees so few pictures."

"I think everybody who has seen them will agree with me in saying the fewer the better," said Bellingham, ready for all subjects. "The dinner this year was as great bosh as usual. But there is a very good story about an R.A. who asked a great lady he happened to meet with how she liked the portrait of her husband. It was her Grace of X., or Y., or Z.—never mind who; I dare say you will all guess. She stared at him, as you may suppose. But he insisted. 'Oh yes, he had finished it a month before; and he always understood it was the Duchess herself who had suggested that pose which was so successful!' Fancy the unfortunate fellow's feelings when he saw what he had done! And I hope her Grace gave it hot and hot to the Duke."

"There, Aubrey, that will do; that is enough of your funny stories. They are not pretty stories at all, though sometimes they make one laugh when one oughtn't," said Mrs. Belling-ham. "Those clubs of yours are not at all nice places, as my sister-in-law says—and talk of women's gossip! But now and then it is like a sniff of salts, you know, or a vinaigrette, which is not nice in itself, but wakes one up. Now we must be going to-morrow, or the day after to-morrow; and I think, as you are here, Aubrey, we might as well go to Perth, and then make a little round through the Highlands. I dare say you are going somewhere shooting as soon as the moors are open. We cannot do much mountain work, because of the sad circumstances and our crape; but we might stay for a week in one place and a week in another, and so make our way to the Grange about the end of August. That would be a very good time. The very hot weather will be over, and it will be best not to try Margaret too much with the heat of an English summer. I wish you would not always interrupt me, Grace. There is never any heat in Scotland. It is rather fine now, and warmish, and quite pleasant; but as for a scorching sun, and that sort of thing— You are very quiet, Margaret. Has Ludovic been scolding you? You ought to leave that to me, Ludovic; a man has always a heavier hand. I always said, if I had been blessed with children, I never should have let their father correct them. Men mean very well, but they have a heavy hand."

"But not dearest Loodie!" cried Miss Leslie; "he always was the kindest! and dear Jean knows as well as any of us—"

"Yes, I know that a man's hand is always heavier than he thinks, whether it is a simple scolding or something more serious. Margaret looks like a little mouse, with all the spirits out of her. If she comes in like that after walks with you, Ludovic, I don't think I will trust her with you again."

"Margaret has not been very lively lately," said kind Lady Leslie. "She has not been keeping us all in amusement, like Mrs. Bellingham. I think I will take the two girls away with me this afternoon, if you have no objections, Jean. I am going to the Manse to see Mrs. Burnside, and the walk will do Margaret good."

"Will you speak to Mrs. Burnside, please, about giving Aubrey a bed?" Mrs. Bellingham said; and Lady Leslie, who was anxious about her husband's interview with his sister, and not at all anxious to cultivate Aubrey's acquaintance, hurried them away. She had a hasty interview with Ludovic before she went out, who was very anxious she should take the business into her own hands. What was to be done? Would it be better to say nothing at all about it, but trust to the "long, long time," and the distance, and the development of the girl's mind?

"But it would be better for her to marry Rob Glen than Aubrey Bellingham, with all his nasty stories," Lady Leslie said, indignantly.

"What was the fellow talking about?" asked Ludovic. He had not paid any attention, save for one moment, at the sound of that too remarkable name; but it had not come to anything except "havers," and he had resumed his own thoughts. Lady Leslie, however, did not let her victim off so easily. She insisted that he should see Rob Glen, and warn him of the disapproval of the family; and this at last, with many sighs

and groans, the unfortunate head of the family consented to do.

"I have been watching her all the time," said the stranger, when he had been taken by the two ladies to the West Chamber, "and I approve. She is not very lively, and I dare say she will never be amusing (begging your pardons, my dear aunts, for so plain a speech); but she is very pretty, and what you call interesting; and a little money, though it is not much, is always acceptable. I have not come off hitherto, notwithstanding my merits. You put me up at too high a price, you ladies; and I have gone through a good many seasons without ever fetching that fancy price. So if you think I have any chance, really I don't mind. I will go in for Miss Margaret seriously, and I will not tell her naughty stories, but bring her up in the way she should go."

"No; you must be more careful how you talk before young ladies," said Mrs. Bellingham. "People here are not used to it. My sister-in-law is a very good little body, but quite untrained, as you would see. Yes, Aubrey, it would make me happy to see dear Margaret in your hands. I am sure you would always be kind to her. And it is a very nice little property, and could be improved; and she would make you a very nice little wife. It would just be the kind of thing to make me feel I had all I wished for, if I could provide for my little sister and for you, Aubrey, my husband's godchild, at the same time."

"Oh, we can't have you take the Nunc Dimittis view," he said, "that is out of the question; but I am quite willing, if she is; and if she isn't after a while, with all my opportunities, I shall be a precious fool, Aunt Jean. By-the-way, it is a little odd, if you come to think of it, marrying into a previous generation, as I should be doing if she'd have me—marrying my aunt, isn't it? I think it's within the forbidden degrees."

"Margaret your aunt, dear Aubrey? Darling Margaret is not quite eighteen; so how could that be?" said Miss Leslie; "and do you mean that this is what you were thinking of? Oh, I wondered what dear Jean, with her own clever head, wanted Aubrey for—Jean, who can manage everything. But how can you tell whether you will love her, dear Aubrey? You cannot always love where you wish to; and I never would give my consent, never for a moment, to a match which was not—"

"What nonsense is she talking?" said Mrs. Bellingham. She had gone to get Margaret's lace to exhibit, and this was why Grace had found the occasion to address Aubrey at such length, "a match which was not—something or other; I am sure, Aubrey, you will fall in love, as everybody does before they marry. I suppose you don't want to shut up little Margaret in a prison with you and me, Grace, and keep her money, that her husband might not get the use of it? That would be just like you old maids. But I mean Margaret to have a good husband, and live a happy life."

"Dearest Jean!" said Miss Grace, with tears. "I keep dear Margaret unmarried, or want her money! She shall have all I have when I die; and as for being an old maid—"

This was a very unkind cut indeed, and Miss Leslie was unable to resist the impulse to cry.

Her tears were not so interesting as Margaret's, for her nose became red, and her short-sighted eyes muddy. "I am sure I have not done anything to deserve this," she said, and sobbed; while Jean told her not to be so silly, and, without paying any more attention, held up the point de Venise, which had belonged to Margaret's mother, in her plump hands.

"Look at that, Aubrey! If all goes well, you may have a wife with *that* upon her wedding-dress. Dear me, I think I would almost marry myself to have it. Is it not lovely? But Margaret will not care a bit; no one does at her age. She would think a bit of common Valenciennes from a shop just as pretty, or perhaps, Lord knows, imitation would please her. I had a piece myself in my trousseau not half so good as that, nor half so much of it, but still *lace*, you know, real lace; and I let it lie about, and wore net ruffs and things. Even I! so you may fancy what Margaret will do. But if it was her mother's (and Bell swears it was), she has a right to it," Mrs. Bellingham said, with integrity beyond praise.

"It is very nice, Aunt Jean," said Aubrey, holding it to the light; "but I think you are a little too enthusiastic. If it is point de Venise, it is very late work—not the best. I should be disposed to say it was point de France—very pretty all the same, and valuable in its way. Now look at that stitch: I don't think you would find that in real old Venetian. I think that is a French stitch. But it is very nice," he added, looking at it critically, "very nice: on a dark velvet or brocade, it would look very well. As for putting it over white satin, I never should consent to such a thing. Light point de Flandres, or modern Brussels, or Malines, I shouldn't mind; but Venetian point, no. You ladies have your own ideas; but I wouldn't allow it, not if my opinion was asked."

"You see, you allow it is Venetian, after all."

"Or point de France. It is very much the same thing. Sometimes you can scarcely tell that it has travelled over the Alps. But I think I have an eye for lace. Any china?" said Aubrey, walking to a door in the panelling and opening it coolly. "Ay, I thought it was a cupboard. But here's only common stuff."

"The best tea-things!" said Miss Grace, with a little shriek, "that have always been kept there ever since I was a child."

"In that case, perhaps they are better than they appear," said Aubrey, calmly; and after a closer inspection, he decided that this was the case. They were Chelsea, "but not much." From this it will be seen that young Mr. Bellingham was a young man of extended and various information. He went up-stairs to the high room with them, and was really excited by the old clothes. The house, though he appreciated its curiousness, did not otherwise attract the young man. "If one could spend a few thousands on old oak and tapestry, it might be made very nice," he acknowledged; but there were some old cups and saucers here and there in the various rooms which pleased him. And as he accompanied the ladies up and down, and examined everything, he gave an occasional thought to Margaret, which ought to have made her proud, had she been aware of the distinction. She would do very well. She was not at all the

kind of person whom, in such circumstances, it would have been natural to see. A red-haired young woman, with high cheek-bones—was not that the recognized type of a Scotch heiress? Aubrey knew that the conventional type does not always hold; but he had thought of Miss Leslie's nose and her short sight, and he had also thought of his aunt's plumpness, and that peculiarity of tone which many Scotchwomen in England attain, with the proud consciousness of having lost all their native accent.

There are few things so disagreeably provincial as this tone, which is not Scotch, which is the very triumph and proclaimed conviction of having shaken off Scotch and acquired the finest of Southern speech. Aubrey had been afraid of all these things; but Margaret had not come up to the conventional requirements of her position. Her soft native Fife, even with its modulations, did not alarm him like Aunt Jean's high English, and her nose would never be like that of Aunt Grace. Altogether, she was an unexceptionable heiress, sweet and sorrowful, and "interesting." It was a commonplace sort of word, but yet even a superfine young man is sometimes obliged to use such ordinary mediums of expression. For a man who, previously set up at much too high a figure (to quote his own metaphor), and commanding no offers, was ready to accept a moderate fortune even under disadvantageous conditions, the thought of a nice little property, weighted only by Margaret, was very consolatory indeed.

CHAPTER XXVII.

NEXT day was Sunday, the last day that Margaret was to spend at home; not like the brilliant Sunday on which old Sir Ludovic, for the last time, attended "a diet of worship" in the parish church, and was reminded of his latter end by good Dr. Burnside; but gray, and dull, and cloudy, with no light on the horizon, and the whole landscape, hill and valley and sea, all expressed in different tones of a flat lead color, the change of all others which most affects the landscape. In Fife, as has been candidly allowed, the features of the country have no splendor or native nobleness; and accordingly there is no power in them to resist this invasion of grayness. Mr. Aubrey Bellingham, though he did pretend to "go in" for the beauties of nature, intimated very plainly his discontent with the scene before him.

"Anything poorer in the way of landscape I don't know that I ever saw," he said, and sighed, when he was made to take his place in the old carriage to be driven to Fifeton, to the "English Chapel." It was six miles off; whereas the parish church, with the Norman chancel, was scarcely one. But, as Mrs. Bellingham said, if you do not hold by your church, what is to become of you?

"Only the common people go there," she said—"the farmers, and so forth. The gentry are *all* Episcopalian. My brother, Sir Ludovic, may go now and then for the sake of example, and because Dr. Burnside is an old family friend; but Sir Claude, and everybody of importance, you will find at our church. All the *élite* go there. I can't think what the gentry were thinking of, to allow the Presbyterians to seize the endowments. It is quite the other way in England, where it is the common people who are dissenters, and *we* have a church which is really fit for ladies and gentlemen to go to. But things are all very queer in Scotland, Aubrey. That is one thing, I suppose, that gives the common people such very independent ways."

"Well, Aunt Jean, let us be thankful we were not born to set it right," said Aubrey, reconciled to see that his six-miles' drive was to be in company with Margaret. But she, in her deep mourning, did not afford much good diversion during the drive. The fact that it was the last day—the last day! had at length penetrated her mind; and a vague horror of what might happen, of something hanging over her which she did not understand, of leave-takings, and engagements to be entered into and promises to be made, had come over Margaret like a cloud. She had passively obeyed her sisters' orders, and followed them into the carriage, though not without an acute recollection of her last drive in that carriage by her father's side at a time when she was not passive at all, but liked her own way and had it, and was not aware how happy she was.

Margaret took all the other changes as secondary to the one great change, and did not feel them as an old man's darling, a somewhat spoiled child, accustomed to unlimited indulgence for all her fancies, might have been expected to do. But her individuality came back to her, and with it a sense of unknown troubles to be encountered, as she leaned back in her corner, saying nothing. She drew herself as far as possible away from Aubrey Bellingham, and she let her veil drop, with its heavy burden of crape, and took refuge within herself. She had to part with her home, and Bell and John, the attendants of her life, but, more alarming still and strange, she had to part with Rob Glen. Ludovic's interposition had increased tenfold the importance of everything about Rob Glen, the circumstances of which she had thought so little when the first step had been taken. How could she have thought of the young man's position, or of any consequences that might follow, at the moment when her father lay dying? Rob had been very kind; his tenderness, his caresses, had gone to her heart. There were indeed moments, after the first, when they no longer impressed her with such a sense of kindness, when she would have been glad enough to avoid the close contact, and when the touch of his arm round her gave Margaret a sense of shy shrinking, rather than of the utter confidence and soothing which she had felt at first—and when she had not liked to vex him by resistance, but had edged and shrunk away, and made herself as small as possible to avoid the embarrassing pressure.

But all this vague shyness and shrinking had changed at their last interview, when Margaret, in generous impetuosity, and terror lest he should think she considered herself raised above him by her fortune, had taken the matter into her own hands and made all the vague ties definite. What an extraordinary sensation it was to feel that she belonged to him—she, Margaret Leslie, to him, Rob Glen! She could not realize or understand it, but felt, with a sense of giddiness through her whole being, that something existed which bound her to him forever. Yes, no doubt, when you came to think of it, that was what it meant. She had not been aware of it at first, but this no doubt was how it was. And Ludovic's questioning had made it all so much more real. After what her brother had said, there was no avoiding the certainty.

Between Rob Glen and herself was an invisible link, woven so closely that nothing could undo it. How changed all the world was! Once it lay free and bright and open before her, with but one restriction, and that her natural obedience to her father and loyalty to her home. Now, with a giddiness and dazzling in her eyes, she felt how different it all was. She had no longer any home, and the world was closed up to her by that figure of Rob Glen. She did not know that she objected to him, or disliked his presence, but it made everything different. And chiefly it made her giddy, so that she herself and the whole universe seemed to be going round and round—Rob Glen. She was not sure, even —but all was confusion in her mind—that she thought of him now just as she had thought of him in those old, old times, when he had sat among the potatoes and made his picture; when he had seemed so clever, such a genius, such a poet, making a common bit of paper into a landscape, in which the sun would shine and the wind blow forever.

That side of the subject was dim to her now. Rob was no longer an artist doing wonders before her eyes, but a man whose touch made her shrink, yet held her fast; one whom she was more shy of, yet more bound to, than to anybody else in the world; from whom she would like to steal a little farther off, if she could do it unnoticed, yet move a step nearer to, should he find her out. This strange jumble of feeling seemed to be brought to a climax by the thought that she was going away to-morrow. To-night —there was no avoiding the necessity—she must go again and meet him, and explain everything to him, and part with him. What might he say, or make her do and say? She could not wound his feelings by refusing, by letting him see that she shrank from him. She felt that she must yield to him, not to hurt his feelings. A mingled sense of sympathy and gratitude, and (though the word is so inadequate) politeness, made it seem terrible to Margaret to withdraw from her lover.

To betray to a person who loves you that his gaze, his touch, his close vicinity is distasteful, what a dreadful thing to do—what a wound to his feelings, and his pride, and his fondness! If he would not do it; if he would keep a little farther off, and keep his arms by his side like other people, how much more pleasant; but to be so unsympathetic, so unfeeling, as to show him that you did not like what he meant in such great kindness! this was more than Margaret could do. As she sat back in the carriage and was carried along through the gray landscape, with a whiff of Mrs. Bellingham's *mille-fleurs* pervading the atmosphere, and a sea of crape all about her, and the voices of the others flowing on, Margaret, whom they thought so impassive, was turning over this question, with flushes of strange confusion and trouble. What would he say? what would he ask of her? what promises would she have to make, and pledges to give? To give him up was a thing that did not enter into her mind; she could not have done anything so cruel; but she looked forward to the next meeting with an alarm which was very vivid, while at the same time she was aware that it was quite inevitable that she must see him, and that in all likelihood she would do what he wanted her to do.

This pervading consciousness confused Margaret much in respect to the morning's service, and the people who came up to her and pressed her hand, and said things they meant to be kind. It was a little chapel, very like, as Mrs. Bellingham said indignantly, the chapels which the dissenters had in England; and to see all the common folk going to the big church with the steeple, to which they were called by all the discordancy of loudly clanging bells, while the carriages drew up before that little non-conforming tabernacle, was very offensive to all right-minded people.

"Things must have been dreadfully mismanaged, Aubrey, at the time when all was settled," Mrs. Bellingham said, very seriously; "for you see for yourself all the best people were there. One advantage is that it is much pleasanter sitting among a congregation that is *all* ladies and gentlemen; but surely, surely, taking the most liberal view of it, it is more suitable that *we* should have the churches, and the common people be dissenters, as they are in England? I would not prevent them—I would let them have their way; but naturally it is not we that should give place to them, but they to us."

"But, dearest Jean, we were all once—"

"And when you think—Grace, I wish you would let me get in a word—that we really cannot get a very good set of clergy because there is no money to give them, while the Presbyterians have got it all, though it comes out of our pockets! I have never studied history as I ought to have done, for really education was not so much attended to in our days; but I am sure the Scots gentry must have been very badly treated. For that John Knox, you know, sprang of the common people himself, and they were all he cared about, and no pains were taken, none at all, to suit the Church to the better classes. But Margaret has been more seen to-day; and we have had more condolences and sympathy from our own kind of people at this one service than we would have had at the parish church in twenty years."

These shakings of hands, however, and the words of sympathy were too much for Margaret, who was not perhaps in the best condition for being inspected and condoled with, after all the secret agitation of this long, silent drive, and who had to be sent home, finally, alone, while her sisters and their attendant stopped half-way to take luncheon with Sir Claude.

"You will send back the carriage for us, Margaret, since you don't feel equal to staying? Of course, it is a very different thing to her, who never was away from him, to what it is to us, who had not been with him for years," Mrs. Bellingham said, while Miss Leslie lingered at the carriage-door, and could not make up her mind to leave her dearest Margaret.

"I think I ought to go with her, dear child. Don't you think so, dear Aubrey? But then Sir Claude and Lady Jane are so kind; and then it will be such a trouble sending back the carriage. Darling Margaret, are you sure, are you quite sure you don't mind going alone? for I will come with you in a minute. I don't really care to stay at all, but for Jean, who always likes a change; and dear Sir Claude is so kind; and it will be a change, you know, for dear Aubrey—the chief people in Fife!" she added, anxiously putting her nose into the carriage, "if you are quite sure, dearest Margaret, that you don't mind."

Free of the crape, and of that sense of a multitude which belongs to a closely packed carriage, Margaret went home very much more tranquilly in her corner, and cried, and was relieved as the heavy old vehicle rolled along between the well-known hedge-rows, and passed the well-known church upon its mound where her old father lay sleeping the sleep of the weary and the just. She gazed out wistfully through her tears at the path round the old apse of the church where she had walked with him so lately, and close to which he was now laid. In these days no idea of floral decorations had visited Scotch grave-yards, and the great gray stone-work of the Leslie tomb, rearing its seventeenth-century skulls and crossbones against the old twisted Norman arches, was not favorable to any loving deposit of this kind. But a rose-bush that grew by the side door had thrown a long tendril round the gray wall, which was drooping with a single half-opened rose upon it straight across those melancholy emblems, pointing, as it seemed to Margaret, to the very spot where old Sir Ludovic lay. This went to her heart, poor child. They were taking her away, but the rose would remain and shed its leaves over the place, and make it sweet; and kind eyes would look at it, and kind people would talk of old Sir Ludovic, and be sorry for his poor little Peggy, whose life was so changed.

There is something in the pang of self-pity in a young mind which is more poignant, and yet more sweet, than any other sorrow. There is nothing so ready to bring the tears that give relief. They would talk about her, all the kind poor people; not the ladies and the gentlemen, perhaps, who went to the English chapel, and of whom Jean was so fond, but a great many people in the high town and the "laigh toun" whom Margaret knew intimately, and the family in the Manse, Dr. Burnside and his wife and Randal. Randal had been kind too. How he had run for the doctor that day, though it was of no use! and how many things he had done after, not stopping, Margaret thought, to talk to her, but always doing what was most wanted! Ah! —this thought brought her to the other end of the circle again with a spring. It was always herself, Margaret remembered, that Rob had thought of, always her first. She began to go over all the course of events as the carriage rolled on, too quickly now, to Earl's-hall. Had she forgotten, she asked herself, that time when he came to her father's aid on the church-yard path —how careful he had been of the old man—and how much trouble he had taken to please him afterward? Thinking of her own troubles, she had forgotten half that Rob had done. How kind he had been! and Sir Ludovic had liked him—he had got to be fond of him; surely he

7

had been fond of him! He had allowed her to be with Rob, drawing, talking, as much as she pleased. He had never said "You must give up Rob Glen." Perhaps, indeed, *that* was what her father meant. What did it matter about being what people called a gentleman? Sir Claude was all that; but except when he sent a servant to ask how Sir Ludovic was, what had he ever done, though Grace said he was so kind? The great people had all been the same. They had sent a servant; they had sent their carriages to the funeral. But Rob had held up her father when he stumbled, and had come to talk to him and amuse him, and had made a picture of him which was more to Margaret than all the National Gallery. Oh, that was what it was to be kind! The carriage heaving horribly as it turned into the rut inside the gate, stopped Margaret in the full current of these thoughts. But they were a great support to her in the prospect that lay before her, the farewell scene that she knew she would have to go through, when he would be so sorry, and she would not know what to say.

The Leslies, like so many kind people, dined earlier than usual on Sundays. They dined at five, to the great discomfort of the party who had lunched with Sir Claude, and who arrived just in time for this second meal. Mr. Aubrey Bellingham thought it was done in deference to the national desire to be uncomfortable on Sunday, and submitted with a shrug of his shoulders; but Mrs. Bellingham, having more right to express an opinion, did so frankly, and with much indignation. She said:

"I know it's Mary's way in Edinburgh; and there may be excuses where there is a young family, and servants have to be considered. Of course they are not rich, and servants insist on being considered when they know they have you in their power; but at Earl's-hall, and when *we* are here! I think it is very unnecessary. Last Sunday we were not thinking of dinner, and I am sure I cannot tell you when we had it; but just when people are recovering their spirits, and when a cheerful meal is your best restorative! It may be very good of Mary to consider her servants, but I must say she might just as well, for once in a way, have considered you and me."

"But, dearest Jean! dear Mary is the most unselfish! She does not mind any inconvenience—"

"Oh, inconvenience! don't speak to me—she *likes* it!" cried Mrs. Jean, indignant. "She is just the kind of woman that relishes a tea-dinner, and all that sort of thing; and if she can make out that she saves sixpence, what a thing that is! And Ludovic just lets her do what she likes. She is getting him into all her huggermugger ways. If a woman has not more self-respect, she ought, at least, to have some respect for her husband. But everything is made to give in to the children and the servants, in that house. I could have put up with it, not that I ever like it, in Edinburgh, for there one knows what one has to expect. But here, where Bell and John were so used to my father—and when *we* are in the house, and without even asking my opinion, and the excellent luncheon we have just had! she might have thought of Aubrey, who is not accustomed to any nonsense of consideration for ser-

vants; but I always said, though she is a good enough wife to Ludovic, that she was a woman of no perception," Mrs. Bellingham said.

After this little storm, the untimely dinner was marred by some sulkiness on Jean's part, as was perhaps natural. And though Aubrey made himself very agreeable, with the most noble and Christian forgiveness of injuries, devoting himself to little Effie, whom he regaled with historiettes of a less piquant description than those of his *début*, yet there was a general irritability about the simple meal which, it must be allowed, often attends that well-meant expedient for the keeping of Sunday. The company dispersed early, flocking off to their rooms, where Mrs. Bellingham, with her foot up, instructed her maid as to her packing, and once more turned over the packet of lace which had fallen to her share. Margaret, when she had seen the rest of the party go away, fled too, to escape another interview with her brother, who looked, she thought, as if meditating a renewal of his remonstrances, and, having watched her opportunity, stole softly down-stairs. Even Bell was still busy after the dinner. Her chair stood in the court outside the door, but she had not yet come out to enjoy her favorite seat. And Bell's heart was so heavy that her work went but slowly. She had no thought of anything but Miss Margaret, who to-morrow was to be taken away.

Margaret stole out like one who had learned that she was guilty. Never before had she emerged so stealthily from the shadow of the old house. She did not go the usual way, to run the risk of being seen, but crept round by the garden-wall, as she had done sometimes when returning, when Rob was with her. There was a feeble attempt at a sunset, though the sun had not shone all day, and consequently had no right to his usual pomps, but in the west there was a redness breaking through the gray, which brightened the face of the country, and changed the character of the landscape. Under the trees it fell like lamps of rich gold, escaping here and there through broken openings in the clouds, and warming the wood with gleams of color which had looked so dark and wind-scathed in the morning. Margaret went softly, threading through the colonnades of the great fir trunks, and sat down on the little mossy knoll under the silver-fir. She placed herself so that she could not be seen from the house, but yet could spy through the branches the approach of any danger from that side.

It was the first time she had been first at the place of meeting, and her heart beat as she sat and waited. She, who had shrunk from the prospect of this meeting, she became alarmed now lest he should not come, and longed for him with a kind of sick anxiety. Oh that he would come, that she might get it over! She did not know what it was to be, but instinctively felt that there must be something painful in this last meeting. The last! She would not be sorry to have met, perhaps, when she was away and had no longer any chance of seeing him. She would understand better what he meant, and what she herself meant; and there is something which subdues the pride in thus waiting for one who does not come. She did not seem so sure that it was he who cared, that it was he only who would break his heart, as she sat there alone;

and she had almost lost herself in fancies more bitter than any she had yet known—in dreamy realization of her loneliness and a sense that no one, perhaps, would care much when she went away. Who did care? Not Ludovic, who wished her to do well, but would not have suffered much had Margaret died with her father; nor his wife, who was very kind, but had so many girls of her own; nor Effie, though she would cry and think she was sorry. Nobody would care; and Jean and Grace would often find her a trouble; and nobody in the world belonged to Margaret, cared for her above everything else, was happy when she was happy, and grieved when she was sorry;—nobody—except, perhaps, him alone.

"Margaret!" A low eager voice that seemed the very essence of subdued delight, trembling with satisfaction and happiness, and he suddenly made a spring to her side from under the trees, through which he had been threading his way to the place of meeting. He threw himself on his knees by her, and seized and kissed her hands a hundred times. "You here before me! waiting for me! To think I should have lost a moment of the little time I may have you! I shall never forgive myself; but I thought it was too early for you, even now."

"Oh, I have not been waiting long," she said. "It was because we dined so early; and then they were all—tired."

"Except my Margaret. God bless my Margaret, that came out and took the trouble to wait for me! How often I have sat here and watched for the sweep of your dress at the corner of the house, for the least sign of you! And to think that you should have been first to-night, and waiting—"

"Why should not I wait," she said, "as well as you? And to-morrow I am going away."

"To-morrow!" he cried, in a voice of despair. "How am I to endure it? how am I to go on without you? I am afraid to think of it, my darling. Margaret! Margaret! what are you going to say to me to give me strength to get through to-morrow, and all the days after it, till we meet again?"

Now it has come! said Margaret to herself; and she felt with astonishment that the emergency seemed to give her possession of her faculties. "I do not know," she said, steadily, "what you want me to do or say. I shall be very sorry to go away and to—part from you. But what can I do? My sisters have the right to do what they think proper with me; and I think I ought, too, to go and see my own house. I would like to take Bell or somebody, but they will not let me. And now that Ludovic is here and his family, it is natural that I should go away."

"Yes; but first say something to comfort me, Margaret. I did not suppose you could stay here forever: but tell me you love me, and will be faithful to me. Tell me when I may come after you?"

"Come after me?" she exclaimed, with a certain dismay.

"Did you not think I would come after you? Did you think I could stay in one country while you were in another—I, who have had the happiness of seeing you every day? But it is better this should end, though it is like to break my heart, for we should have lost time, and been

content just with seeing each other; and now, Margaret, my darling, we must settle something. Tell me what I may do? To wait till you are of age is a lifetime. If I come to England after you in about three months, when you are in your own house, will you receive me and tell your sisters what I am to you? Margaret! you are not frightened, darling? You did not think I would let my love go away and carry my heart with her without settling something? You could not have been so cruel!"

"I do not want to be cruel," she said; "but oh! wouldn't it do to wait—to wait a little? It is only three years; I am very near eighteen. I shall be eighteen in November; and three years go so quickly. Why do you look at me like that? I am not unkind. It is only that I think; it is only that—oh! I am sure that would be the best!"

"Three years!" he said; "you might as well bid me wait thirty years. How can I be sure you will not forget me long before three years are out? What! live without knowing anything of you—without seeing you, for three centuries—it would be all the same. Tell me to go out into St. Andrew's Bay in a storm, and be cast away on the rocks—tell me to drown myself in the Eden—as you please, Margaret! I think it is in me to do it if you bid me; but wait for three years and never see you—never know what you are thinking, never hear the sound of your voice? I had rather go and hang myself at once!" cried Rob. He was walking up and down under the shadow of the trees. He was very much excited. After coming so far, after holding her in his hand, as he thought, was he going to lose her at the last?

"I did not mean that"—she stood leaning against the fir, very much troubled—"what can I do? Oh, what am I to do?"

"You must not ask me to be content without you," he said, "for I cannot—I cannot. It is not possible for me to give you up and live without you now. If you had sent me away at the very first, perhaps— But after all that has passed, Margaret, after feeling that you were mine. to ask me to go away and give you up—now!"

"I did not say give me up; I said—"

"You said three years, darling—three lifetimes; you could not mean anything so dreadful! You would not kill me, would you? It is like taking my heart out of my breast. What good would there be in the world for me? What could I do? What would I be fit for? Margaret, Margaret! you could not have the heart to treat me so!"

"What can I do?" she said, trembling. "Ludovic has found out about you, and he asked me to give you up. I did not mean to tell you, but I cannot help it. He says they will never, never consent. And what am I to do? How can I fight with them? I said I would not give you up. I said it would break your heart."

"And so it would, my darling!" he cried, putting his arm round her; "and, oh, my Margaret, yours too!"

Margaret made no reply to this. She withdrew the least little step—but how could she hurt his feelings?

"That was why I said three years," she said;

"three years is not so very long. Poor Jeanie in the house, did you ever see Jeanie? She is—very fond of some one; and she has not heard of him at all or seen him, for two years. It would pass very fast. You would become a great painter—and then; but Jeanie does not know if she will ever see him again; and his name is Rob, too, like you."

"What has Jeanie to do with it?" he cried, with a look of dismay. Then he caught her arm and drew her away. "There is some one coming from the house; let us not wait here, but come down the other side of the wood. I must not be interrupted now. I have a great deal more to say to you, Margaret, my Margaret, this last night before we part."

CHAPTER XXVIII.

Rob had a great deal to say, but it was chiefly repetition of what he had said before. He drew her arm within his, and they wandered down by the edge of the wood and into the fields. That last little accidental outbreak of sunshine was over, and all once more was grayness and monotones. There was nobody about; the evening was not tempting enough to bring out walkers. In the kirktown people were out "about the doors," sitting on the kirk steps, keeping up a confused little hum of conversation, quieter than usual as suited the Sabbath night; and the people who had gardens strolled about them in domestic stillness, and commented upon the coming apples; but it was not the fashion in Stratheden to take walks on Sunday evening. The fields were very silent and still; and so absorbed were the two in their conversation that they wandered far out of the woods of Earl's-hall, and were skirting the fields about the farm before they were aware. Rob's plan was to go to London, to make what progress he could with his drawing, to study and work, and achieve success; the last went without saying. Margaret was as certain of it as that the sun would rise to-morrow. But she was not equally certain of the other part of the programme, which was that he should go to the Grange—her house where she was to live—and be produced there as her betrothed husband, and introduced to her sisters.

This prospect alarmed her more than she could say. She did not want him to come to the Grange. She did not know what to say about writing to him. The idea brought a hot blush to her face. Margaret was not quite sure that she could write a letter that she would like Rob Glen to see. He was very clever, and she did not think she could write a very pretty letter. In short, she was unpractical and unmanageable to the last degree, and Rob had some excuse for being impatient. She had no idea what could be done, except that she might perhaps come to Earl's-hall and see him there, and that three years was not so very long. He lost himself in arguments, in eloquent appeals to her; and she had nothing very eloquent to say in return. After a while she was silenced, and made very little answer at all, but walked along by his side demurely, with her thick gauze veil drooping over her face, and heard all he had to say, saying yes now and then, and

sometimes no. Her position was very simple; and though he proved to her that it was untenable by a hundred arguments, and showed her that some other plan was necessary, he did not drive Margaret out of it.

What could she do? she asked, wringing her hands. Ludovic was against them, and Jean would be much more against them. She dared not let Jean know. Even her brother himself had said that Jean must not know. And, to tell the truth, Rob himself was of the opinion that it would be better to keep this secret from Mrs. Bellingham; but yet he thought he might at least be allowed to visit at the Grange, as an old friend, if nothing more. They got through a series of by-ways into the field path, where their first meeting had been, and Rob was trying, for the hundredth time, to obtain some promise of intercourse from Margaret, when suddenly some one coming behind them laid a hand upon a shoulder of each. Rob gave a violent start and turned round, while Margaret, with a little cry, shrank back into the shadow of the hedge-row.

"My certy!" said the intruder; "this is a fine occupation, Rob, my man, for a Sabbath nicht!" And then she, too, gave a cry of surprise, more pretended than real, but in which there was a little genuine fright. "Eh, bless me, it's Miss Margret, and so far from hame!" she cried.

"Mother! what are you doing here?" cried Rob. But as for Margaret she was relieved. She had thought nothing less for the moment than that Jean was upon her, or, at the very least, Bell coming out to seek and bring her back. Mrs. Glen was not a person of whom she stood in any fear, and she would not tell or interfere to let Jean know, for Rob's sake. So that Margaret turned round from the hedge-row with a relieved soul, and said,

"Oh, is it you, Mrs. Glen?" with a new sense of ease in her tone.

"Deed and it is just me, my bonnie young lady. I hear you are going away, Miss Margret, and many a sore heart you will leave in the country-side. You're so near the farm, you must come in and I will make you a cup of tea in a moment. It's real gray and dull, and there's a feel in the air like rain. Come your ways to the farm, Miss Margret, my bonnie dear; and after that Rob will take you home."

Margaret made no resistance to this proposal. She had been walking for some time, and she was tired, and even the idea of the tea was welcome. She went in after Mrs. Glen with some misgivings as to the length of her absence, but a sense of relief on that point too; for it had always been a good excuse to Bell, and even to her father, that she had accepted the civility of one of their humbler neighbors. "It pleases them; and so long as they are decent folk they will never but be awfu' keen to take care of Miss Margret: and she knows none but decent folk," Bell had said. The cup of tea in the farm-parlor would be as good a reason for Margaret's absence as Sir Claude's luncheon-table was for her sisters'. To be sure, in former days there had been no son at Mrs. Glen's to make such visits dangerous. She went in with a sense of unexpected relief and sat down, very glad to find herself at rest in the parlor, where a little fire was burning. To be sure, Rob would walk home with her and renew his entreaties; but he could not, she thought, continue them in his mother's presence, and the relief was great.

"Mony a time have you come in here to get your tea, Miss Margret. I've seen Rob come ben carrying ye in his arms. I mind one time you were greeting for tiredness, a poor wee missie, and your shoe lost in the burn; that lad was aye your slave, Miss Margret, from the time you were no bigger than the table."

"Oh, I remember," said Margaret; "I thought Bell would scold me, and I did not know how I was to go home without my shoe."

"You went home in that lad's arms, my bonnie dear, for all he stands there so blate, looking at ye as if you were an angel; he wasna aye sae blate. You went home in his arms, and gave him a good kiss, and thought no shame. But you were only six then, and now you're eighteen. Oh ay, my dear, I can tell your age to a day. You were born the same week as my youngest that died, a cauld November, and that sent your bonnie young mother to her grave. It was an awfu' draughty house, and no a place for a delicate young woman, that auld house at Earl's-hall. Fine, I mind; and Rob there he's five years older. From the time you could toddle he aye thought you the chief wonder o' the world."

"Mother, you that know so much you had better know all," said Rob. "I think her the chief wonder of the world still."

"You need not tell me that, my bonnie man; as if I could not see it in your een!" Margaret stirred uneasily while this conversation went on over her head. She had never thought of having this engagement told to anybody, of being talked about to anybody. She got up with a little gasp, feeling as if there was not air enough to breathe. If they would not surround her so, close her up, all these people; oh, if they would only let her alone! She tried to turn away to escape before Rob should have said any more—but, before she clearly understood what was passing, found herself suddenly in the arms of Mrs. Glen.

"Oh, my pretty miss! my bonnie young lady! is this all true that I hear?" Rob's mother cried, with effusive surprise and delight. "Did I ever think, when I rose out of my bed this morning, that I was to hear such wonderful news afore the night? Eh, Miss Margret, my dear, I wish ye much joy, and I think ye'll have it, for he's a good lad; and you, ye smiling loon, I need not wish you joy, for you're just leaping out of yourself with happiness and content."

"And I think I have good reason," cried Rob, coming up in his turn and receiving her out of his mother's embrace. Oh, how horribly out of place Margaret felt between them! Never in her life had she felt the dignity of being Margaret Leslie, old Sir Ludovic's daughter, as she did at that moment. Her cheeks burned crimson; she shrank into herself, to escape from the embracing arms. What had she to do here? How had she strayed so far from home? It was all she could do not to break forth into passionate tears of disgust and repugnance. Oh, Margaret thought, if she could but get away! if she could but run home all the way and never stop! if she could but beg Jean to leave Earl's-hall instantly that very night! But she could not do any of these things. She had to stand still, with eyes cast down and crimson cheeks, hearing them

talk of her. It was to them she seemed to belong now; and how could she get away?

"Now give us your advice, mother," said Rob, "we cannot tell what to do. The Leslies are prejudiced, as may easily be supposed, especially the old ladies (oh that Jean and Grace had but heard themselves called old ladies!), and Margaret wants me to wait the three years till she comes of age. She wants me to trust to chances of seeing her and hearing of her—not even to have any regular correspondence. I would cut off my right hand to please her, but how am I to live without seeing her, mother? We had been talking and consulting, and wandering on, a little farther and a little farther, till we did not know where we were going. But now that we are here, give us your advice. Will you be for me, I wonder, or on Margaret's side?"

He had called her Margaret often before, and she was quite used to it; why did it suddenly become so offensive and insupportable now?

"You see," said Mrs. Glen, "there is a great deal to be said on both sides." Mrs. Glen was very much excited, her eyes gleaming, her heart beating. It seemed to her that she had the fate of these two young people in her hands, and might now clinch the matter and establish her son's good-fortune if Providence would but inspire her with the right thing to say. "There is this for our bonnie Miss Margret, that she would be all her lane to bear the opposition o' thae ladies, and hard it would be for a delicate young thing no used to struggle for herself; and there's that for you, Rob, that nae doubt it would be a terrible trial to worship the ground she treads on as you do, and never to see her for three lang years. Now let me think a moment, bairns, while this dear lassie takes her cup of tea."

Margaret could not refuse the cup of tea. How could she assert herself and withdraw from them, and let them know that she was not to be taken possession of and called a dear lassie by Mrs. Glen? Her heart was in revolt; but she was far too shy, far too polite to make a visible resistance. She drew back into the room as far as she could out of the fitful gleams of the fire-light, and she shrank from Rob's arm, which was on the back of her chair; but still she took the tea and sat still, bearing with all they said and did. It was the last time; but oh, what trouble she had got into without meaning it! Suddenly it had come to be salvation and deliverance to Margaret that she was going away.

"Now, bairns," said Mrs. Glen, "listen to me. I think I have found what you want. The grand thing is that you should be faithful to each other, and mind upon each other. It's no being parted that does harm. Three years will flee away like three days, and you will be young, young, ower young to be married at the end; and you would do more than that, Rob Glen, for your bonnie Margaret; weel I ken that. So here is just what you must do. You must give each other a bit writing, saying that ye'll marry at the end of three years—you to her, Rob, and her to you. And then you will be out of all doubt, and troth-plight, the one to the other, before God and man."

"Mother!" cried Rob, starting up from where he had been bending over Margaret, with a wild glow of mingled rage, terror, and hope in his eyes. The suggestion gave him a shock. He did not know anything about the law on that point, nor whether there was more validity in such a promise than in any other love-pledge. But he was struck with sudden alarm at the idea of doing something which might afterward be brought against him, and a certain generosity and honor not extinguished in his mind made him realize Margaret's helpless condition between his mother and himself, and her ignorance and her youth; while at the same time, to secure her, to make certain of her, gave him a tug of temptation, a wild sensation of delight. "No, no," he cried, hoarsely, "I could not make her do it;" then paused, and looked at her with the eager wildness of passion in his eyes.

But Margaret was perfectly calm. No passion was woke in her—scarcely any understanding of what this meant. A bit writing? Oh yes, what would that matter, so long as she could get away?

"It is getting dark," she said; "they will not know where I am; they will be wondering. Will I do it now, whatever you want me to do, and go home?"

"Margaret, my love!" he cried, "I thought you were frightened; I thought you were shrinking from me; and here is your sweet consent more ready than even mine!"

"Oh, it is not that," she said, a little alarmed by the praise and by the demonstrations that accompanied it. "But it is getting dark, and it is late; and oh, I am so anxious to get home."

Rob wrung his hands. "She doesn't understand what we mean, mother; I can't take advantage of her. She thinks of nothing but to get home."

"You gomerel!" said his mother, between her teeth; and then she turned a smiling face upon Margaret. "Just that, my bonnie miss," she said; "a woman's heart's aye ready to save sorrow to them that's fond of her. It's time you were home, my sweet lady. Just you write it down to make him easy in his mind, and then he will take you back to Earl's-hall."

"Must I write it myself?" Margaret said; and it came across her with a wave of blushing that she did not write at all nicely—not so well as she ought. "And what am I to say? I don't know what to say." Then she gave another glance at the window, which showed the night drawing near, the darkness increasing every moment, with that noiseless, breathless pleasure which the night seems to take in getting dark when we are far from home. She got up with a sudden, hasty impulse. "Oh, if you please, Mrs. Glen, if you will be as quick as ever you can! for I must run all the way."

"That will I, my darlin' lady," said the delighted mother. It was she who had the whole doing of it, and the pride of having suggested it. Rob stood by, quite pale, his eyes blazing with excitement, his mind half paralyzed with trouble and terror, hope to have, reluctance to take, fear of something unmanly, something dishonorable, intensified by the eagerness of expectation, with which he looked for what was to come. He stood "like a stock stane," his mother said afterward, his lips parted, his eyes staring, in her way as she rushed to the desk at the other side of the room to find what was wanted. "You eedeeot!" she said, as she pushed him aside, in an angry undertone. Had he not the sense even

to help in what was all for his own advantage? Margaret pulled off her black glove and took the pen in her hand. She knew she would write it very badly, very unevenly—not even in a straight line; but if she had to do it before she could run home, it was better to get it over.

"Oh, but I never wrote anything before," she said; "Mrs. Glen, what must I say?"

"I never wrote the like of that before," cried Mrs. Glen; "and there's Rob even—too happy to help us." She had meant to use another word to describe his spasm of irresolution and apprehension, but remembered in time that he must not be contemned in Margaret's eyes. "It will be just this, my bonnie dear: 'I, Margaret Leslie, give my word before God and man, to marry Robert Glen as soon as I come of age. So help me God. Amen.'"

"Don't put that," cried Rob, making a hasty step toward her. "Don't let her put that." But then he turned away in such passion and transport of shame, satisfaction, horror, and disgust as no words could tell, and covered his face with his hands.

"Not that last," said Margaret, stumbling, in her eagerness, over the words, and glad to leave out whatever she could. "Oh, it is very badly written. I never could write well. Mrs. Glen, will that do?"

"And now your bonnie name here," said the originator of the scheme, scarcely able to restrain her triumph. And as Margaret, with a trembling hand, crossed the last t, and put a blot for a dot over the i, in her distracted signature, she received a resounding kiss upon her cheek which was as the report of a pistol to her. She gave a little cry of terror, and threw down the pen, and turned away. "Oh, good-bye!" she cried, "good-bye. I must not stay another moment. I must run all the way."

Rob did not say a word—he hurried after her, with long strides, keeping up with her as she flew along, in her fright, by the hedge-row. "Oh, they must have missed me by this time. They will be wondering where I have been," she said, breathless. Rob set his teeth in the dark. Never in his life had he been so humiliated. Though she had pledged herself to him, she was not thinking of him; and in all the experiences of his life he had never yet known this supreme mortification. He had been loved where he had wooed. The other girls whom Rob had addressed had forgotten everything for him. He half hated her, though he loved her, and felt a fierce eagerness to have her—to make her his altogether—to snatch her from the great people who looked down upon him—to make himself master of her fate. But this furious kind of love was only the excitement of the moment. At the bottom of his heart he was fond of Margaret (as he had been of other Margarets before). He could not bear the idea of losing her, of parting from her like this, in wild haste, without any of the lingering caresses of parting.

"Is this how you are going away from me, Margaret," he cried, "flying—as if you were glad to part, not sorry, when we don't know when we may meet again?"

"Oh, it is not that I am glad; it is only that they will wonder—they will not know where I have been."

"Will you ever be as breathless running to

me as you are to run away from me?" he cried. "Stop, Margaret! one moment before we come near the gate, and say good-bye."

She yielded with panting breath. That sacred kiss of parting—which, to do him justice, he gave with all the fervor that became the occasion, giving, as he felt, his very heart with it—how glad she was to escape from it, and run on!

"Oh no! I will not forget—I could not forget!" she cried.

Who was this, once more in the lovers' way? A dark figure, who, they could see, by the movement of his head, turned to look at them, but went on without taking any notice. Margaret, anxious as she was, recognized Randal Burnside, and wondered that he did not notice her, then was glad to think that he could not know her. Rob had other thoughts. "Again found out—and by the same fellow!" he said to himself, and gnashed his teeth. Randal was going over to Earl's-hall, a familiar visitor, while he, the betrothed husband of the daughter of Earl's-hall, had to skulk about the house in the dark, and take leave of his love under cover of the night. Not without bitter humiliations was this hour of his triumph.

"We must wait till he is out of sight," he said, hoarsely, holding her back. It was like holding an eager greyhound in the leash. "Oh, Margaret," he said, and despite and vexation filled his heart, "you are not thinking of me at all—and here we have to part! You were not in such a hurry when you used to cry upon my shoulder, and take a little comfort from my love!"

This, and the necessity of keeping back till Randal had passed, touched the girl's heart.

"It is not my fault that I am in such a hurry," she said. "Oh, you were kind—kind—kinder than any one. I will never forget it, Rob."

"It was not kindness," he said, "it was love."

"Yes, Rob." She put her soft cheek to his with compunction in her heart. She had been so eager to get away, and yet how kind he had been—kinder than any one! Thus there came a little comfort for him after all.

But just then, with a sudden flutter, as of a bird roused from the branches, some one came out through the gate, which Randal had not closed behind him—a figure of a woman indistinguishable against the dimness of the twilight, with a little thrill and tremor about her, which somehow made itself felt though she could not be seen.

"Is that you, Miss Margret? Bell sent me to look for you," she said, with the same thrill and quiver in her voice.

Rob Glen started violently. It was a new shock to him, and he had already met with many shocks to his nerves that night. Her name came to his lips with a cry; but he had sufficient sense of the position to stop himself. Jeanie! was it possible, in the malice of fate, that this was the Jeanie of whom Margaret had told him? He grasped her in his arms for a moment with vehemence, partly because of that sudden startling interruption, and, with one quickly breathed farewell on her cheek, turned and went away.

"Oh, Jeanie, yes, it is me. I am very, very sorry. I did not want to be so late. Have they found out that I was away? have they been looking for me?" cried Margaret. It was not, perhaps, in the nature of things that Jeanie should be unmoved in her reply.

"You're no looking after the gentleman," she said. "He's gone and left you, feared for me; and you've given him no good-bye. You needna be feared for me, Miss Margret. Cry him back, and bid him farewell, as a lass should to her lad. I'm nae traitor. You needna be feared that Jeanie will betray ye. It's no in my heart."

"Oh, but he's gone, Jeanie," said Margaret, with a ring of relief in her voice. "And oh, I'm glad to be at home! They made me stay when I wanted to be back. Oh, how dark it is! Give me your hand, Jeanie, for I cannot see where you are among the trees."

Jeanie held out her hand in silence and reluctantly, and Margaret, groping, found it, and took hold of it.

"You are all trembling," she said.

"And if I am all trembling, it's easy enough to ken why. Standing out in the dark among the black trees, and thinking of them that's gone to their rest, and waiting for one that was not wanting me. Eh, it's no so long since you had other things in your head, Miss Margret—your old papa, that was as kind as ever father was. But nobody thinks muckle about old Sir Ludovic now."

"Oh, Jeanie! I think upon him night and day!" cried Margaret; and what with the reproach, and what with her weariness and the past excitement, she fell into sudden tears.

"Is that you, my bonnie lamb?" said another voice; and Bell came out of the gloom, where she, too, had been on the watch. "It's cold and it's dreary, and you're worn to death," she said. "Oh, Miss Margret, where have you been, my bonnie doo, wandering about the house, and greeting till your bit heart is sair? Weel, I ken your heart is sair, and mine too. What will we do without you, John and me? You are just the light of our eyes, as you were to the auld maister, auld Sir Ludovic, that was a guid maister to him and to me. Eh, to think this should be the last night, after sae many years!"

"But, Bell," said Margaret, calmed by the sense of lawful protection and the shadow of home, "it is not the last night for you?"

"Ay, my bonnie pet, it's that or little else. When you're gane, Miss Margret, a' will be gane. And my lady's a good woman; but I couldna put up with her, and she couldna put up with me. We're no fit for ither service, neither me nor John—na, no even in your house, my bonnie lamb, for I know that's what you're gaun to say. Nae new house nor new ways for John and me. We're to flit into a bit cot o' our ain, and there we'll bide till the Lord calls, and we gang east to the kirk-yard. God bless ye, my bonnie bairn. Run up the stairs; nobody kens you were away; for weel I divined," said Bell, with an earnestness that filled Margaret's soul with the sense of guilt—"weel I divined that ye would have little heart for company this sorrowful night."

CHAPTER XXIX.

WHEN Margaret stole into the long room, where the family were assembled that evening, she heard a little discussion going on about herself. Ludovic had risen up, and was standing with an uneasy look upon his face, preparing to go in search of her, while Jean was asking who had seen Margaret last. Randal Burnside had come in only a few minutes before, and was still standing with his hat in his hand; and he it was who was explaining when Margaret entered.

"I saw her with Bell as I came in," he said (which was so far true that he lingered till Bell had met her). "I fear she has been making some sad pilgrimages about the house. Has she ever left Earl's-hall before?"

"Never—not for a single day," said kind Lady Leslie; and there was a little pause of commiseration. "Poor Margaret!" they all said, in their various tones.

They were seated at one end of the long room, two lamps making a partial illumination about them, while the surrounding space lay in gloom. The books on the walls shone dimly in the ineffectual light, the dim sky glimmered darkly through the windows, opening this little in-door world to the world without. Mrs. Bellingham had got her feet up on a second chair, for there were no sofas in the long room. Sunday was a tiring day, and Lady Leslie had yawned several times, and would have liked had it been bed-time. She was a woman of very good principles, and she did not like to think of worldly affairs on Sundays; but it was very hard, at the same time, to get them out of her head. As for Miss Leslie, she had got a volume of sacred poetry, which had many beautiful pieces. She remembered to have said some of them to her dear papa on the Sunday evenings of old, between thirty and forty years ago; and though it was a long time since, she had been crying a little to herself over the thought. Effie was, perhaps, the only thoroughly awake member of the family; for it had just been intimated to her that her aunt Jean, after all, had invited her to go to the Highlands to be Margaret's companion, and her heart was beating high with pleasure. Aubrey had whispered to her his satisfaction too. "Thank Heaven you are coming," he said; "we shall not be so very funereal after all." It was while she was still full of smiles from this whisper, and while Randal stood with his hat in his hand, giving that little explanation about Margaret, that Margaret herself stole in, with a little involuntary swing of the door of the West Chamber, through which she came, which made them all start. Margaret was very pale and worn out, with dark lines under her eyes; and she came at an opportune time, when they were all sorry for her. Instead of scolding, Lady Leslie came up and kissed her.

"My dear," she said, "we all know how hard it must be for you to-night;" and when the ready tears brimmed up to the girl's heavy eyes, the good woman nearly cried too. Her heart yearned over the motherless creature thus going away from all she had ever known.

This kiss, and the little murmur of sympathy, and the kind looks they all cast upon her, had the strangest effect upon Margaret. She gave a little startled cry, and looked round upon them with a momentary impulse of desperation. It had never occurred to her that she was deceiving any one before. But now, coming in worn with excitement and trouble of so different a kind, all at once there burst upon Margaret a sense of the wickedness, the guiltiness, the falsehood she was practising. She had never thought of it before. But now when she gave that startled look round, crying "Oh!" with a pang of compunction and wondering self-accusation, the whole enormity of it rushed on her mind. She felt that she ought to have stood up in the midst of the group in the centre of the room, even "before the gentlemen," and have owned the truth. "I am not innocent as you think me, it is not poor papa I am crying for. I was not so much as thinking of papa," was what she ought to have said. But there was only one individual present who had the least understanding of her, or even guessed what the start and the exclamation could mean. When she opened those great eyes wide in her sudden horror of what she was doing, Lady Leslie, a little frightened lest grief should be taking the wilder form of passion, unknown to the placid mind, in this poor little uneducated, undisciplined girl, did all she could to soothe her with gentle words. "We are all a little dull to-night," she said. "My dear, I am sure the best thing you can do is to go to bed."

"Oh yes," said Mrs. Bellingham, "we are all going to bed. Though it is not a day when one is supposed to do very much, yet there is no day in the week more tiring than Sunday. We always keep early hours on Sunday. By all means, Margaret, go to your room and get a good rest before to-morrow. You have been making a figure of yourself, crying, and you are not fit to be seen; though, indeed, we might all have been crying if we had not felt that it would never do to give way. When you think," said Jean, sitting back majestically, with her feet upon the second chair, "of all that has happened since we came here, and that nobody can tell whether we will ever meet under this old roof again!"

"Let us hope that Margaret will come back often; and I am sure she will always find her brother's house a home," said Lady Leslie, still holding her hand and patting her shoulder kindly. All these words came into her mind in a confusion which prevented her from realizing what they meant. She saw Jean shake her head, and demand sadly how that could be, if Ludovic were to sell the house, as he had just been saying? But even this extraordinary suggestion did not wake Margaret's preoccupied mind. They all said "Hush!" looking at her. It was supposed among them that the only one who would really suffer by the sale of Earl's-hall was Margaret, and that to hear of the idea would be more than she could bear. But in her confused condition she took no notice of anything. She did not seem to care for Earl's-hall, or for the family trouble, or for anything in the world except this strange thing which absorbed her, and which none of them knew. The lamps and the circle of faces were like a phantasmagoria before her eyes, a wreath of white sparks in the darkness, all pale, all indistinct against the dim background. Randal only became a little more real to her by dint of what seemed to her the reproachful look he gave her. She thought it was a reproachful look. He had seen her out-of-doors, though he had not taken any notice of her. She remembered now that he had not even showed her the civility of taking off his hat.

"He has no respect for me any more," Margaret said to herself; and this thought went deep, with a pang, to her very heart.

Bell was waiting for her in her room, where already her boxes were packed, and most of her preparations made; and poor Margaret, her mind all confused with a sense that what was supposed to occupy and engross her was scarcely in her thoughts at all, gave herself up into the old woman's hard yet tender hands, as passive as a child, with all the ease that perfect confidence gives. She was not afraid of Bell, nor did she feel the guilt of keeping from her that uncomfortable secret which was no happiness to her, poor child, and which she would so gladly have pushed aside from her own mind had it been possible. "Eh, I wonder if onybody will ever take the pride in it that I have done," Bell said, taking down her young mistress's hair, and letting it fall in long, soft undulation of silky brown over her hands. She turned her head away while she brushed, that no tear might drop upon it. "Na, naebody will take the same pride in it as me: for I've been a' ye've had to bring ye up from a bairn, my bonnie, bonnie darlin': and nae ither woman can ever be that. It's like taking the heart out o' my breast to see you turn your back on Earl's-hall."

The same words had been said to her not very long before, and in a way which ought to have touched her more deeply. Margaret trembled a little with the recollection. "But I will come back again, Bell, and see you," she said, with a far more ready response. She pulled down the old woman's arms about her neck, and clung to her. "Oh, I will come back!" she cried; "Bell, there will never be anybody in the world like you."

"You maunna say that, my bonnie lamb. Many, many there are in the world better worth thinking upon than the like o' me. I am no sae selfish a creature as that; but you'll keep a corner for your old Bell, Miss Margret, ay, and auld John too. He's just speechless with greetin': but he canna yield to shed a tear—and a temper like the auld enemy himsel'. But it's no temper, it's his heart that's breaking. You'll no forget the auld man? and whiles ye'll write us a word to say you're well and happy, and getting up your heart?"

"How will I ever get up my heart," cried Margaret, "in a strange place, with nobody, nobody—not one that cares for me?"

"Whisht, whisht, my darling! You'll find plenty that will care for you—maybe ower many, my bonnie doo—for you'll be a rich lady and have a grand house, far finer than puir Earl's-ha'. And oh, Miss Margret, above a' take you great care wha you set your heart on. There's some that are fair to see and little good at the heart, and a young creature is easy deceived. You mustna go by looks, and you mustna let your heart be tangled with the first that comes. Eh, if Sir Ludovic had but lived a little longer, and gotten you a good man afore he slippit away!"

Margaret was silenced, and could not say a word. If he had known *this*, what would he have thought of it? Would he have handed his little Peggy over to the first that came? Would he have chosen for her, and made this confusing harassing bondage into something legitimate and holy? Margaret received the thought of that possibility with a gasp, not of wishing, but of terror. It seemed to her as if she had escaped something from which there could have been no escape.

"But that's far from your thoughts as yet," said Bell, "and it's no me that will trouble your bonnie head with the like o' that before the time; and the ladies will take great care—I'm no feared but what they will take great care. They will keep poor lads away, and poor lads are aye the maist danger. Here I'm just doing what I said I wouldna do! But eh, we're silly folk; we canna see how the bairns are to be guided that gang from us: as if God would bide in Fife as well as the like o' me: as if he wasna aye there to haud my darlin' by the hand!"

Bell paused to dry her eyes, and to twist in a knot for the night the long locks of the pretty hair in which nobody again would ever take so much pride.

"And, Miss Margret," she said, "you'll no let some light-headed thing of a maid tear thae bonnie locks out o' your head with her curlings and frizzings? Sir Ludovic couldna endure them. He would aye have it like silk, shining in the sun. He never could bide to see it neglected. The ladies even, though they're no so young as they once were, did you ever see such heads? But yours is as God made it, and as bonnie as a flower. And you'll aye mind your duty, my bonnie darlin', and your prayers, and remember your Creator in the days o' your youth. And dinna think ower muckle about your dresses, nor about lads. That will come in its time. I'm just beginning again, though I said I wouldna do it! But oh, to think it's the last night, and I'll never put you to your bed again, nor gie you good advice, nor keep you from the cauld, nor take it upon me to find fault with my bonnie young lady! I canna tell what will be the use of me mair when my bonnie bird flies away."

"Oh, Bell, I will come back; I will come back!"

"Ay, you'll come back, my darlin' bairn; but if you come a hundred times, and a hundred to that, you'll never be the same, Miss Margret. The Lord bless you, my bonnie lamb—but you'll never be the same."

Whether this was a very good preparation for the long night's rest which Mrs. Bellingham thought necessary for travellers, may perhaps be doubted. But Margaret soon cried herself to sleep when Bell withdrew. She was too much exhausted with excitement to be further excited, and this gentle chapter of domestic life, the return of the faces and voices, and looks and feelings familiar to her, gave some comfort to the girl's overworn brain. They interfered between her and that strange scene in the farm-house. They formed a new event, a something which had happened since, to soften to her the trouble and commotion of that strange interruption of her life. She slept, and woke in the morning with a sense of relief which at first she could scarcely account for. What was it of comfort and amelioration that had happened to her? Was it all a dream that her father was dead, that her youthful existence was closed? No, it was that she was going away. Margaret shuddered and trembled with wonder to think that it was possible this could be a relief to her. But yet it was so. She could not doubt it, she could not deny it to herself. When she ought to have been broken-hearted, she was glad. To go away, to escape from all that was so secret and so strange was so much a comfort to her, that she had almost forgotten that she was leaving home at the same time, going out upon a strange and unrealized existence, leaving the friends of her infancy, the house she was born in, all the familiar circumstances of her life, and her father's grave, where he had been laid so lately.

Margaret felt vaguely with her mind that all these farewells ought to have broken her heart, and she shed a few tears because Bell did so, because old John, speechless and lowering like a thunder-cloud, turned his back upon her and could not say good-bye. John had tossed her trunks on to the cart with the rest with absolute violence, as if he would have liked to break them to pieces; his face was dark with woe which wore the semblance of wrath. He turned his back upon her when she went to shake hands with him, and Margaret turned from the door of the old gray house with tears dropping like rain, but oh! for her hard heart! with an unreasonable, unfeeling sensation of relief, glad to get away from Earl's-hall and Rob Glen, and all that might follow. They thought it was perhaps the society of Effie which had "made it so much easier" for her; and Mrs. Bellingham congratulated herself on her own discrimination in having thus pleased Ludovic and consoled Margaret.

Dr. Burnside and his wife, who came to the railway to see the party off, applauded her tenderly, and bade God bless her for a brave girl who was bearing her burden as a Christian ought. Did Randal know better what it was that supported her, and made even the sight of the grave, high up upon the mound, a possible thing to bear? Did he know why it was that she went away almost eagerly, glad to be free? She gave him a wistful, inquiring look, as he stood by himself a little apart, looking at the group with serious eyes. Randal was the last to divine what her real feelings were, but how could Margaret tell this? He thought she was calmed and stilled by the consciousness of a new bond formed, and a new love that was her own, and was grieved for her, feeling all the vexations she must encounter before this love could be acknowledged, and doubting in his heart whether Rob Glen, he who could press his suit at such a moment and keep his secret, was a lover worth acknowledging. But Randal had no right to interfere. He looked at her with pity in his eyes, and thought he understood, and was very sorry, while she, looking at him wistfully, wondered, did not he know?

Thus Margaret went away from her home and her childhood, and from those bonds which she had bound upon herself without understanding them, and which still, without understanding, she was afraid of and uneasy under. Sir Ludovic and his wife left Earl's-hall at the same time to join their children in Edinburgh, and there to make other calculations of all they could, and all they could not, do. Perhaps when they were at a distance, the problem would

seem less difficult. Earl's-hall was left silent and solitary, standing up gray against the light, the old windows wide open, the chambers all empty, nobody stirring but Jeanie, who was putting all things into the order and rigidness of death. Bell, for her part, sat down-stairs in her vaulted room, with her apron thrown over her head; and John had gone out, though it was still morning, "to look at the pitawties," with a lowering brow, but eyes that saw nothing through the mist of unwilling tears.

That very night Rob Glen came back to his seat under the silver fir, and gazed at the vacant house with eager and restless eyes. He was not serene, like his mother, but unhappy and dissatisfied, and with a great doubt as to the efficacy of all that had been done. Margaret had mortified him to the heart, even in giving him her promise. He was a man who had been loved; and to be thus accepted with reluctance gave a stab to his pride which it was hard to bear. And perhaps it was this sentiment which brought him, angry and impatient and mortified, back to the neighborhood of the house from which his new love had just gone away, but where, he could not but recollect, his old love still was. Jeanie had gone about her work all day with that arrow in her heart. She had known very well what was coming, had watched it even as it came, and sadly contemplated the transference to her young mistress of all that had been so dear to herself. She had followed the course of the story almost as distinctly as if she had been present at all their interviews; seeing something, for her turret had glimpses of the wood, and guessing more, for did not Jeanie know? But yet to see them together had been for the moment more than Jeanie could bear. It had seemed an insult to her that Rob should come, leading her successor, to the very house in which she was; and her more charitable certainty that he did not know of her presence there had gone out of her mind in the sharpness of the shock. And when her work was over, Jeanie too went out, with a natural impulse of misery, to the same spot where she had seen them together. "No fear that he'll come here the night," Jeanie said to herself, bitterly; and lo! before the thought had been more than formed in her mind, Rob was by her side. She gave a cry, and sprang from him in anger; but Rob was not the man to let a girl fly from him over whom he had ancient rights of wooing. His countenance was downcast enough before. He put into it a look of contrition and melancholy patience now.

"Jeanie," he said, "will you say nothing, not a word of forgiveness, to an old friend?"

"What can the like of me say that could be pleasant?" said Jeanie; "you're far ower grand a gentleman, Maister Glen, to have anything to say to the like of me."

"You know very well that you are doing me a great deal of injustice," he said, sadly; "but I will not defend myself. If I had but known that you were here—but I did not know."

"I never heard that you took much trouble to ask," said Jeanie; "and wherefore should you? You were aye far above me. There was a time when I was silly, and thought little of that; but I ken better now."

"I don't know that I am above anybody;

there are many people that are above me," he
said, with a sigh, and a look of dreary vacancy
beyond her, which deeply provoked yet interested the girl in spite of herself.

"Ay," she said, "you will feel for other folk
now; you will ken what it means now. But
I've naething to say to you, Mnister Glen, and
I'm wishing ye nae harm. A's lang ended that
ever was between you and me."

"Are you sure of that, Jeanie?" he said.

It was not in Rob's nature to let any one escape from him upon whom he had ever had a
hold.

"Ay, I'm sure of it," she cried; "and you
are but a leer and a deceiver if you dare speak
to me in that voice, after what I've seen with
my ain een — after the way I've seen ye with
Miss Margret! Oh, she's ower good for you,
ower innocent for one that hasna a true heart!
Last night, no further gane, I saw you here
with my bonnie young lady; and now, if I
would let you, that's how you would speak to
me."

"Jeanie," he said, "it's all just that you are
saying; but how do you know how I was led to
it? You could not see that. She came out, in
her trouble, to cry here, and I was here when
she came. Could I see her cry and not try to
comfort her? I don't pretend to be strong, to
be able to resist temptation. I should have
thought of you, but you were not here; I did
not know where you were. And she, poor
child, was in great need of some one to rest
upon, some one to console her. That was how
it came about. You know me. I did not forget you; but she was there, and in want of
some one to be a comfort to her. I am confess-
ing to you like a Catholic to his priest; for all
that you say there is nothing between us now."

"Oh!" she cried, "speak to me no more,
Rob Glen. I canna tell what's ill and what's
well, when you talk and talk, with that voice
that would wile a bird from the tree."

"Why do you find such fault with my voice?"
he said, coming a little nearer. "It may be as
you say, Jeanie, that all is ended; but, at least,
your good heart will do me justice. You were
away, and here was a poor young creature in
sore trouble. Say I've been foolish, say my life
has gone away from me into another's hands;
but do not say that I forgot my Jeanie; that I
never did—that I will never do."

"Oh, dinna speak to me!" cried the girl—
"dinna speak to me! I'm neither your Jeanie,
nor I will not give an ear to anything you can
say."

"Then I will wait till you change your mind,"
he said; and as she turned hastily toward the
house, Rob went with her, gentle as a woman,
respectful, with a sort of deprecation and melancholy softness. Perhaps she was right, he would
allow, with a soft tone of sorrow. Life might
be changed, the die was cast; but still it was
not in Rob's nature to let any one drop. He
talked to her with a tone of studious gentleness
and quiet. "At least we may be friends," he
said.

CHAPTER XXX.

THE party of travellers went to Perth, and
from thence wandered among the hills and
woods, and by the wild and lonely glens, to
which that gate of the Highlands gives an entrance. It was all new to Margaret. In all her
life she had seen nothing more imposing than
the lion crest of Arthur's Seat, as seen across the
stately breadth of the Firth, the low twin heads
of the Lomonds, or, in the far distance among
the mists, the long withdrawing line of the
Grampians. When she saw these misty hills
nearer, when she watched the clouds at play
upon them, and counted the flying shadows, and
shared the instantaneous brightening of the sun-
glints, what wonder that Margaret felt her heart
rise in her breast notwithstanding all the trouble
there. She had not thought it possible that the
world could be so lovely. The weather was fine,
with now and then a rainy day, and the days
were still long, though midsummer was past.

Mrs. Bellingham and Miss Leslie were good
travellers. Given two comfortable places in a
carriage, and weather at all tolerable, and they
were ready to drive anywhere, and to go on
from morning to night. A bag fitted with all
manner of conveniences, a novel, a piece of
knitting, and plenty of shawls, was all they demanded. Even when it rained they could make
themselves very comfortable in the hotels, finding out who everybody was—and did not object
even to walking within limits. And they knew
about everything: which were the best routes,
and how much the carriages ought to cost in
which they preferred travelling; for it did not
suit these ladies to go in coaches or other public
vehicles along with the raskal multitude—and
indeed, as it was still only July, the raskal multitude had as yet scarcely started on its peregri-
nations. As soon as they felt that their crape
was safe under the shelter of large water-proofs
they were happy. Mrs. Bellingham took the
best seat with undaunted composure; but Miss
Leslie thought it necessary to go through a good
many processes of explanation or apology before
she placed herself by her sister's side.

"Oh no! I cannot think of always taking that
place: really, Margaret, you must have it to-
day. You can see the view so much better.
Dearest Jean, do make dear Margaret take my
place. She sat all yesterday with her back to
the horses; and I don't mind, not in the very
least. I would much rather sit with my back to
the horses. I never have been used to monopo-
lize the best place."

"Hold your tongue, Grace, and get in," said
Mrs. Bellingham. "I suppose you mean that
I do—and I think, at my age, it is my place to
have the best seat. You are only wasting our
time, now that we really have a fine day. Now
this is very comfortable. It is the kind of thing
I always enjoy: a decent carriage, and horses
that are not bad—I have seen better, but we
might have a great deal worse—and two nice
girls opposite, and a gentleman at hand whatever happens, and as lovely a drive before us as
heart could desire. We will stop for lunch at
Kenmore, Aubrey; do you know Kenmore? It
is close to Taymouth, which is as beautiful a
place as any you could see. It always reminds
me of Windsor Castle, except that it lies low,

and Windsor is on a hill. We go by the side of Loch Tay, which is a beautiful loch, Margaret; not so pictnresque as some you will see farther west, but beautiful for all that. Now, Grace, the girls have settled themselves, and Aubrey is on the box. Are we to wait for you all day? You always keep us waiting when every one is ready to start."

"It is only because I wanted some one to have this seat," said Miss Grace, anxiously. "I have been this way before, and the dear girls have not; or Aubrey, perhaps, dear Aubrey would rather be here than on the box? It would be much more amusing for you all, dear Jean, than to have me. Oh!" said the trembling lady, as her more energetic sister dragged her in with a grip of her arm, and the door was closed upon her. She kept asking Margaret and Effie all the day to change places with her, and kept the party in a fidget; "for, you see, I have been this way before," she said. It was a bright day, and Loch Tay lay before them, a sheet of light, between pale and golden, its fringe of trees wet with past rain, and big Ben Lawers rising huge into the blue air.

Margaret felt that she had to make an effort to retain the sadness that she had kept round her like a mantle. How could she laugh? how could she let them talk, and chime in with irrestainable reply and remark, when only such a little while ago—not yet a month ago?—she said to herself. But when things had come so far as this, it was not to be supposed that the little veil of natural sentiment could keep her eyes always drooping. Her face began to glow again, to change from white to red, and back into that delicate paleness which was habitual to her. The clouds and the mists cleared away from her brown eyes. The scent of the young birches, the plash of the water on the shore, the soft shower of rain-drops now and then shaken out over their heads by some mischievous breeze as they passed; the atmosphere so heavenly clear, the sun so gay and friendly, beguiled her out of her trouble.

In grief, as in sickness, there is a moment when the burden is sensibly lightened, the bonds relax for the first time. This moment came to Margaret now. She was terrified to feel how light her heart was, and what an involuntary glow of exhilaration had come over her. Nothing had happened to make her glad. She was only rising again, in spite of herself, into the beauty of the common day, into the light and brightness of her youth. And indeed, but for the sense that she ought not to be happy, Margaret might well have felt the well-being of the moment enough for her. The fresh air, and the pleasant progress, and all the beautiful sights around her, were brightened by Effie's bright countenance, full of smiles and delight, and by the other companion on the box, who leaned over them to shower down a flood of comments upon everything — comments which were generally amusing enough, and often witty to Margaret's simple ears. And even the self-contented comfort of Jean, sitting well back in her corner, with her eau-de-cologne, her purse, her little paper-knife, her novel lest the drive should get dull, and Miss Grace's anxious regret to have the best side, and desire that some one would "change seats with her," were full of fun, full of amusement to the inexperienced girl. Nature betray-

ed her into laughter now and then, into smiles between times.

It was only a month yet, not quite a month, since old Sir Ludovic died; but was it Margaret's fault that she was only eighteen? These four weeks had lasted the length of generations. Now they were creeping into their natural length again, into mornings and evenings, soft and swift as the passage of the clouds. And the country was so fresh and sweet, and all the world so amusing in its varied humors. Her heart came back again into renewed life, with a little thrill and tremor of unconscious yet half-guilty pleasure. She could not be churlish enough to close herself up against all the seductions of nature and gentle persuasions of her youth.

Killin was one of the places where the party had arranged to stay, or, rather, where Mrs. Bellingham had arranged to stay. To have one person with a decided will and taste, and all the rest obedient in natural subjection or good-humored ease, is the grand necessity for such an expedition. Mrs. Bellingham fulfilled all these requirements. She knew what she herself liked, and was very well disposed to make other people accept that, as the standard of beauty. And luckily Jean had been on Loch Tay before, and had arbitrarily decided, like a despot of intelligence, that on Loch Tay Killin was the place to stay. She sat up in her carriage with a pleased importance as they drove in through the homely cottages, thatched, and tiled, and mossy, through the genial odor of peat in the blue air, past the swift flowing of the brown golden stream which winds its way into the loch round that island where the dead Campbells have their mansion as lordly as Taymouth, and how much more safe and sweet. Jean sat up in her place with a pleased relaxation of her countenance as the carriage drove round to the inn-door where Steward, her maid, who had gone by the coach with all the boxes of the party, stood in attendance behind the smiling landlord, but heading the homely waiters and chamber-maids. Steward knew her place. To be mistress of a Highland inn would not at all have displeased her; but she knew very well that she was of a different and higher order of being from those smiling Highland maids with their doubtful English, and the anxious waiter who had so many parties to look after, and lost his wits now and then when the coach was crowded. A party taking so many rooms, and not illiberal in their way, though Mrs. Bellingham looked sharply after the bills, gave importance to everybody connected with them.

"You got my letter, Mr. MacGillivray?" said Mrs. Bellingham.

"Ay, my leddy; oh, ay, my leddy; and I hope ye'll find everything to your satisfaction," said the landlord, opening the door with anxious obsequiousness, as if Jean had been the Queen herself, Miss Leslie could not but remark. It was a pleasant moment. The sun was declining westward; the roar of the waterfall above the bridge came fitfully upon the air; the rush of the nearer stream sounded clear and close at hand; the cottage children ran in picturesque little russet groups to gaze at the new-comers. On the other hand, Ben Lawers, clumsy but grand, heaved upward against the sky and cut its arch in two. The trees filled in all the crevices about, and in the distance Glen Dochart glimmered far away, opening up between the hills a golden path into the west.

"Make haste, children," said Mrs. Bellingham, "for we will have to dine at the *table-d'hôte*; and that I know by experience waits for nobody, and a very funny business it is. But it's a great pity we're a month too early, and you'll get no grouse."

"That is a mistake indeed," said Aubrey; "but, after all, we are only a fortnight too early, and the time may come when we shall have better luck."

"And oh, darling Margaret," said Miss Leslie, "I have had such a beautiful view! I am so sorry, I cannot tell you how sorry, I am that neither you nor dear Effie would take my seat!"

It had been a most successful day, with no clang or bustle of railways, but only the horses' measured trot; the roll of the wheels; the flash of the sunshiny loch; the honest Highland sunshine, sweet as heavenly light can be, but never scorching, only kindly warming, cheering, smiling, upon the wayfarer. And now it was very pleasant to see the friendly people at their doors: the Highland maids, happy to please you, with their kind voices and looks of friendly interest; the waiter, bothered to death, poor man, but anxious, too, that you should eat and show an appetite. Nowhere else is there such homely interest in the chance guest. Perhaps the bill is a trifle high: is it a trifle high? Not any higher than in England, though perhaps just a little more than in the big, inhuman Swiss caravansary where all the Cockney world is crowding. There are caravansaries in the Highlands too, but not at Killin. There, still, the maids smile kindly, and cannot bide that you should not be happy; and the waiter (though drawn three ways at the same moment) is troubled if you do not "enjoy your dinner." And the peat smoke rises in aromatic wreaths into the clear blue air, and the river flows golden in the sunshine, but above the bridge tumbles in foaming cataracts; and broad and large, with a homely magnificence, the loch spreads out its waters under the sun or moon.

After the meal, grandly entitled a *table-d'hôte*, to which our party sat down in friendly conjunction with a stranger pair, whom Mrs. Bellingham was very condescending to, and whom it was odd not to know intimately, as they did to each other all the honors of the family dinner, Jean retired to the most comfortable room, where Steward brought her writing things, and her books and knitting. "I will put up my feet a little," she said, "but I advise the rest of you to go out for a walk. You should never lose a fine evening in the Highlands, Aubrey, for you never know what to-morrow may be. I know the place as well as I know my Bible. Go up to the bridge and look at the water-fall, for it is considered very fine; and there is a man, where the boats lie, who sells Scotch pearls; you can tell him to bring them up to show us after you come in again. But go out and take a walk first, and get the good of the fine evening. I will just put up my feet."

"And, dearest Jean, as Aubrey is a kind of cousin—or perhaps it is a kind of nephew—to darling Margaret, don't you think I may stay with you? for it would be very selfish of me,

dear Effie, and dear Margaret, to leave dearest Aunt Jean alone."

The younger people strayed out without waiting for the conclusion of the controversy which was thus opened between the ladies; for Mrs. Bellingham was quite able to dispense with her sister's society, though kind Miss Grace, with many a whisper behind her back, declared that she did not at all mind, but that it would never do to leave dear Jean alone. They went out discussing their own curious relationships with a great deal of natural amusement; for there was no doubt that Effie at seventeen and a half was the unquestionable niece of Margaret, who had not yet arrived at her eighteenth birthday. "And as Miss Leslie is my aunt Grace, it is unquestionable that Miss Margaret Leslie must be my aunt Margaret, most venerable of titles," said Aubrey, taking off his hat and making her a reverential bow. He protested that no Christian name could be added to the title of aunt which could produce so profound an impression of age and awe. Aunt Grace might sound skittish and youthful, and Aunt Jean be no more than matronly; but nothing less than a white-haired grandmother could do justice (they all allowed) to the name of Aunt Margaret. Effie, who was a great novel-reader, reckoned upon her fingers how many there were to be found in books.

Thus discussing, they went lightly along through the soft Highland evening all scented with the peat. The sky was still blue and clear, but in the village street it was almost dark, glimmers of the never-extinguished fires shining cheerfully from the cottage-windows, and the few passengers about looking at each other with puckered eyelids, "as an old tailor looks at the eye of his needle," according to Dante. Some one contemplating them thus, with contracted pupils and projected head, attracted the notice of the girls as they went along, in a little pause after their laughter—some one with a fishing-basket over his shoulder—and came to a sudden pause before them.

"Randal Burnside!" Margaret cried, with a little start. And Randal made a very elaborate explanation as to how he had been under an old engagement to come here to fish, and how much surprised he was to see them arriving whom he had parted from only about ten days before.

"I could not believe my eyes," he said.

Why should not he believe his eyes? Mrs. Bellingham, when told of this explanation, declared indignantly that she had herself told him of her intention to stay a few days at Killin.

"What should he be surprised at?" she asked; but this was a question to which nobody could reply.

He turned with them, as was natural, and they all continued their walk together. There were no lamps nor other worldly vulgarities in Killin; there was no railway even, in those days, invading the silence of the hills—nothing but the cottages, low, homely places, in pleasant tones of gray, and red, and brown, with soft blue pennons of the aromatic peat-reek floating over them, and clouds of white convolvulus threaded up and down their homely walls—and the big shadows of the hills forming the background, or, when you reached higher ground, the silver brightness of the loch. And how quiet it was! the distant

108 THE PRIMROSE PATH.

roar of the wild water only heightening, as with a great abstract voice of nature, taking no note of humanity, the tranquillity and softened dimness of the village. The little group took in the stranger and increased itself, then unconsciously sundered and formed into two and two.

Was it not the merest accident that the two in advance were merry Effie and the gay Englishman, and the two behind Randal and Margaret? Nothing could have been more natural. But Margaret's hesitating laughter was quenched henceforward. She was half ashamed of it, as not befitting her orphanhood and her black dress: and then she could not but think of the other evening, not so very long ago, when Randal's appearance had startled her before: the time when he had not taken any notice, not even taken off his hat. Margaret had never got over the humiliation of that greeting withheld. He had seen her, for she had heard him say so: but then and there, she felt, Randal must have lost his respect for her—Randal who had known her all her life. Even in the excitement of the moment this had given Margaret a wound; and she had not got over it, though that evening had so many recollections that were painful to her. Two or three times now in the soft gloom, as they walked along side by side, she raised her head and gave her a furtive, timid glance, with the words on her lips, "Why did you take no notice that night?" But though her mind was full of it, she had not the courage to ask the question. Effie and Aubrey went on before, their voices sounding softly through the night; but Randal did not say very much, and Margaret nothing at all. The spell of the momentary gayety was broken. A little moisture even stole into her eyes under cover of the night; and yet she was not unhappy, if only she could have had the courage to ask why it was that he "took no notice." They went as far as the bridge and stood there, looking at the torrent as it foamed down, leaping and dashing in white clouds over the rocks.

Margaret had never seen such a scene; even the brawling cataracts of the Tummel and Garry, which had been her first experience of the kind, were not like this. In the midst of the wild commotion a knot of stately firs held themselves aloof, intrenched in a citadel of rock amidst all the rage of the torrents, the wild water raging on every side, but the tree-island, coldly proud, scarcely owning, by a quiver of its leaflets, the influence of so much passion roused. Randal said something to her as he stood by her, but she could not hear a syllable. She looked up at him and shook her head, and he smiled. Somehow he did not look (though it was so dark that she could scarcely see) as if he had lost his respect for her, after all.

"What a row," said Aubrey, as they came away, "for such a cupful of water! If it had been Niagara, there might have been some excuse."

"That is just like the Highlands," said Randal, with that partial offence which always moves a Scotsman when it is suggested by any impertinent stranger that his country is not the equal in every respect of every other country under the sun. "It is not Niagara, and Ben Lawers is not Mont Blanc; but they impose upon us all the same."

"Hush!" said Margaret; "don't talk; one is enough." What she said was not very intelligible, but, indeed, the one voice was enough in the air. It seemed to her to declaim some great poem, some wild chant, like a sublime Ossian. The others went chattering on before, delighted with themselves and their jokes. And when the rush of the wild stream had sunk into a murmur, Margaret herself began again to wonder. "Why did he take no notice that night?"

Next day Randal joined them quite early. It was not a good day for fishing, he said. It was too bright. Besides, if they were only going to stay a day or two, he could make up for his idleness afterward. He had got a boat ready, and was bent on taking the ladies to Finlarig, and afterward upon the loch.

"Of course, we are going to Finlarig, Randal," said Mrs. Bellingham. "Do you think I have never been here before? Good-morning, Duncan Macgregor. Have you any of your pearls to-day? Oh yes! I should like to look at them. The little ones are beautiful, but the big ones are too milky. I like the small size best. You can come up and see us after dinner to-night, and bring them with you. Duncan and I are old friends. Many a pearl I have got from him, and had them set afterward at Sanderson's, in Princes Street. I invented the setting myself, and it was very much admired—just a gold thread twisted round them. Margaret, you don't wear any rings. I must have one made for you. Duncan Macgregor had much better come with us, Randal. I have no confidence in gentlemen rowers. You will go off with the girls as soon as we get to Finlarig, and then where shall we be?"

"You will have your devoted nephew, Aunt Jean. My aunts are the aim and object of my life. I never think of anything else, sleeping or waking. How can you talk of being left alone so long as you have me?"

"I prefer Duncan Macgregor," said Aunt Jean; "and as for your aunts, as you call them, you have only one. And I don't want to see you pushed out of your place by that lad, Randul Burnside," she added, in a whisper. "Just you keep your eyes upon him, Aubrey. I can't think what business he has here."

Mrs. Bellingham's prophecy was so far fulfilled that the young men and the girls did somehow, as is their use and wont, manage to separate themselves from their elder companions, one of whom, at least, had every desire to further this separation. It was Randal who was the cicerone of the party, and who led them through the winding path to that secluded, sheltered palace of peace where the dead Campbells rest. They were not thinking much about the Campbells. Who, indeed, thinks of the silent occupants, be they Pharaohs, be they Highland caterans, of those still dwellings of the dead? The Campbells lie in lordly guardianship of their loch and their trees, with their clan within call, and their castle scarcely out of hearing, and all kinds of Highland bravery—honeysuckles and wild roses in the summer, barberries and rowans in the autumn, flaunting upon the half-ruined wall that surrounds their tomb.

The young people strayed that way—two of them full of talk and laughter, two of them quiet enough. Why it was that Effie and Aubrey fell together it would be difficult (yet not very difficult) to say; but the reason why Margaret stayed her steps for those of Randal was easy enough. She wanted, constantly wanted, to ask him why he took no notice *that* night. For this reason she lingered while the others went on, looking at him now and then with a shy, eager look, which at once puzzled the young man, and filled his heart with a dangerous interest. She wanted to ask him something—what was it she wanted to ask him? Randal was on his guard, he felt. He had been warned effectually enough. Margaret was not for him. Even if he had wanted her (which he did not, he said to himself with a little indignation), was not he forestalled? Had not her heart been caught in its first flight? He might be sorry, but that did not matter much: the deed was done. And he was fully warned, completely forestalled, even if he had wished for anything else. But what was it she wanted to say? Probably, in the innocence of her heart, something about *that* fellow, for whom, poor thing, she must fancy—she who knew nobody, because she loved him—that every one cared.

They came at last to a little sheltered glade close to the little river, with its golden brown water. There was a beautiful barberry growing in a corner, which Margaret had caught sight of. She wanted a branch of it to put in her hat, she said—until she remembered that her hat was covered with crape. But Randal was cutting the scarlet grapes before that evident incongruity had occurred to her. She sat alone upon a bit of the broken wall close by, among ferns and ivy, and watched him.

"Oh," she said, "I am so sorry I have given you the trouble. I forgot that it was crape I was wearing. It is very strange that one should ever be able to forget."

"But you are—by moments."

"Yes; it shows how little one knows. I thought I would die."

"But that could not be," said Randal, kindly. "The world would come to an end very quickly if grief killed; but it does not, even the most terrible."

"And you will think mine was not like that," said Margaret. "But I do not forget him! oh, I do not forget him! only—I do not know how it is—my mind will not keep to one thing. I suppose," she said, with a deep sigh, "it is because I have not very much mind at all."

"Nay, you accuse yourself unjustly," he said, with a half smile; "after the shock of a great event, a great trouble, there comes a time of quiet—"

"Oh!" she said, finding herself, by no doing of hers, brought to the point she desired, and turning to him with a sudden start, "Randal, I would like to tell you something. I thought I should have told them all *that* night when I came in, but I had not the courage."

"What is it?" Randal threw a twig of his barberries into the stream and watched it carried along, tossing on the swift current. She was going to speak to him of her love, the poor child; and his heart revolted against such a confidence. He could not look at her. Girls receive the confidences of men with interest, but it is very seldom indeed that a young man plays the same part to a girl.

"When I came in *that* night you all thought my heart was breaking because I was going away, and I did not dare to say otherwise. But oh, Randal! it was not *that*!"

"I understand." He threw in another branch of the barberries and watched it intently, turning his head away from her. "It was another kind of parting that made you cry; you were thinking of—"

"Oh, I was thinking—how glad, how glad I would be just to get away, only to get away!"

"Margaret!" he turned round and looked at her quickly now. She was not embarrassed nor blushing, as if the words could bear some happier meaning, but quite pale and serious, looking at the water as he had been doing. Though he had known her all her life, he had of late given up calling her by her Christian name. It was the surprise that forced it from his lips.

"It sounds like wickedness," she said, fervently. "I can see that, but I do not mean any ill. I could not help it; things had been so strange. How could I help trembling and crying? All had gone wrong, some way. And oh, I was glad, so glad to get away, to be free! But if I had said so you would all have thought me— I don't know what you would have thought me. But it came into my head that perhaps you guessed my true meaning, and thought it was a lie I was telling, and had no more respect for me."

"Respect for you! That is not the word I would have used, Margaret. I have always—liked you—taken an interest in you ever since you were a little baby. How could I lose what you call respect?"

"But you looked like it, Randal. Why did you pass me in the gloaming and never say a word, nor even nod your head, or take off your hat?"

"Margaret!" he cried, in great confusion, "I —I thought you did not want to be recognized. I—thought you would like to think I had not seen you—I thought—"

"How could I do that?" said Margaret, seriously; "for that could not have been true. I have wondered ever since if you thought me—a —a—bad girl, Randal? Oh! I think I have no heart! I can laugh, though papa has only been gone a month. I—almost— forget sometimes that I am so unhappy; but I am not a bad girl, Randal. You might always take off your hat to me. You need not think shame to speak to me—"

"Margaret, for Heaven's sake! who could have imagined you would take it so? I thought you had some one with you whom you cared for more than any one else, and that you would rather I took no notice. I did not think I had any right to interfere between him and you."

"No," said Margaret, with a deep sigh, "I suppose nobody could do that;" and after a pause she resumed, half smiling—"But you should not look as if you thought shame of your friends, Randal; you should take off your hat, even when a girl is not very wise. I thought you had no respect for me after that night."

Margaret pronounced the word *wise* as if it had been written *wice*, which the reader who is Scotch will be aware is a word with a quite distinct meaning of its own; a girl who is not *wice* means a girl who is wildly silly, without any sense—perhaps with not all her wits about her. What would Sir Ludovic have thought had he heard a speech so outrageously Scotch from his little Peggy? How he would have smiled, how he would have scolded! Randal remembered the old man's amused reproofs; but his heart was too much troubled to permit him to smile. And the inference that lay in Margaret's words was more than his intelligence could fathom. He was thrown into the wildest commotion of curiosity, anxiety, and wonder. Was it possible that there was no love, after all, between her and Rob Glen? or what did her joy in escaping, her sigh at the thought that no one could interfere, mean? He answered her at last in a strain quite confused and wide of the purpose, like a man in a dream.

"If I should ever be able to do anything for you, to be of any use to you, Margaret, will you send for me? will you let me know? Whatever it may be, and wherever I may be," he cried, in his confusion, "if you ever tell me you want me, I will come to you if I am at the end of the world!"

She looked up at him with faint surprise, yet gratitude. "Yes, Randal," she said; "now I know that you have not lost your respect for me. But how should I ever want anything?" she added, with a smile; "there is Jean always to take care of me, you know."

———◆———

CHAPTER XXXI.

MRS. BELLINGHAM did not stay long at Killin. How it came about could never be discovered; but wherever the party went, in whatsoever admirable order they set out, it was discovered on their return that Aubrey was somehow at the side, not of Margaret, but of Effie Leslie. His aunt took him severely to task when this dereliction from all the rules of duty had been made evident by the experience of several successive days. Aubrey did not deny or defy his aunt's lawful authority. "It is all that fellow," he said, "continually poking in before me, wherever we go, with his Margaret, Margaret! as if she belonged to him. I hate these men who have known a nice girl from the time she was *that* high. They are always in the way."

"And do you really allow yourself to be put off your plans so easily—you, Aubrey, a man of the world? If I were you, I would soon let Mr. Randal Burnside find his proper place. Let him take care of Effie. Effie would do for him very well. She is the second daughter, and they are not very rich, and her sister has made but a poorish sort of marriage. Effie might do worse than put up with Randal Burnside. It would be doing them all a good turn if you would be firm, Aubrey, and insist on doing what we all wish."

"Surely," said Aubrey, "nothing can be more easy. I hope I know as well as anybody how to keep a presuming fellow in his right place." But, comforting as this assurance was, the very same thing happened the next day, and Mrs. Bellingham was not only angry, but disturbed by it. She called Aubrey into her room at quite a late hour, when she was sitting in all the sanctity of her dressing-gown. Perhaps

their tempers were a little disturbed by the fact that they were both chilly—he with his walk by the side of the loch to finish a cigar, she in the before-mentioned dressing-gown, which, being but muslin, was a little too light for the latitude of Killin.

"The same thing over again, Aubrey," she said; "always that little flirt of an Effie. I declare I never see you pay the slightest attention to Margaret; and when you know how much all your friends wish you to settle—"

"All right, Aunt Jean," said Aubrey, with a tone of injury. "It is all those girls that will derange the most careful calculations. They are both of a height, they are both all black; it is only when you hear their voices that you can tell which is which: and if one will go off in one direction while you have settled all your plans for the other—"

"Ah, Aubrey, I am afraid it is just the old story," said Mrs. Bellingham, shaking her head; "you like the wrong one the best."

"That is a trifle," said the dutiful nephew; "we were not born to follow our inclinations. The wrong always suits the best, that goes without saying; but I hope I am not quite a fool, and I was not born yesterday. Your Effie may be all very well to chatter with, but what should I do with her? I should not choose to starve for her sake, nor I don't suppose she would for mine. It is Margaret for my money; or perhaps the other way would be more like the fact: it is her money for me. But what can a fellow do with the best intentions, if the other three make a point of thwarting him? The only thing to be done is this: send the little one home, and turn that other man about his business: when there are only two of us, we are bound to be civil to each other," Aubrey said, with fine ease, turning over the bottles on his aunt's toilet-table. Mrs. Bellingham was struck by the thorough-going honesty of this suggestion.

"Well, that sounds very fair, Aubrey," she said. "I would not expect you to say more. And, to be sure, when a girl makes a dead set at you, it is very difficult for a young man to keep quite clear. We must not do anything violent, you know, and it makes me much more comfortable to hear you speak so sensibly. Randal Burnside, of course, will be left behind here, and Effie can go home from Stirling or Glasgow. And as we leave in two days, there will be no great harm done. But after that, my dear boy, I do hope you will not lose your time."

"Trust me for that!" he said. "Do you really use such an antediluvian cosmetic as Kalydor, Aunt Jean—you whom I always believed to be in advance of the age? *Crème de thé* is a great deal better. Without it I could never have made up my mind to face the rude winds of the North. Have a little of mine and try; I am sure you will never use the other again."

"Oh, thank you, Aubrey; but I am very well satisfied with my own," said Mrs. Bellingham, who did not choose that anything belonging to her should be called antediluvian. "It is more refreshing than anything when one has been a long time in the air. Then that is settled, and I shall not have to speak of it again, I hope. But if I were you—a university man and a club man—I would show that I was more than a match for Randal Burnside, who never was at anything but a Scotch college, and can't belong to anything better than one of those places in Princes Street. I would not allow myself to be put out of my way by a provincial. I should be ashamed to give in like that, if I was such a young man as you."

Aubrey shrugged his shoulders, and offered no further defence; and the remaining two days were passed happily enough, Margaret and Randal remaining upon terms of confidential intimacy, without any word on either side to make the situation more plain. *She* felt that she had committed her secret to his trust, and was partially supported in consequence in the bearing of it—and encouraged to forget it, which she did accordingly with a secret ease and relief beyond all words—while he, too, felt that something had been confided to him, something far more serious than she seemed to be aware of; and yet did not know what it was. Thus, while she was perfectly at her ease with him, Randal was not so happy. He could not ask her a question, could not even let her see that he remembered the half-involuntary confidence, yet felt the most eager desire to know fully what it was which had been confided to him. How could he help her, how could he be of use to her if he did not know? This pleasant fiction of being "of use," and the eager prayer he had made to her to call him whenever and wherever she wanted him, was it not the natural protest of honest affection against the premature bond which had forestalled itself, which had no right to have come in the way of the real hero? He did not himself know that this was the origin of his anxiety about Margaret, his strong wish "to be of use." How could he be of use? how interfere between the girl and her lover—he whose only possible standing-ground by Margaret's side would be that of a lover too?

But Randal, though he was very clear-sighted in general, had but a confused vision of things relating to himself, and deluded himself with the idea that he might "be of use," might help her, and do a great deal for her—if he only knew! And he did know that some kind of tie existed between her and Rob Glen, but no more. Whether it was wholly clandestine, as it appeared, whether "the fellow" had secured her to himself under any vow of secrecy, whether anybody belonging to her knew, or suspected, Randal could not tell. And the frankness with which she had admitted himself to some sort of participation in the mystery made it more confusing and bewildering still. He could not put any question to her on the subject, but shrank from the very thought of such an interrogation with a mixture of pain and shame, feeling his own delicacy wounded. That Margaret should have a secret at all was intolerable. He could not bear to be her confidant, to hear her acknowledge anything that marred the simple ideal of her maidenhood; and yet how was he "to be of use," if he did not know?

She, for her part, was greatly relieved by the little snatch of conversation which had conveyed so much. He had not lost his respect for her. He did not "think shame" of her. This was very comforting to Margaret. She had made it all quite clear, she thought, how things had gone wrong, and how it was a relief more than a sorrow to leave her home; and now she could be

quite at her ease with Randal, who *knew*. Having thus spoken of it, too, made the burden of it very much lighter. The thing itself was over for the present; and it must be a long time, a very long time, before she would be forced to return to that matter. Perhaps, some time or other, she might be forced to return to it; but not for such a long, long time.

Thus all seemed easy for the moment, and Margaret thrust her foolishness behind her, and managed to forget. They had two more cheerful days. They took long walks into Glen Dochart, and went out on the loch in the evenings; and Effie sang, who had a pretty voice and had been taught; whereas Margaret had a pretty voice, but had not been taught, and was fired with great ambition. And Aubrey took upon him to make researches into the crockery-ware in the cottages, by way of looking for old china, of which, he assured them, he often "picked up" interesting "bits," at next to no price at all, in the neighborhood of Bellingham Court. It did not answer, however, in Perthshire, and Randal and the two girls being Scotch, had to interfere to rescue him from Janet Campbell, at the post-office, who thought nothing less than that the man was mad, and intended to break her "pigs," which is the genuine name of crockery in Scotland.

All these things amused them mightily, and filled up the days, which were not invariably fine, but checkered by showers and even storms—which latter amused the party as much as anything, since there was a perpetual necessity for consultations of all kinds, and for pilgrimages in twos and threes to the window, and to the door, to see if it was going to be fine. During all this time Mrs. Bellingham persistently labored to control fate, and to pair her young people according to her previous determination. That Randal and Effie should have taken to each other would have been a perfectly reasonable and suitable arrangement, and Jean felt that she could meet her brother and his wife with a pleasant sense of triumph, had she been the means under Providence of arranging so very suitable a match. He was a very pleasant young man, well educated, sufficiently well-born, with a little money and a good profession—what could a girl's parents ask for more? But it is inconceivable how blind such creatures are, how little disposed to see what is best for them. With all the pains that she took to prevent it, the wrong two were always finding themselves in each other's way.

And perhaps it helped this result that Miss Leslie, all unconsciously, and in the finest spirit of self-sacrifice, did everything she could to thwart her sister, and to throw the wrong person in the way. It went so to her heart to see Margaret smiling, as she talked to Randal, that she walked all the way home from the bridge by herself, though it was getting dark, and she was nervous to leave the two to themselves. "They will like their own company better than mine," Miss Leslie said to herself. And when Jean asked sharply what had become of Aubrey, Grace quaked, but did not reply that she had seen him taking Effie down the river in the gleam of compunctious brightness, after the afternoon's rain.

"Dear Jean," she said, "you must not be

8

anxious. I am sure he will be back directly, almost directly."

"Anxious!" cried Mrs. Bellingham. It was hard upon so sensible a woman to have to deal with persons so entirely unreasonable. Then Randal let fall various intimations that he had a great fancy for seeing Loch Katrine again.

"The fishing here is not so good as I expected," he said. "I think I shall go further west."

"I would not do that if I were you," Mrs. Bellingham said, with a very serious face. "I would not be so long away from your good father and mother. Of course you will be going somewhere to shoot after the 12th. So is Aubrey. Ladies have not much chance in comparison with the grouse. And, do you know, I thought them very much *failed*, both of them. They are getting old people, Randal. I am sure you are a good son, and would do anything you can to please them; and I could see that your good mother did not like you to come away for the fishing, though she would not say anything. As for Loch Katrine, I don't think it all likely that we shall be able to make it out."

Randal was at no loss to understand what this meant. He smiled to himself to think how mistaken she was, and how little it really mattered who went or stayed, so far as Margaret was concerned; but, after all, why should he follow Margaret? why should he run the risk of making himself hate Rob Glen, and wonder at his "luck" more than he did now? However, he said to himself, there ought not to be any danger of that. He did not think there was any danger. What danger could there be when there was a clear understanding that some one else was master of the field? But still, he could not suppose that the moment of fate, the tragical moment at which he could be of use to Margaret, was coming now. And why should he insist upon going where he was not wanted? So he yielded and sighed, and took his dismissal, though both the girls protested.

"Oh, why will you go and spoil the party?" cried Effie.

"My dear," said Mrs. Bellingham, "I am afraid there will not be much more of the party, for your papa is going to meet us in Glasgow to take you home."

This threw a cloud over poor little Effie, who went to her own room in tears. Was it over, then, this beautiful holiday? Margaret said good-bye to Randal with a cloudy look between smiles and tears.

"You will never pass me by again as if I was not good enough to be spoken to?" she said, with a little broken laugh; and he once more hurriedly adjured her "if she should ever want anything," "if she should want a friend to stand by her." Margaret smiled, and gave him her hand like a young princess. "But how can I ever want anybody," she said, "when there is Jean?" which was not so satisfactory. He felt more lonely, more dismal, more altogether out of place than there was any reason for, when, finally, Mrs. Bellingham packed her little comforts into the carriage, and Miss Grace entreated everybody to take her place, and the travellers rolled away, waving their hands to him as he stood at the inn door.

It is always a dismal thing to stand at the door of an inn and see the greater part of the party who have been rambling, walking, talking, laughing, and crying together, drive away. Randal felt his heart sink in his breast. To be sure, Margaret Leslie was nothing to him, except a child whom he had known all his life. He stood there and fell a thinking, while the landlord nodded and winked to the waiter, and the maids behind pitied the poor young gentleman. How well he remembered the little motherless baby in her black ribbons, whom his mother had once placed in his astonished arms! He had told Margaret of it only yesterday; but he did not tell her what Mrs. Burnside said. "It will be time enough for you to marry, Randal, when she is old enough to be your wife," the prudent mother had said. She would never be his wife now, nor anybody's who could understand her who was worthy of her. To think of that creature falling to the lot of Rob Glen! The blood rushed to Randal's face, and he clenched his hands unawares; then, coming to himself, seized his fishing-tackle, which had been of so little use, and hurried away.

And Margaret was very quiet all the day after, leaving Effie to respond to Aubrey's witticisms from the box. It had come to be the habit that Effie should reply. Mrs. Bellingham was just as comfortably placed as usual, and had her eau-de-cologne, and her paper-knife, and plenty of shillings in her purse for the Highland tolls, and everything as she liked it; but she was not so amiable as in the earlier part of the journey. For one thing, there was not at all a satisfactory place for luncheon, and the wind was cold, and she had not the kind of large pin she liked to fasten her shawl.

"We are going to have a wet August," she said. "When August is wet, the best thing to do is to get out of Scotland. It is bad enough anywhere, but it is abominable in the Highlands. There are the same sort of looking tourists you find in Chamouni, only poorer, and it is cold, which it is not in Switzerland; at least, it is not always cold in Switzerland. Your papa, Effie, is to meet us in Glasgow on Tuesday, and then I think we shall go South."

Nobody said anything against this sentence. There are days when the wind is more keen than usual, when the rain is wetter, and the mud muddier. This was one of these days. It came down in torrents in the middle of the journey; and before the hood of the carriage could be got up a large piece of Mrs. Bellingham's crape on the side next the wind had been soaked and ruined forever. This, her sister thought, was her own fault, in that she had incautiously thrown aside her water-proof; but she herself held it to be Effie's, who had thrown a shawl over that water-proof, "carefully concealing it," the aggrieved lady said. To have your crape ruined when you have just gone into mourning is a grievance enough to upset any lady's temper, and it cannot be said that any of the party enjoyed the drive on this ill-fated day.

After this the pleasure of the expedition grew less and less. Sir Ludovic, who met the party in Glasgow, took an opportunity to take Margaret aside, and talked to her with a grave face.

"I hope you will see how wrong you are, Margaret," he said, "about that lad. I have seen him, and he is as firm as a rock because of your encouragement. Do you think it is a right thing for a young girl like you to give such a man encouragement, and dispose of yourself without the knowledge of one of your friends? I told him I would never give my consent; but he as good as said he did not care a pin for my consent; that he had got yours, and that was all he wanted. But there is one thing I must insist upon, Margaret, and that is that you will hold no clandestine intercourse with him. It would not be —delicate, and it would not be honorable. It is only to save you that I don't tell Jean. Jean would be neither to hold nor to bind. I don't know what Jean might not do; but unless you will promise me that there shall be no correspondence, it is my duty to tell Jean."

"I don't wish to have any correspondence," said Margaret, drooping her head, with a burning blush. Oh, if they would but let her forget it all! But this was what they would not do.

"If you will give me your promise to that "— he said; and in his pleasure at what seemed to him his little sister's dutifulness, Sir Ludovic took her hand into his and gave a fatherly kiss on her forehead; all which his sisters contemplated with wondering eyes.

"Dear Ludovic, how kind you are to darling Margaret!" cried Miss Grace, running to him and bestowing a kiss of her own by way of thanks.

"I see no need for all this kissing," said Mrs. Bellingham; "what is the meaning of it? I hope, Ludovic, you are not encouraging Margaret to make you her confessor, and to have secrets and mysteries from Grace and me, who are her natural guardians and her best friends!"

CHAPTER XXXII.

It was on a bright day in the end of August that Margaret Leslie arrived at the Grange, which was her own house, her mother's birthplace, and her future home. They had been rather more than a month on the way, and had last come from Mrs. Bellingham's house, which was in the neighborhood of Bellingham Court— not the great house of her district, but very near and closely related to that reigning mansion. Mrs. Bellingham had not been without grievances in her life. Indeed, had one of two events happened which she had every reason to expect would happen, her present position would have been different and much more satisfactory. Had her husband lived only a year longer, she would have been Lady Bellingham of the Court, the foremost lady in the county; and had she been the mother of a son, that son would have been Sir Somebody, and his mother would still have been — during his inevitably long minority at least — the mistress of the great house. But these two natural events did not happen. Jean was the mother of neither son nor daughter, and her husband, the eldest son—old Sir Anthony's heir—had cheated her effectually out of all share in the splendors of the house—which splendors, indeed, had been much more attractive than himself—by dying most spitefully a year before his father. If it had been a year after, she would not have minded so much. But as it was, there was nothing for it but to retire to the Dower House, and to see her next sister-in-law,

with whom she had not been on very affectionate terms, become Lady Bellingham, and enter into possession of everything. It may be supposed that this was no slight trial; but Jean, every one allowed, had behaved like a heroine. In the moment of deep and real affliction which followed old Sir Anthony's death, she had taken the situation under review, and considered it very deeply. The first suggestion naturally had been that she should return home, or at least settle in the neighborhood of her father's house. But Jean reflected that her father was not only old but poor, that his house was very limited in accommodation, and that when her present gloom and crape were over, there was neither amusement nor occupation to be had at Earl's-hall, such as might oil the wheels of life and enable everything to go smoothly. Fife was not lively, nor was Earl's-hall attractive; whereas in the neighborhood of the Court, though it would be hard to see another woman reigning there, there was always likely to be something going on, and the family was of the first consequence in the district, not shabby and worn-out like the poor Leslies. Having come to this decision, Mrs. Bellingham had taken her measures accordingly. She had thrown off at once the natural air of grievance which everybody had excused in her after such disappointments. Instead of troubling the new Lady Bellingham in her arrangements, she had thrown herself heartily into the work, and aided her in every way in her power. "I don't mean to say that it is not a disappointment," she said; "I hoped, of course—I don't deny it—to be mistress here myself. I have worked for it: through all Sir Anthony's illness, I am sure, I never was less attentive to him because I knew I should be turned out as soon as he was released from his sufferings."

"No, I am sure you never were," said the new Sir Anthony, warmly.

"And I should have liked to be my lady, I don't deny it. If my poor Aubrey had lived, I should have enjoyed the position quite as much as you I hope will enjoy it, my dear."

"Oh, enjoy it! think of the responsibility!" cried the new Lady Bellingham.

"I should not have minded the responsibility; but Providence has settled otherwise—you have it, and I have not. But don't think I am going to be disagreeable on that account. I will move into the Dower House as soon as you please, and I will do everything I can to help you in settling down. I know how to struggle for my rights when it is necessary," Mrs. Bellingham had said, not without a warning glance at Sir Anthony, "but, thank Heaven, I also know how to submit."

In this spirit she had begun her life, and with the same noble meaning had lived many years a kind of secondary star in the Bellingham firmament, shining independently, but never in opposition. A close connection with the Court made the Dower House important, and she kept up that connection. She was always serviceable, giving as well as receiving, maintaining her own position, even while she magnified it by that of the great house; and, in short, nothing, all her friends allowed, could be more perfect than her behavior, which was everything a sister's ought to be, and everything that could be desired in an aunt. The Dower House was a pretty house, and Mrs. Bellingham's jointure was sufficient to permit her a comfortable little carriage, a nice little establishment, with the means of giving excellent dinners when she chose, and enjoying life in a dignified and most comfortable way. On the other hand, she dined very often at the Court, and had the use of their superfluous luxuries, and a share in everything that was going on, which increased at once her comfort and her consequence. This was the position in which she stood to her relations and neighbors. She felt now that she was about to repay them a hundred-fold for all the little advantages they had thrown in her way by providing for Aubrey, who was her husband's godson, and the least successful member of the family. Aubrey was very accomplished, very charming, very idle. He could not be got to do anything, except make himself agreeable, and he had never even done that to any purpose. When Mrs. Bellingham heard that her father was dying, her first thought was of this. But she was a woman who could keep her own counsel. She sent Aubrey a check, and directions for his route: she threw facilities in his way, of which he did not, perhaps, quite make the use she expected; but still things had mended in the latter part of their journey, and Margaret and he had been very good friends when they parted, and all was well in train in pursuit of this purpose. Mrs. Bellingham carried her young sister to the Dower House, and showed her the greatness of the Court. It was vacant for the moment, but its imposing size and splendor filled Margaret with admiration.

"All this would have been mine, Margaret, if my poor dear Aubrey had lived. You may think what a grief it was to me to lose him," said Jean, with a sigh. "And that is why I take such deep interest in Aubrey, who was his godson, you know. This is Aubrey's home."

"Dearest Jean! how much more we ought to think of her, and try to please her, darling Margaret," said Miss Leslie; "when we see how much she has lost."

And when they had gone over all the empty stately rooms, and looked at all the portraits—docile Margaret receiving the tale of family grandeur with unquestioning assent—and had made acquaintance with the lesser world of the Dower House, its paddock, its gardens, its conservatory, all the little comforts and elegancies which were so dear to the sisters, it was time to set out for the Grange, that Margaret might see her own house. It had been settled that Mrs. Bellingham and Miss Leslie should go there with her to take possession of it, and to see what changes would require to be made, to fit it for occupation—and that they were to remain with her there as long as the fine weather lasted, going back to the Dower House for winter and Christmas. The Grange lay in another county, and was some distance from the house of the Bellingham's, with which it communicated only by a very circuitous route. In old days, when the ladies would have been obliged to post, it would have taken days instead of hours to get to it, and yet it would have proved a nearer way. They had to go to the nearest town and then take a train going north, in order to find at the junction a train going south, in which they could proceed to the end of their journey. And what between the changes, and the waiting here and there, this journey occupied most part of the day. It was dark when they drove from the little town where the railway ended, through a succession of dim roads and lanes and under overshadowing trees that made the twilight dimness greater, to the Grange: which presented no recognizable feature, but was merely a large shadow in the gloom surrounded by shadows less solid—ghosts of waving trees and high hedge-rows. There was a woman visible at the little lodge, who came out and opened the gate and courtesied to the strangers, leaving her cottage door open and showing a cheerful glow of fire-light, and a tiny little girl of three or four years old, standing against the light and gazing at the carriage; but this was the only gleam of cheerfulness that dwelt in Margaret's mind. The child's face was scarcely visible, but its little sturdy figure against the fire-light, with two small feet well apart, and the most wondering curiosity in its entire pose, made the forlorn little mistress of the place smile as she went through those gates which led to her home. After this there was a long avenue to drive through, with great trees overshadowing the carriage, and tossing their branches about in the night wind. It had been a very hot day, and the breeze which had sprung up was very grateful, but the moaning it made in the branches was very melancholy, and affected poor Margaret's imagination. "How the wind soughs," she said, with full use of the dreary guttural. She was sitting in the front seat of the cab as it jolted along amidst all those waving shadows, and Margaret felt very sad, she did not know why. She had been curious about her sister's house, and interested, and had liked the novelty and perpetual change; but she did not feel any curiosity, nothing but sadness, in coming to this place, which was her own, though there was nobody here to welcome her. How the wind soughed! no other word could express so well the wild moan and wailing, which is an exaggeration by nature of the sound which the French call tears in the voice. It went to Margaret's heart: the tears came into her voice, too, and filled her eyes in the darkness. All was melancholy in this home-coming to nothing but darkness and the unknown — the wind tossing about the branches and complaining to the night, the sound of water somewhere, complaining too, with a feeble tinkle—the sky invisible, except in a speck here and there, just light enough to show how the branches were tossing overhead. The young traveller drooped her head in her corner, and felt her courage and her heart fail.

"Margaret," said Jean's voice out of the darkness, from the other side of the carriage, "you must learn to remember now that you are not a Scotch country girl in Fife, but an English young lady with a character to keep up—a landed proprietor. Don't talk that vulgar Scotch. If you use such language here nobody will understand you; and they will think you a girl without any education, which would be most painful for all your relatives, and a slur upon poor papa's memory. Therefore remember, no Scotch."

This altogether completed Margaret's downfall. The gloom, the sobbing wind, the contrast between this home-coming and all that is ordinarily implied in the word, were enough in themselves to overwhelm so young a creature, still so short a way removed from the first grief of her life; but the reproof was of a kind which made the contrast still more poignant. Nothing in all his intercourse with his favorite child had been so tender or so characteristic as Sir Ludovic's soft, laughing animadversions upon that very point—"My little Peggy, you must not be so Scotch!" How often had he said it, his face lighted up with tenderest laughter, his reproof more sweet than other people's praise. But how different it sounded when Jean said it! Something came climbing into Margaret's throat and choked her. When the carriage stopped with a jar and a crash, as it did at that moment at the scarcely discernible door, she could not wait for its opening, or till the coachman should scramble from his perch, but flung the carriage door open, and jumped out, eager for movement of any kind; her forehead throbbing with pain over her eyebrows, the sob in her throat, and a sudden gush of salt-water, hot and bitter, blinding her eyes. What could be more unlucky than to alight thus before the closed door and not be able to see it for tears? It opened, however, while Margaret began to help Steward, who had groped her way from the box, to get out the innumerable small articles with which the cab was crowded. The country girl, who appeared at the door with a candle protected by a long glass shade in her hand, did not imagine for a moment that the slim creature not so big as herself, with the armful of cloaks and shawls, was her mistress. She addressed herself to the ladies in the carriage, as was natural.

"If you please, ma'am," she said, making a courtesy, "Miss Parker have gone to bed with a bad headache; but please there's tea in the parlor, and all your rooms is ready."

Margaret, however, scarcely saw the dark wainscoted room into which she followed her sisters, hearing their voices and exclamations as in a dream. It only seemed to Margaret to look very dark, very cold, with its gleams of reflections. Her little white-panelled room at home was far more cheerful than this dark place. She heard them say it was lovely! perfect! in such good keeping! without paying any attention. It was not in keeping with Margaret. In all her life she had never felt such a poor little melancholy stranger, such a desolate childish atom in an unknown world, as during this first hour in the house which belonged to her, the place where she was absolute mistress.

Finding that there was nothing to be made of her, that she would neither eat the plentiful fare on the table, nor admire the china in the great open cupboards, nor make herself amiable in any way, Mrs. Bellingham gave her a cup of warm tea and sent her to bed; where Steward, with a little pity, deferring her mistress's unpacking, benevolently followed to help her to undress. They had put her into a large, low, many-latticed room, with that mixture in it of venerable mansion and homely cottage which is the dream of such rural houses; but in the darkness made visible by two poor candles, even that was little more cheerful than the dark parlor with its wainscot. At Earl's-hall, even in August, there might have been a little friendly fire to make a stranger at home; but in "the South—!" How many a pang of cold have we all supported in much warmer latitudes than England, for very shame because of "the South!"

Naturally, however, Margaret could not sleep,

though she was glad to be alone. She kept her candle lighted, to bear her company with something of a child's dread of the darkness, and lay thinking with eyes preternaturally awake, now that the tears had been all wept out. She thought of everything—of Earl's-hall, and the rhythm of the pines which were not like that rainy melancholy sough, and of those moments in the wood when she had gone out with her eyes just so hot with tears unshed, and just such a fiery throbbing of pain in her forehead, and choking in her throat. And oh, how kind he had been! he had not thought of himself, but only of comforting her. How he had drawn her to him, made her lean upon him, taken off the weight of her sorrow. How hard-hearted she had been to poor Rob, never thinking of him all these days, glad to escape from the thought of him. And he had been so kind! A great compunction came into her mind. How much he had been mingled in the twist of her life at that time which of all other times had been the most momentous in it! and how was it possible that when that crisis was over her very fancy should have so fled from him, her thoughts thrust him away? Poor Rob! and he had been so kind! Margaret begged his pardon in her heart with great self-reproach, but it did not occur to her to make him any amends. She had no desire to call him back to her, to see him again, to write to him. Oh no! she drew her breath hard, with a sudden panic: why should she write to him? It was not necessary. She could not write at all a nice letter such as would be a pleasure to any one. But the thought seemed to catch her very breath, her heart began to thump again, and her brow to burn and throb.

"Are you asleep, dear Margaret?" said Grace, coming in. "I just ran up-stairs for a moment to see. Dearest Jean is going over the rooms, to see what sort of rooms they are—not that we can see very much at night; and, of course, darling Margaret, I should like much better, and so would dear Jean, to wait till you were with us yourself; and if you would like me to stay with you, I would much rather stay. I shouldn't at all mind giving it up. So far as one can see, it is the dearest old place, so old-fashioned! and such china, and old armor in the hall!—real armor, just as delightful as what you see in Wardour Street. Dear Jean is so pleased. Now do go to sleep, darling Margaret, go to sleep. The wainscot parlor is the dearest old room, just like a picture. I am to go out and join dear Jean on the stairs when I hear her coming up. She is talking to Steward about unpacking, for dear Jean is very particular about her unpacking. Are you asleep, darling?—not yet? but you must really go to sleep, and be quite fresh for to-morrow. That is right, shut your eyes, and I will shade the candle; or perhaps it would be better to have a night-light; I think I must try to get you a night-light. There is dear Jean coming up the stairs. She enjoys anything like this. That is her voice coming up. You can always hear dear Jean's voice, walking about a house. At the Dower House, when I am in my room, I always hear her at night starting to see that all the doors and windows are safe. She begins with the scullery and goes everywhere. Dear Jean is energetic to a fault. She does not mind what trouble she takes. Now you are asleep, darling Margaret, quite fast: hush — hush!" said Miss Grace, patting her shoulder softly. It was not a very sensible proceeding, but it soothed Margaret. She turned round her cheek, still wet with tears, with a soft laugh, which was half derision and half pleasure.

"I am fast asleep; now run, Grace, run, or Jean will scold you."

"Oh, it is not that I am afraid! but really, really if you are going to sleep, and don't want me to stay — I will stay in a moment if you would like it, darling Margaret; but perhaps I should only keep you from sleeping, and dear Jean—"

"Where has she run to now?" they could hear Jean's voice saying at a distance, and Miss Grace gave her young sister a hasty kiss and hurried away. Margaret lay still and listened for a long time while Jean's voice perambulated the house, going everywhere. It gave a new sort of brisk activity to the dark and cold place. Up and down and about the passages went the high-pitched tones, commenting on everything. It was seldom that Margaret could make out what they said. But the sound made a cheer and comfort, a sense of society and protection. By-and-by she got drowsy with those cheerful echoes in her ears, and dropped at last into the deep sleep of youth, with a sense of this peaceful patrolling all about her, the darkness lighted by gleams of the candles they carried, and by Jean's voice.

And in the morning what a flood of sunshine filled the room! lavish, extravagant sunshine pouring in, as if it had nothing else to do; which indeed was pretty nearly the case, as all the harvest was housed about the Grange, and there was not much, except light matters of fruit, for that magnificent sun to do, nothing but to ripen the peaches on the walls and the apples on the trees, and wake for a joke, with a blaze and illumination which might have done for a king, a little bit of a slim girl in the low-roofed chamber with its many windows. Margaret woke all in a moment, as you wake with a start when some one stands and looks at you fixedly, penetrating the strongest bond of drowsiness. She sprang up, her mind already full of excitement as she recollected where she was: in the Grange, in her own house! a curious thrill of pleasure, and wonder, and eager curiosity came over her. She got up and dressed hastily in her eagerness to see her surroundings.

From her windows she looked out upon nothing but trees, a walled garden on one side, a little park on the other, a glimpse of a small stream with a little wooden bridge over it, and trees, and more trees as far as the eye could go. Her eye went as far as eye could go in that unconscious appeal for something to rest upon which is instinctively made by all who are accustomed to hills; but there was no blue line upon the horizon, no undulation to relieve her. The only inequality was in the trees, which were some lower and some more lofty—in tufts of rich foliage everywhere, shading the landscape like a delicate drawing. Though it would not be September till next day, yet there were already traces here and there that autumn had tinted the woods with that "fiery finger." It was nothing more than a touch; but it brightened the picture. How different from the parched elms and oaks

all bare with the wind, and the dark unchanging firs in the Earl's-hall woods!

The house was still asleep when she stole downstairs, half afraid of herself, down the oak staircase, with its heavy balustrade. She was the only thing waking in the silent house, which still was so full of living, waking sunshine. She seemed to herself to be the last survivor — the only inhabitant. Timorously she stole down, finding shutters at all the windows, bolts at all the doors. At Earl's-hall who ever dreamed of a bolt or a bar! The door was "snecked" when John thought of it, but often enough was left on the latch, so that any one might have come in; but very different were the precautions here. She stole about on tiptoe, peeping here and there, feeling herself an intruder, totally unable to believe that all this was hers; and very much frightened by the noise she made, undid the heavy fastenings and opened the great door, which creaked and clanged as if calling for help against some invader.

The dew was still sparkling on the flowers when she issued forth into the fresh air of the morning, doubly refreshed with last night's showers. The birds were singing, nations and tribes of them, in every tree. They made such a din round her as she stepped out that she could scarcely hear herself thinking. Instinctively Margaret ran down to the little brook, which she called (to herself) the burn. And there, looking back, she stood entranced with a novel delight. She had never before seen anything like it. A great old rambling simple-minded English house, of old brick with a bloom on it, and touches of lichen, golden and gray: covered with verdure, nothing new or petty; the very honeysuckles grown into huge trees, forests of the simplest white clematis, the traveller's joy, with its wild wreaths and sweet clusters of flowers, roses in their second bloom mounting up to the old chimneys, which had retreated into great bushes of ivy; and everywhere through a hundred folds and wreaths of green — everywhere the mellow redness of the old house itself peeping through. Margaret clasped her hands in delight. The landscape was nothing but trees, and had little interest for her; but the house! It was itself like a great flower, all warm and strong. And this was hers! She could not believe it. She stood rapt, and gazed at the perfect place — a mass of flowers and leafage, and bloomy old walls. It was a poem in homely red and brown, an autumnal sonnet. And this was hers! She could not believe it—it was too beautiful to be true.

CHAPTER XXXIII.

AFTER this there ensued a moment of great quiet and pleasant domestic life. Miss Parker, who was the house-keeper, was a very legitimate member of the class which nobody had then thought of calling Lady-help, but which flourished in the shadow and protection of a family as Poor Relation. She was a distant cousin of Margaret's mother, who, having no money and no talents of any serviceable sort, had been kindly provided for in this very natural domestic office; and the good woman took a great deal of interest in Margaret, and would not have at all disliked to inspire her with rebellion, and persuade her to make a stand for "her own place" in her own house. That the other family, the other side of the house, should be regnant at the Grange, making Margaret appear like the daughter rather than the mistress, offended her in every point; but as she was not a wicked woman, and Margaret not a rebellious girl, these little intentions of malice came to nothing, and Jean commenced an unquestioned and on the whole beneficent sway with little resistance. As for Margaret herself, the novelty of everything filled her life with fresh springs of enjoyment, and gave her a genuine new beginning, not counter to the natural, nor in any way antagonistic, but yet genuinely novel, fresh, and unconnected with any painful or disturbing recollection.

The soft unlikeness of the leafy English landscape round, to all she had been used to, was not more marked than the other differences of her life. When she went along the rural road the little girls courtesied to her, and so did the women at the cottage-doors; they stood obsequious in their own houses, when she went to see them, as if she had been the Queen; not like the cottagers about Earl's-hall, to whom she was only Miss Margaret, who courtesied to nobody, and who were more likely to offer the little girl "a piece" or a "drink of milk" than to take the surreptitious shillings which Margaret at the Grange was so delighted to find herself able to give. "But they will be affronted!" she said, in horror, when this liberality was first suggested to her; such a difference was there between Fife and "the South." Then, within reach, there lay a beautiful little church, in which there were monuments and memorial marbles without number to the Sedleys, the family of her mother, the owners of the Grange, and where an anxious new incumbent had established daily service, to which he was very anxious the Leslies at the Grange should come by way of setting a good example. To this admirable man, who thought that within the four seas there was no salvation except in the Anglican Communion, Margaret unguardedly avowed, knowing no harm in it, that she had been brought up in the Church of Scotland, and was not very familiar with the prayer-book. Oh, what daggers Jean looked at her, poor Margaret not knowing why! Mrs. Bellingham made haste to explain.

"My father was old-fashioned, Mr. St. John, and never would give up the old kirk. I think he thought it was right to go, to countenance the common people. I always say it is a disgrace, that it is they who have the parish churches in Scotland, just the set of people who are dissenters here; but I assure you all the gentry go to the English Church."

Mr. St. John, though he was a little appalled by that generalization, and did not like to learn that "the common people" were dissenters, or that any church but the Anglican could be called "old," yet nevertheless was not so shocked as he might have been, thinking, good man, that the common people in Fife probably spoke Gaelic, and that this was the reason why they had their service separate from the gentry. He began immediately to talk to Margaret about the beauty and pathos of Celtic music, which bewildered her extremely, for naturally Margaret Leslie, who had scarcely ever been out of the East

Neuk till her father's death, had never heard a word of Gaelic in her life.

And now at last Bell's fondest desires were carried out. The little town which was near, and which the lessening limits of this history forbid us to touch upon, was a cathedral town full of music and with many educational advantages; for there were numerous schools in the neighborhood, and masters came from town to supply the demand two or three times a week. Margaret began to play upon the "piany," as Bell had always longed to have her do, and to speak French. We cannot assert that she made very much progress in the former accomplishment with her untrained fingers and brief patience; but she had a pretty voice and learned to sing, which is perhaps a rarer gift, though it cannot be denied that she abused this privilege and went about the house and the garden, and even the park, singing at the top of her voice, till her sisters were provoked into expostulation. "What is the use of teaching you," Jean cried, "when you go singing, singing—skirling they would call it in Fife—straining all your high notes? When I was a girl like you, I was never allowed to open my mouth except for practising, and when there was an occasion for it. It is all gone now, but I assure you when I was twenty I was considered to have a very pretty voice. I wish yours may ever be as good. It will not be so long if you go straining it in this way. Do you think the birds want to hear you singing?" cried Mrs. Bellingham, with scorn.

"Oh, dearest Jean! but dear Margaret has much more of a voice than we ever had. We used to sing duets—"

"Yes, Grace had a little chirp of a second—just what you will come to, Margaret," said Mrs. Bellingham, "if you go on as you are doing, straining all your high tones."

As for the French, they found fault with her pronunciation, which was natural enough; but perhaps it was not so natural that Mrs. Bellingham should find fault with the irreproachable accent of Monsieur Dubois, a Parisian, pur sang, who had taught princesses in his day. "No, Margaret, my dear; you may go on with him, for any kind of French is better than none, when you are so far behind with your education. But I am sure he is taking all these good people in with his fine certificates and testimonials. His French cannot be good, for I don't understand a word he says!" Thus the autumn went on: the trees about the Grange got aglow, and began to blaze with glorious colors, and Margaret with her crape getting shabby (crape gets shabby so soon, heaven be praised!) ran about the house, the park, the country roads, and the village, scolded, petted, taken care of, watched over, teased and worried, and made much of, as she had never been before. She had been the child at Earl's-hall, whose innocent faults everybody had smiled at, whose innocent virtues had met the same fate, who was indeed the spring of everybody's happiness, the most cherished, the most beloved—but yet, so to speak, of no importance at all. Here it was different; here everything hinged on Margaret. Jean, though she was a despot, insisted loudly on the fact that she was but a despot-regent, and Margaret's name was put to everything, and Margaret's supremacy upheld, though Margaret herself was scolded.

What difference it might have made in this state of affairs, had little Margaret, Sir Ludovic's orphan child, been dependent upon her sisters, as, but for that mother of hers of whom Margaret knew nothing, she well might have been, it would be impossible to say. They would have done her "every justice;" they would have taught her to sing and scolded her for singing; they would have called in Monsieur Dubois, and then declared his French could not be good; all these things would have happened all the same, and they would have meddled with and dictated to, and teased, and tried, their little sister. But whether the process would have been as bearable as it was under the present circumstances, who can tell? The dependent might have felt that insupportable which tempted the heiress into laughter, and disclosed a fund of mirth within which she did not know she possessed.

One thing, however, Jean would not have done had Margaret been penniless, which she did for Margaret as the young lady of the Grange. She certainly would not have invited Aubrey, after his return from Scotland, to come and see the new horse that had been bought for Margaret, and to superintend her instructions in that kind. The girl had ridden at home, cantering about the country, all unattended, on a gray pony, in a gray garment, which bore but a faint resemblance to the pretty habit in which she was now clothed; but she had never mounted anything like the prancing steed which was now to be called hers. The sisters were a great deal too careful of her to allow this fiery steed to be mounted until after Margaret and the horse had received all kinds of preparation for the conjunction; but when the ladies came out to superintend the start, and watched while Aubrey, newly arrived, put the slim light creature upon her horse, Jean and Grace felt a movement of pride in her, which made the more emotional sister cry, and swelled Mrs. Bellingham's bosom with triumph. "Take care of her," she said to her nephew with a meaning glance, "for you will not find many like her." "I will take care," said Aubrey, returning the look. This Mrs. Bellingham would not have done had Margaret been only her little sister without any fortune, instead of the young lady of the Grange.

It was a very pleasant ride, and it was so different from all her former exercises of the kind that it became one of those points in Margaret's life which tell like milestones when one looks back. She did not talk very much after the first delighted outbreak of pleasure; but in her heart went back to the stage of the gray pony, and with a startled sense of the change in everything round her, contemplated herself. What change had passed upon her? Was it only that she was a little taller, a little older, transplanted into new surroundings, separated altogether by death and distance from the group of old people who had been all her world? Not altogether that: there were other changes too important to be fully fathomed during a ride through the green lanes, and under the falling leaves. She rode along, hearing vaguely what Aubrey said to her, making only what response was necessary, wondering over this being who was, yet was not, herself. She had forgotten all about herself so far as that was possible in the novelty of this new chapter of her career. She had lived only from day to day,

from moment to moment, not asking herself what she was doing, how she was changing; and lo she was changed. She found it out all in a moment. It bewildered and turned her head, and made her so giddy, that her companion thought she had taken a panic and was going to fall. He started and put out his hand to hold her. "Oh, it is nothing," Margaret said; "it is over now; it was all so strange." "What was strange? You are ill, you are giddy, you have got nervous." "Yes, I am giddy; but neither ill nor nervous. I am giddy to think—oh, how strange it is! Do you remember, Mr. Aubrey, when we were in the Highlands in August?" "Nearly three months ago. Indeed, I remember very well. Do you think it is likely I should forget?" "Oh, I don't suppose it was much to you," said Margaret, with an abstraction of tone which prevented him, though very willing, from accepting this as provocative of something like flirtation. "It was myself that I was thinking of, and it made me giddy. Since that time I am quite different. Since then I have grown up." "I don't see very much difference," said Aubrey, contemplating her with those pleased looks of unspoken admiration which he knew did not in general afford an ungrateful mode of homage. "Oh! perhaps I have not grown much taller; but this is more than tallness. Do you remember Earl's-hall, Mr. Aubrey? It is not really, is it, so very far away?" "I should not say so—about fifteen or sixteen hours' journey, if the railway went straight, without that horrid interval of the Firth." "Oh, that was not what I was meaning!" said Margaret, turning her head away a little coldly. And though he went on talking, she did not pay much attention. She came home with dreamy eyes, and suffered him to lift her off her horse, and went straight up to her room, leaving him. They had not ridden quite so far as they intended, and the ladies had not got home from their drive.

As Margaret went up-stairs, carrying her train over her arm, she met Miss Parker, her poor relation, on the stairs, who gave a jump at the sight of her, and uttered a cry. "Oh, my dear, I thought you were a ghost!" she said. "Why should I be a ghost? I don't feel like a ghost. Come in and tell me," said Margaret, opening the door of her room. Miss Parker had palpitations, and this was quite enough to bring one of them on. "I never thought you were like your poor mamma before," cried the house-keeper in her agitation, "not a bit like. You are just like the Leslies, not her features at all; but in that habit, and in the very same hat and feathers!" Margaret took off her hat at these words, and Miss Parker breathed a little more freely. "Ah, that is better, that is not so startling. You were as like her, as like her—" "Why should not I be like her? Poor mamma, it is hard upon her having nothing but me to leave in the world, that I should be so unkind as not to be like her," said Margaret, musing, half thinking through the midst of this conversation how strange it was that Earl's-hall should seem so very far away.

"I remember her as well as if it were yesterday," said Miss Parker, "coming up that very stair after her last ride with—oh, I should not speak of him to you! It was before she had ever seen Sir Ludovic, your papa."

"Her last ride with—whom?" Margaret's cheeks grew crimson. Somehow it seemed to be half herself about whom she was hearing—herself in her mother.

"Oh, my dear! I don't know if I ought to tell you all that story. They were a sort of cousins, as I was to them both. He had no money, poor fellow; but otherwise so suitable! just of an age, brought up much the same—and she was an heiress, if he had nothing. They tried to put it into her head that he was not good enough for her. And then they put it into his head (they succeeded there) that a man ought not to owe his living to his wife. So he would go away, let her say what she pleased. Oh, I remember that night when they took their last ride together. She came up-stairs and met me in her riding-habit, in just such a hat and feathers, and her face pale with thinking, like yours, my dear. She changed color, too, like you (ah, there it goes!), all in a moment changing from white to red."

"And what happened," cried Margaret, breathless.

"Well, my dear, nothing more than this happened— He went away. He went to India with his regiment; he thought he might get on there, perhaps, and get his promotion, and come back for her (she was not of age then). But he never came back, poor fellow—he died in less than a year."

"And she—she?" Margaret became breathless with anxiety and interest. She had not known her mother had any story; and how strange it was—half as if it might be herself!

"She felt it very much, my dear. She put on mourning for him—indeed, she had to do that, for he was her cousin. Memorial windows were just coming into fashion, and she put up a window to his memory in the church. Well, then! after a while, she went to Scotland, and met with Sir Ludovic. He was not young, but he was a most striking-looking gentleman—and—well, I need not tell you any more. You know, as well as I can tell you, that *he* was your papa."

"Poor papa!" said Margaret, her eyes filling, though she had said "poor mamma" a moment before. "Did she care for him at all?"

"Oh, my dear! she was *in love* with him, a great deal more in love with him than she ever was with poor Edward. She *would* have him. Of course it was pointed out to her that he was poor, too, and living so far away, and a Scotchman, which is almost like a foreigner, and quantities of poor relations. She must have liked him more than she did poor Edward, for she would not listen, not for a moment; even when it was said that he was old, she cried, 'What do I care?' Oh, you must not think there was any doubt on that point. She was very fond of your papa. That is poor Edward's picture in the corner," said Miss Parker, crying a little, "he never had eyes for any one when she was there; but he was my cousin too."

Margaret got up tremulously, and went to look at the portrait. It was a feeble little water-color: a young man in a coat which had once

been intended to be red, but which had become the palest of pink. When she looked at his insignificant good-looking features, she could not but remember her father's with a glow of pride. But Miss Parker was crying softly in the corner of the sofa. Why does it always happen that people are at cross-purposes in loving? Miss Parker would have been very happy with Edward: why was it not she but the other whom the young soldier loved? It made Margaret sad to think of it. And then all at once there came into her mind, like a pebble cast into tranquil water, Rob Glen. Something in the features of poor Edward, who had died in the jungle, recalled Rob to her mind. Her heart began to beat. Perhaps, no doubt, there was some one who would be very happy to have Rob, who would think him the noblest man in existence. And Margaret gave a little shiver. Suddenly it came to her mind with overpowering force that, notwithstanding all these changes, notwithstanding the difference in herself, notwithstanding the Grange and all its novel life, she, this new Margaret, who was so different from the old Margaret, was bound to Rob Glen. It seemed to her that she had never understood the position before. Miss Parker had gone away crying, poor, sentimental, middle-aged lady! and Margaret sat down on the sofa when she had left it, with dismay in her heart, and gazed at Edward's water-color with blank discomfiture. There seemed to rise before her the little parlor in the farm—every detail of its homely aspect; the red and blue cloth on the table, the uncomfortable scratching of the pen with which she wrote her promise, the bit of paper smoothed out by Mrs. Glen's hand, the little common earthenware ink-bottle.

She had not been aware before that she remembered all these things; but now they started to the light, as if they were things of importance, all visible before her, remade. How was it possible that she could have put them all away out of her memory so long? She had thought of him now and then, chiefly with compunctions, feeling herself ungrateful to him who had been so kind. But it was not with any compunction now that she remembered him, but with sudden alarm and sense of an incongruity beyond all words. Supposing Edward had not died, but had come back from the jungle after her mother had met Sir Ludovic, what would she have thought? how would she have felt? would she have welcomed him or fled from him? But then I—have never seen—any one, Margaret said to herself. She blushed, though she was alone. There was nothing in that—her color was always coming and going—and even this momentary change of sentiment relieved her a little. The horror was to have remembered, all of a sudden, in this calm and quiet—Rob Glen.

When such a sudden revelation as this occurs, it is astonishing how heaven and earth concur to keep the impression up. Next evening their dinner was more lively than usual. To keep Aubrey company over his wine, Mrs. Bellingham had invited Mr. St. John, the young rector (though they were in such deep mourning, your parish clergyman is never out of place, he is not company), to dine with them; and there was a little more care than usual about the flowers on the table (since the garden-flowers were exhausted, Jean had restricted the article of flowers), and a more elaborate meal than was ever put upon the table for the three ladies. Mr. St. John was High-Church, and had been supposed to incline toward celibacy for the clergy, but of late his principles had been wavering. The elder ladies at the Grange had given him no rest on the subject; they had declared the idea to be Popish, infidelistic, heathen. Not marry? Grace in particular had almost wept over this strange theory. What was to become of a parish without a lady to look after it; and by this time Mr. St. John had been considerably moved by one of two things, either by the arguments of Mrs. Bellingham and Miss Leslie, or by the consideration that the Grange was very near the rectory; that it was a very nice little property, the largest house in the parish, its inhabitants the most important family; and that its heiress was eighteen, and very pretty, though brought up a Presbyterian, and probably, therefore, quite unregenerate, and as good as unbaptized. He sat opposite Margaret at the table, while Aubrey Bellingham sat by her, and the young priest felt an unchristian warmth of enmity arise in his bosom toward the stranger. But this put him on his mettle, and the talk was very lively and sometimes amusing; it made Margaret forget the fright of recollection that had seized her. The two young men remained but a very short time in the dining-room after the ladies had left, and Mr. St. John had just managed to get possession of a seat beside Margaret and to resume the question of the Celtic music, which he had so skilfully hit upon at one of their earlier meetings, as a subject sure to interest her, when an incident occurred that threw back all her thoughts vividly into their former channel.

"Don't you think that the invariably pathetic character of their music reflects the lending tendency of the race?" Mr. St. John had just said; and she was actually making what she felt to be a very foolish answer.

"I have heard the pipes playing," she was saying, "but not often; and except reels, I don't know any— Did you call me, Jean?"

"Here is a parcel for you, a large parcel by the railway," said Mrs. Bellingham. "Yes, really; it is not for me, as I thought, but for you, Margaret. What can it be, I wonder? It has got Edinburgh on the ticket, and a great many other marks. Bland, will you please undo it carefully, and take away all the brown paper and wrappings. I dare say it is a present, Margaret; it looks to me like a present. I should say it was a picture; perhaps something Ludovic may have sent you from Earl's-hall. Was there any picture you were fond of that can have been sent to you from Earl's-hall?"

"Dearest Margaret, it will be one of the portraits. How kind of dear Ludovic to think of you. Surely you have a right to it," said Miss Leslie; and even the young men drew near with the lively curiosity which such an arrival always creates. The very name of picture made Margaret tremble; she approached the large white square which Bland—Jean's most respectable servant—had carefully freed from the rough sheets of card-board and brown paper in which it had been so carefully packed, with the thrill of a presentiment. Miss Leslie's fingers quivered with impatience to cut the last string, to unfold the last enclosure, but a heroic sense of duty to

Margaret kept her back. It was Margaret's parcel: she it was who had the right to disclose the secret, to have the first exquisite flutter of discovery. Grace knew the value of these little sensations against the gray background of monotonous life. But it seemed to Margaret that she knew what it was, even although she had no recollection for the moment what it could be. She unfolded the last cover with a trembling hand.

Ah! It was Earl's-hall, the old house, exactly as it had been that sunshiny morning before any trouble came—when little Margaret, thinking no evil, went skimming over the furrows of the potatoes, running up and down as light as air, hovering about the artist whose work seemed to her so divine. What an ocean of time and change had swept over her since then! She gave a tremulous cry full of wonder and anguish, as she saw at a glance what it was. They all gathered round her, looking over her shoulder. There it stood, with the sun shining full upon it, the old gray house: the big ivy leaves giving out gleams of reflection, the light blazing upon Bell's white apron—for Bell, too, was there: he had forgotten nothing. Margaret's heart gave a beat so wild that the little group round her must have heard it, she thought.

"Earl's-hall!" said both the ladies together. "And, dear me, Margaret, where has this come from?" said Mrs. Bellingham; "Ludovic had no picture like this. It is beautifully mounted, and quite fresh and new; it must be just finished. It is very pretty. There is the terrace in the tower, you can just make it out—and there are the windows of the long room; and there, I declare, is my room, just a corner of it, and somebody sitting at the door—why, it is something like Bell! Who can have sent you such a beautiful present, Margaret? Who can it be from?"

Margaret gained a little time while her sister spoke; but she was almost too much agitated to be able to say anything, and she did not know what to say.

"It was a friend," she said, with trembling lips. "It was done—before— It was not finished." And then, taking courage from desperation, she added, "May I take it up-stairs?"

What so natural as that she should be overwhelmed by the sudden sight of her old home? Grace rushed to her with open arms. "Let me carry it for you; let me go with you, darling Margaret," she said. But the girl fled from her, almost pushing her away in the nervous impatience of agitation. Even Jean was moved. She called back her sister imperatively, yet with a softened voice.

"Let her alone; let her carry it herself. Come here, Grace, and let the child alone," said Mrs. Bellingham. "The sight of the old place has been too much for her, coming so suddenly —and not much wonder. After all, it is but four months. But I should like to know who did it, and who sent it," she added. That was the thought that was foremost with Aubrey too.

CHAPTER XXXIV.

This incident completed the painful process which was going on in Margaret's mind. The little visionary link of kindness, tenderness, gratitude, which had existed between herself and Rob Glen had been really broken by the shock administered to her on the evening when she pledged herself to him forever; but she had never attempted to realize her feelings, or inquire into them—rather had been glad to forget them, to push away from her and postpone all consideration of the subject which all at once had become so painful, so full of difficulty and confusion. She had avoided even the idea of any communication with him. When Ludovic spoke to her of correspondence, it had seemed impossible that the pledge he asked for could be necessary, or that there should be any question of correspondence. She had never thought of it, never meant it. There was her promise against her which sometime or other must be redeemed. There was the fact that Rob had parted from her like a lover, a thing which it now made her blush hotly to recollect, but which then had seemed part of the confused strangeness of everything—a proof of his "kindness," that kindness for which she had never been so grateful as she ought to have been. These were appalling certainties which overshadowed her life; but then, nothing could come of them for a long time, that was certain; three immense lifetimes of years stood between her and anything that could be done to her in consequence.

And how familiar we all become with the Damocles sword of an impending, but uncertain event!—Margaret had been able to escape for a long time, and had put all thought of it aside. But her mother's story had recalled one aspect of her own, and here was another, bursting upon her distinct and vivid, which could not be pushed aside, which must be faced, and even explained. Heaven help her! She carried away the big drawing in her arms, her heart thumping against the card-board wildly with suffocating force, her head throbbing, her mind in the most violent commotion. Had there been nothing else, no doubt the sudden recalling of all her thoughts to her old home, without any warning, in a moment, must have had a certain effect upon her. Even Jean had fully acknowledged this. It was natural that she should feel it. But something much more agitating, something more even than the bewildering thought of all that had happened in the last few weeks of her stay at Earl's-hall, came upon her with the first glimpse of the picture. Recollections rushed upon her like a torrent, recollections even more confusing, more painful than these. The drawing itself was a memorial of the time when there was no trouble at all involved, when Rob, newly discovered, was a curiosity and delight to the young creature in quest of something new, to whom he was a godsend; and this it was which suddenly came before her now.

There is no such anguish of retrospection as that with which the very young look back upon moments in which they feel they have made themselves ridiculous, and given their fellow-creatures an inferior, inadequate representation of them. This it was which overwhelmed Margaret now. She had acquired a little knowledge, if from nothing else, from the conversation of Mrs. Bellingham, which had modified her innocence. She had heard of girls who "flung themselves at the heads" of men. She had heard of those who gave too much "encouragement," who "led on" reluctant wooers. This talk had passed lightly enough over her head, always full of dreams; but yet it had left a deposit as so much light talk does.

When first her eyes fell upon the picture, this was the thought that rushed upon her. Almost before the ready tear had formed which came at the sight of Earl's-hall, before the quick pang of grief for the loss of all which the old house represented to her, before the sense of fatal bondage and entanglement which was her special burden, had time to make itself felt—came, with a flood of agony and shame, a realization of herself as she had been when Rob Glen had seated himself at the end of the potato field to make this drawing.

Other things that had happened to her had not involved any fault of hers; she did not even feel that she was seriously to blame for the forging of the chain that bound her—but this, this had been her own doing. She it was who had wooed him to Earl's-hall; she had asked him to come, and to come again; she had persuaded him to a hundred things he never would have thought of by himself. But for her he would not have returned day by day, getting more and more familiar. When she rushed about everywhere for the things he wanted, when she admired everything he did with such passionate enthusiasm, when she could hang over his shoulder watching every line he drew, what had she been doing? "Flinging herself at his head," "leading him on," "encouraging him," oh, and more than encouraging him! as Ludovic had said. This was worse even than the bondage in which it had resulted. Her face was covered with burning blushes; her soul overflowed with shame.

Oh, how well she recollected the ridiculous ardor with which she had taken up her old playfellow; the sense of some new delightful event which had come into her life when she met him, and discovered his sketches, and appropriated him, as it were, to her own amusement and pleasure! What a change he had made in the childish monotony and quiet! She remembered how she had brought him to the house, how she had coaxed her father for him, how she had fluttered about him as he sat there beginning his drawing. If he said he wanted anything, how she flew to get it. How she watched every line over his shoulder; how she praised him with all simple sincerity. (Margaret still thought the picture beautiful, more beautiful than anything she had ever seen.) She seemed to see herself, oh, so over-eager, over-bold, unmaidenly! Was it wonderful that he should think her ready to do everything he asked her—ready to make any sacrifice, to separate herself from all belonging to her for his sake?

There is always a certain consolation, a certain power which upholds and supports, in the consciousness of suffering for something which is not one's own fault. To have been the victim of some wonderful combination of circumstances, to have been caught in some snare, which all your skill was not able to elude, that is far from being the worst that can befall any one. But to see in your conduct the germ of all your sufferings, to perceive how you have yourself led lightly up, dancing and singing, to the precipice over which you are about to be pitched—this is the most appalling ordeal of all. Margaret grew hot all over, with a blush that tingled to her finger points, and seemed to scorch her from head to foot. Whose fault was it, all the self-betrayal that followed, the horrible bond that bound her soul, and which she did not even venture to think of; whose fault was it but her own?

"Margaret, dear Margaret, dearest Jean has sent me to ask, are you not coming down-stairs again? We all feel for you, darling—and oh, do you think it is nothing to us? Dear Jean puts great force upon herself, she has such a strong will, and commands it; but we all feel the same. Oh, what a beautiful picture it is! What a dear, dear old house! How it brings back our youth, and dearest, dearest papa!"

Miss Leslie put her nose to the picture as if she would have kissed it. She felt in the depths of her artless soul that this was her duty to old Sir Ludovic, of whom poor Grace had known little enough for twenty years before. The tear came quite easily, which she dried with her white handkerchief, pressing it to her eyes. Not for anything in the world would she have failed of this duty to her dearest papa. Jean thought chiefly of crape, and was content with that way of expressing her sentiments; but within the first year, within, indeed, the first six months, to mention her father without the tear he had a right to, would have been to Grace a cruel dereliction from natural duty. After a twelve-month, when the family put off crape, it would no doubt cease to be necessary—though always, she felt, a right thing—to pay that tribute of tears.

Margaret stood by, and looked on with a dreary helplessness. She had no tears for her father, no room for him even in her overladen and guilty soul. And this she felt acutely, with a pang the more, feeling as if all love had died out of her heart, and nothing but darkness and confusion, and ingratitude and insensibility, was in her and about her. She took up the picture with a slight shudder, as she touched it, and put it away in the corner where hung the faded portrait of her mother's young lover.

This touch of contact with the story of one who had gone before her, whom somehow—she scarcely knew how—she could not help identifying with herself, gave her a little fanciful consolation. Margaret did not long, as so many girls have done, to have a mother to flee to, and in whom to confide all her troubles; but it seemed to her, in some confused way, that it must have been but a previous chapter in her own life, which had passed under this same roof, in this same house, twenty years ago. She seemed almost dimly to recollect it, as she recollected (but far more vividly) that time of folly in which she had "encouraged" and "led on" Rob Glen.

It was better for her to obey Jean's call, to go down-stairs and try to forget it all, for a moment, than to stay here and drive herself wild, wondering what he might do next, and what, oh what! it would be necessary for her to do. Grace, who was a little disappointed not to find her dissolved in tears, recommended that she should bathe her eyes, and brought her some water, and took a great deal of pains to obliterate the traces of weeping which did not exist. She tucked Margaret's hand under her arm, and patted it and held it fast.

"My poor darling!" she said, cooing over the unresponsive girl. Jean, too, who was not given to much exhibition of feeling, received her, when she came back, with something like tenderness.

"Put a chair for Margaret by the fire, Aubrey," she said, "the child will be cold coming through all those passages; that is the worst of an old house, there are so many passages, and a draught in every one of them. I would not say a word against old houses, which are of course all the fashion, and very picturesque, and all that; but I must say I think you suffer from draughts. And what good is the fireplace in the hall? the heat all goes up that big chimney. It does not come into the house at all. I would like hot-water pipes, but they are a great expense, and of course you would all tell me they were out of keeping. So is gas out of keeping. Oh, you need not cry out; I don't mean in the drawing-room, of course, which is a thing only done in Scotland, and quite out of the question; but to wander about those passages in the dark, and never to stir a step without a candle in your hand! I think it a great trouble, I must allow."

"Your ancestral home, Miss Leslie," said Mr. St. John, who had secured a place in front of the fire, "must be a true mediæval monument. I am very much interested in domestic architecture. And so I am sure you must be, familiar with two such houses—"

"People who possess old houses seldom care for them," said Aubrey, taking up a position on the other side. "You know what my aunt says about gas and hot-water pipes. Tell me," he said, half whispering, stooping over her, to the great indignation of the clergyman, "what I must call you. I must reserve the endearing title of aunt for the family circle, but I can't say Miss Leslie, you know, for you are not Miss Leslie; and Margaret, tout court, would be a presumption."

"Everybody calls me Margaret," she said.

"That man did at Killin. I felt disposed to pitch him into the loch when I heard him; but probably," said Aubrey, laughing, "there might have been two words to that, don't you think? Perhaps, if it had come to a struggle, it would have been I who was most likely to taste the waters of the loch."

"Oh, Randal is very good-natured," said Margaret, making an effort to recover herself, "and perhaps he would not have known what you meant if you had spoken about a loch. I never saw this house till just a little while ago," she added to Mr. St. John, anxious to be civil. "I never was out of Fife."

"And the Northern architecture is different from ours; more rude, is it not? I have heard that people often get confused, and attach an earlier date to a building than it really has any right to."

"It is kind of you to say the man at Killin was good-natured," said Aubrey, on the other side; "of course, you think I would not have given him much trouble. It seemed to me that everybody showed an extraordinary amount of confidence in that man at Killin. He pretended to be fishing, but he never fished. I suspect his fishing related to—who shall we say—your little cousin? Nay, I am making a mistake again; I always forget that you belong to the previous generation—your niece."

"Effie!" cried Margaret, completely roused, so great was her surprise. "Oh! but it was always—it was never—Effie—" Here she made a pause, bewildered, and caught Mr. St. John's eye. "Oh, I beg your pardon," she cried, with a sudden blush; "I—don't know about architecture. I have not had—very much education," she answered, looking piteously at her sisters for aid.

"Oh, dearest Jean! I think I must really go and tell Mr. St. John—"

"Hold your tongue!" said Mrs. Bellingham, holding her sister fast by her dress; "let the child make it out for herself. Do you think they mind about her education? Who cares for education? Men always like a girl to know nothing. Just keep out of the way and stop meddling."

This aside was inaudible to the group round the fire; though Mr. St. John's admirable enunciation made all he said quite distinct to them, and Mrs. Bellingham's sharp ears were very conscious of Aubrey's whispering—which was ill-bred, but of no effect—on the other side of Margaret's chair.

Mr. St. John gave a little laugh of respectful derision and flattery.

"In the present age of learned ladies it is quite a relief to hear such a statement," he said, "though I should not like to trust in your want of education. But this country is very rich architecturally, and I should be delighted to offer my humble services as cicerone. I should like to convert you to the pure English Elizabethan—"

"It must have been Miss Effie," said Aubrey; "who else? for Aunt Grace, though charming—And it stands to reason that a man who says he has gone to a certain place for fishing, yet never touches a rod, must have ulterior motives. And Aunt Jean is of opinion that these two would make a very pretty pair."

Why Aubrey said this it would be hard to tell; whether from malice, as meaning to prick her into annoyance, or whether out of simple mischief, anyhow it roused Margaret.

"Oh, I do not know if Jean would care—I am sure you are—very kind," she said, vacantly, to Mr. St. John; then more rapidly to the other hand: "I am almost sure you are mistaken. Neither Jean nor Effie knew Randal—that is, to call knowing; he was—quite a stranger. I don't think he knew Effie at all."

"These are just the most favorable circumstances for a flirtation," said Aubrey; "but look, they are all on the alert, and Aunt Jean is making signs to me. It is evident they mean you to talk to him, not me. When he goes away, let us return to Miss Effie and the man at Killin."

"Oh, I don't want to talk about them!" cried Margaret—here at least there was nothing to make her shrink from Jean's inspection; she said this quite out loud, so that all the company heard. Because she had one thing to conceal, was it not natural that she should take particular pains to show that there was nothing to conceal? She did not want any one to whisper to her.

And there was besides, there could be no doubt, a certain tone of pique and provoked annoyance in Margaret's voice.

"I was saying," said Mr. St. John, mildly, "that in our own church there is a great deal that is interesting; and if you would allow me to take you over it some day, you and Mrs. Bellingham or Miss Leslie, I should not despair of interesting you. Besides, there are so many of your ancestors commemorated there. I hope we may succeed in making your mother-country very interesting to you," he said, lowering his tone. It was a great relief to the young clergyman when "that fellow" went away from the heiress's side.

"Oh, I like it very well," Margaret said.

"But I am very ambitious, Miss Leslie; very well is indifferent. I want you to like it more than that; I want you to love it, to prefer it to the other," he said, with fervor in his voice. "And now I must say good-night." He held out his hand bending toward her, and Margaret, looking up, caught his eye: she gave a little start, and shrank backward at the very moment of giving him her hand. Why should he look like that—like him whom she was so anxious to forget? She dropped his hand almost before she touched it, in the nervous tremor which came over her. Why should he look like Rob Glen? Was he in the conspiracy against her to make her remember? She could scarcely keep in a little cry which rose to her lips in her sudden pain. Poor Mr. St. John! anything farther from his mind than to make her think of any other suitor could not be. But Mrs. Bellingham, who was more clear-sighted, saw the look, and put an interpretation upon it of a different kind. When Mr. St. John had gone, attended to the door by Aubrey at his aunt's earnest request, Mrs. Bellingham came and placed herself where Mr. St. John had been, in front of the fire.

"That man," she said, solemnly, when he was gone, "is after Margaret too. Oh! you need not make such signs to me, Grace; I know perfectly well what I am saying. I never would speak about lovers to girls in an ordinary way; the monkeys find out all that for themselves quite fast enough—do you think there is anything that I could teach Effie on that point? But Margaret's is a peculiar case: she ought to know how to distinguish those who are sincere —she ought to know that it is not entirely for herself that men make those eyes at her. Oh, I saw him very well; I perceived what he meant by it. You have a very nice fortune, my dear, and a very nice house, and you will have to pay the penalty like others. You will very soon know the signs as well as I do; and I can tell you that *that* man is after you too."

"Dearest Jean!" said Grace, "he may be a little High-Church, more high than I approve, but he is a very nice young man. Whom could Margaret have better than a good, nice-looking, young clergyman? They are more domestic and more at home, and more with their wives—"

"Fiddle-faddling eternally in a drawing-room," said Mrs. Bellingham; "always in a woman's way wherever she turns. No, my dear, whoever you marry, Margaret, don't marry a clergyman; a man like that always purring about the fireside would drive me mad in a month."

"Is it St. John who is in question?" said Aubrey, coming back. "Was he provided for my amusement? or is he daily bread at the Grange already? I don't see how so pretty-behaved a person could drive any one mad; he is a great deal safer than your last *protégé*, the man at Killin."

"I don't mean to discuss such questions with you, Aubrey," said Mrs. Bellingham; "it is late, and I think if you will light our candles for us, we will say good-night. And I will go with you, Margaret, and look at that picture again; it was a very pretty picture. I must have it framed for you; there is a place in the wainscot parlor where it would hang very well. Who did you say sent it to you? or did you tell me? I did not know that there ever was anybody at Earl's-hall that could draw so well."

"Dear Jean," said Grace, thinking it a good opportunity to appear in Margaret's defence, "let her alone, let the poor child alone to-night; she is too tired for anything. Are you not too tired, darling Margaret? I am sure you want to go to bed."

"I hope I know better than to overtire her," said Jean, with some offence; "there is no need for you to come, Grace. Where have you put the picture, Margaret? Why, you have put it with its face to the wall! Is that to save it from the dust, or because you don't like to see it? My dear, I don't want to be unkind, but this is really carrying things too far. You don't mean to say you have taken a dislike to Earl's-hall?"

"No," Margaret said, under her breath; though it seemed to her that to look at the picture again was more than she could bear.

"And it is a very pretty picture," said Jean, turning it round and sitting down on the sofa to look at it—"a very pretty picture! By-and-by you will be very glad to have it. And who was it you said did it? I never thought Randal Burnside was an artist. Perhaps he got one of the people to do it who are always at Sir Claude's. But, my dear, if that is so, I can't let you take a present from a young man like Randal Burnside."

"It was not Randal"—Margaret was eager to clear him: "he never sent me anything in a present; he would not think of me at all. It was—once when he came to make a picture of papa, which is beautiful— He was a young man from the farm."

"A young man from the farm!"

"Rob Glen," said Margaret, almost choked, yet forcing herself to speak. "Papa said he might do it. I did not know anything about it, but I suppose he must have finished it; and here it is." It seemed a simple statement enough, if she had not been so breathless, and changed color so continually, and looked so haggard about the eyes.

Mrs. Bellingham heard this account with a blank face.

"Rob Glen!" she said; "Rob Glen! where have I heard the name before? Was it the servants at Earl's-hall, or was it Ludovic, or—who was it? Papa said he might do it? Dear me! papa might have known better, Margaret, though I am sure I don't want to blame him. I have to be paid for, I suppose; and how very strange it should have been sent like this, with-

out a word! He will send a bill, most likely. How strange I should not have heard anything about this artist! Was there any price mentioned that you remember, Margaret? They ask such sums of money for one of those trifling sketches. It is nice enough, but I am sure it is not worth the half of what we shall have to give for it. When there is no bargain made beforehand, it is astonishing the charges they will make; and papa really had no money for such nonsense: he ought not to have ordered it; but perhaps he thought it would be a gratification to you. Can you remember at all, Margaret, if anything was said about the price?"

"Oh no, no—there was to be no price. It was not like that. He asked to do it, and papa let him do it. Nobody thought of any money."

"But, my dear!" said Jean—"my dear! you are a little simpleton; but you could not think, I hope, of taking the man's work and giving him *nothing* for it? That is out of the question—quite out of the question. I never heard of such a thing," said Mrs. Bellingham. The words seemed to penetrate through all Margaret's being. She trembled, notwithstanding all her efforts to control herself. What could she reply? Take a man's work and give him *nothing* for it; but it was not money that Rob would take.

"Of course it could not be expected that you should know anything of business," said Jean, "and poor papa was already feeling ill, perhaps, and out of his ordinary way. I dare say a letter will come by the next post to explain it. And if not, you must give me the young man's address, and I will write and ask, or we might send word to Ludovic. Aubrey is a very good judge of such things; we can ask Aubrey to-morrow what he thinks the value should be. Now, Margaret, you are trembling from head to foot—you are as white as a sheet; you have a nervous look about your eyes that it always frightens me to see. My dear, what is to become of you," cried Jean, "if you let every little thing upset you? It was in the course of nature that we should lose papa—he was an old man; and, I believe, though he was never a man who talked much about religion, that he was well prepared. And as for Earl's-hall, you would not grudge that to Ludovic? It is his right as the only son. It shows great weakness, my dear, both of body and mind, that you should be upset like this only by a picture of Earl's-hall."

Margaret listened with all that struggle of conflicting feelings which produces hysteria in people unused to control themselves. The choking in the throat, the burning of those unshed tears about her eyes, the trouble in her heart, was more than she could bear. She could not make any reply. She could not even see her sister's face; the room reeled round with her; everything grew dark. To save her balance, she threw herself suddenly upon the firm figure before her, clutching at Jean's support, throwing her arms round her with a movement of desperation. Few people had ever clung wildly to Mrs. Bellingham in moments of insufferable emotion. She was quite overcome by this involuntary appeal to her. She took her young sister into her arms, all unconscious of the cause of her misery, and caressed and soothed her, and stayed by her till she had calmed down, and was able to escape from her trouble in bed. Jean believed in bed as a cure for most evils.

"You must not give way," she said—"indeed, my dear, you must not give way; but a good night's sleep will be the best thing for you; lie still and rest."

"What a tender-hearted thing it is!" she said, going down-stairs again for a last word with Aubrey, after this agitating task was over. "I declare she has quite upset me, too; though it is scarcely possible, after being so long away from home, that I could feel as she does. She is a great deal too feeling for her own comfort. But, Aubrey, you must not lose your time, my dear boy; you must push on. It would be the greatest 'divert' to her, as they say in Scotland, if you could only get her to fall in love with you. I have the greatest confidence in falling in love."

"And so have I—when they will do it," said Aubrey, puffing out a long plume of smoke from his cigar.

CHAPTER XXXV.

CURIOUSLY enough, Margaret's first thought, when she woke in the morning, was not of the picture nor of all the consequences which it seemed to threaten. Sometimes the most trifling matter will thrust itself in, before those giant cares, which generally wait by our bed-sides, to surprise us when we first open our eyes. And the first thing she thought of, strangely enough, was Aubrey's suggestion of last night—Effie! What could he mean by it? Effie had been his own companion, not Randal's. Randal had not walked or talked with, or sought any one, except— It was very strange, indeed, how any one could suppose that Effie— He did not *know* her. Of all the party, the one he knew best was certainly herself. She must certainly be best aware of what his feelings were—of what he had been thinking about! It annoyed her to think that Aubrey should have so little perception, should know so little about it, though Jean had such confidence in him. There was a little irritation in her mind about this point, which quite pushed to the front and made itself appear more important than it was. She could not help making a little survey of the circumstances, of all that had happened—and it had just occurred to her to recollect the offer of service and help that Randal had made her. This had made her half smile at the moment, and since then she had smiled more than once at the idea that she could want his help. She had said, "Jean will manage everything;" and yet he had said it with fervid meaning, with a look of anxious concern.

Ah! she sprang up in her bed, and clasped her hands together. The occasion had come; but she could not consult Randal, nor any one. She must struggle through it by herself, as best she could, holding her peace, saying nothing. That was the only safety for her. But Margaret was surprised to find that when she turned the picture round again, and looked at it trembling, as though it had been capable of doing her bodily harm, she did not feel so much power in it as she had done the day before. It did not sting her the second time. She looked at it almost tranquilly, seeing in it no dreadful accuser, bringing before her all her own past levity and

folly, but only a memorial of a time and a place which indeed made her heart beat with keen emotion and with pain, but not with the overwhelming, sickening passion of misery which had been like death to her last night.

She could not understand how this was, for the circumstances had not changed in any way; and there was still evidently before her the difficulty of making Jean understand how it was that this picture could be accepted without payment, and keeping her, energetic as she was, from interfering in her own person. There was still this difficulty; and all that made the future so alarming, the dread of other surprises that might follow this, was undiminished; but yet, instead of turning the picture to the wall again, in sick horror of it and fear of it as of a ghost, Margaret left it in the recess, uncovered, the corner of the broad rim of white touching the little faded water-color portrait. That touch gave her a certain soothing and consolation. It was not the same kind of trouble as her own; probably the other girl who had been engaged to that poor fellow without loving him had not been at all to blame; but yet there his portrait stood, a memorial of other uneasy thoughts that had gone on in this same chamber. Probably *she* blamed herself too, though not as Margaret was doing. But certainly, anyhow, she must have sat thinking, and cried in the same corner of that sofa, and looked at the pale painted face. Margaret leaned the cause of her trouble against the frame of that dead and gone one, which the other girl had lived through, and felt that there was consolation in the tomb. What so visionary, so painful, so foolish even, that will not console at eighteen when it happens to offer a parallel to our own distresses?

And it was with renewed courage and a great deal more composure than she could have hoped for, that Margaret went down-stairs. They all came to meet her with kindly questions how she was. "But I, for one, think it quite unnecessary to put any such question," said Aubrey. He looked at her with a lingering look of pleasure. He did not object to Margaret. She was not "his style;" but still he did not object to her, and this morning he admired her, as she came down-stairs in her morning freshness, her black dress bringing out the delicate tints of her complexion. Jean had told him that he had better lose no time; and the fact of Mr. St. John's evident intentions had quickened Aubrey's. The good which another man was trying to secure became more valuable in his eyes. She was certainly very pretty, he said to himself, a delicate little creature, like a pale rose—not altogether a white rose, but that delicate blush which is not definable by any vulgar name of color; and her silky hair was piquant among all the frizzy unkempt heads that were more fashionable. On the whole, he had not the least objection to make what "running" he could for Margaret. She was worth winning, with her beautiful old house, and her pretty little income, though she was not quite his style.

"Here is a fat letter for you," he said; "we have all been grumbling over our letters. Aunt Jean, I think, would like to read them all, to see if they were fit to be delivered to us; she takes all the charge of our moral as well as of our physical well-being. I saw her look at this very narrowly, as if she had the greatest mind to break the seal. *That* is of course a figure of speech nowadays. I mean to open the envelope; it is very fat and tempting to the curious spectator. I should like myself to know what was in it; it must be from some dear confidential young lady friend."

Margaret looked at the letter with a little thrill of alarm. She did not get many letters, and every one that came was a slight excitement; but when she had looked at it she laid it down very calmly. "It is from Bell," she said. She knew very well what Bell would say to her. She would tell her about the brown cow and the chickens, and how John was with his rheumatism; and there was no great hurry to read it for a few minutes, until they had ceased to take so much notice of her. Margaret knew that after a minute or two her sisters would be fully occupied with their own concerns.

"Aubrey is talking nonsense, Margaret, as he generally does," said Mrs. Bellingham. "The idea that I would open anybody's letter! not but what I think it a very right thing of young people to show their letters to their parents, or to those who stand in the place of parents; it shows a right sort of confidence, and I confess, for my part, I always like to see it; but I am not the sort of person that would ever force confidence. It is nothing, I always say, unless it comes spontaneously. I wonder if Bell will tell you anything about that picture that arrived last night, Margaret? I saw your letter was from Bell, and that is what made me look at it, as Aubrey says, though he always exaggerates. Of course, I knew Bell and you had no secrets, Margaret. I really think if you had been out of the way I should have done violence to my own feelings and gone the length of opening it, just to see if there was anything to explain what that young man could mean by sending it without a word."

"Oh!" said Aubrey, "it was a young man, then, was it, who made the drawing? it is satisfactory to know that it was a young man."

"Why is it satisfactory to know that he is a young man? I can't say that I see that at all; it is neither satisfactory nor unsatisfactory: it is not a person in our condition of life, so that it does not matter in the least to Margaret. Why do you say it is satisfactory to know that he is a young man?"

"Well, because then there is hope that he will do better when he is older," said Aubrey. "You all seemed to like it so much that I did not venture to say anything; but it is not great in point of art. I have no doubt it is a most faithful representation of the place, but it is nothing to speak of, you know, in the point of art."

"Oh, really, do you think so?" cried Mrs. Bellingham; "then you would not think it worth a very high price, Aubrey? I am very glad of that—for I thought we might be obliged to offer a large sum—"

"It is a beautiful picture," said Margaret, hotly; she could not bear anything to be said against this rooted belief of hers; its presence alarmed and troubled her, but she would not have it undervalued. "If it were to be sold it would be worth a great deal of money—it is a beautiful picture; but there is nothing about

selling it," she cried, a flush rising into her cheeks. "It was done for—papa: money would not buy it—and him that painted it was not thinking about money." Her pronouns, poor child, were wrong, but her heart was right. Rob Glen was her greatest terror on earth, but she would be just to him all the same.

"But that is just what I cannot be satisfied about," said Jean. "If you pay a man for his work, why there you are! but if you don't pay him, or give him anything as an equivalent, why where are you? Every man must be paid one way or another. Open Bell's letter, Margaret, and tell me if she says anything about it. I shall have to write to Ludovic, or to the young man himself, if we do not know what he means."

Margaret opened Bell's letter with a hand that trembled a little. She did not expect to find anything there on the subject which had so deeply occupied her; but still, to open this thick enclosure before Jean, whose mind was so much set upon it that something was to be found there, and who would watch her while she read it, and ask to see Bell's humble epistle, was very alarming. She opened it with a tremulousness which she could scarcely disguise. Bell had folded her letter, which was written on a large sheet of paper, in the way in which letters had been folded before the days of envelopes, and consequently it was with some little delay and difficulty that a trembling hand opened the big folds. But Margaret was suddenly petrified, frozen to her very heart with terror, when she saw another letter lying enclosed—a tiny letter of a very different aspect from Bell's. She dared not move—she dared not do anything to show the greatness of the shock she had received. The danger was not of a kind that she dared disclose. The paper shook in her hands convulsively, and then they became preternaturally still and steady. She did not know Rob Glen's handwriting, but she knew that this was from him by instinct, by inspiration of her terror. What was she to do? Her face she felt grow crimson, then fell into a chill of paleness; and when she lifted her eyes in a momentary glance of panic to see if Jean was looking at her, she met the eyes of Aubrey, and without knowing what she did, in a kind of delirium made a terrified, instantaneous appeal to him. Her thoughts were too hurried, her desperation too complete even to make her conscious that the appeal was unreasonable, or, indeed, aware that she had made it, till the thing was done; and next moment all became dim before her eyes, though she still kept her balance desperately upon her seat, and held the papers firmly in her hands.

Aubrey was not insensible or unkind: he was startled by the look; for whatever Margaret's emotion might mean it was evidently something very real and terrible for the young, inexperienced creature who put this involuntary trust in him. He said instantly:

"Have you finished breakfast, Aunt Jean?—for if so, I want you to look at some things of mine—a parcel I received this morning. Christmas is coming, and with all that crew of children at the Court, a man is put to his wit's end: come into my room and give me your advice about them. Oh yes, of course they are rubbish; what can I buy but rubbish on my little scrap of money? But come and give me your opinion."

"Wait a minute, my dear boy, wait a minute; you shall have my opinion with the greatest of pleasure; but I want to hear what Bell says."

Upon this he got up, and walking solemnly to her, offered his arm. "Who is Bell? I decline to yield the *pas* to Bell. Come now with me, and Bell will do afterward; if it takes so long to read as it promises from the size of it, I should have to wait till to-morrow, and that does not suit me at all. Whisper! there is a scrap of Sèvres, Rose du Barri, and one or two small rags of lace."

"Oh!" Mrs. Bellingham uttered a cry. She made a little dart toward Margaret to inspect the letter over her shoulder, thus hoping to secure both the advantages offered; but before she could carry out her intention, her hand was caught fast in Aubrey's arm. "I want *you* to see them all *first*," he whispered in her ear.

"I do think dear Aubrey might have asked me too," said Miss Grace, querulously; "I don't know that there is so much difference, though it is Jean, to be sure, who is his real aunt. But then, perhaps, dearest Margaret, you know, he might not like to ask me, an unmarried lady, to go into his room. Yes, yes, dear Aubrey, I see exactly what he meant—he gave me a look as he went away, as much as to say, I will explain it all afterward. Naturally, you know, he would not ask me, being an unmarried lady, to go into his room. Where are you going, my dear—where are you going? You have not eaten anything, darling Margaret; you have not even taken your tea."

But it was not difficult to escape from Grace; and Margaret, with a sense of desperation, snatched a cloak from the hall and stole out, wending her way among the shrubbery to the most retired spot she could think of. She would not go to her room, where her sister would inevitably come after her. She had thrust Bell's big letter—innocent production, penned out of the fulness of Bell's heart, which was as big as the letter—into her pocket. And she dared not look at the other till she had got safe into some corner where nobody would see her, some covert where she would be free from inspection. The cold wind revived her, and a little spiteful rain came damp upon her face, bringing back a little of its color; but she was unconscious of both wind and rain. She went to a little breezy summer-house in a corner of the grounds; and then she bethought herself that the gravel-paths were dry there, and Jean might easily follow; so she retraced her steps hurriedly, and pulled the hood of her cloak over her head, and ran across the little bridge over the stream, to the park, where all the ground was still thickly sprinkled with the autumn carpet of yellow leaves. The grass was wet, the rain came spitefully in her face, but she did not mind. When she was in the midst of the big clump of elms, where the leaves were almost gone, she stopped and paused a moment to rest, with her back against a tree. Jean would never follow her there; the wet grass and universal dampness spreading round her made her safe. She opened her fingers in which she had held it fast, the innocent-looking little missive. With

what a beating heart she opened it! Oh, how foolish, foolish she had been to bind all her life, for ever and ever, and she not eighteen! And here it was that she read her first love-letter—her heart beating, but not with pleasure; her bosom heaving with terror, and dismay, and pain.

"Margaret, my own darling, where have you gone from me? Why do you not send me a word in charity? It is three months since you went away! Is it possible that in all that time you have never thought of me, nor thought how miserable I was, deprived of you and of all knowledge of you? You have put my love to a tremendous test, though it is strong enough to bear that, and a great deal more. But oh, my love, don't make me so unhappy! Shake me off, you cannot; make me forget, you cannot. My love is too tender and too constant to fail; but you can make me very wretched, Margaret, and that is what you are doing. I have waited and waited, and looked every day for a letter—the merest little scrap would have made me happy. I knew you could not write often or much; but one word, surely I might have had one word. I am just finishing the drawing you liked, the view of Earl's-hall, hoping that, notwithstanding all changes, you may like it still, and that it may remind you of the happy time when we first knew each other, when nobody thought of parting us. Your dear old father would never have parted us; he would have preferred your happiness to everything. He would rather have chosen a loving husband to take care of his little Peggy, than all the world could give her. Your brother thinks otherwise, my darling, and I don't blame him; but I know what old Sir Ludovic would have thought. And you will not let them turn you against me, my sweetest Margaret; you will not give me up because I am poor? That is a thing I would scarcely believe, if you said it with your own dear lips. Margaret Leslie give up her betrothed husband because he had nothing! I never would believe it. But I know your delicate sense of honor, my own dear girl. You do not like to write to me in secret for the sake of the people you are living among. I understand how you feel, and you are right—I know you are right; but, my sweet love, remember that to please them you are killing me, and I don't feel that I can bear it much longer. The silence is becoming too much; it is making an end of me. One word—one sweet loving word, my own Margaret, just to keep me alive! I feel that I am getting desperate. If I do not have one word from you I cannot answer for myself, even if it be for my own destruction; if I do not hear of you, I must come and see you. I must get sight of you. Three months without a word—without a message, is enough to kill any one who loves as I do. I say to myself, she cannot have forgotten me, she cannot have forsaken me. she is too true, too faithful to her word; and then another day comes, and I get desperate. Half a dozen times I have been ready to start off to go after you, to watch about your house, only to get a glimpse of you. Write to me, my Margaret, put me out of my misery—only one word—!"

Then, in a postscript, it was added that he had asked Bell to send this for once, in order that her friends, her unkind friends, who wanted to separate her from him, might not find out he had written, and that he had sent the drawing—and that once more he begged for one word, only one word in reply. It was written under two dates, one some weeks before the other. Margaret stood with her back against the elm-tree, and read it with a flutter of terror. Oh, what would she do if he were to carry out his threat, if he were to come and watch about the house, and look for her! Was that a thing that might happen any time, when she was walking through the lanes, even here in her own little park under her elm-trees? Might he come at any moment and do as he used to do at Earl's-hall? Oh! Margaret started from her shelter and clinched her hands, and stamped her foot on the wet, yielding grass! Oh! should it ever have to be gone through again, all that it made her blush so hotly to think of? The blush that was usually so evanescent got fixed in hot crimson of excitement on her cheek. If he came, it seemed to her that it was she who must fly—anywhere—to the end of the world: but yet he had a right to come, and some time he would come, and she would not be able to say a word against it. "Oh, what shall I do? what shall I do?" cried Margaret to herself. Would he not let her even have her three years to herself? He might wait, surely he might wait for three years!

But it would be impossible to give any idea of the confused muddle of pain and helpless, instinctive resistance in her thoughts. A hot flush of resentment against him for daring to use the name her father had ever called her by—a kind of speechless fury and indignation, burst out in the midst of all her other excitements. How dared he do it, Rob Glen, who was nobody, who was not even a gentleman? And then she covered her face with her hands, and cried out with horror and bewilderment to think that this was her opinion of one to whom she had pledged herself, to whom she would belong almost more than to her father himself. And she had no one to go to, no one she could confide in, no one whose help she could ask. And what help would avail her? She must keep her word, she must fulfil her promise—at the end of three years.

She never even contemplated the possibility of breaking her word; but at present why could he not let her alone? Had she not begged him to let her alone? She sank down by the foot of the elm, not even noting the wet, and cried. Crying could do no good, she knew that; but yet it relieved her mind. She was hemmed in and encompassed with danger. Perhaps he might come, might appear suddenly in her path, with arms ready to take hold of her, with those caresses which made her shrink, even in imagination, with shame and pain. There had never been a time—except the first moment when she was too broken-hearted, too miserable to care what happened to her—that she had not shrunk from his tenderness. And how could she bear it now? Terror came upon her breathless and speechless; here even, under these very trees, he might appear suddenly. A stifled shriek came out of her oppressed heart at the thought. It seemed to her that she could never move anywhere with safety, without a sense of terror again.

And then there were lesser but very apparent dangers. Jean would ask her what Bell had said; she would ask, perhaps, to see Bell's let-

ter, in which there was a sentence which was as bad as telling all. Bell wrote: "I am sending to you, my dear Miss Margret, a note that Rob Glen—him that you had to come so much to Earl's-hall before my dear old maister died—has asked me to send. Lothe, lothe was I to do it! It may be something misbecoming the like of you to receive. But I will send it this one time. For a young lady like you to be writing of letters with a young gentleman of her own kind is a thing I would not encourage; but Rob Glen is more a match for your maid, Miss Margret, than he is for you. And it's real impudent of him to ask me; but as he says it's something about one of his pictures, I do it for this one time." If Jean asked to see Bell's letter, would not this betray her? So that her path was surrounded by perils both great and small. After a while, weary, wet, and draggled, with her dress clinging to her, and her cloak dripping, she returned across the sodden grass. Jean, she knew, would be busy for the moment with household cares, and it seemed to Margaret that, if she lost no time, she might still make an attempt to avert the fate that threatened. She went to her own room, holding up as best she could her poor black dress with its spoiled crape, and, still crimson and hot with her excitement, wrote two letters in the time which she ordinarily took to arrange the preliminaries of one. She wrote to Rob as follows, with a terseness of expression partly dictated by the terror of him that had taken possession of her mind, partly by the headstrong haste in which she wrote.

"DEAR ROB,—I could not write, and I cannot now, because I promised to Ludovic. You must not come; oh, don't come, if you have any pity for me! My life would be made miserable. How is it possible I could forget you? You don't forget anything in such a short time—and how could I ever forget? Oh, it has cost me too much! Please, please do not come. I am quite well, and you must not—indeed you must not—mind my not writing, for I promised Ludovic. Good-bye, dear Rob; I do not want to hurt you. I always knew that you were very kind; but you must not—indeed, indeed, you must not—think of coming to me here."

Her wet dress, her spoiled crape, clung about her limbs; her wet shoes were like two pools, in which her cold little feet were soaked. As is usual at such moments of excitement, her head was burning but her feet cold. Nevertheless, she wrote another little note to Bell, telling her that she was quite right not to send any letters, and begging that if she saw Mr. Randal Burnside she would ask him to speak to Mr. Glen. Bell was to say that Margaret had told her to make this extraordinary request—and Mr. Randal Burnside would understand. Nothing could be more incoherent than this last letter, for Margaret did not half know what she meant Randal to do or say; but he had promised to help her; he had told her to call him whenever she wanted him. Was her poor little head getting feverish and light? She went out again, stealing, in her wet garments, once more down-stairs, leaving a dimness upon the polished wood, and walked all the way through the gradually increasing rain to the post-office in the village, where she put in her two letters. She was aching all over, her head hot and light, her feet cold and heavy, her crape all soaked and ruined, her hands too feeble to hold up her dress, which clung about her ankles, and made her stumble at every step, before she got home.

CHAPTER XXXVI.

THE time that had passed so peacefully over Margaret, bringing so many new experiences, new scenes, and enlarged acquaintance with her own circumstances and advantages, had not gone with equal satisfaction over Rob Glen. Margaret's pledge to him—that pledge which she had given so easily, and which his mother prized so deeply—had been nothing but painful and shameful to him. Conscience has curious varieties in different persons, even in persons so nearly related as mother and son. Rob felt no sting in his moral consciousness from the fact that he had led Margaret to commit herself in her moment of trouble, and had taken advantage of the very abandonment of her grief to assume the position of a lover, the mere fact of which gave him a hold over her which nothing else could have given. To do him justice, he would have taken the same position with any comely poor girl whom he had encountered in equal distress ; but the poor lass would probably have thought little of it, whereas to Margaret's more delicate nature there was all the reality of an unbreakable bond in the embrace and kiss with which he had taken possession of her, before she was aware. But Rob felt no trouble in his conscience in this respect. It did not occur to him that he had surprised her, and taken advantage of her sorrow and loneliness and bewilderment; but in respect to the pledge which his mother had with so little trouble got from her, his conscience did speak. Margaret, it was true, had thought nothing of it; she had felt that all was done already, that her fate was fixed and irrevocable, that she could not go back—and what did her name on a piece of paper signify? But here was where Rob's honor, such as it was, came in ; he hated that piece of paper. He was deeply mortified by Margaret's readiness to consent to everything so long as she could get free from his mother and himself. The written bond seemed to put him in a false position, to lessen him in his own eyes. He would have nothing to say to it.

"Keep it yourself, if you like it, now that you have got it—it is none of my doing," he had said, throwing it from him. Mrs. Glen secured it with a cry of dismay, as it was fluttering toward the fire.

"Ay, I'll keep it," she said ; "and ye'll be fain some day to come questing to me for your bit o' paper, as ye call it, that you never would have had if your mother had been as thoughtless as yoursel'."

"Mother!" he said, furious, "do you think I would hold a girl to her written promise, if she did not want to keep her word ?"

"I canna say what you would do," said Mrs. Glen ; "you're just a great gomerel, that's what you are. Ye have mair confidence in her being in love with ye, a lang leggit ne'er-do-weel, than in onything that's reasonable : but, Robbie, my man, love comes and love goes. You're no bad-looking, and you have the gift of the gab, which goes a lang way—and maybe she'll stick to ye, as you think, against a' her friends can say ; but for me, I've aye a great confidence in what's put down in black and white, and I wouldna say but you would be fain to come to me for my bit o' paper, for a' so muckle as you despise it now."

"Never will I build my faith on such a foundation—never will I hold Margaret to her bond !" cried Rob ; but his mother locked the precious bit of paper in the old secretary which stood in the parlor, with a cynical disregard to his protestations.

"It's there in the left-hand drawer, if anything should happen to me; if you should ever want it, you'll ken where to find it," she said.

And several weeks went on without any impatience on the part of either in respect to Margaret ; even the conversation which Rob had with the new Sir Ludovic, who summoned him curtly to give up all idea of his sister, had rather encouraged than depressed him ; for it was evident that Margaret had showed no signs of yielding, and her brother was not even her guardian, and had no power whatever over her. When he thus ascertained from Sir Ludovic's inadvertent admission that Margaret had remained steadfast, Rob had metaphorically snapped his fingers at the Baronet. He had been perfectly civil, but he had given Sir Ludovic to understand that he cared little enough for his disapprobation. "If I was in your position I should no doubt feel the same," he had said with fierce candor ; "I should think that Margaret was about to throw herself away ; but she does not think so, which is the great matter."

"She will think so when she comes to her senses—when she is fit to form an opinion," Sir Ludovic cried ; and Rob had smilingly assured him that he was contented to wait and put this to the proof. But after that interview, when Earl's-hall was dismantled and left vacant, and everything belonging to the Leslies seemed about to disappear, and not a word came out of the distance in which Margaret was, both Rob and his mother began to be uneasy. Rob had not calculated upon any correspondence ; but yet he had felt that somehow or other she would manage to communicate with him, and to find some means by which he could communicate with her. Girls of Margaret's condition do not submit to entire separation as those of Jeanie's do ; and when day after day passed, and week after week, it was natural that he should become uneasy. Nor was the anxiety which he felt as a lover unshared by the cooler spectator. Mrs. Glen began to ply him with questions, anxious, fretful, scornful, derisive.

"Ony word to-day, Rob?" she would say ; "I saw you gang out to meet the lassie with the post." "Dear, dear, Rob, I hope our bonnie young lady may be well!" would be the burden of the next inquiry—and then came sharper utterances: "Lord! if I was a lad like you, I wouldna stick there waiting and waiting, but I would ken the reason." "Do you think that's the way to court a lass, even if she be a lady ? I would give her no peace if it were me ; I would let her see that I wasna the one to play fast and loose with." These repeated assaults were followed by practical consequences quite as disagreeable. Instead of the indulgence with which he had been for some time treated, the tacit consent given to his do-nothingness, the patience of his mother, though it went sorely against the grain, with an existence which produced no profit and was of no use—he began to be once more the object of those bitter criticisms and flying insults which she knew so well how to make use of, to the exasperation of the compelled listener. "What it is to be a man and a good scholar!" she would say. "I couldna sit hand-idle, looking at other folk working—no! if it were to save my life. Eh, ay, there's a wonderful difference atween them that are born to earn their living, and them that are content to live on their friends. I hope the time will never come when that will be my lot. But no one of a' my friends would help me, that's one thing, certain, though there are some that have aye the luck to get somebody to toil and moil, while they live pleasantly and gang lightly. It is the way of the world." Another time she would burst out with all the fervor of roused temper. "Lord, man, how can ye sit there and see every creature in the house working but yoursel'? I would sooner weed the turnips or frichten the craws—but you're of less use than a bairn of three years auld."

Rob steeled himself as best he could against these blighting words. He would stroll forth whistling by way of defiance and be absent the whole day, absent at meal-times when his mother exacted punctuality, and late of returning at night. It was a struggle of constant exasperation between them. He had no money and no means of getting any, or he would gladly have left the farm, where there was no longer even anything to amuse him, anything to give him the semblance of a pursuit. To be sure, he worked languidly at his drawings still, and resumed the interrupted sketch of Earl's-hall which had occupied so important a place in his recent history.

To have before you the hope of being rich in three years, of being able to enter another sphere and cast away from you all those vulgar necessities of work which fill the lives of most people—to have ease before you, happiness, social elevation, but only on the other side of that long chasm of time, which for the moment you can see no way of getting through—it is impossible to imagine a more tantalizing position. Say that it is utterly mean and miserable of any man to fix his entire hopes upon an elevation procured in such a way; but Rob was not conscious of this. A rich wife, who was also pretty and young, seemed to him a most satisfactory way of making a fortune. Had she been old and ugly the case would have been different; but he had no more hesitation about enriching himself by means of Margaret, than he had felt in securing Margaret to himself in the incaution and prostration of her grief. His conscience and his honor had in these particulars nothing to say. But as day after day went on and he received nothing from Margaret to prove his power over her, no stolen letter, no secret assurance of her love and faithfulness, Rob's mind became more and more uneasy, and his thoughts more and more anxious. She was the sheet-anchor of his safety, without which he must return into a chaos all the more dark that it had been irradiated by such a hope.

And this suspense, while it made his position at home more and more uncomfortable every day, did not improve his mental condition, as may be easily supposed. He had entertained plans, before he had perceived how easily he might step upward by aid of Margaret's hand, of seeking his fortune in London, and either by means of pen or pencil, or both together, making out some kind of future for himself. But why should he take this trouble, and expose himself to the rich man's contumely, etc., when, by-and-by, he might himself appear among the best (as his ignorant fancy suggested), a patron of art instead of a feeble professor of it—a fine amateur, with all the condescension toward artists which it is in the power of the wealthy to show? This was an ignoble thought, and he was partially conscious that it was so; but there was a latent love of indolence in him which is always fostered by such prospects of undeserved and unearned aggrandizement as now flaunted before his eyes. Why should he work laboriously to gain a little advancement for himself, when by mere patience and waiting he might reach to such advancement as the most Herculean work of his could not bring him to? And the suspense in which he was worked upon his mind and led him on in this evil path. He could do nothing till he had heard from her; and she would write, she must write, any day.

These motives altogether, and the want of money to do anything for himself, and even the reproaches of his mother, who denounced him for eating the bread of idleness without affording him any means to attempt a better existence—which latter acted by hardening his heart and making him feel a defiant satisfaction in thwarting her—all drove him deeper and deeper into the slipshod habits of an unoccupied life. He got up late, happy to escape a *tête-à-tête* breakfast with his mother, and her sneers and reproaches, at the cost of Jenny's integrity, who smuggled him in a much better breakfast than his mother's while the mistress was busy about her dairy or in her poultry-yard; he dawdled over his sketches, doing a little dilettante work as pleased him; then he would stroll out and perhaps walk across the country to some other farm-house, where he was sure of a hospitable invitation to share the family dinner, and an excellent reception from the mother and daughters, to whom it was no trouble to make himself agreeable; or he would go to the Manse, and resume the often interrupted discussion about his "difficulties" with Dr. Burnside, who was anxious to be "of use" to Rob, and to be instrumental, as he said, in bringing him back to the right way.

These discussions amused both parties greatly—the Minister, as affording him a means of bringing forth from their ancient armory those polemical weapons in which every man who has ever attempted to wield them, takes a secret pride—and the young sceptic, by reason of the delightful sense of superiority with which he felt able to see through his adversary's weakness, and sense of power in being able to crush him when he wished to do so. Often these controversies, too, which were continually renewed and never-ending, got Rob a dinner, and saved him from the domestic horrors of the farm. And by-and-by there happened another accident which threw him still more into the way of mischief, as happens so often to those who dally with temptation. He had made his peace with Jeanie on that melancholy night after Margaret's departure. She had been angry; but she had been persuaded to hear his story—to understand him, to see how it was that he had been "drawn into" the present circumstances of his life—and finally to be sorry for him who had gone astray because unaware that she was near, and because of poor little Margaret's need of comfort and solace.

Did not Jeanie know how he could console a poor girl in trouble with that tongue of his, that would wile a bird from a tree? She had forgiven him, and they had parted in melancholy kindness, recognizing that fate, not any fault of theirs, had separated them. When the household at Earl's-hall was broken up, Jeanie had returned to her father; and not long after she had, as was most natural, encountered Rob in a lonely lane, where she was taking a melancholy evening walk. What could be more natural? She could not sit and talk with the wives at their doors, when the soft autumn twilight, so full of wistful suggestion, dropped softly over the "laigh toun." Jeanie was too much in the midst of her own life, too much absorbed by the dramatic uncertainties of fate, to be capable of that tranquil amusement. There were not many people in the Kirkton who cared for the exercise of a walk. The men might stray out a hundred yards beyond the village, on one side or the other, with their evening pipe, but the women kept at "the doors;" they had enough of exercise in the care of their families and in "redding up the house."

Thus Jeanie, even if she had wanted a companion, would have been unlikely to find one; and indeed it was much more to her mind to stray forth alone, very melancholy, with her head full of Rob, and all her old anger and indignation softened into indulgence and pity. He was made like that, could he help it? He could not see trouble anywhere without doing what he could to console the sufferer. Jeanie knew this well—and how tender a comforter he was. And poor Miss Margaret was so young and so bonnie, and in such sore trouble; and oh, it was easy to see, Jeanie thought to herself, how soft her heart was to him! No wonder; he would wile a bird from the tree. They met while she was in this softened mood; and Rob was one who never neglected the good the gods provided of this sort. He in his turn had recourse to Jeanie for consolation, throwing himself upon that feminine mercy and sympathy which never had yet failed him. And Jeanie cried, and was dismally flattered by his confidence in the midst of her suffering, and told him all she had heard from Bell about Margaret's movements, and forgot herself, poor girl, in the intensity of fellow-feeling and understanding.

Next time they met it was not by accident; and Rob, while growing more and more anxious about the new love, which meant more than happiness to him, which meant likewise fortune and an altogether elevated and loftier life, took the comfort of the old love which was thus thrown in his way, and found life much more tolerable from the fact that he could talk over his distresses with Jeanie. He could confide to her his

mother's taunts, and the hardness of his life at home, till Jeanie almost felt that to see him married to Margaret would be an advantage to herself, though she cried over it bitterly enough when she was alone. But what did she matter, after all, a poor lass? Jeanie thought she could put up with anything to see him happy.

"A bonnie end your drawing and your painting and a' your idleness is coming to," said Mrs. Glen, one November morning, while Rob obscured all the light in the little parlor window, putting the last touches to that drawing of Earl's-hall. "A bonnie way of spending your life. Eh, man! I would sooner sweep the house, or clean the rooms! What is the good o' a' this fyking and splairging? and what is to be the end of your bonnie miss that a' this idle work was to win? I'll warrant she thinks she's gotten clear off, and got a' she wanted, and no need to do a hand's turn for you, in recompense of a' that you have thrown away upon her."

"You have a very poor opinion of Margaret," he said, "if you think so little of her. You can scarcely want her for a daughter-in-law."

"Me!" said Mrs. Glen; "am I wanting her? I hope I have mair sense than to put my trust in daughters-in-law. 'A gude green turf's a fine gude mither,' that's a' the most of them are thinking. Na! she might gang to—Jerusalem for me, if it wasna that her siller is the only way I can think of to get you bread, ye weirdless lad. When you have no mother to keep a roof over your head, what is to become of you? The Lord be thanked there's no a weirdless one in my family but yoursel'. Do I want the lass or her siller—no me! But I'm real glad I've got yon bond over her, for you and no for me."

He frowned as he always did at the mention of this. "I am going to pack up this drawing and send it to Miss Leslie," he said.

"The picter! in a present!" Mrs. Glen stood for a moment taken by surprise, and a little bewildered by the suddenness of the suggestion. "I'm no that sure but what it's a good notion," she said, slowly; "them that dinna ken might say it was throwing good money after bad; but I'm no that sure. In a present? What might you get for that now if you were to sell it? for there's plenty folk, I hear, that are fuilish enough to give good solid siller for a wheen scarts upon paper." She had the most exalted idea of her son's skill, and secretly admired his work with enthusiasm—with all the naive appreciation of a "picture" which is natural to the uninstructed but not dull understanding—though she would not have betrayed her admiration for the world.

"What might I get for it?" said Rob, looking critically yet complacently, with his head a little upon one side, at the finished drawing. "Well —if I were known, if I had got a connection among the picture-dealers, perhaps—let us say twenty pounds."

"Twenty pound!" (she drew a long breath of awe and wonder); "and you'll go and give that light-headed lassie, in a present, a thing that might bring you in twenty pound!"

Rob did not explain that the bringing in of twenty pounds was an extremely problematical event. He got up with a little thrill of excitement and easy superficial feeling. "I would give her," he said, "just to hear from her—just to have her back again—just to have her hand in mine—I would give her everything I have in the world!"

"Ay, ay, my bonnie man," said his mother, impressed for the moment by this little flourish of trumpets. But she added, "And it would not be that hard to do it, if she'll only return you back your compliment, Rob, and do as muckle for you!"

This was how the sending of the picture "in a present" was decided upon, as a touching, if dumb appeal, to Margaret's recollection—not to say as "laying her under an obligation," which it would be necessary to take some notice of; for both mother and son fully appreciated this side of the question, which also forced itself at once upon Mrs. Bellingham's practical and sensible eyes. Mrs. Glen, for her part, entertained a secret hope that Margaret would have sense enough to see the necessity of giving not only thanks and renewed affection, but perhaps something else "in a present," which would make a not inadequate balance to Rob's gift. This was how things were managed by all reasonable people, that neither side might be "under an obligation" of too serious a character. But she was wise enough to say nothing of this to her son, though it is just possible that the thought may have glanced across his mind too. And about the letter which he sent immediately afterward, through Bell, and which produced such results for Margaret, Rob, on his side, said nothing at all.

CHAPTER XXXVII.

BELL had left Earl's-hall when the house was dismantled, a melancholy operation, which was proceeded with soon after the departure of the ladies. Old Sir Ludovic's library was sent over to Edinburgh, where the greater part had been sold and dispersed. It was, in its way, a valuable library, containing many rare editions and old works of price, a costly taste, which the present Sir Ludovic did not share. Whatever was done with the old house, his wife and he agreed that to get rid of the books would be always an advantage. If they kept it, the long room must be either divided into two, or at least arranged, for the comfort of the family, in a manner impossible at present while it was blocked up with shelves in every corner, and a succession of heavy bookcases.

In these innocent regions it was not necessary to keep servants in charge of an empty house out of alarm for the safety of its contents. Is it not the simple custom, even of householders in Edinburgh, secure in the honesty of their population, to lock their doors for all precaution, and leave emptiness to take care of itself? There was not much fear for Earl's-hall. If Aubrey Bellingham had known, indeed, that the various "bits" of china that he admired, and the old dresses in the "aumie" in the high room, and the bits of forlorn old tapestry that wantoned in the wind, were thus left without any protection, it is very possible that he might have organized a gang of æsthetic cracksmen to seize upon those treasures; but they were not in danger from any one in Fife.

Bell and John, or rather, to speak correctly, John and Bell, taking with them their brown cow and all the chickens, removed into a cottage which they had acquired some years before, on the road to the Kirkton, with one or two fields attached to it, and a neat little barn, byre, and poultry-yard. This had been for a long time past the object of their hopes, their Land of Promise, to which they looked forward as their recompense for years of long labor; and it was pleasant, there could be no doubt, to establish the brown cow in the byre and see her "like my leddy in her drawin'-room," Bell said, making herself comfortable in her new habitation. But it is a very different thing to have only "a but and a ben," when you have been virtual mistress of a fine old house like Earl's-hall; and although Bell had always prided herself upon her willingness "to turn her hand to anything," it did not quite please her to do all the little sweepings and dustings, and fulfil every duty of her little ménage, after having Jeanie under her, to whom she could refer all the rougher work which did not please herself. But above all, it was hard upon Bell that she had no longer "the family" to occupy her thoughts, to call forth her criticisms, and rouse her temper now and then, and give her a never-failing subject of interest and animadversion. Bell had a daughter of her own, who had been married as long as she could remember, it appeared to the old woman, and who had no children to give her mother a new hold upon life; and when she had finished her work and sat down in the evening "outside the door," but with a totally different prospect from that she had been familiar with so long, Bell would talk to any neighbor that chanced to pass that way, and paused to cheer her up—about "my family" and even about "my ladies," though they were the same whom she had talked of a little while ago with nothing but the definite article to distinguish them, and of whom she had never been fond, though they had risen so much in her estimation now, and she generally concluded the audience by a sudden relapse into crying on the subject of "my Miss Margaret" which filled the Kirkton half with pity for "the poor old body that had been so long in one place, and couldna bide to be parted from them," and half with indignation that she should "think mair o' a young lady that wasna a drap's blood to her, than of her ain." Mrs. Dreghorn, Bell's daughter, who kept the "grocery shop" in the "inigh toun," was strongly of this opinion. "My mother thinks nothing o' me in comparison with her Miss Margret—aye her Miss Margret!" said this good woman; but as Mrs. Dreghorn was forty, it may perhaps be allowed to be a different sentiment which Margaret called forth, from that steady-going affection on equal, or nearly equal terms, which subsisted between herself and her mother. Bell could not speak of her child without a moistening of the eyes. "My bonnie bairn!" she was never tired of talking of her, and of the letters Margaret wrote to her; Bell was perhaps the only one of Margaret's correspondents of whom she was not at all afraid.

Bell, however, was very much bewildered by the hasty, incoherent little epistle which she received in reply to hers, which had contained the letter of Rob Glen. "If you see Mr. Randal Burnside, will you ask him to speak to Mr. Glen? Say I told you to ask him, dear Bell; oh, be sure I said you were to ask him! and Mr. Randal will understand." What did this mean? Bell grew frightened, and for her part could not understand. The first step in the matter had been strange enough: that Rob Glen should have ventured to forward a letter to Miss Margaret, was of itself a strange and inexplicable fact. But it might be, as he said, about his picture; it might be about some price which old Sir Ludovic had offered. In such circumstances writing might be necessary, and he might not like, perhaps, to write to "the ladies themselves." But Margaret's message made the mystery more mysterious still. It confounded Bell so much that she said nothing about it to John, but wrote with much trouble and pain another letter, begging her young lady "not to trouble her bonnie head about young men; but to leave them to themselves, as being another kind of God's creatures, innocent enough in their way, but not the best of company for bonnie young ladies like her darling."

When, however, Bell had entered this protest, she immediately bent her mind to the due carrying out of Margaret's request. Randal had adopted the habit of coming over from Edinburgh in the end of the week and staying till Monday, a praiseworthy habit which his mother much encouraged, and of which she too spoke with tears in her eyes (so weak are women!) as proving her son to be the very best son in the world, and the very prop and staff of old age to "the doctor and me." It was true enough that he was the delight and support of the old couple in the Manse, of whom one was as yet not particularly old. And if Randal was fond of golf, and arranged "a foursome" for all the Saturdays of his visits, upon the Links which were within reach, in what respect did that affect the matter? A man may be a "keen golfer," let us hope, and a very good son as well.

"Is there ony news at the Kirkton?" Bell said, when John came in, throwing off an old furred coat that had been old Sir Ludovic's; for John's bones were getting cranky with rheumatism, and his blood thin, as happens to every man. The fur glistened as he came into the warm room with his breath, which the cold without had fixed like beads upon every little hair. John put it away carefully on its peg, and came "into" the fire, and put himself into his big wooden arm-chair before he replied—

"Naething of consequence; there's a change o' the ministry looked for afore lang, but that's been maistly aye the case as lang as I can mind. Either they're gaun out, or they're coming in; they're a' much alike as far as I can see."

"I wouldna say that," said Bell, who was more of a partisan than her husband. "There's our ain side—and there's the tither side, and our ain's muckle the best. It's them I would stand by through thick and thin—I'm nane o' your indifferent masses," said the old woman; "but it wasna politics I was thinking of. Did you see naebody that you and me kens?"

"Naebody that you and me kens? I saw a' body that you and me kens," said John, taking a very large mouthful of the vowel, which he pronounced aw—"first Katie and her man, just in their ordinar; and syne John Robertson at his door, complaining that he never could find Jeanie; and syne John Armstrong, a bonnie laddy, very strang, shoeing ane of Sir Claude's horses that's to hunt the morn; and syne—"

"Touts, I dinna want a dictionary," said Bell, probably meaning directory; "naebody mair particular than John here and John there? as if I was wanting a list o' a' the Johns! Weel I wat there's plenty o' ye, young and auld, and great and sma'."

"Is't the wives you're so keen about? I can tell ye naething o' the women; there were few about the doors at this time o' the night, and them just taupies, that would have been mair in their place, getting ready their man's supper, or putting their bairns to their beds."

"Eh, man John, but ye've awfu' little invention," said Bell. "If it had been me that had been to the Kirkton, I would have heard some story or other to divert you with that were biding at hame. But ye canna get mair out of a man than Providence has put intill him," she said, with a sigh of resignation; then added, as by a sudden thought, "You wouldna see ony of the Manse family about?"

"Ay did I," said John, provoked to hear any doubt thrown upon his capacity of seeing the Manse family. "I saw the gig trundling up the bit little avenue with Mr. Randal and his little portmanteau that I could have carried in ae hand. But Robert's just a useless creature that will have out a horse for naething, sooner than up with a bit small affair upon his shoulder and carry 't. It's bad for the horse and it's worse for the man, to let him go on in such weirdless ways."

"So Randal Burnside's back again?" said Bell. She did not pay much attention to John's further animadversions upon Robert, who was the man-of-all-work at the Manse. Having at last got at the scrap of information she wanted, she got up and bestirred herself about the supper, and listened to just as much as interested her and no more. In this way at his own fireside, without even Jeanie to disturb him, and no bell to break the thread of his discourse, John loved to talk.

The next day was Saturday, which Bell allowed to pass without any attempt to execute her commission; but when Sunday came, after the service was over, the sermon ended, and the kirk "skailing," in all decency and good order, she seized her opportunity. "Will you speak a word, Mr. Randal?" she said, lingering behind the rest. "Na, no afore n' the folk; but if you'll come round to me at poor Sir Ludovic's tomb yonder, where I'm gaun to see if ony weeding's wanted."

Randal gave a hasty assent. His heart began to beat, in sympathy, perhaps, with Margaret's heart, which had beat so wildly when she gave the commission now about to be communicated to him. He got free of the people, doubly tiresome at this moment, who insisted on shaking hands with the Minister's son as part of the performance. "Eh, what a sermon the Doctor's given us!" the kind women said. Perhaps Randal had not been so much impressed by his father's eloquence; but he was very eager to make an end of these weekly salutations and congratulations. He hurried back to Bell, with such an increase and quickening of all the currents of his blood, that the old woman looked with surprise upon his glorified countenance. "I never thought he was such a bonnie lad," Bell said to herself. As for Randal, he tried very hard, but with no success, to persuade himself that what she wanted with him must be some trifling business of her own. But his heart travelled on to Margaret, and to some chance message from her, with a determination which he could not resist.

"Well, Bell, what is it?" he said.

"I am real obliged to you, Mr. Randal. It's no my business, and it's a thing I canna approve of, that mann be said to begin with. Mr. Randal, I was writing to my young lady, to Miss Margret—"

"Yes?" said Randal, a little breathless, and impatient of the suspense.

"Ay, just that—and ye'll no guess what happened. Rob Glen, that's him that is Mrs. Glen's son at Earl's-lee farm, a lad that was to be a minister—you'll ken him by name at least—Rob Glen?"

"Yes, I know him;" Randal felt as if she had thrown a deluge of cold water upon him; his very heart was chilled. "Oh yes," he said, coldly, "I know Rob Glen."

"Well, sir, what does that lad do but come to me with a bit letter in his hand. 'When ye're writing to Miss Margret, will ye send her that for me?' he said. You may think how I glowered at him. 'For Miss Margret!' I said. He gave me a kind of fierce look, and 'Just for Miss Margret,' he says. You might have laid me on the floor with a puff o' your breath. Miss Margret! so young as she is, far ower young to get letters from ony man, far less a lad like Rob Glen."

"But why are you telling me this?" said Randal, half angry, half miserable. "I hope you will not tell it to any one else."

"I will tell it to no one else, Mr. Randal; I'm no one to talk. I have to tell you because I'm bidden to tell you. When I looked like that at the lad, he said it was about a picture that he had drawn of auld Earl's-ha'. And weel I minded the drawing of that picture, and the work my bonnie lady made about it. Well, I sent the letter, and yesterday morning, nae farther gane, I got twa-three lines from her, a' blotted and blurred, poor lamb. I'm thinking the ladies mann have been at her—her that never had a hard word from man or woman! 'Bell,' she says, 'if you see Mr. Randal Burnside, will you tell him to speak to Mr. Glen? Say it was me that bade ye, and then he'll ken fine what I mean.' I hope ye do ken what she means, Mr. Randal, for it's mair than I do; and I canna approve for a young lady, and such a young thing as Miss Margret, ony such troke with young men."

Randal's face had been almost as changeable as Margaret's while these words floated on. He reddened, and paled, and brightened, and was overshadowed, one change following another like the clouds on the sky. Finally, the last result was a mixture of confusion and bewilderment, with eager interest, which it is difficult to describe. "I fear I don't understand at all, Bell," he cried. "Was that all? Was there no more than that?"

"No another word; but a' blurred and blotted, as if she had been in an awfu' hurry. And ye canna understand? She said you would ken fine."

"I think I understand a little," Randal said, ruefully. He had asked her to call upon him whenever there was anything in which she want-

ed help, and here it was evident she wanted help; but of what kind? Was he to help her lover, or to discourage him? But of this Margaret gave no intimation. The office in itself was embarrassing enough, and what man ever received a more mysterious commission? She had appealed to him for aid, and who so willing to give it? But what kind of aid it was she wanted he could not tell. "I know in a way," he said, "I know she wants me to do something, but what? Never mind, I will do my best to find out; and when you write to her, Bell, my good woman, will you tell her—"

"Na, na," said Bell, briskly, "no a word. I've had enough to do with that kind of thing. I'll carry no message, nor I'll take charge o' no letters; na, na, lads are a destruction to everything. And no a lad even that might be evened to the like of her. Na, na, Mr. Randal, it might be the mamst innocent message in the world; I'm no blaming you, but I canna undertake no more."

"And I think you are quite right," he said, confusedly; "but—what did she want him to do?" He went away in great perplexity and excitement, which it was very difficult to shut up within his own bosom. To speak to Glen—that was his commission; but with what object? To help Margaret, poor little Margaret caught in the toils, and who had no one to help her; but what did she want him to do?

Randal went out after afternoon church was over, the "second diet of worship," as his father called it. It was not a promising evening for a walk. The short November day was closing in; the foggy atmosphere was heavy and chill—the clouds so low that they seemed within the reach of his hand. Hedge-rows and trees were all coated with a chill dew which soon would whiten with the night's frost; everything was wet underfoot. Even in the "laigh toun" few of the people were "about the doors." Gleams of ruddy fire-light showed through the cottage windows, often over a moving mass of heads, of different sizes, the children sitting about "reading their books" as became a Sabbath evening, and the elders on either side of the fire carrying on solemn "cracks," each individual furnishing a remark in slow succession. In-doors there was something drowsy and Sabbatical in the air; but there was nothing drowsy or comfortable out-of-doors. Randal walked toward the farm in the grim gray winterly twilight, wondering whether he could make any plausible errand to the house, or how he was to make sure of seeing Rob. But Fortune favored him in this respect, as indeed Fortune could scarcely help favoring any one who, wanting Rob Glen, walked in the twilight toward Earl's-lee. When he was within a field or two of the farm-house, Randal became aware of two figures in the shadow of a hedge-row, and of a murmur of voices. He divined that it was a "lad and lass." Lads and lasses are nowhere more common spectacles, "courting" nowhere a more clearly recognized fact than in Fife. Randal took care not to look at them or disturb them; and by-and-by he saw a little figure detach itself out of the shadows and run across the field. Who could it be? Their fervor of love-making must be warm indeed to enable them to bear the miseries of this "drear-nighted November." He went on with a certain sympathy and a little sigh. Randal did not feel as if there could ever be any occasion for "courting" on his part. He was vaguely excited; but sadness, more than any other feeling, filled his mind; if he saw Rob before him, what was he to say to him? "Ah, Glen!" he exclaimed, "is that you?" while yet this question was fresh in his mind.

Rob came forward from the shadow with evident discomfiture. He recognized the new-comer sooner than Randal knew him. Was he, then, the man who had been whispering behind the hedge, from whose side that little female figure, not, he thought, unknown to Randal either, had flitted so hurriedly away? Hot indignation rose in Randal's veins.

"Can it be you?" he said, with a sudden mingling of displeasure and contempt with the surprise in his voice.

"Not a pleasant evening for a walk," said Rob. He was uneasy too, but he did not see what he could do better than talk, and forestall if possible any objection the other might seem disposed to make. "I dropped something in the ditch," he said, accusing as he excused himself, "but it is evidently too dark to hope to find it now."

"You are still staying here?" said Randal, still more contemptuous of the lie, and feeling a secret desire, which almost mastered him, to push his companion into the chill ooze under the hedge-row. "Though the country," he added, "has not the same attraction as when we met last."

"No," said Rob, with a slight falter, "that is true; but necessity has no law. I am here because—I have nothing to do elsewhere. I am not so lucky as you, to be able to hold by and follow out the trade to which I have been bred."

"That is a misfortune, certainly."

"Yes, it is a misfortune—and such a misfortune in my case as you can scarcely realize. I have disappointed my friends and put them out of temper. There could be no harm in abandoning the law, but there is great harm in abandoning the Church."

"There is always harm, I suppose," said Randal, "in throwing up the career in which our training can tell. Church or law, it does not so much matter; there is always disappointment in such a drawing back."

"Perhaps that is true; but most in the first, and most of all in my class. Yes," said Rob, suddenly, "you may say there is less attraction now. The last night we met, it was just before the Leslies left Earl's-hall."

"I remember the night," said Randal, with some irrestrainable bitterness in his tone.

"I am sure you do. I felt it in your tone to-night. You disapproved of me then; and now," said Rob, with an air almost of derision, and he laughed a little nervous, self-conscious laugh.

"I don't pretend to any right either of approval or disapproval," said Randal. Anger was rising hotter and hotter within him; but what was it she wanted him to do?

"No right; but people don't wait for that," said Rob. He was not comfortable nor happy about his good-fortune. He had got Margaret's note, and it had stung him deeply. And here was one who could communicate with her, though he could not—who belonged to her sphere, which he did not. "We all approve or disapprove by instinct, whatever right we may have. If you had felt more sympathy with me, I might have found a friend in you," Rob went on, after a pause. "When two people, so different in external circumstances as Margaret and myself, love each other, a mutual friend is of the greatest advantage to both."

The blood rushed to Randal's face in the darkness. He felt the veins fill and throb upon his forehead, and fury took possession of his heart. He could have seized the fellow by the throat who thus wantonly and without necessity had introduced Margaret's name. But then—who could tell?—this office of mutual friend might be the very thing she had intended him to take.

"I cannot see what use I could be—"

"You could be of the greatest use. You could find out for me, without suspicion, a hundred things I want to know; or, if you fell under the suspicion of being after Margaret yourself," said Rob, with the unconscious vulgarity which he had never been able to get over, "there would be no harm done. They would not turn you to the door for it. You see our correspondence has to be of a very limited character till she is of age."

"Do you think," said Randal, hotly, "that to carry on such a correspondence at all is right or honorable without the sanction of the friends? No creature so young" (he kept to words as impersonal as possible, not feeling able to use a pronoun to indicate Margaret, whose sacred name ought never to have been breathed) "can understand what such a correspondence is. Glen, since you ask me, as a man of honor you ought not to do it. I am sure you ought not to do it."

"It is all very well talking," said Rob, "but what am I to do? Lose sight of her altogether—for three long years?"

"Is that the time fixed?" said Randal, with dismay.

"When she comes of age. Then, whatever happens, I have sufficient faith that all will go merry as a marriage-bell. But in the mean time—" Rob said, half-bragging, half-mournfully: he was in reality in the lowest depths of discouragement; but the last person to whom he would have confided this was Randal Burnside.

Randal was struck with a sudden thought. "Look here," he said, somewhat hoarsely, "I have given you my opinion, which I have no right to do; but you may make some use of me in return, if you like. Look here, Glen; I'll get you something to do in my uncle's office in Edinburgh, which will be better than hanging on here, if you'll have patience and wait till the time you mention, and take my advice."

Was this what she wanted him to do? The effort was a great one; for Randal felt a loathing grow over him for the under-bred fellow to whom such celestial good-fortune and unexampled happiness had fallen. To annoy and harass himself with the constant sight of him in order to leave her free and unmolested, it was a sacrifice of which Margaret would never know the full difficulty. Was this what she wanted him to do?

CHAPTER XXXVIII.

AUBREY BELLINGHAM was in the hall at the Grange when Margaret, all wet and weary, came in from that journey to the post-office. She was very anxious to get to the shelter of her own room, not only because she was feeling ill and wretched, but for the more immediately important reason that she was feverishly anxious to get rid of her wet dress before Jean should see her; for Margaret knew that Jean would more easily forgive a slight moral backsliding than her dishevelled appearance, blown about by the wind and soaked by the rain, and not without traces of the mud. She was ashamed of her own plight, though she had been too tired and had felt too miserable the latter half of the road, to keep up the struggle with the elements. Her feet made a splashing noise upon the tiles as she came in, and were cold as two pieces of lead; so were the hands, with one of which she had tried to keep up her umbrella, till it was blown inside out, when she gave up the struggle. A faint glimmer of anger rose in her when she saw Aubrey, all trim and dry and *point devise* as he always was, evidently waiting for her with the intention of speaking to her in the hall.

"How wet you are!" he said; "I could not believe my eyes when I saw you out in this rain. Could nobody have gone to the village instead of you? Why did you not send me?"

"Oh, *you*, Mr. Aubrey? It would have been worse for you than me," said Margaret. "I never thought much of the weather; but I cannot wait now to talk. I must run and change my dress. Jean," she added, ruefully looking at her spoiled trimmings, "will be angry about the crape."

"I hope I managed rightly," he said, following her to the stair. "I hope I did what you wanted?"

Margaret gazed at him with blank, wide-open eyes. What had he done? She had forgotten the silent appeal she had made to him in her pain. Aubrey was a man of sense, and he perceived that to insist upon this good office which he had in reality done out of pure good-nature, without any thought of interest, was more likely to hurt than to help him now; so he added hurriedly, "I did not see how wet you are; I cannot detain you an instant longer. Why didn't you send me? You will be ill after this."

"Oh! I never take cold," said Margaret; but how glad she was to struggle up-stairs, holding up the clinging skirts of her wet dress. Fortunately, Mrs. Bellingham, who had a thorough instinct of comfort, kept fires in all the bedrooms, so that Margaret had the glimmer of a little brightness to console her in the bodily misery which for the moment prevailed over all the distresses of her mind. She took off her wet clothing with great haste, and with an impulse to hide it, to keep it from Jean's keen eyes; and when she "was fit to be seen," she sat down to think how she could explain that hurried errand to Jean. The post-bag went from the Grange twice a day, in a regular and orderly manner, as it ought. What need had she to rush through the rain with her letters? But this problem proved too much for poor Margaret's brain: her head kept getting hotter and hotter; her feet, notwithstanding the fire, would not get warm; her

bosom seemed bound as by an iron chain; she could not get her breath. What could be the matter with her? Jean had said she had a cold on the previous night; she supposed it must be that—a bad cold; how stupid and how wretched she felt. She sank back into the corner of the sofa which was opposite the fire; it was very lazy of her to do so, she knew, in broad daylight, when there was all the day's work to do. Margaret planned to herself that she would do it to-morrow—her practising and her French exercises, and all the little studies with which, under Mrs. Bellingham's energetic guidance, she was making up for her neglected education. She would do them to-morrow—yes, to-morrow; but was not to-morrow Sunday, when you cannot work? Was not night coming, in which you could do no work? Was not— Here Margaret seemed to break off with a start, and found that she had been dozing, dozing in the middle of the day, in broad daylight! It seemed impossible. She woke wretched, as young and healthy creatures do after such a feverish sleep. How could anybody sleep in the day? and how, of all wonders, was it that Margaret herself had slept in the day? It seemed something incredible; but before she knew what was coming, in those troubled wanderings, she had dropped again into another snatch of uncanny sleep. She did not hear the luncheon bell, nor if she had heard it would she have had energy enough to go down-stairs, or, indeed, to get up from her seat; and when Miss Leslie, coming up, hurried into the room, in wonder and alarm, to call her, Margaret was found propped up in the corner of the sofa, all flushed and confused, her pretty hair falling out of its fastenings, her hands hot and feverish. She woke with a start when her sister opened the door. "Oh! where am I? where am I?" she cried. After this there was nothing but alarm in the house. The doctor was sent for, and Miss Grace, who had cried herself almost into hysterics, could do nothing but kiss her little sister, and ask, in a melancholy voice, "Are you better—do you think you are a little better, darling Margaret?" was turned out and sent away, while Jean hastily took the place of nurse. If Jean had a fault as a nurse, it was that she required so many preparations. She assured Margaret it was nothing at all but a feverish cold, and that it would be better to-morrow; but she provisioned the room, as John had provisioned old Sir Ludovic's, as for a siege of six weeks at least, and took her place in a dressing-gown and large cap by the bedside, like a woman who had made up her mind to hold out to the end. Margaret, however, was too ill to be alarmed by these precautions; she was too ill to mind anything except the pain which had her by the throat, and checked her breathing and filled her veins with fire. It was not a bad cold only, but that sublimation and intensification of cold which carries death and destruction under the name of congestion of the lungs. She was very ill for a week, during which time Mrs. Bellingham kept heroically by her bedside, resolute to keep out Grace and to fight the malady in the correct and enlightened way. Aubrey had to search through all the adjoining town, from shop to shop, for a thermometer good enough to satisfy his aunt, which she received from his hands in all the mingled solemnity and familiarity of her nursing-dress.

"I am sure the Red Cross has nothing half so imposing," he said, in his flippant way; "you would strike an army with awe." He himself had but a dull time of it down-stairs. He remained till Margaret was out of danger—very kindly solicitous—but when the crisis was over he withdrew. "You see I can make no progress now," he said, on the occasion of an interview which Mrs. Bellingham awarded him, when the good news was proclaimed; "but perhaps a week or two hence I may come in with the chicken and champagne, and help to amuse the convalescent. One may make a great deal of running with a convalescent, Aunt Jean."

"I wonder how you can talk so lightly, when we have just escaped such a danger," said Mrs. Bellingham. "Not only Margaret, poor dear, but the property would have gone to quite a distant branch of the family, and even the savings of the minority. I can't bear to think what might have happened. But you can do nothing now, it is true; you may as well go and return when you will be of use. But mind and go to the very best shop you can find in town, and get me a really good thermometer. I put no faith in anything that is bought in the country." And that night, for the first time, Mrs. Bellingham permitted herself to go to bed.

It would be needless to follow Margaret through all the feverish thoughts that assailed her, or even those more coherent ones that came after the first stupor of illness. She recovered the power of thought now and then by intervals, as the fever abated, and then, no doubt, soft, dreamy musings, half dismal, half pleasant, of a pretty grave somewhere which would cut all the knots that bound her, and make all things clear, came into her mind. If she were to die, how little would it matter whether Jean was angry, whether Ludovic scolded! They would all forgive her, even if she had been silly. And though poor Rob, to whom her heart melted, as the one person whom she felt sure (besides Bell) to be very fond of her, would, no doubt, "break his heart" over that grave of hers, it would, she thought, be less hard for him, than to find out how little pleasure she took in the bond between them, and to bear the brunt of that struggle which she had so little heart to encounter—the struggle with Ludovic and Jean. And then another thing: what would it matter if Aubrey were right after all, and it was really Effie, Effie that Randal Burnside cared about? They would be happy, no doubt; and they would sometimes give a sigh to poor little Margaret, and tell each other that they never thought she would live long.

This wrung Margaret's heart with an exquisite pity for her poor young tender self, cut down like a flower. And as the fever recurred, she would lose herself in wonderings where they would bury her; if they would take her down to the Kirkton, and lay her with her father in the breezy mound where she would be able to see her own hills, and hear, on stormy nights, the moaning of the sea? And then it would seem to Margaret that she was being rolled and jolted through a vast darkness going toward that last home of the Leslies—dead at eighteen, but yet feeling and seeing everything, and half pleased with the universal pity. Over all these wanderings of sick and feverish fancy Jean presided in her big cap, the shadow of which against the wall—sometimes rigidly steady, with a steadiness that only Jean could possess, sometimes nodding so that Margaret trembled, feeling that nothing could survive so great a downfall—ran through them all. Jean, in her big cap, was very tender to the girl. She was very quiet in her movements, and, notwithstanding the nodding of the cap, very vigilant, never forgetting an hour or dose.

The strangest week it was!—the time sometimes looking not an hour, since she had begun to doze in the corner of the sofa, sometimes looking like a year, during which she had been wandering through dreariest wilds of confusion and pain. When she came to herself at last, without any choking, without any suffering, but utterly weak and passive, Margaret did not quite know whether she was glad that she was better, or disappointed to feel that everything outside her was just of as much consequence as ever; that she would have to marry Rob Glen, and submit to Jean's scolding, and wonder if it was true about Randal and Effie—just the same.

But she did not recover in the speedy and satisfactory way which was desired. When she got what her anxious attendants called almost well, and got up and with an effort got herself dressed, it was astonishing to find how few wishes she had. She did not want anything. She did not care about going down-stairs, did not want to get out, and was quite content to be let alone in her corner of the sofa, reading sometimes, still oftener doing nothing at all. At this point of her convalescence it was that Jean had retired, leaving the remainder of the nursing to Grace, who, with a great grievance at her heart on the score of being shut out of the sick-room, took the place now offered her with enthusiasm, and did her best to administer the wines and jellies, the beef-tea, the concentrated nourishment of all kinds which were wanted to make her charge strong again. One day, however, Jean, returning from some outside occupation, found the sick-room in a grievous state of agitation. Margaret had fainted, for no particular cause that any one knew; and Grace and Miss Parker stood weeping over her, scarcely capable of doing anything but weep.

"Her mother, bless her, was just like that," Miss Parker was saying. "I often thought afterward if we had taken her abroad for the winter it might have been the saving of her. The doctor said so, but no one would believe it. Oh, if we had only taken her abroad!"

This was said in the intervals of fanning Margaret, who lay extended on the sofa as pale as marble, while Grace held salts to her nose. Margaret came to herself as her sister came into the room, with a shiver and long sigh, and Jean, rushing in, cleared away the two incapable persons and resumed the charge of affairs. But, like a wise woman, she took a hint even from her inferiors. When she had restored poor Margaret and made all quiet and comfortable round her, and ordained that she was not to talk or be talked to, Jean's heart throbbed with terror. Not only did Margaret herself seem in renewed danger, but there was the estate to be considered, which would go away to a distant cousin, and do no one (as Mrs. Bellingham said) any good. When the doctor came, she consulted him with great anxiety on the subject. "Yes," the doctor said; "no doubt it would be very good for her to go to Mentone for the winter." He would not say she was in any particular danger now, but delicate, very delicate; all the Sedleys had been delicate, and it must not be forgotten that her mother died young. All this made Jean tremble. The girl herself, though she had been almost a stranger to her a little while ago, had got hold of her fussy but kind nature. She had nursed Margaret successfully through a serious illness; was she to submit to have her snatched out of her hands now for no reason at all, with no disease to justify the catastrophe? Jean said No stoutly. She would not submit.

"My dear, I am going to take you to Mentone," she said. "I hope you will like it. It is very pretty, you know, and all that. There are a great many invalids; but, poor things, they can't help being invalids. I am very sorry we sha'n't enjoy Christmas at the Court; that is a thing that would have done you good. But, to be sure, as we are still wearing deep mourning, we could only have gone to the family parties, which are not very amusing. Grace, you may as well begin your packing; you always take such a time. I am going to take Margaret to Mentone."

"Oh!" cried Grace, ready to cry, "dearest Jean! then the doctor thought that dear Margaret—"

"The doctor thought nothing about Margaret," cried Mrs. Bellingham. "The doctor thought what I told him. I said Mentone would do the child good after her illness, and all that has happened, and he agreed, of course. That is all they can do. They tell you to go if they think you will like it. If they think you will not like it, they recommend you to stay at home. I'll take Aubrey with me; he will always amuse Margaret."

"And, dearest Margaret, how good it is of dear Jean to settle it all! Do you think you will like—"

"Like! of course she will like it," said Jean. "We shall start in a week; so you had better speak to Steward about your packing. A day will do for Margaret and me."

"Mentone? that is Italy!" said pale Margaret, with a little glow rising upon her face; and then she put her pale little hands together, which were as small as a child's, and said to herself, inaudibly, "That is *away!*"

She got a little better from that hour. All the circumstances of her bondage, all the risk of discovery, the chance of agitating letters, such as those which had been the cause of the exposure that had ended in her illness, had come rushing back upon her memory. And it was a sudden intimation of some letters that had been put aside for her that had caused her faint, overpowering her, in her weakness, with sudden agitation. Letters! What might they be? She dared not ask for them. She dared not say anything about them in case of questions which she could not answer. He might be coming, for aught she knew, to haunt the neighborhood of the house, to watch for her, to waylay her, to claim and take possession of her, whether she liked or not. It is not to be described what a soft gush of ease and relief and quiet came over her, when she realized that she was now to be taken *away*. Away! out of reach of all painful

visitors, where it would be too far for him to come after her, where she would be safe. Margaret mended from that hour. And when, by means of Miss Parker, of whom she was not afraid, she managed that evening, while Jean and Grace were at dinner, to get possession of the letters, and found one from Bell giving an account of the execution of her commission, and another from Randal, her heart threw off its burden, although Randal's letter filled her with strange yet pleasant excitement. She was not frightened by it as she had been by Rob's letter; but felt, on the contrary, a great thrill of eagerness and wonder. Would he say anything about Effie? This, however, was all Randal said:

"DEAR MARGARET,—If I may call my old playfellow so, I got your message, and thank you most cordially for it. I understood it, though I did not know what you wanted me to do. But I will tell you what I did. I saw him: he was anxious and complaining. I advised him to have patience, not to attempt to write, which would probably put you in a false position, and offered him a place in my uncle's office. He has accepted, and he will take my advice. If this is not what you meant, let me know by one word. I thought it was for the best; but if silence is disagreeable to you, it is I that am to be blamed, not any one else. Thank you, with all my heart, for understanding that I would serve you, if there was any need, with my life. Yours ever,
      "RANDAL BURNSIDE."

How her heart bounded! She seemed to have found some one who would set things right, who would manage those disturbed affairs for her. It did not occur to her that she had no right to put such a charge upon Randal, or make him her agent. That idea never entered her mind. How well he had divined what she wanted! The way in which he told her of it was very curt and brief, it is true, and she felt disposed to wonder why he had put it in such few words; but it relieved her of all her fears. It was in Randal's hands now. Randal would not let *him* come to worry her. Randal would save her from all this trouble. Jean heard her laugh, as she was coming up-stairs—heard her laugh, the little monkey! and Mrs. Bellingham was so glad that she could not be angry, though had this outburst happened twenty-four hours sooner, she probably would not have taken her away.

And she was quite equal to the journey when the day came, though she was still weak and white. One incident occurred, however, before they started, which very much surprised Margaret. She was in the wainscot parlor, alone, reclining among her cushions, when Mr. St. John came in. The elder ladies were out, and Margaret had been left alone. Perhaps it was Miss Grace who had suggested this to the gentle Anglican. He came in and sat down beside her, with eyes enlarged by emotion and anxiety; and after he told her how much sympathy her illness had brought out, and how many people had asked for her, and how fervently they had all thought of her when the prayer for sick persons came in the Litany, Mr. St. John startled Margaret beyond measure by suddenly telling her that he loved her, and asking if she would be his wife. "Me?" she cried, with wondering, questioning eyes, in profoundest bewilderment and surprise, and with her usual Scotch indifference to her pronouns. She grew paler than ever with horror. "Oh, it cannot be so!" she said, shaking her head. But this gave her a shock of surprise and pain. She did not want to hurt anybody's feelings. Could it be anything in her that made this painful thing happen over again?

CHAPTER XXXIX.

AUBREY joined the travellers in London. It was very self-denying of him, very kind, to give up all the festivities at the Court, and all his many Christmas invitations, in order to accompany and take care of a party of ladies on a journey to Mentone, his aunt said; "I will not say that it is not a sacrifice to myself to give up Christmas at the Court. I don't grudge the sacrifice, my dear, for your sake, and for the sake of your health; but I will not say it is nothing and does not matter, as Grace does. Don't you believe, either, that it does not matter to Grace. She likes her amusement just as well as the rest of us, though, to be sure, our mourning would make a difference. But Aubrey is a young man, and has as many engagements as he can set his face to; and we are nothing but a couple of old aunts, and you a bit of a little girl. Yet when he can be of use he never hesitates. You ought to be very grateful, Margaret, for all he is doing for you."

"And so I am," said Margaret: it was very kind. And though Aubrey, when he arrived, scouted the notion, and declared that he would go anywhere to get rid of the festivities of the Court, this did not make any impression upon the ladies, who praised his self-denial to the echo. As for Margaret, there could be no doubt that his presence made the expedition very much more agreeable to her. Jean and Grace were very kind; but Jean was a little overpowering in her manifold arrangements, and Grace's tenderness did not always fall in with the girl's humor, who was apt to be impatient now and then. Margaret got better day by day; and there was so great a load lifted from her mind that she was able to enjoy everything as she had never done before. No chance now that she should be followed and pursued by any attendant of whom she would be afraid. Every step they took made that more impossible. She seemed to get out of the range of Rob Glen altogether when she crossed the Channel, not to say that Randal had already made her deliverance certain.

She dwelt upon this action of Randal in many a musing, with mingled admiration and gratitude. How clever it was of him to divine what she wanted to be done! The confusion of the moment had been partly to blame for the incoherent message she had sent; but it was not altogether the confusion of the moment. There had been, besides, a reluctance to mention the name of Rob Glen to Randal, a desire to imply, rather than to state distinctly, what she wanted him to do. The vagueness was at least partly voluntary, and partly she did not know what she wanted to be done. She wanted something, some one to interpose who should know better than herself, who should be able to see what was

most expedient. What claim had she on Randal that he should have done so much for her? And what inspiration could it be that made him divine so exactly what she wanted—exactly what she wanted!—not to hurt Rob's feelings? Oh no, very far from that. If she had not been unwilling to hurt Rob's feelings, it would never have been in his power to give her so much alarm as he had done.

Margaret sat and thought over all this as they crossed the bit of sea between Dover and Calais. Jean and Grace had betaken themselves to a deck cabin, where they lay each on a sofa, scarcely venturing to congratulate each other that the sea was not quite so bad as usual, but prepared for every emergency, and Aubrey had gone to the other end to smoke a cigar. Margaret, in her excitement, had scorned the deck cabin, which both her sisters protested had been secured entirely for her. She was, though she did not as yet know it, one of those happy people who are excited, not prostrated, by the sea. She felt that she would like to walk about the decks with Aubrey; but all that had been permitted to her was to sit in the most sheltered corner, done up in shawls and wraps, so as to lessen all chances of taking cold. And after a while, when the first thrill of excitement calmed down, and she began to get accustomed to her own emotion, and the fact that she had left England, and the extraordinary certainty that these were the shores of France to which she was going, the extreme isolation of the moment drove Margaret back, as is so often the case, upon her most private thoughts. The exhilaration of her being, which was partly convalescence and partly change, she attributed entirely to the fact that, for the moment, she was free—delivered from the danger that had seemed about to overwhelm her.

This consciousness seemed to triumph over everything—her grief which was still so recent, her illness, all the ills her flesh was heir to. And as Margaret's mind was growing amidst all this agitation, it was now, at this moment, in the middle of the Channel, that the thought suddenly occurred to her: if she had been a sensible girl—if she had not been a very foolish girl, how much better it would have been to pay no heed to Rob Glen's feelings—to cut at once this bond which was all his making, which had been woven between them without any wish of hers—which she had always rebelled against, except those first nights when she had scarcely been aware what he was saying, or what doing—when she had received his declarations of love almost without hearing them, and allowed his kisses on her cheek with no more perception of their meaning than that he wanted to be "kind" and comfort her. There had been no lover's interview between them in which Margaret had not—a little —shrank from him. She had held herself away as far as she could from his embracing arm. She had averted her cheek as much as possible; but it had been impossible for her to fling away from him, to deliver herself altogether at the cost of Rob's feelings. This she had not strength of mind to do. But now she perceived that it would have been better had she done it—had she said plain No, when he declared his love with all the hyperbole of passion.

Margaret knew she did not love him, certainly not in that way; but how she had shrunk from saying it—from letting him feel that she did not care for him as he cared for her! How it would have hurt his feelings! Rather put up with some little excess of affection for herself, she thought, than humiliate him in this way! And now was the first time when she really asked herself, Would it not have been better to say the truth? The question flushed Margaret's cheek with crimson, then sent back all her blood in a sudden flood upon her heart. She did not venture to contemplate the possibility of having done this —of having actually said to him, "It is a mistake; you are very—very kind, but I am not in love with you."

The mere idea of it appalled her. How cruel it would have been! How he would have "thought shame!" How his feelings would have been hurt! But still—but still—perhaps it would have been better. She had just become pale and chill all over with the horrible possibility of having given such pain as this, when Aubrey's voice startled her. He was saying, anxiously,

"I am afraid you are ill. I am afraid you are feeling cold. Won't you go into the cabin and lie down? We shall be there in half an hour."

"Oh no!" said Margaret, her paleness disappearing in another sudden blush. The days of her blushing—her changes of countenance, which were like the coming and going of the shadows— had come back. "Oh no! I am not cold; and I am not ill. I like it. But I—was thinking—"

"I wonder if I might offer you a penny for your thoughts? I dare say they are worth a great deal more than that. Would you like to have mine? They are not worth the half of a penny. I was thinking what poor creatures we all are—how unamiable we are on board of a steamboat (the most of us). Look what pictures of misery these people are! It is not rough, but they cannot believe that it may not be rough any moment; when there is a pitch—there—like that!" said Aubrey, himself looking a little queer. "They think, now it is coming! All their strength of mind, all their philosophy, if they have any, cannot resist one heave of that green water. Ugh—here's another!" he cried, relapsing out of his fine moral tone into abject sensationalism. Margaret laughed as merrily, with her eyes dancing, as if there was no Rob Glen in the world.

"But I don't care," she cried. "I like it: when it seems to go from under your feet, and then bounds like a greyhound."

"Don't speak of it," he said, faintly. "And why is it you are so superior to the rest of us? Not because you are so much brighter, and purer, and better—"

"Oh no!" cried Margaret, interrupting him, shaking her head and smiling. "Oh no! for I am not that—"

"You should not contradict people who are older than yourself—it is not good manners," he said, solemnly. "You are all that, I allow; but that is not the reason. It is simply because of some little physical peculiarity, some excellence of digestion, or so forth, if one may venture to use such a word: not because it is *you*—which I should think quite a natural and proper reason. No, for I have seen a creature as fair and as good almost as you are, Margaret (our travel-

lers' names are Margaret and Aubrey, you know —that's understood), I have seen a beautiful young girl, everything that was sweet and charming, lying dishevelled, speechless, a prey to nameless horrors. Ah! that was a bad one!" said the young man, unable to conceal that he himself had become extremely pale.

"Oh! I am very sorry for her," said Margaret, forgetting the compliment in the interest of the story. "Who was she, Mr. Aubrey?" and she turned her sympathetic eyes full upon him, which was almost more than, in his present state of sensation, he could bear; but, happily, Calais was within a stone's-throw; and that is a circumstance which steels the suffering to endurance. He got up, saying, "I think I must look after the aunts."

Margaret looked after him with a warm gush of sympathy. Who was this beautiful young girl who had been so ill? Was poor Aubrey, too, "in love?" She felt disposed to laugh a little, as is natural in the circumstances; for does not every one laugh when a love-story is suddenly produced? But she was deeply interested, and at once felt a kindred sympathy and affectionate interest opening up in her bosom. Poor Aubrey! Had anything happened, she wondered, to the beautiful young girl who was everything that was sweet and charming? Was not that enough to make everybody take an interest in her at once?

Margaret got no immediate satisfaction, however, about that beautiful young girl, but she often thought of her; and when she saw any shadow come over Aubrey's face, she immediately set it down to the credit of this anonymous young lady. For the moment, however, she was herself carried away by the excitement of being "abroad." But, alas! is not the very first of all sensations "abroad" a bewildering sense that it is just the same world as at home, and that "foreigners" are nothing else than men and women very much like the rest of us? For the first hour Margaret was in a kind of wonderland. The new, unusual sound of the language, the different looks of the people, delighted her, and she could understand what they were saying; though both Jean and Grace declared it to be such bad French that they never attempted to understand. "Is it very bad French?" she whispered to Aubrey; "perhaps that is why I know what they mean." And he gave her a comical look which made Margaret inarticulate with suppressed laughter. Thus the two young people became sworn allies, and understood each other. But, after the first hour, the old familiar lines of the world she had been previously acquainted with came back to Margaret. The people, though they were dressed differently and spoke French, were the same kind of men and women as she had always known. Indeed, the old women in their white caps looked as if they had just come from Fife.

"That is just what they were at home," she said again to Aubrey: "the old wives—those that never mind the fashions—even Bell!" There were some of the old women on the French roads, and at the stations, so like Bell that the sight of them brought tears to Margaret's eyes.

"Who is Bell? I have so often heard of Bell. Bell has been put forward again and again, till I am afraid of her. I am sure you are afraid of her; and Aunt Jean, too, though she will not say so."

"Oh, not me!" cried Margaret, uncertain as ever about her pronouns; "Bell is—she is just *Bell.* She was our house-keeper; she was everything to me; she brought me up. I never recollect any one else. Afraid of Bell—oh! no, no. But I would not like Bell to know," said Margaret, slowly, "if I did anything that was bad—anything that was *real* wrong—"

"You never will," said Aubrey, "so it doesn't matter; but I should call that being afraid of her. Now there are some people whom you only go to when you *have* done something that is *real wrong.*"

"Are there? I don't know. It was Bell that brought me up, more than any one else. She is living now near—on the way to the Kirkton. But you will not take any interest in that."

"I take the greatest interest," said Aubrey; and it so chanced that this conversation, broken off in the railway, was renewed again when they were settled at Mentone, where again old women were to be found like Bell. They passed rapidly through Paris, and settled at once in the place that was supposed to be good for Margaret. But by the time they reached the sunny Riviera Margaret had thrown off all trace of indisposition, and evidently wanted nothing but air and sunshine, and a little petting, like other flowers. They had a little villa on the edge of that brightest sea; and there along a path bordered by a hedge of aloes, and with a great stone-pine at the end, its solemn dome of foliage and its great column of trunk relieved against the Mediterranean blue, the two young people took a great many walks together.

One of these evenings specially stamped itself on their memories; the sky was flushed rose-red with the sunset, and all the sounds in the air were soft, as summer only makes them in England: there was a tinkle going on close at hand from a convent-bell, and there was a soft sound of voices from the beach—voices, of which the inflections, the accents, were all dramatic, though they could not tell a word that was said. It was the enchanted hour, the time of natural magic and poetry; and Aubrey, though he was not at all poetical, felt it a little more than he could have believed possible. He had found out how pretty Margaret was—how much prettier, day by day. It was not that there was any striking beauty in her that conquered with a glance; but every morning when she appeared down-stairs, with her color coming and going, with her brown eyes full of such eagerness and lovely wonder, "she grew upon you," Aubrey said. He had thought her very tolerable even at first—no particular drawback to her income and her estate. But by this time he took a great deal of interest in her. She was never the same; always changing from serious to gay, from red to white, from quiet to eagerness. He was interested, never wearied. He had not really found it much of a sacrifice to accompany the ladies, after all. The place was a bore; but then, fortunately, Margaret no longer required to be kept at this place; there was a reasonable hope of moving on to places in which there was more amusement; and Margaret was really amusing, very amusing, as girls go. There was a variety about her which kept your interest alive.

"Did you ever do anything that was real wrong?" said Margaret, dreamily, looking out toward the horizon where the rose of the sky met the blue of the sea. She was rather thinking aloud, than realizing the scope of what she said; and it is doubtful whether the girl ever realized the difference between a girl and a man—the very different sense that *real wrong* might have to him, or the equivocal meaning which such words might bear to a listener of so much more experience in the world.

He laughed, startling Margaret from her dreamy musing. "Alas!" he said, "a great many times, I am afraid. Did you? But I don't suppose you know what wrong means."

"Yes," she said, drawing a deep breath, "I am not in fun; once: and it seems as if you never can get better of it. I don't know if it is any excuse that I did it because I did not like to hurt a person's feelings."

"What was it?" he said, lightly; "a little fib—a statement that was not quite justified by fact? These are the angelical errors that count for wrong among creatures like you."

"Then what do you call wrong, if that is not wrong? Aubrey, it was more wicked than that: but I am not going to tell you what it was. I have been dreadfully sorry ever since I did it. But I feel a little easier, a little happier now."

"Perhaps you broke a bit of old Dresden?" he said, "or lost that Venice point Aunt Jean showed me. I should never forgive you for such sins, Margaret. No wonder you are reluctant to confess them. You are happier because nobody could be unhappy in this delicious evening, walking as we are. It is only in such a scene that I could look with complacency upon the heartless destroyer of china, the careless guardian of lace—"

"You are only laughing at me," she said; "I think you are always laughing. Don't you think there is anything in the world more serious than china and lace?"

"Very few things, Margaret. Few things so dear, which you will allow is very serious, and few things so easily injured."

"But oh, Aubrey! I think that is almost wicked, to love a thing that cannot love you again, as much as—more than things that have life."

"I don't do that, Margaret." He looked at her so earnestly that she was almost abashed, yet, fearing nothing, went on, moved by the flowing of her own newly awakened thoughts. "You and Jean, you talk as if a little bit of a cup or a plate—what we call pigs in Fife—was of more importance— What are you laughing at, Aubrey?—because I said pigs? But it is the common word."

"My dear little Margaret," he said, "don't make me laugh, with your pigs. Lecture me. Let us go and sit under the pine and look out upon the sea, and do you preach me a little sermon about real right and real wrong. I am just in the mood to profit by it now."

"You are doing what papa used to do," said Margaret, half laughing, half crying; "he would always make a fool of me. And how should I lecture you? You must know much better than I do."

"I ought, I suppose," he said. The pine stood on a little point, one of those innumerable fairy headlands that line that lovely coast, the sea lapping softly, three parts round, the foot of the cliff on which it holds its place. The air was more fresh there than anywhere else. The pine held high its clump of big branches and sharp evergreen needles high over their heads: behind them was a bosquet of shrubs which almost hid them as they sat together. The blue sea thus softly whispering below upon the beach, the delicate rose that tinted the sky, the great pine isolated and splendid, how could they recall to Margaret the dark wood, all worn with the winds, the mossy knoll, the big elbows of the silver fir, the moan of the Northern sea with which she had been so familiar? The one scene, though made up of almost the same details, bore no more resemblance to the other than Aubrey Bellingham did to Rob Glen: and where could a greater difference be?

"Yes," he said; "so far as wrong is concerned, I should suppose so. I must be better up in that than you are; but, all the same, I should like you to teach me. Let it be about the right; there you are strong. What must I do to cease to be a useless dilettante—as you say I am?"

"Me? I never said so, Aubrey—not such a word. I never said such a word."

"But you meant it. Tell me, Margaret: if I can cease to be a dilettante and a trifling person, what would you have me be?"

He bent toward her, looking into her eyes, and half put out his hand to take hers; and Margaret, startled, saw once more what it had so much bewildered her to see in Mr. St. John, the same look which she knew in the eyes of Rob Glen. What an amount of experience she was acquiring, ever renewed and extended! This frightened her greatly. She drew away from him upon the garden-seat, and kept her hands clasped firmly together, and beyond the reach of any other hand.

"I do not want you to be anything," she said, "you are very well as you are. You might think upon—perhaps you might think upon—the common folk a little more. When you came to Earl's-hall we did not know what you meant; and sometimes even now Jean and you— I know most about the common folk, they are just as interesting as the others."

"Ah," he said, laughing, but a little discomfited, "you mean the poor. Must I take to visiting the poor?"

"I suppose you call them the poor, in England," said Margaret, doubtfully, "but you know a great deal better than I do, Aubrey; for one thing, you are older. I think perhaps Jean will think I ought to go in now."

"Certainly, I am a great deal older; but not so very much, either. I am twenty-five—just about the right age to go with eighteen. Yes, tell me a little more. I shall recollect about—what do you call them? the common people—not the poor. Go on, my moralist; I am ready to be taught."

"I think I hear Grace calling," she said, rising to her feet. "I am sure Jean will think the wind is getting cold, and that I should have gone in before."

"The wind is as soft as summer," he said, with a little excitement, "and the evening as sweet as—yourself. Wait a little, only a few minutes; there is something I wish so much to say to you."

"Oh, Mr. Aubrey!" she said, frightened. "Do not say it! I would rather you did not say it. Once I did very wrong, not wishing to hurt a person's feelings; but that is what I must never do any more."

"Are you sure," he said, rising too, with a sudden flush of anger, "that you know what I was going to say?"

Margaret paused, with an alarmed look at him, the color wavering in her cheeks, her eyes very anxious, her lips a little apart.

"What I was going to say," he continued, pointedly, "was, that I fear I must soon leave the villa, and the fine weather, and your delightful society. This kind of holiday life cannot endure forever."

"Oh!" She uttered her favorite exclamation with a look of distress and, he thought, disappointment. This was balm to Aubrey's heart.

"Yes, I am sorry, too. But what can be done when duty calls? My office is getting clamorous, and there is nothing for a man to do here. Now, perhaps, we had better carry out your intention, and go back to Aunt Jean."

And they walked through the garden back to the house, with scarcely a word spoken between them. One way or the other way, both were equally uncomfortable modes of managing such a crisis. She had hurt his feelings! It was better than all that followed the episode of Rob Glen; but still it was not a pleasant way.

CHAPTER XL.

AND it was true that the very next morning Aubrey declared his intention of going away. "My chief finds that the office cannot get on without me," he said, pretending to have had letters by the morning mail; while Margaret sat, not daring to look up, feeling more guilty than she could say. Her consciousness that she was to blame even carried the day over her determined belief in the sincerity and absolute truthfulness of every one about her. Twenty-four hours since she would have accepted Aubrey's statement as a matter-of-fact which left no room for doubt or comment. But now she could not but feel that she had something to do with it, that she had hurt his feelings, which made Margaret feel very guilty and wretched. He had been so kind to them, to her and her sisters, and sacrificed a great many pleasant things to come with them: and this was all her gratitude! She did not like to lift her eyes. When Jean and Grace both rushed into wailing and lamentations, she said nothing. She tried to swallow her tea, though it nearly choked her, but she could not speak.

As for Mrs. Bellingham, she said not half so much to her nephew then as she did after breakfast, when she had him to herself.

"You can't be going to do anything so foolish, Aubrey, my dear Aubrey!" she said; "why, you are making progress day by day! If ever a girl was delighted with a young man, and pleased to be with him, and happy in his society, Margaret is that girl. And you know how anxious I am, and how it would please everybody at the Court to see you provided for."

"You are very kind, Aunt Jean," he said, with a flush of angry color. "I know you mean nothing that is not amiable and kind; but I think, all the same, I might be provided for in some other way."

Jean, though she was so strong-minded, felt very much disposed to cry at this failure of all her wishes.

"I don't understand you at all," she said; "I am sure there was nothing meant that was the least disagreeable to your feelings. Margaret, though I say it that perhaps shouldn't, is as nice a girl as you will find anywhere; and though her education has been neglected, nobody need be ashamed of her. And you seemed to be quite pleased; and I am sure she is really fond of you."

"Yes, that is one of your Scotticisms," he said; "you mean that as long as I am serviceable, and don't ask too much, Margaret likes me well enough. I don't say anything against that—"

This time Mrs. Bellingham really did put up her handkerchief to her eyes. "I never expected to hear of my Scotticisms from you, Aubrey," she said. "Of course I am Scotch—there is no doubt about it—and I would never be one to deny my country. But I did think that, after spending by far the greater part of my life in England, I might have been free of any such abuse as that."

"My dear Aunt Jean, do you think I meant abuse? I mean that Margaret likes me well enough as a friend—which you call being fond of me. I shouldn't wonder if she would herself say, with all the innocence in the world, that she was fond of me, knowing perfectly what she means; but then I should put a different meaning on such words. She will never be fond of me in my sense; and so, as I have still a little pride left (though you might not think so), it is clear that I cannot be provided for, as you say, in that way."

"What is the matter with you, Aubrey? Has anything happened between Margaret and you. Have you said anything, or has she said anything?"

Aubrey saw he had gone too far, and had almost committed himself; and he did not want any one to think that a mere ingénue, a bread-and-butter girl like Margaret, had repulsed or discouraged so accomplished a gentleman as himself. He said, with a little laugh, "My dear aunt, what are you thinking of? That has not been at all necessary. Margaret and I are the best friends in the world. I am 'very fond of her,' as you say. She is a charming little girl. But your scheme will not do; that is all. Was not I quite willing to be provided for? But it will never come to anything. Oh yes, I suppose the chief might be smoothed down; there is nothing so very important going on at the office: but what is the good of it? Margaret and I will stroll up and down the beach, and listen to the band, and all that, and be very fond of each other; but we will never get a step farther than we are now."

"I know what it is," said Mrs. Bellingham—"you are bored; that is the whole business; and I don't wonder. To see all the poor things about, with their sick faces, is enough to make

anybody ill. And Margaret, the little monkey, after giving us such a fright, is just as well as I am. Some one was speaking to me the other day about the villa. I dare say we could get it off our hands quite easily; and in that case, if we go on to some place which is more amusing, will you change your mind—or, let us say, reconsider your decision?"

He shook his head and shrugged his shoulders, and then he remembered his interests like a young man of sense. "Well, perhaps I will reconsider my decision," he said.

After this the party went on into Italy, and saw a great many things that filled Margaret with delight and wonder. She expanded like a flower, as the spring came on—that Italian spring which is as youth to whosoever can receive it with an unburdened soul. And to Margaret, who already possessed youth, it was not only delight, but mental growth and expansion of the whole being. Aubrey left them for a time, but returned again to escort them home in that month of May which is the climax of all the splendors of spring. The interval between his going and his coming back did a great deal more for Aubrey than any attentions of his could have done. They were in Florence when he left them, where Mrs. Bellingham and Miss Leslie had already found a number of acquaintances, and where soon they were deep in afternoon teas and social evenings, as if they had been at home.

Margaret had no education which fitted her for the delights of this life, and she could not run about alone in the solemn Italian city as she had done at home; and she missed her companion, who, though he was not clever nor particularly well-informed, understood how to set afloat those half-thoughtful, half-bantering conversations which youth loves, and in which young talkers can soar to heights of wise or foolish speculation, or drop into nonsense, at their pleasure: an art in which, it is needless to say, neither Mrs. Jean nor Miss Grace was skilled; and now and then he had an accès of enthusiasm equally beyond the range of the ladies, who walked about, guide-book in hand, and insisted that nothing should be omitted. "Margaret, Margaret! you are running away without seeing half of the pictures. I am only at No. 310," Mrs. Bellingham would say. But when Aubrey was there, the girl was emancipated, and allowed to gaze her soul away upon what she liked and what he liked. How she missed him! She was quite ready, as he said, to declare with fervor that she was "very fond" of Aubrey, and welcomed him when he came back with genuine pleasure. "Oh, how glad I am you are to be with us now till we get home!" she said.

Aubrey looked at her with a glance which was half angry and half affectionate. "You are a little deceiver," he said; "you like me to be with you only so long as I am useful. I am a kind of courier; that is all the good of me."

"Oh no," cried Margaret, "I cannot tell you how much I missed you. It is because you are so kind."

"It is because of me, not because of you," he said, with a frown and a laugh; "and so it always will be, women are so"—he was going to say selfish; but when he caught Margaret's eyes puckered with emotion and wistfulness, looking anxiously at him, he stopped short and changed the word—"ridiculous," he added, not knowing what she meant, and feeling a little, just a very little, prick in his heart that it was so, and that Margaret only found him agreeable for his good qualities, and not from any inclination toward him within her own being. Her eager reception of him, however, woke a sentiment in him which was not unlike love; he was pleased by the brightness of her welcome: and to be unable to make a girl fall in love with you, a simple girl of eighteen who has never seen anybody, after months of companionship—a girl, too, whom to marry would be to provide for yourself for life—this, there can be no doubt, is humbling to a man of accomplishment and experience. So Aubrey made up his mind to another effort, with more determination, if with less lively hope. He would not quarrel with her if in the long-run she still refused to fall in love with him, but he began to hope that a different result might be attained. He liked Margaret, and Margaret liked him, without any disguise; and, after all, there was no telling: perhaps perseverance on his part, and the habit of referring to him perpetually, and getting a great deal of her pleasure through him, might bring about a satisfactory state of things at the last.

They reached London in the beginning of June, when everything looked at its brightest. What a change Margaret felt in herself! She was no longer the little girl who had been allowed to grow up in all the simplicity of a country maiden, untaught and unsophisticated, at Earl's-hall. She had seen a great many things and places, though that mere fact does not make very much difference. She had learned to think; and there had grown about her that little subtle atmosphere of personal experience which can rarely be acquired in the little world of home. It was not possible for her to identify herself with her old sisters as she might have done with her mother. From the first they had been separate existences, detached from her, though in close incidental conjunction, and so kind to her. She was grateful to them, and loved them as she could, but she was very conscious of the isolations of her existence; and how could she help the little criticisms, the little laughters, the amusement which their "ways" could afford only to one whose life was not involved in theirs, and whose duty to them was less than the most sacred? Such detachedness has much to do with the energy of personal existence. Margaret had begun to feel herself, and to know what her life was, during the hours of solitude that were inevitable; and through the long period of partial companionship in which she went and came, docile and quiet in the train of Jean and Grace, without feeling herself ever identified with them, her own being was slowly developing within her. She had begun to see what the position was that she was born to occupy, and to foresee dimly duties which she had no natural guide to instruct her in, no natural representative to do for her, but which would have to be done otherwise than as Jean and Grace would bid.

These grave foreshadowings of the future came, however, but by glimpses upon Margaret. She had no desire to think of the future: over it there was a shadow which she did not know how to meet. She held it as much as she could at arm's-length, still with a dumb faith in circumstances, in something which might still happen to deliver her. So entirely had she succeeded in this, that the alarming image of Rob Glen, which every time she thought of him had more and more terrors for her, had not even troubled her in any vision for weeks before the party recrossed the Channel on their way home. But on that passage, as they came back, Margaret suddenly remembered the thought that had occurred to her there as she went away. It was a breezy day, and the sea was not smooth: Jean and Grace lay on sofas in the deck cabin, indifferent to Margaret, and everything else in earth and heaven. Aubrey, not much more strong in this particular, had taken himself and his miseries out of the way. Margaret, in happy exemption, sat alone. But this was not a happy exemption, as it happened; for suddenly there leaped into her mind a recollection of the question she had asked herself first, in this very steamboat, on this very ocean, five months ago—Would it not have been better to disregard Rob Glen's feelings and tell him the truth? "Yes," she said now to herself, firmly, though with pale lips, and a shadow immediately fell over the brightness: the time was coming when her fortitude would be put to the test, when she must meet him and decide what was to be the course of her life—and every tick of her watch, every throb of her pulse, every bound of the boat, was bringing her nearer—nearer to this terrible moment, and to Rob Glen.

They stopped in London for a few days to "do some shopping"—perennial necessity which haunts every mortal—and "to see the exhibitions." This was a thing which Mrs. Bellingham considered absolutely necessary. She had not failed to go through the Royal Academy, with her catalogue in her hand, marking the pictures she liked, once in the last twenty years. Nobody in society could avoid doing this. Whether you cared for them or not, it was indispensable that you should see them—they are always a topic of conversation afterward; and Mrs. Bellingham had seen a dull party redeemed, quite redeemed, by a little knowledge of the exhibitions.

"Oh yes, dearest Margaret, we must stay; dear Jean never misses the pictures, and you and dear Aubrey must see them. Dearest Jean says that all young people should see them; certainly they are very beautiful and humanizing, and will do us all a great deal of good. We are to start as soon as we have had our luncheon. I should have liked to go in the morning, but dear Jean likes to see the people as well as the pictures; and, darling Margaret, you that have never seen anything, that will be so good for you too."

"Not your hat, Margaret, your *bonnet!*" said Mrs. Bellingham; "we are in town: it is not like Florence or Paris, or any of those foreign places where we were visitors. Here you must understand that we are in *town*. Next year we will come up for the season, when we are out of mourning (or almost out of mourning), and you must be presented and all that; but there is nothing to be done in crape: it would be altogether out of the question, and a disrespect to papa. But, such as it is, put on your bonnet, my dear Margaret. We shall see nobody—but we may see a good many people; and you must never forget that you are in *town* now."

The bonnet was put on accordingly, and the ladies went to the Academy, with Aubrey in attendance as usual. Perhaps he did not like it so well as in foreign places, for they were a little travel-worn, and their crape not so fresh as it ought to be; but still the faithful Aubrey was faithful, and went. He knew that if anybody saw him (and of course somebody would see him), it would be supposed that he had expectations from the old aunt in her imperfect crape; or the truth would creep out about Margaret, and he would be forgiven everything when it was known that it was an heiress upon whom he was in attendance. Such facts as these change the external aspect of affairs.

It was a bright day, warm and cheerful, and the Academy, of course, was crowded. Aubrey did not consider that it was his duty to follow Mrs. Bellingham while she made her conscientious round; but he kept close by Margaret, who was half frightened by the jostling and crowd, and could not see anything, and had a vague sense of dread she could not tell why. "I am afraid you have a headache," Aubrey said; but Margaret did not feel that it would be honest to take refuge in that common safeguard of a headache. It was something more like a heartache that she had, though she could not tell why. She was standing looking round her vaguely enough, tired and waiting for a seat, in the great room, in a corner not so crowded as the rest, and Aubrey was coming up hurriedly to tell her of a sudden vacancy on one of the benches, when he was arrested by the sudden change in her countenance. Her eyes, which had been wandering vaguely over a prospect which afforded her but little interest, suddenly cleared and kindled; her face, which had been so pale, was suddenly lighted by one of those flushes of color which changed Margaret's aspect so completely; her lips, which had been so serious, parted with the brightest of smiles. She made a step forward, all lighted up with pleasure, and held out her hand. Aubrey stopped suddenly short in his advance, and looked suspiciously, keenly at the new-comer who produced this change on her. He was not a man who was addicted even to the most innocent of oaths; but this time his feelings were too much for him. "By Jove! the man of Killin," he said; and he was so much startled that the words were uttered half aloud.

"Randal!" Margaret said, all smiling, holding out her hand. "Oh! I did not think I should see any one I knew—much less you. How little one can tell! I had been wanting to go away."

The simplicity of pleasure with which she said this took Randal by surprise. He clasped her hand and held it in his own for a moment with a corresponding self-betrayal. "It seemed too good to be true," he said; and they stood together for a moment so completely absorbed in this sudden delight of seeing each other, that Aubrey gave way to another vulgarism quite unlike his good-breeding: he made as though he would have whistled that long note of wonder and discovery which is one of the primeval signs invented before language. "When did this come about?" Aubrey said to himself; and his surprise was so genuine that he could do nothing but stand half petrified, and watch the course of this singular interview going on in all simplicity before his eyes.

"Jean and Grace are both here," said Mar-

garet, "and Aubrey—Aubrey, whom you saw with us last summer. Oh, Randal, have you just come from home? Are they all quite well? Is it long since you saw Bell? Is Earl's-hall very dreary, standing empty? Oh! I would like to hear about everything. Will you come and see us? But tell me, now, are you staying in London, and what was it that brought you here, just this very afternoon, when I was coming too?"

"My good angel, I think," said Randal, fervently; and again the color rushed over her face, and she smiled—as Aubrey thought he had never seen her smile before.

"Let us say a kind fairy," said Margaret; "but will you come and see us where we are living? For here there is no quiet place to talk. Don't go away though, Randal: Jean and Grace would like to see you—and I too."

"Is it likely that I should want to go away?" he said; and then his face paled a little, and he added: "There is some one else you want to ask me about, Margaret. You will not need to trust to me for information at second-hand." Then he lowered his voice, and said, bending toward her, "Glen is here."

"Oh!" Aubrey could see the usual little exclamation prolonged almost into a cry. She grew quite pale with a dead pallor of fright. "Oh, Randal, take him away; or take me away. What shall I do?" she cried.

"Do you not wish to see him, Margaret?"

"Oh no, no, Randal! Turn round; pretend to be looking at the pictures. What shall I do? Oh, do not let him know I am here! It was that made me ill before. It was—all a mistake, Randal. Oh, I felt sure when I came out to-day something was going to happen; and then when I saw you I thought how silly I had been—that it was something good that had happened: now here is the right reading of it. Oh, Randal, you helped me before; can you not help me again now?"

"I will do anything, whatever you wish," he said; "but, Margaret, if this is your feeling, it is scarcely fair to Glen; I think he ought to know."

"Yes, yes," she said, but in too great a panic to know what she was saying; "which will be the best? Should I stay here while you take him away, Randal? I could stand close to the pictures and put down my veil; or will you take me away? Oh, think, please, for I do not seem able to think! But he would be sure to know me if he saw me with you. Aubrey—oh, here is Aubrey," she said, seizing his arm as he approached; "he will take me: and, Randal, come—will you come to-night?"

"Where?" said Randal, putting out his hand to detain her. Aubrey, with a somewhat surly nod of recognition which the other was scarcely aware of, gave him the address; and almost dragged through the crowd by Margaret's eagerness, went away with her, not ill-pleased, notwithstanding this disagreeable evidence of some mystery he did not understand, to carry her off from the man she had smiled upon so brightly. She had dropped her veil, which was half crape, over her face, and, holding her head down and clinging to his arm, drew him through the crowd.

"Are you ill?" he said; "what is the matter, Margaret?" But she made no reply; and

it was only when he had found Mrs. Bellingham's hired carriage, which was waiting outside,
and put her into it, that she seemed to be able
to speak. Even then she would not let him go.
"Will you come home with me?" she said,
with a sweetness of appeal and a wistful look
which Aubrey, with some indignation, felt to be
false, after the reception she had given to "that
Scotch fellow," yet could not resist.
"I am afraid you must be ill," he said, half
sullenly—"yes, if you wish it, I will go with
you; but Aunt Jean, I am afraid, will think this
very strange."
"There was some one that I did not want to
see. Ah!" she cried, putting up her hands to
her face and sinking back into a corner of the
carriage. Aubrey, looking out where her terrified glance had fallen, saw a man turn round and
stare after them as they drove away; but he
could not see who or what kind of man this was.

CHAPTER XLI.

WHEN Rob Glen accepted the offer that Randal made him and agreed to the conditions, it
was done partly in despite, partly in impatience,
partly because the novelty tempted him, in the
state of discouragement and irritation which
Margaret's troubled response had thrown him
into. He had not ceased to be "in love" with
her, nor was the impassioned letter he had addressed to her really false, notwithstanding his
constant confidential interviews with Jeanie,
which would have been the direst offence to
Margaret had they been known, or had she really cared for him as he supposed and hoped her
to do. Had she been within reach, Rob would
have been really as much in love with Margaret
as ever; but he was angry and hurt by her indifference, and humiliated, he who had won so
much love in his day, that she did not receive
his letter with pleasure. Even if she had seen
the inexpediency or impossibility of continuing
the correspondence, he could not forgive her that
she had no word of thanks to send him for the
letter, which might have made a girl happy, no
breathing of soft response to its impassioned
strain. He was pleased to punish her, to revenge himself by the hasty pledge not to write
again. Yes, he would punish her. Next time
she received one of these letters it should be
after months of weary waiting, when she would
thank him as she ought.
It was absolutely impossible for Rob to realize that it would be a relief to Margaret not to
hear from him at all. The idea was incredible.
Never before in all his experience had he met
with a girl who was quite insensible to his wooing, and Margaret, who was so young, so artless! She might be afraid to snatch that painful joy; the perils of a clandestine correspondence might alarm instead of exciting her; but
that she should not like it, was beyond all Rob's
acquaintance with human nature, and altogether
incredible to him. And thus he would punish
her. Edinburgh too would no doubt be more
cheerful than the farm in the depth of winter,
when his mother's ill-humor and the absence of
all amusement would aggravate the short days
and long, cold nights, in which even a stroll with

Jeanie was no longer practicable. Mrs. Glen,
too, looked favorably on the idea. It would
"pass the time." "And you'll be in the way of
seeing a good kind of folk," his mother said;
"plenty of gentry is aye about thae lawyers'
offices. They're in want o' siller, or they're
wanting to get rid o' their siller; and I wouldna
lose a chance of a good acquaintance. Then,
when the time comes, and when you set up in
your ain house with your lady-wife, you'll no be
without friends."
"Friends made in an Edinburgh writer's office, of what use will they be in the heart of
England?" said Rob, with lofty superiority; but
he was not displeased by the suggestion. He
no more thought it possible that, with his talents, he could fail to "win forward," as his
mother said, than he thought it possible that
Margaret could really be indifferent to such a
glowing composition as the love-letter he had
sent her. The only thing in the whole matter
that he felt any reluctance about was, how he
was to break it to Jeanie, whose sweetness, as
his confidential friend and adviser, had been very
soothing and consolatory to him. As the decision had to be made at once, there was not even
much time in which to break it to Jeanie. He
strolled past her father's cottage in the high
town on one of the nights when Margaret lay at
her worst in a haze of fever, with her life appar-
ently hanging on a thread. But none of all the
little knot of people at the Kirkton, whose lives
were tangled with hers, were as yet aware of
anything that had occurred to her. Rob went
slowly past the little window, all glowing with
fire-light, where John Robertson sat tired with
his work, while Jeanie put away the cups and
saucers after their tea. By-and-by it would be
necessary to light "the candle," for he had still
a job to finish before bedtime; but what did
they want with the candle when they were at
their tea? Fire-light was quite enough for the
scanty meal and the conversation which went
on, not without a divided attention on Jeanie's
part; for she could not but think that she heard
a step outside which she knew.
"I think I will run out for two or three minutes and see Katie Dewar, when you are settled
to your work, faither," Jeanie said; "she is always complaining, and it's a fine night," she added, with a little compunction, looking out through
the uncurtained window. The sense of deceiving, however, was not at all strong or urgent in
her, for such little deceits about a lover's meeting
are leniently dealt with in Jeanie's sphere.
"You'll no be very long, Jeanie." Her father
had a sufficiently good notion of what was going
on, and, as he was quite unconscious of any complication in Rob Glen's affections, and quite confident in his daughter's purity and goodness, it
did not disturb him much. "Mind that it's a
cold night, and dinna loiter about."
"I'll no be very long, faither." Jeanie threw
a shawl round her, but left her pretty head, with
its golden-brown curling hair, uncovered. If it
was very cold it was always easy to throw a fold
of the shawl over her head. She went out, with
her heart beating—not altogether with pleasure.
To be with him was still a kind of happiness, and
it was better even to be the confidant of his
engagement with another — which Rob had so
cunningly implied would never have existed had

Jeanie's presence hereabouts been known—than to have nothing at all to do with him. She stole along, half flying, in the shadow of the houses, and finally came out into the cold moonlight, at the corner beyond the little square, where she could see some one waiting. Poor Jeanie! her pleasure and her sadness, and the mixture of the sweet with the bitter which was in these interviews, had become a kind of essential elixir to her life.

"Jeanie," he said, after their first greetings were over, "I am going away."

"Going away!" She had to grasp at his arm to support herself. "Ay," she said, drearily, after a pause, "nae doubt; I aye kent that was how it would have to be."

"I only knew it myself yesterday," he said; "I have not lost a moment in telling you. How did you know that this was how it would be?"

"Oh, I kent it," she said, holding her hands clasped to support herself; "it was easy to divine—it was no such a mystery. Weel, Maister Glen, ye'll go to her ye've chosen, and ye'll be real happy with her. She's bonnie, and she's good, and she'll give ye more, far more, than the like of us could give you. I wish ye luck with a' my heart. Ay, a' my heart! baith her and you."

Jeanie withdrew a step from his side as she spoke, and her voice took something of the soft wail of the dove in the inflections and modulations which mark the native tongue of Fife. It was in a kind of soft cadence that she spoke—too soft to be tragic, but pitiful and wailing, the most pathetic of utterances. Jeanie did not rebel—it was natural, it was right; but the blow went to her heart.

"My foolish Jeanie," he said; "what are you thinking of? Do you think it is Margaret that has sent for me? Do you think she is going to acknowledge me all at once, and that all our troubles are over? No, my dear; you are too simple and too good, my bonnie Jeanie. It is not that. Margaret takes no notice of me. I am going to Edinburgh—to a situation, not for ease, not very far away—and not to her, Jeanie. You must not give me up so soon."

He put his arm round her, and drew her close to him; and Jeanie, though full of better resolutions, was weak with the shock she had just received. She was thankful to lean against him for a moment.

"No that—not to her? when she could settle a' if she pleased. Eh, Rob, ladies are no like—they're no like—"

"You, Jeanie? No; who is like you? Always kind—whatever happens, always ready to forgive. What is that in the Bible, 'Suffereth long, and is kind.' I think that must have been made for you."

"Oh!" said Jeanie—like Margaret, in the soft long breath of that ejaculation—"we shouldna quote Scripture, you and me! for what we are doing is a' wrang. Oh, Rob, it's a' wrang! You that are troth-plighted to another lass—though she is a lady—and me, that—"

"Yes, you that—what of you, Jeanie? not pledged, you must not say so, to another man."

"And if I was," she cried, "what would you have to do with it? it would be but justice. Na, na, that's no what I'm meaning, as weel ye ken. My heart has never had room but for ane. No

—me that should ken better. Oh, dinna, dinna, I canna have it! Me that should have kent better was what I meant to say."

"Why should you know better? How can we tell what will happen in three years? And till three years are over nothing is settled," he said, with a secret thrill of anxiety and pain in his heart to remember that this, unlike much that he said, was altogether true.

"It's true," she said, shaking her head. "My heart's that heavy I can think of nothing but harm; we may a' be dead in three years; and oh, I wish it might be over with me!"

"I cannot have you speak like this," he said. "I am going to Edinburgh—you don't seem to care to hear—to a situation Randal Burnside has offered me. I don't know that I will stay in it long. Very likely it will only be a stepping-stone to something better. I will see you when I come back, which will be often, Jeanie; and indeed I think you might come over to see your friends in Edinburgh—you must have friends in Edinburgh—and see me."

"I'll not do that," said Jeanie, decidedly.

"You'll not do that? I don't think that is quite kind. But never mind, I will come home—often—on Saturday, like Randal Burnside."

"Will you be in the same line as Maister Randal, Rob?"

"I think not just the same line. He pleads, you know, Jeanie, in the Parliament House, before the judges, and I will have to manage cases before they get there. It is a very important business. Failing what I was brought up to—the pulpit, and all that I was trained for—I think my people will be more pleased with the law than anything else. It is always respectable; it is one of the learned professions. I will not deny that it is a very good opening, Jeanie."

"And when do you go away?"

"This week," he said. "I don't want to lose any more time; I have lost all my summer. It would have been better for me if I had never come home. I would have missed you, Jeanie; but then I might have avoided other things that can never be got rid of now."

"Oh!" she said, her heart wrung with the suggestion, pleased with the regret, wounded with the comparison; "I wonder if you would say just the same of me to her as of her to me?"

"How could I, when you are so little like each other?" he said. "But, Jeanie, let us think of ourselves; let us not bring in her, or any one. My bonnie Jeanie, when I come back I shall always find you here?"

"I canna tell—the cobbling's no just a grand trade, and what will feed ane does not yet serve two. I think I will maybe take a new place—at the New-Year."

"But not to take you from the Kirkton, Jeanie—not to take you away from me?"

"If it was to take me far, far away—to London, or to America, or to New Zealand, where so many are going—and I wish my faither would think of it," she said, softly. "Oh! I've great reason to pray, 'Lead me not into temptation,' for I would be far, far better away."

"You are not like yourself to-night, Jeanie. Why should you lecture me to-night, just when you have to say good-bye to me—good-bye for a little while?"

"It would be far, far better if it was good-bye

forever," she said; "but eh, Rob, I canna understand mysel'. I would be glad if it was me that was to go—ay would I. I would go to New Zealand, if my faither would but come, the morn; but when it's you, a' my strength fails me, my heart goes sinking away from me, my head begins to turn round. I know it's right, but I canna bide it, Rob!"

"My poor little Jeanie," he said, caressingly. "And I cannot bide it, if you speak of what a man likes; but it is better for me that I should not be wasting my time. I should be doing some work that will be worth a man's while. What is money, Jeanie? I shall have plenty of money. But I ought to be known, I ought to think of my name."

"Oh, that's true," she said. "I know well you're no a lad to spend your life in a quiet country place. And that just shows me more and more the difference between you and me, Rob. I shouldna call you Rob—I should say Maister Glen."

"Will you write to me, Jeanie? That was why we lost sight of each other. I did not know where you were; but now I will often send you a letter, and then, on the Saturdays, I will probably come over with Randal Burnside."

"Rob, Mr. Randal is a gentleman, and so will you be a gentleman. No, oh no; you and me should say farewell. I'll aye think upon you. I'll pray for you night and morning; but dinna speak about you and me. We're like the twa roads at Earl's-ha' that creep thegither under the trees, and then pairt, ane west, the ither east. Oh, Rob!" said Jeanie, with streaming eyes, "no good will ever come of this. Let us summon up a good courage and pairt. Here we should pairt. No, I'll no grudge you a kiss, for it will be the last. It's a' been mecsery and confusion, but if we pairt the warst will be past. Say Farewell, and God bless you, Jeanie!—and ah! with all my heart, I'll say the same to you."

"You are trembling so that you can scarcely stand," he said. "Do you think I will let you leave me like this? I cannot part from you, Jeanie, and why should I? It would break my heart."

"It has broken mine," said Jeanie, fervently; "but rather a broken heart as a false life. Rob, Rob, haud me nae longer, but let me gang to my faither. I'm safe when I'm with him."

But it was not for a long hour after this that Jeanie returned to her father, conducted as near as he could venture to go by her lover, who grew more and more earnest the more he was resisted. She went in very softly, with a flushed and glowing cheek, stealing into the cottage not to disturb the solitary inmate who sat working on by the light of his dim candle.

"Is that you, Jeanie?" he said, placidly; "and how is Katie Dewar, poor body?" This question went to the bottom of her guilty heart.

"I'll no tell you a lie, faither; I wasna near Katie Dewar. It's a fine night, and the moon shining; I gaed down the road, and then a little up the road, and then—"

"Oh, ay, my lass, I ken weel what that means," he said; "but I can trust my Jeanie, the Lord be praised for it. I'm just done with my job, and it's been a lang job. When the supper's ready I'll blow out the candle, and then if you've onything to tell me—"

"I have naething to tell you," she cried. But as they sat together over their supper, which was of "stoved" potatoes, a savory dish unknown to richer tables, Jeanie pressed upon her father once more with incomprehensible energy and earnestness the idea of New Zealand, which had already two or three times been talked of between them before.

Rob, however, left her with little alarm as to New Zealand. He was deeply gratified by that attachment to himself which made her ready to put up with everything, even the bond which bound him to another; and the struggle in Jeanie's mind between what she wished and what she thought right, which ended in the triumph of himself, Rob, over all other powers and arguments, was very sweet and consolatory to him. It healed the wounds of his *amour propre*. If Margaret did not give him the devotion he deserved, Jeanie gave him a devotion which he did not hesitate to confess he had not deserved, and this reconciled him to himself. The maid made up for the short-comings of the mistress, and perhaps Jeanie's simple worship even gave a little license to Margaret as to the great lady, from whom, in her ladyhood and greatness, the same kind of love was not to be expected. She had things in her power to bestow more substantial than Jeanie's tenderness, and with these she had vowed in due time to crown this favorite of fortune. Rob was a sort of Sultan in his way, and liked the idea of getting from these two women the best they had. He went away from Stratheden a few days after, with his heart quite soft and tender to his Jeanie. He would not forget her this time. He would write to her and say to her what he could not say to Margaret. He would keep a refuge for himself in her soft heart, whatever happened. And, indeed, who could tell what might happen in three years?

While he thus made a settlement which quite pleased him in his affairs of the heart, the other part of his life was not quite so satisfactory. The position which he took in the office of Randal's uncle in Edinburgh was naturally that of a beginner, and he did not "win forward" as he had hoped. When clients came, they preferred to see the principal of the office, and instead of making acquaintance among the gentry, Rob found that all he had to do with them was opening the door to them when they came in, or showing them the way out when they left the office.

He did not say much about this, nor did he reveal his discontent to Randal, having sufficient good-sense to learn by experience, and perceiving that this was indeed quite natural and the only thing to be expected, as soon as circumstances had impressed it upon him. But struggles with reason and circumstances of this kind, if they invariably end in an increase of hardly acquired knowledge, and are thus, perhaps, instructive in the highest degree, are not pleasant. And Rob having made no advance in "position," and having no important work confided to him, but only, as was natural, the most elementary and routine business, soon became heartily sick of the office and of himself. He returned more hotly to his former hopes, as he felt the folly of this, and soon began to be conscious of the utter incongruity between his prospects and his present position. He tried to console himself like any child, by imagining to himself scenes of delightful revenge for all those "spurns which patient merit of the unworthy takes." When he was Margaret's husband, and the possessor of her fortune, he planned to himself how he too would become a client of the employers who now treated him so coolly. What piece of business would he intrust to them? He would make them buy in Earl's-hall if it ever came to be sold. He would consult them about the investment of the long accumulations of Margaret's minority. But in the mean time, while these grandeurs were not his, the office became more and more irksome to him.

He had lost the habit of work during those idle months at home, where love-making had been his only serious occupation, and indeed he had never had the habits of work necessary here, the routine of certain hours and clearly defined duties, which the more free and less regular work of education is in general so little akin to. He had not been what is called idle in his studies; but then these are always vague, and a young man may make up the defective work of the day at night or at odd moments, which a clerk in an office never can do. After a while, Rob had become so entirely disgusted with the humbleness of his position and the character of his work—so deeply impressed by the incongruity of his present with the future he looked forward to—and so indignantly conscious of powers within him which were capable of something better than this, that he threw up the situation which it had taken Randal no small trouble to get for him, and, without warning, suddenly set out for London, carrying with him his sketches and some slight and frothy literary essays which he had written, with the full intention of becoming a painter and an author, and taking the world by storm. The payment of three months' salary had given him the means for this; and he felt that it was the only way, and that he had known all along it was the only way, to acquire for himself fame and fortune. He had by this time heard of Margaret's illness, and of her absence; but even had he thought of doing so, he had no means of following her into the expense and mystery of that unknown world which the ignorant know as "abroad." Indeed, to do him justice, he went to London with no intention of molesting Margaret, but only with a very fixed determination of making himself known—of coming to some personal glory or profit which should make up to him for the personal failure of the past. Rob had been in London for about a month on that eventful day when Randal Burnside, who was in town upon business, had met him in the Exhibition. They had met not without a certain friendliness; and Randal, curious to know what he was doing, and still more curious to ascertain how much he knew about Margaret, and if he was keeping his promise in respect to her, had engaged Rob to dine with him, and had parted from him only a few minutes before he met Margaret herself.

Meantime Rob, having finished his inspection of the pictures, and convinced himself that there were many there much inferior to his own, though he could find no purchasers for them, was issuing somewhat moodily forth, when a slight figure in black hurrying down the steps before him, and clinging closely to the arm of a man

whom he thought he had seen before, yet did not recognize, caught his eye. He stood and looked after them while the carriage was called, his curiosity awakened he could scarcely tell why. He had followed them down to the pavement, and had just reached it when Aubrey put Margaret into the carriage; and all at once a vision of that well-known face, all tremulous and eager, avoiding, as he thought, his suddenly excited gaze, rose before him. In another moment the carriage was dashing along more quickly than is usual in the streets of London. Rob stood with a gasp gazing after it, and did not come to himself till it was too late to attempt the frantic expedient of jumping into a hansom and rushing after it. He did so when he realized what it was that had happened; but by this time it was too late, and he had not remarked the appearance of the carriage, but only the face in it. Margaret! The sight put sudden fire into his veins. He must see her; he must claim her. It was irrational and monstrous that a girl who was his promised wife should be entirely separated from him. Whether it was her own will or that of her friends, he would not submit to it any more.

———

CHAPTER XLII.

IT was Rob, perhaps, who had the most right to be excited by this unexpected vision; but Randal, who had no right, was also driven half wild by it, and altogether lost his head as he stood gazing blankly about him, and saw Margaret, rather dragging Aubrey after her than being conducted by him, thread through the crowd with such an eager impulse of flight. Few young men could have refused to be a little biassed and shaken from their equilibrium by the sweetness of such a reception as he had just received. The brightening of her countenance, the look of pleasure that overspread her face, the gleam of sweet friendliness and welcome would have been pleasant from any one; but from her who had already touched his fancy and interested his heart—from her to whom already he had given a devotion which was of the nature of friendship rather than love—it was more than pleasant, it set every nerve tingling. His devotion had borne a kind of character of friendship, he thought; for was not love hopeless on her side, pledged as she was? And yet he could not do less than serve her for the sake of her childhood, for the sake of all the associations of the past, but chiefly for the sake of herself, so sweet as she was, so tender, and lovely, and young—the kind of creature whom it would be sweet to shield from all trouble.

It had wrung his heart before now to think how little he could do for Margaret, having no right to stand by her. What right had he to interfere? He was not even a connection like Aubrey, whom he called "that English fellow," just as Aubrey called him "that Scotch fellow" and "the man of Killin." He had to stand by and see her go out into the world with nobody who understood her, her life already fettered by bonds so unsuitable, so foolishly formed, but beyond all power of his to interfere. And now to receive such a welcome from her, to see her face so lit up with pleasure to greet him, went to

Randal's very heart. It seemed to send a corresponding light over his whole being: he did not ask himself what it meant; but it was not possible that Margaret's sudden unaffected lighting up at sight of himself, and her unaccountable horror and terror and flight at the name of Glen, should not have stirred all manner of strange emotions in Randal. He made a virtue of patience for an hour or two until he thought it certain that her sisters would also have gone home, and then he hastened to the address Aubrey had unwillingly given him, missing, by so doing, an excited visit from Rob Glen, who, after driving wildly through the bewildering streets in hopeless confusion, bethought himself that Randal might know where Margaret was likely to be found. They missed each other on the crowded way, and Randal went on, with his head full of dreams, in a kind of intoxication of beatitude and wonder. What a change since this morning had come over the young man's life!

When, however, he reached the place where the ladies were staying, it was into the midst of confusion and excitement that Randal found himself suddenly thrown. Mrs. Bellingham was walking about the room in great commotion, Miss Grace crying softly on a sofa. They received him without surprise as people already too much excited to find any new event unexpected or strange.

"How do you do, Randal?" said Mrs. Bellingham; "I am sorry to say we have scarcely time to receive you as we should like. We had settled ourselves for a week in town, and got very nice rooms and everything; and I had quantities of things to do—the work of a year, I may say. We have no clothes, not an article to put on, and there were a hundred things I wanted. But all is thrown into disorder, all is unsettled, and I sha'n't be able to do anything. We must go back to the Grange at once without a moment's delay."

"Dearest Jean!" said Miss Grace, with streaming eyes, "you know you said we must just give ourselves up to dear Margaret; and if it makes her ill to stay in London, how can it be helped? Let me go with dearest Margaret, and do you stay and do your shopping—"

"As if I would trust her out of my hands! especially if she is going to be ill again. But here is the thing that puzzles me. Did you ever hear of Margaret being ill, Randal, at Earl's-hall? But here is a girl that was as strong as —as strong as a little pony—in Fife, and she gets congestion of the lungs as soon as she comes to the South, and cannot stay two days in London! I never heard anything like it—of course I am very sorry for Margaret. What have I been doing but devoting myself to her for the last five months? And she was just blooming —would you not have called her blooming, Aubrey? But London does not agree with her. Fancy London not agreeing with a girl! I don't know when I have been so much put out in all my life."

"Is—Miss Leslie—ill?" said Randal, not knowing how to shape the question.

"Yes; she grew faint and ill just after we met you," said Aubrey, looking at him with steady composure. "I thought the best thing to do was to get her out of that beastly atmosphere at once."

"Oh, you did quite right, Aubrey; I am not in the least blaming you. Much better, in such a case, to leave at once; for if she had fainted outright, in the middle of the crowd, that would have been a pretty business! I never was used to girls who fainted," said Mrs. Bellingham, plaintively. "I have known them to get bad headaches when there was nothing going on; but fainting, just when we were all amusing ourselves—and we have got a box at the opera to-night! it really is enough to send one out of one's wits—a box at the opera! and you know what a chance that is."

"But, dearest Jean! do you go; I will stay with dear Margaret. I shall not mind it; indeed, I shall not mind it much; and you know she has been persuaded; she has given up the idea of going home to-night."

"Going to-night was simply impossible! we are not all born idiots!" said Mrs. Bellingham, with a vigor of language which betrayed her nationality. Then, calming down a little, she seated herself and began to pour out the tea, which had been neglected. "I am sure I beg your pardon, Randal, for letting you see me in such a 'fuff.' But it is provoking, you will allow. And as for going to the opera by myself, or with only Grace, instead of having a pretty, fresh young girl by our side that everybody would remark! I declare one would need to have the patience of a saint not to feel it. Oh, ill? No, I don't think she is very ill; just upset, you know. Indeed, I should have said it was more like a fright than anything else; but Aubrey says there was nothing—no accident, nor runaway horse, nor man killed. I've seen that happen in London streets, and very awful it was."

"No," said Aubrey, steadily, "there was nothing of that sort; but the atmosphere was bad enough for anything; and then the fatigue of the journey—"

"Do you take sugar in your tea, Randal? So many people take no sugar, it is always a trouble to recollect what you young people take and what you don't take. Well, I suppose we will just have to make up our minds to it. Steward can stay with Margaret to-night, and we will go. It is no use throwing away a box at the height of the season."

"But, dearest Jean, let me stay with dear Margaret. I don't really mind. I am sure I don't mind—"

"And to-morrow we must just go back," said Mrs. Bellingham, sweeping on in the larger current of her discourse. "You must remember me very kindly to your excellent father and mother, Randal. I hope we shall see them in the autumn. We are pretty sure to be in Fife in the autumn. Margaret will be distressed not to see you; but, after all that has happened, I thought the best place for her was just her bed; so I made her lie down, and I don't like to disturb her. She will be quite distressed not to see you, when you have been so kind as to take up your time calling—which really is a thing, with people only up in town for a few days, that I never expect. You must have so many things to do."

This Randal took as a hint that he had at present "taken up his time" and hers long enough, and he went away horribly disappointed, tingling with pain as he had done with pleasure and excitement when he came, yet, but for the disappointment, not so entirely cast down as he might have been. Margaret's determined flight, her abandonment of the place where Rob Glen was, even though that place was London—large enough, it might be supposed, to permit two strangers to inhabit it at the same time without meeting—and her evident horror of the engagement between them, made Randal's spirits rise more than his disappointment subdued them. This bondage once cleared away, and Rob Glen dropped back again into the regions to which he belonged, who could tell what might happen?

There was but one thing that abode a prominent alarm in his mind, after the first sting of disappointment was over, and that was "the other fellow," who lied so calmly on Margaret's behalf. Was he in her confidence too? Randal felt that to possess her confidence as he himself did was as great a privilege as any man could have; but somehow, curiously enough, it did not seem to him either so sacred or so seemly that Aubrey should possess it too. He felt that the suggestion of this wounded him for Margaret's sake. She ought not to take a young man into her confidence — it was not quite delicate, quite like the perfection of Margaret. This was the only thing that really and permanently troubled him as he went away.

And he had not been long back in his hotel when, a little before the dinner hour at which he expected Rob to appear, the chief hero of the whole entanglement suddenly made his appearance in a very evident state of excitement. Rob was pale, his eyes wild with anxiety, his hair hanging dishevelled over his forehead, as he wiped it with his handkerchief, and his coat covered with dust. He looked eagerly round, though he did not know himself what he expected to see. He waited till the door was closed, and then he said hurriedly, "Burnside, I have seen Margaret: I saw her coming out of the Academy when I met you this morning. I have been rushing about half over London after her, and I cannot find her. Have you heard anything or seen anything, or can you guess where she is likely to be?"

"'Sit down, Glen."

"Sit down!—that is no answer. I don't feel as if I could sit down until I have spoken to her. Tell me where you think she can be."

"Glen, I want to speak to you. I have something to say to you. They are gone, or going away, that much I heard. I saw Mrs. Bellingham this afternoon, and she told me that her sister was ill again, and that they were off at once. She found that London did not agree with her."

"Ill again?—gone away!" said Rob, hoarsely: then he threw down his hat upon the table with an exclamation of annoyance and pain. "It is not treating me fairly. I ought to see her," he cried, and threw himself, weary and angry, upon the nearest chair.

"I think so too," said Randal, seriously. "I think you ought to see her. I don't want to hurt your feelings, Glen; but I think you should see her, and make her tell you candidly the state of affairs."

"What do you mean by the state of affairs? If it is that her family are opposed to the existence of any tie between her and me, that is no new discovery. I know that, and *she* knows that I know it."

"That was not all I meant, Glen—that is bad enough. You know my opinion. As a man of honor, I think you have a duty even to the family; but this is different. She is not happy. I think you ought to have a full explanation, and —set things on a right footing."

"What does setting things on a right footing mean?" Rob said, with an attempt at a sneer, which was more like a snarl of despair. He had not found it such easy work "making his way" in London. His money was running short, and he had nothing to do, and no prospect of being able to support himself much longer. Margaret was his sheet-anchor, his sole hope in the future. He thought, too, that the rapid dash away of the carriage was not accidental, that she had seen him and driven him wild; and this bitter reflection embittered him, and made him ready to take offence at anything or nothing. He was miserable altogether, excited, distracted, anxious — and tired to death besides. He had taken nothing since the morning, having rushed off in wild pursuit of her instead of getting his usual mid-day meal. He bent down his head upon his folded arms, after that angry question, and thus defeated all Randal's disposition to find fault or blame him, if there had been any such disposition in Randal's mind.

On the contrary, however, the young man's heart, softened by the gleam of brightness that had seemed to come upon his own life out of Margaret's eyes, melted altogether over the unlucky presumptuous lover, the fool who had rushed in "where angels might fear to tread," the unfortunate one who had lost all chance of that prize at which he had snatched too quickly and too roughly. Randal forgot to think of his presumption, of his doubtful conduct, and all his offences against good taste and the highest standard of honor, in sheer pity for the downfall of him who had soared so high. He laid his hand upon the other's shoulder.

"Glen," he said, "you are not the first who has made a mistake, or who has been the victim of a mistake. That is no disparagement to you: it is only continuing in the mistake that would be blamable. You and she—let her name be sacred—I do not like even to refer to her—"

"Who? Margaret?" said Rob, defiant. He would have his way, whatever the other might think. "I have no reason to be so shy about her name. Advice is very seldom palatable in the best of circumstances; but between me and Margaret—" Because Randal had deprecated the use of her name, he insisted on using it. He had a kind of insolent satisfaction in turning it over and over. "Between me and Margaret," he said, with a laugh, "there is no need of advice, that I know of—we understand each other. Mistake there is none between Margaret and me."

Randal bowed very gravely—he did not smile. The color wavered over his face—then departed. "In that case there is nothing to be said."

"Not a word; Margaret and I understand each other. Margaret— I suppose I can wash my hands somewhere before dinner. I am as dusty as a lamplighter with rushing about."

And they dined together, talking of everything in the world except Margaret, and thinking of nothing else. It was a relief to Randal that her name was no longer on the lips of his uncongenial companion; but yet the silence brought in a more eager and painful wonder as to what he was going to do. But Randal could not renew the subject, and Rob did not. He went away early, without having once again referred to the matter which occupied both their thoughts.

He lived in a humble room in one of the streets which run from the Strand to the river—not an unpleasant place, for his window commanded the Thames; but it was a very long walk from Randal's hotel. He went slowly through the streets, through all the loitering crowds of the summer evening, which were no longer bustling and busy, but had an air of repose and enjoyment about them. Rob loitered too, but not from any sense of the pleasantness of the air, or the season. He had no one to care whether he came in or not, and it was easier to think, and think again, over this difficult question which must be decided one way or another, in the open air, than it was within-doors, shut up with a question which he had debated so often. If Margaret was weary of the bargain, if she shrank from him and avoided him, what should he do? One moment he thought of casting her off proudly, of showing her what he thought of her fickleness, and taunting her with her Englishman, "that fellow" who was always with her. This would have been the most consolatory to his feelings. But, on the other hand, to point out to her the cowardice, the dishonor of breaking her word, the strength of the pledge which she could not escape from, was better in another sense. Why should she be permitted to forsake him because she had changed her mind? What right had she to change her mind? Was it a less sin in a woman than in a man to break a promise, to think nothing of a vow? A man would not be allowed to escape scathless from such a perjury, why should a girl? And as he walked along the street, mortified, humbled, breathing forth fumes of anger and pain, there even gleamed before Rob's eyes the scrap of paper, the promise on which his mother counted, which was locked in the secretary in the farm-parlor. He had hated the vulgar sharpness which had exacted that promise from Margaret, he had scouted it as a means of keeping any hold upon her. But now, when he felt so strong a desire to punish her, such an eager, vindictive determination not to let her go free, even this came into his mind. Not to secure her by it—which was his mother's thought, but at least to punish her by it. He would send for it, he thought; he would keep it by him as a scourge, not as a compulsion. He would let all her friends see at least how far she had gone, how she had pledged herself, and how she was forsworn.

While he was pursuing these thoughts, loitering along through the soft summer night, jostled by the sauntering crowds who could not walk, even in the London streets, at that soft hour as they did during the day, his ear was suddenly caught by the intonations, so different from those around, the low-pitched, lingering vowels, and half chanting measure of his natural tongue. Not only Scotch but Fife were the sounds that reached his ears: now the heavy rolling bass of a man, then a softer voice. Good heavens! who was it? A tall, feeble-looking,

large-boned man, a trim little figure by his side, moving lightly and yet languidly, like her voice, which had caught Rob's ear by reason of something pathetic in it. The words she said were words of ordinary wonder and curiosity, such as became a country lass in the street of London; but the tone was sad and went to the heart, notwithstanding the little laugh with which it was sometimes interrupted. Was it possible? He turned round and followed them eagerly, growing more and more certain of their identity, scheming to get a glimpse of their faces, and make certainty sure. Jeanie! how came she here? He stepped forward as soon as he was certain of her, and laid his hand lightly on her shoulder. She started and turned round with a low cry. A gleam of delight came over her face. Her soft eyes lighted up with sudden warmth and gladness. It was the same change that had taken place on Margaret's face while Aubrey Bellingham—who was not the cause—watched it with disagreeable surprise; but this was warmer and more brilliant, more evanescent too; for Jeanie's countenance fell the next moment, and trouble, like a gray shadow, came over her face.

"Jeanie!" cried Rob, "how on earth have you come here? What has brought you here? Where are you staying? What are you going to do? I cannot believe my eyes!"

She stood trembling before him, unable to raise her eyes, overcome by the happiness of seeing him, the wretchedness of parting—a wretchedness which she thought, poor girl, she had eluded, with all the conflict of feeling it must have brought. She tried to speak, but she could only smile at him faintly, and begin to cry.

"Maister Glen," said her father, "you maun speak to me; Jeanie has had enough of fash and sorrow. We are on our way—to please her, no for ony wish of mine—on a lang voyage. We're strangers and pilgrims here in this muckle London, as I never realized the state before."

"On a long voyage!" Rob, though he had got through so much emotion one time and another, felt his heart stand still and a cold sensation of dismay steal over him. Had he not been keeping himself a refuge in Jeanie's heart, whatever might happen? He said, "This is a terrible surprise. I never thought you would have taken such a step as this, Jeanie, without letting me know."

"Maister Glen," said Jeanie, adopting her father's solemn mode of address, and hastily brushing the tears from her cheek, "wherever I gang, what's that to you?" Her voice was scarcely audible; he had half to guess at what she said.

"It is a great deal to me," he cried; "I never thought you would treat me so: going away without a word of warning, without saying good-bye, without letting me know you had any thought of it!"

A thrill of pain penetrated Rob's heart. It was half ludicrous, but he did not see anything ludicrous in it. They were both flying from him, one on either side, the two girls with whom his fate was woven—one for want of love, the other for too much love. Rob saw no humor in the position, but he felt the poignancy and sting of it piercing through and through his heart. Should he be abandoned altogether, then; left entirely alone, without any love at all? But his whole nature rose up fiercely against this. He would not submit to it. If not one, then the other. "It cannot be, it cannot be. I will not let you go," he said.

"Maister Glen," said her father, "I canna rightly tell what has been between Jeanie and you. You're better off than she is in this world, and your friends might have reason to complain if you bound yourself to a poor cobbler's daughter. But this I ken, you have brought my Jeanie more trouble than pleasure. Gang your ways, my man, and let us gang ours. Jeanie, bid Mr. Glen farewell."

"I will say no farewell till I know more about it," he said. "Where are you staying? I must see more of you, I must hear all about it. We are old friends at least, John Robertson; you cannot deny me that."

"Old enough friends; but what o' that? It's no years, but kindness, that I look to. We're biding up west a bittie, with a decent woman from Cupar. I'm putting no force upon Jeanie to take her away. It's a' her ain doing; and if her and you have onything you want to say, I'll no forbid the saying of it; but I dinna advise thae last words and thae lang farewells," said John Robertson, shaking his head. Jeanie looked up at him wistfully, with a sad smile in her wet eyes.

"Let him come this ae night, faither—this ae night," she said, in her plaintive voice; "maist likely it will be the last."

———

CHAPTER XLIII.

RANDAL BURNSIDE was found at the station in the morning, though the train was an early one, to see the ladies away; which, as the travellers were only Margaret and Grace, and as this was one of the things impossible to Aubrey, who could not get up in the morning, was a kindness very much appreciated. It had finally been decided, after much consultation, that as nothing ever happened at the Grange, and as even Mr. St. John was absent, Grace might be sufficient guardian for Margaret for the few days longer which Mrs. Bellingham was compelled by her shopping to remain in town. There was Miss Parker, who would keep her right on one hand, and there was Bland, the most respectable of butlers, on the other, to guide her steps. So, with a flutter of mingled disappointment and exhilaration, Miss Leslie had assumed the charge of her young sister. It was a great relief to Grace's mind to see "a gentleman" at the station, ready to relieve her of all anxieties in respect to the luggage, and she thought it "a great attention" on his part. He was very useful, as she always said afterward. Not only did he secure them in a carriage in the very centre of the train (which was such a safeguard in case of accidents) and look after the luggage, but he waited till the very last moment, though it was wasting his time sadly; and young men, when they are in London only for a few days, really have no time, as Miss Grace knew. She smiled upon him most sweetly, and entreated him not to wait; but he kept his post; it was a great attention.

"And if you should want anything," Randal said, with great meaning, "I shall be in town,

at the Wrangham, for ten days longer." This was repeated as he stood with his hand upon the carriage door just before the train started.

"I am sure, Randal, we are very much obliged," said Miss Leslie; "but you see dear Jean is in town behind us, and she will do all our commissions, if there is anything wanted. Dearest Margaret and I will not want very much, and dear Jean knows about everything; but I am sure it is very kind of you, and a great attention—" And as the train was gliding away out of the station, she put out her head again to beg that he would give her very kind regards, when he saw them, to his dear papa and mamma.

Margaret's mind had been preoccupied with a dread of seeing some one else waiting to prevent her escape, and it was not till the train was in motion that she felt safe, and sufficiently relieved to wave her hand in answer to Randal's parting salutation. What a thing it is to be out of pain when you have been suffering, and out of anxiety when you have been racked with that torture! Margaret leaned back in the corner, feeling the relief to the bottom of her heart. And it was a beautiful day, the country still all bright with the green of the early summer. When they had got a little way out of town, the faint little shade of disappointment in Miss Leslie's mind over lost shopping and relinquished operas gave way to a sense of unusual exhilaration in being her own mistress, and even more than that, having an important trust in her hands.

"After all," she said, "dearest Margaret, I think it will be very nice to get back to the country, though dear Jean always says a week or two in town is very reviving at this time of the year; but you must not think I am unhappy about coming away, for I really do not mind it much—nothing at all to speak of. I shall always say it was a great attention on the part of Randal Burnside, and I am sure dear Jean will feel it. But how could he think we should want him, or anything he could do for us, when dear Jean is in town? Did you hear him give me his address, dearest Margaret? He said he would be at the Wrangham for ten days more. My word, but that must cost him a pretty penny! The Burnsides must be very well off, when Randal can afford to live at the Wrangham, for it cannot be expected that he can be getting much by his profession yet. We once went to the Wrangham ourselves, but it was too expensive. I think you never go there without finding some Fife person or other. I wonder how they have got their Fife connection. But it amuses me to think that Randal Burnside should give us his address."

Margaret listened to this monologue with but slight attention; neither did she attach any importance to Randal's parting words. She was languid in the great relief of her mind, and quite content to rest in her corner, and listen to Grace's soft ripple of talk, which flowed only with a fulness most delightful to herself, the speaker, who had not for many a long day had such an opportunity of expressing, uninterrupted, her gentle sentiments. She was pleased with her companion, who neither interrupted, nor contradicted, nor did anything but contribute a monosyllable now and then, such as was necessary to carry on what Grace called the conversation. The

Grange was as bright and sweet to the eyes when they got there, as it had been dark and melancholy on their first arrival. Everything was beginning to bloom—the early roses on the walls, the starry blossoms of the little mountain clematis threading along the old dark-red wall, the honeysuckle preparing its big blooms, and the garden borders gay with flowers.

Miss Parker met them smiling upon the steps, and all the servants of the household, which Jean had organized liberally, courtesying behind her, while Bland, as affable as his name, with his own hands opened the carriage door. And to be consulted about everything was very delightful to Miss Leslie. She seized the opportunity to make a few little changes in the garden, which she had long set her heart upon, and even corrected one or two things in-doors, which she had not ventured to touch before. And she wrote to dearest Jean that Miss Parker was very kind, and studied their comfort in every way, and that Cook was behaving very well indeed, and Bland was *most* attentive. All her report was thoroughly satisfactory; and she could not help expressing a hope that dearest Jean would not hurry, but would enjoy herself. And Miss Leslie found Margaret a very pleasant companion, giving "no trouble," and ready to listen for the whole day, if her sister pleased, and Grace was very well pleased to go on. She was very well pleased, too, to go on in her viceroyalty, and very liberal to the old women in the cottages, where Margaret and she paid a great many kindly visits. And, in short, Miss Leslie's feelings were of the most comfortable kind, and her rule, though probably it would have been much less successful in the long-run, and consequently less popular, was for a time, to all the dependants who were permitted to have their own way, a very delightful sway in comparison with that of her sister; and it was very pleasant to herself to be looked up to, more or less, instead of being looked down upon.

"I was always fond of you, dearest Margaret, but I never did you full justice till now," she said, half crying, as it was so natural for her to do when she was moved either happily or otherwise. Dear Jean, no doubt, was a great loss; but then dear Jean was enjoying herself *too*. Thus the beginning of this exile and retreat was very pleasant to both the ladies; and Margaret, with her expanded being, took real possession—with a sense of security and calm which sank into her heart like a benediction—of her own house.

On the third day after their arrival she had gone out into the park alone. It was the afternoon, and very bright and warm — too warm, Grace thought, for walking; but Margaret, in all the ardor of her young strength, found nothing too cold or too hot. She strayed across the park in the full sunshine: her broad straw hat was shade enough, and the long, black gauze veil, which Jean still insisted upon, hung floating behind her. Her dress, though black, was thin and light. She had recovered all the soft splendor of health, though in Margaret it could scarcely be called bloom or glow. A faint rose-tint like the flowers, as delicate and as sweet, was on her cheek going and coming; she had a book clasped under her arm, but she was not at all sure that she meant to read. She made her way through the blaze of the sunshine, defying

it, as foolish girls do, to the clump of trees where she had rushed, in her despair, to read Rob Glen's letter on the wet wintry day when she had caught her illness.

Without premeditation she had started for this shelter; but as she gained the shade and sat down at the foot of the great elm, the whole scene came back to her. Her heart woke, and seemed to echo the frantic beating which had been in it then. What a difference! Winter then, all weeping and dreary; yellow leaves scattered on the grass, naked branches waving in the dank air, against the mud-colored clouds; now nothing but summer — the grass covered with flickering gleams of gold and soft masses of grateful shade, the sky so blue and the leaves so green; and, what was more wonderful still, her heart then so agitated and miserable, now so tranquil and calm. Yes, she said to herself, with a little tremor, but why should she be so tranquil and calm? Nothing was changed; three days ago she had dashed through the London streets in the same frantic flight and horror. Nothing was changed. What did the distance matter, a hundred miles or a thousand, when in fact and reality everything was the same? And distance could not settle it one way or another : running away could not settle it. By word or by letter, must she not make up her mind to do it — absolutely to meet the difficulty herself, to confront the danger, not to run away?

Her book dropped down upon the warm, delicious turf beside her. In any case this, in all likelihood, would have been its fate; but it fell from her hand now with a kind of violence. Yes! it must be settled—not by running away—it must be done somehow, beyond all chance of undoing. Margaret was a child no longer : she had learned at least the rudiments of that great lesson; she had found that those evils which we have brought on ourselves cannot be undone by chance or good-fortune. If she was to reclaim herself, it must be by a conscious struggle and effort; and how was it possible that she could encounter this boldly, forestall the next danger, go out to meet the trouble? If he would but leave her alone, it would not matter so much. She thought she could thrust it away from her and be happy—too grateful to let the days drift by, to enjoy her life till the inevitable moment when the long-dreaded fate must come; and then—?

Margaret's heart began once more to sing wildly in her ears. Then! What was it she must do? She was not as she had been a year ago, when nothing but a frightened acquiescence, compulsion yet submission, to something against which there seemed no possibility of effectual resistance, a dreadful fate which she must make the best of when it came, seemed before her. Now she could no longer contemplate the future so; she would not be passive, but must not, must make some effort for her own emancipation : but not yet! not yet! her fluttering heart seemed to say : though something sterner in her, something stronger, protested and held another strain. "If 'twere done, when 'tis done, then it were well it were done quickly." If a struggle was inevitable, one desperate effort must be made to get herself free, why should she delay and suffer so many agonies in the mean time?

A flutter of daring, a sinking of despair, com-

bated in her; and then arose the horrible question — If she did summon courage enough to
parley with her fate and ask for her freedom,
would he grant it? She had not come so far as
to think anything was possible without his consent. Would he let her go free? If she could
but dare to tell him that she did not love him,
that it was all a mistake, would he believe her,
and be persuaded, and let her go? Awful question to which it was impossible to give an answer.
Margaret felt like a criminal dependent on the
clemency of a monarch, before whom she could
only kneel, and weep, and pray. Would he
hear her? Would he waive his claims — the
claims which she could not deny—and let her go
free?

When she was in the midst of these thoughts,
too much engrossed to heed what might be going on round her, and secure that here nothing
could be going on, the creaking of a branch, as
under a footstep, caught Margaret's ear. She
looked up, but saw nothing to alarm her, and
with that curious deliverance from all fears or
suspicions, and simplicity of trust which is apt
to precede a catastrophe, returned to her fancies
and questions and took no further notice. What
harm could come near her there? She was in
the middle of the park, in an island of shade in
the midst of the blaze of sunshine, out of sight
of the house, out of reach of the gate, a place
shut up and sacred, where no one interfered with
the freedom of the young mistress of all. It
might be a squirrel, it might be a rabbit; what
could it be else? She did not even go so far as
to ask herself what it was; there was not the
break of a moment in her thoughts. Would he
let her free? Her word was pledged to him.
How could she release herself from that solemn
promise? He was her master by reason of this
pledge. Would he be merciful? would he have
pity upon her? would he set her free?

What was that? A voice: "Margaret!"
She seemed to hear it somehow before it really
sounded, so that when the word was uttered it
felt like a repetition. She looked up with a
sudden cry. The voice was close over her head,
and the very air seemed to tremble with it—re-
peating it, "Margaret!" She sprang to her feet
with a wild impulse of flight, requiring no second
glance, no second hearing, to tell her that the
moment of fate had come. She had even made
one hurrying, flying step, with terror in her looks,
her throat suddenly dry and gasping, her strength
and courage gone. Was it he? what was it that
caught at her dress? She darted away in terror indescribable; but just as she did so all the
desperation of her case flashed upon Margaret.
She stopped, and, turning round, looked him in
the face.

There he stood looking at her, leaning against
the tree, holding out his hands—"Margaret!"
he cried. His face was all glowing and moving with emotion—unquestionably with genuine emotion. No cheat ever got by guile such
an expression into his lying face. Rob was not
lying. There was great emotion in his mind.
He who could not look at a girl without trying
to please her felt his first glance at Margaret
reillumine all the first fire of loving in his heart.
He had never seen her look half so beautiful.
The health that was in her cheeks, the development that had come to her whole being, all tend-

ed to make her fairer; and even the improvement of her dress under her sister's careful supervision increased her charm to Rob. He was
keenly alive to all those signs of ladyhood which
separated Margaret from his own sphere, and
which proved not only her superiority, but his
who loved her. She shone upon him like a new
revelation of beauty and grace, tempting in herself—irresistible in that she was so much above
him. But if she had not been at all above him,
Rob still would not have let her go without the
most strenuous effort to retain her. His face
shone with the very enthusiasm of admiration
and happiness. "Margaret! my beautiful darling!" he cried; and he held out his hands, inviting, wooing her to him. "Do not be afraid
of me," he said, with real pathos in his voice.
"Margaret! I will not come a step nearer till
you give me leave—to look at you seems happiness enough."

Oh, what a reproach that look was to the
poor girl, who, frightened and desperate, had
yet intelligence enough left to see that there was
no safety in flight! Happiness enough to look
at her! while she—she, ungrateful—she, hard-
hearted, shrunk from the sight of him! She
could not bear the delight and the petition in
his eyes. Instead of being a supplicant to him
for her freedom, it was he who, for his happiness, was a supplicant to her.

"Oh, do not speak so," she said, wringing her
hands; "do not speak so well of me—I do not
deserve it. Oh, why have you come here?"

"Why should I have come? To see you,
my only love. How do you suppose I could
keep away from you? Margaret, do you think
I am made of stone? do you think I only pretend to love you? You did not think so once
at Earl's-hall," he said, coming very softly a step
nearer to her. His look was wistful, his voice
so soft that Margaret's heart was pierced with a
thousand compunctions. She shrank, without
venturing to step farther back, bending her pli-
ant, slight young figure away from him; and
thus he got her hand before she was aware.
Margaret shrank still farther from his touch,
her whole frame contracting; but the instinct
of constancy and the sense of guilt were too
much for her. She could not withdraw her
hand.

"Oh, Mr. Glen," she said—"oh, Rob," for
he gave her a startled look of wonder and pain,
"what can I say to you? I do not want to be
unkind, and oh, I hope—I hope you don't care
so much, not so very much! Oh," she cried,
breaking out suddenly into the appeal she had
premeditated, "don't you think we have made a
mistake—a great mistake?"

"What mistake, Margaret? Is it because
you are so much richer than we ever thought,
and I so poor? Yes, it was a mistake. I had
no right to lift my hopes so high. But do you
think I remembered that? It was you I was
thinking of—not what you had!"

"What does it matter what I have?" she
said, sadly. "Do you think that was what _I_
was thinking of? Rich or poor, has that anything to do with it? But oh, it is true—I cannot help it—we have made a mistake."

"I have made no mistake," he said; "I
thought you the sweetest and the fairest creature that ever crossed my path, and so you are,

And I loved you, Margaret, and so I do now. A king could not do more. I have not made any mistake."

"Oh!" she cried, with a shiver of desperation running through her, drawing her hand from his, "you may scorn me, you may despise me, but I must say it. It is I, then. Oh, Rob, do not be angry! You have been kind, very kind, as good as an angel to me; but I—I am ungrateful, I have no heart. I cannot, cannot—" Here Margaret, entirely overcome, broke forth into sudden weeping, and covered her face with her hands.

Then he took the step too far, which was all that was wanted. How could he tell it was too far? He would have done it had she been no beautiful lady at all, but a country girl who had been once fond of him, whom he could not allow to escape. He put his arm tenderly round her, and tried to draw her toward him.

Margaret sprang from his side with a quick cry, putting him away with her hands. "Oh no, no, no!" she cried, "that cannot be, that can never be! Do not touch me; do not come near me, Mr. Glen!"

"Margaret!" his tone was full of astonishment and pain; "what does this mean? It seems like a bad dream. It cannot be you that are speaking to me."

And then there was a pause. She could say nothing, her very breathing was choked by the struggling sobs. Oh, how cruel she was, how barbarous, how guilty! And he so tender, so struck with wonder and dismay, gazing at her with eyes full of surprise and sudden misery! Would it not have been better to bear anything, to put up with anything, rather than inflict such cruel pain?

It was Rob who was the first to speak. There was no make-believe in him; it was indeed cruel pain, bitter to his heart and to his self-love. He was mortified and wounded beyond measure. He could not understand how he could be repulsed so. "If this is true," he said, "if it is not some nightmare—if I am not dreaming—what is to become of me? My God! the girl I love, without whom I don't care for my life, my betrothed, my wife that was to be, tells me not to come near her, not to touch her! What does it mean—what does it mean, Margaret? You have been hearing something of me that is false, some slander, some ill stories—"

"No, no! oh no, no! not that, not a word."

"Then what is it, Margaret? If you have any pity, tell me what it is. I have done something to displease you. I have offended you, though Heaven knows I would sooner offend the whole world."

"It is not that: oh, can you not understand, will you not understand? I was so young. I did not know what it meant. Oh, forgive me, Mr. Glen. It is not that I want to be unkind. My heart is broken too. I was never—oh, how can I say it?—I was never—never—but do not be angry!—never so—fond of you as you thought."

She raised her eyes to him as the dreadful truth was said, with the awed and troubled gaze of a child, not knowing what horror of suffering she might see, or what denunciation might blast her where she stood. But Margaret was not prepared for something which was much more difficult to encounter. He listened to her, and a smile came over his face.

"My darling," he said, softly, "never mind; I have love enough for the two of us. We have been parted for a long time, and you have forgotten what you thought once. I think I know better, dear, than you. I was content, and so shall I be again, and quite happy when all these cobwebs are blown away. I will take my chance that you will be fond of me," he said.

This was a turn of the tables for which she was absolutely unprepared. She could do nothing but gaze at him blankly, not finding a single word to reply.

"And you shall be humored, my darling," he said. "I am not such a clown as you think. Do you suppose I don't understand your delicacy, your shyness, my Lady Margaret? Oh, I am not such a clown as you think. I will wait till you give me that dear little hand again. I will be patient till you come to my arms again. Oh no, I will not hurry you, darling. I will wait for you; but you must not ask me," he cried, "you must not expect me, to give up my betrothed wife."

"Dearest Margaret," said another voice behind, which made Margaret start, "I have been looking for you everywhere. Here is a letter from dearest Jean, saying that dear Ludovic is in town, and that she will bring him with her when she comes. Is this gentleman a friend of yours, darling Margaret? You must introduce him to me," Miss Grace said.

CHAPTER XLIV.

Miss Leslie was hospitality itself. This national virtue belonged to all the Leslies, even when they had little means of exercising it; and it was intensified in Grace's case by the fact that she had so seldom any power of independent action. She was like a school-girl suddenly placed at the head of a household, and made absolute mistress in a place where hitherto even her personal freedom had been limited. And the pleasure of making a new acquaintance was doubled by the consciousness that there was no brisk ruler behind her to limit her kindness to the stranger. She insisted that he should come to dinner that evening, since she heard that he was staying in the village. "Of course dear Margaret will like to be able to talk to you about home," she said. It was not often that she had the opportunity of entertaining any one; and though Rob, to do him justice, hesitated for a moment, feeling that his acceptance of the unlooked-for opportunity should depend upon Margaret, still it was scarcely to be expected that he could refuse an invitation so manifestly advantageous to him. Margaret said nothing. She would not reply to his look. She gave Grace a glance of mingled horror and entreaty; but Grace scarcely noticed this, and did not understand it. Margaret walked silently by their side to the house, as if in a dream. She heard them talk, the voices coming to her as through a mist of excitement and pain; but what could she do? When Grace suggested that she should show Mr. Glen the house, she shrank away and declared that she was tired, and was going to her room to rest; but the only result of her defection was, that Grace herself took the part of cicerone, and that

Margaret, shutting herself up in her room, heard them going up and down stairs, Grace's voice leading the way, as Mrs. Bellingham's had done on the first night of their arrival.

"Dearest Margaret, do you know you are almost rude to Mr. Glen?" her sister said, before dinner; "and such a pleasant young man, and so clever and so agreeable. I am sure dear Jean will think him quite an acquisition."

"I hate him!" cried Margaret, with the fervor of despair. When she heard the words which she had uttered in her impatience, a chill of horror came over her. Was it true that she hated him, to whom she was bound by her promise, who loved her and expected her to love him? She went away to the other end of the room, pretending to look for something, and shed a few hot and bitter tears. It was horrible, but in the passion of the moment it seemed true. What was she to do to deliver herself?

"I don't want to see him," she said, coming back, "and Jean would not like to have him here: I know she would not like to have him here."

"You will forgive me, darling Margaret," said Miss Leslie, "but I think I know what dear Jean would like: she would not neglect a stranger. She is always very kind to strangers. How do you do again, Mr. Glen?"

And the evening that followed was dreadful to Margaret. Grace, who liked to study what her companions would like, made a great many little efforts to bring these two together. "They will like to have a little talk," she said, running up-stairs to consult Miss Parker about something imaginary. "They are old friends, and they will like to have a little talk."

Margaret, thus left alone with Rob, grew desperate. She turned to him with a pale face and flashing eyes, taking the initiative for the first time.

"Oh, why did you come?" she cried; "do you think it is like a man to drive a poor girl wild—when I told you that I wanted you to go away? that it was all a mistake—all a mistake!"

"It was no mistake so far as I am concerned," he said. "Margaret, you have given me your hand and your promise; how can you be so cruel as to deny me your heart now?"

"I did not give you anything; I was distracted. I did not know what you were saying," she said; "I did not give you anything. Whatever there was, you took. It was not I—it was not I!"

"Margaret, my darling!" he said, coming close to her, "you cannot mean to be so unkind. Do not let us spend all these precious moments in quarrelling. Will you let me tell her when she comes back?"

Margaret's voice seemed to fail in her throat, and a wild panic came into her eyes. She was afraid of his vicinity; she could not bear any appearance of intimacy, any betrayal of their previous relations. And just then Miss Grace came back, profuse in apologies.

"I had something to say to the house-keeper, Mr. Glen. I thought that dear Margaret, as an old friend, would be able to entertain you for a little while, for I heard you were old friends."

"From our cradles, I think," said Rob, significantly. "Miss Margaret used to go fishing with me when I was a boy, and she a tiny little fairy, whom I thought the most wonderful creature on earth. There are traditions of childhood to which one holds all one's life."

"Ah!" said Grace, "childish friendships are very sweet. At dear Margaret's age they are sometimes not so much appreciated; but as one grows older, one understands the value of them. Are you going to stay for some time in our village, Mr. Glen? And are you making some pretty sketches? That was beautiful, that one of Earl's-hall, that you sent to dear Margaret. Dearest Jean was so much struck by it. I am sure it is a great gift to be able to give so much pleasure."

"I will make a companion sketch of the Grange for you, if you would like it," said Rob; "nothing would give me more pleasure. It is a beautiful old house."

"Oh, Mr. Glen! But you are a great deal too good—much too good! And how could I ever repay—how could I ever thank you!"

Margaret rushed from the room while these compliments were being exchanged. It seemed to her like a scene from some old play which she had seen played before, save that the interest was too sharp and intense, too close to herself, for any play. She felt herself insulted and defied, provoked and wounded. What did he care for her or her feelings? Had he felt the least real consideration for her, he could not have done it. She rushed up the half-lighted stairs to her room, with passion throbbing in her heart. Oh, that Jean were here to send him away! though there was, in reality, nobody whom Margaret was more alarmed for than Jean. Oh, that there was some one whom she could trust in—whom she might dare to speak to! But to whom could she speak? If she did betray this secret, would not she be thought badly of, as of a girl who was not a good girl? How well she remembered the sense of humiliation which had come over her when Randal Burnside took no notice of her presence, and did not even take off his hat! Randal Burnside! The name seemed to go through and through her, tingling in every vein. Ah! was it because of this that he had looked at her so wistfully, when he put her into the railway-carriage, to warn her perhaps of what was coming? Could it be for this that he had told Grace where he was to be found?

The breath seemed to stop on Margaret's lips when this idea occurred to her. She had appealed to Randal before, in her despair, and Randal had helped her; should she appeal to him again? There was a moment's confusion in her brain, everything going round with her, a sound of ringing in her ears. What right had she to call upon Randal? But yet she knew that Randal would reply to her appeal; he would do what he could for her; he would not betray, and, above all, he would not blame her. That was a great deal to say, but it was true. Perhaps (she thought) he would be more sorry than any one else in the world; but he would not blame her. The only other person who *knew* was Ludovic; but to Ludovic she dared not appeal. He would think it was all her own fault; but Randal would not think it was her fault. He would *understand*. She stood for a moment undecided, feeling that she must do something at once, that there was no time to lose; and then she made a sudden dash at her writing-table, scattering the papers on it, in her confusion. She must not think any longer; she must do something, whatever it might be. And how could she write an ordinary letter in such a crisis, with an ordinary beginning and ending, as if there was nothing in it out of the common? She plunged at it, putting nothing but what she was obliged to say.

"He has come here, and I don't know what to do. Oh, could you get him to leave me in peace, as you did before? I have no right to trouble you; but if you have any power over him, oh, will you help me? will you get him to go away? I know I ought not to write to you about this; but I am very unhappy, and who can I go to? Oh, Randal, if you have any power er over him, get him to go away!"

At first she did not sign this at all; then she reflected that he might not know her handwriting, though she knew his. And then she signed it timidly with an M. L. But perhaps he might not know who M. L. was; other names began with the same letters. At last she wrote, very tremulously, her whole name, the Leslie dying into illegibility. She did not, however, think it necessary to carry this herself to the post-office, as she had done the letter to Bell. Grace was not so alarming as Jean, and the post-bag was safe enough, she felt. When she had thus stretched out her hand for help, Margaret was guilty of the first act of positive rebellion she had ever ventured upon. She refused to go downstairs. The maid who took her message said, apologetically, that she had a headache; but Margaret herself made no such pretence. She could not keep up any fiction of gentle disability when the crisis was coming so near. And though she so shrank from confiding her griefs to any one, the girl, in her desperation, felt that the moment was coming in which, if need were, she would have strength to defy all the world.

All was dark in Margaret's room, when Grace, having parted from her visitor, who had done his very best to be amusing, notwithstanding the unsatisfactory circumstances, came softly into her little sister's room and bent over the bed.

"Poor darling!" Miss Leslie said, "how provoking, just when your old friend was here. But he is coming again, dearest Margaret, to-morrow, to begin his sketch. How nice of him to offer to make a sketch—and for me! I never knew anything so kind; for he scarcely knows me."

Thus fate made another coil round her helpless feet.

As for Rob, he went back to the inn in the village scarcely less disturbed than Margaret. He had come to a new chapter in his history. Her coldness, her manifest terror of him, her flight from the room in which he was, provoked him to the utmost. He was less cast down than exasperated by her desire to avoid him. He was not a man, he said to himself, from whom girls generally desired to escape, nor was he one with whom they could play fast and loose. He had not been used to failure. Jeanie, who had a hundred times more reason to be dissatisfied with him than Margaret could have, had been won over by his pleading even at the last mo-

ment, and was waiting now in London for the last interview, which he had insisted upon. And did Margaret think herself so much better than everybody else that she was to continue to fly from him? He was determined to subdue her. She should not cast him off when she pleased, or escape from her word. In the fervor of his feelings he forgot even his own horror at the vulgar expedient his mother had contrived, to bind the girl more effectually. Even that he had made up his mind to use, if need were, to hold as a whip over her. It was no fault of his, but entirely her own fault, if he was thus driven to use every weapon in his armory. He had written to his mother to send it to him before he came to the village, and now expected it every day. Perhaps to-morrow, before he set out for the Grange, it would arrive, and Margaret would see he was not to be trifled with. All this did not make him cease to be "in love with" her. He was prepared to be as fond, nay, more fond than ever, if she would but respond as she ought. No one had ever so used him before, and he would not be beaten by a slip of a girl. If he could not win her back as he had won Jeanie, then he would force her back. She should not beat him. Thus the struggle between them, which had been existing passive and unacknowledged for some time back, had to his consciousness, as well as Margaret's, come to a crisis now.

Next morning she kept out of the way, remaining in her own room, though without any pretence of illness. Margaret was too highly strung, too sensible of the greatness of the emergency, to take refuge in that headache which is always so convenient an excuse; she would not set up such a feeble plea. She kept up-stairs in her room in so great a fever of mental excitement that she seemed to hear and see and feel everything that happened, notwithstanding her withdrawal. She heard him arrive, and she heard Grace's twitterings of welcome; and then she heard the voices outside again, moving about, and divined that they were in search of the best point of view. They found it at last, in sight of Margaret's window, where Rob established himself and all his paraphernalia fully in her view. It was for this reason, indeed, that he had chosen the spot, meaning, with one of his curious failures of perception, to touch her heart by the familiar sight, and call her back to him by the recollection of those early days at Earl's-hall. The attempt exasperated her; it was like the repetition of a familiar trick—the sort of thing he did everywhere. She looked out from behind the curtain with dislike and annoyance which increased every moment. It seemed incredible to her, as she looked out upon him, how she could ever have regarded him as she knew she had once done. All that was commonplace in him, lightly veiled by his cleverness, his skill, his desire to please, appeared now to her disenchanted eyes. The thought that he should ever have addressed her in the tenderest words that one human creature can use to another; that he should ever have held her close to him and kissed her, made her cheek burn, and her very veins fill and swell with shame. But, notwithstanding all her reluctance, she had to go down to luncheon, partly compelled by circumstances, partly by the strange attraction of hostility, and partly by the distress of Grace at the possibility of having to take her lunch "alone with a gentleman!" Margaret went down;· but she kept herself aloof, sitting up stately and silent, all unlike her girlish self, at the table, where Miss Leslie did the honors with anxious hospitality, pressing her guest to eat, and, happily, leaving no room for any words but her own. Grace, however, was too anxious that the young people should enjoy themselves, not to perceive how very little intercourse there was between them, and, after vain attempts to induce Margaret to show Mr. Glen the wainscot parlor, she adopted the old expedient of running out of the room and leaving them together as soon as their meal was over.

"I must just speak to Bland," she said, hurriedly, "I shall not be a moment. Margaret, you will take care of Mr. Glen till I come back."

Margaret, who was herself in the very act of flight, was obliged to stay. She rose from her chair and stood stiffly by it, while Grace ran along the passage. Her heart had begun to beat so loudly that she could scarcely speak, but speak she must; and before the sound of her sister's footsteps had died out of her hearing, she turned upon the companion she had accepted so reluctantly, with breathless excitement.

"Mr. Glen," she said, trembling, "I must speak to you. We cannot go on like this. Oh, why will you not go away? If you will not go away, I must. I will not see you again; I cannot, I cannot do it. For God's sake go away!"

"Why should you be so urgent, Margaret?" he said. "What harm am I doing? It is hard enough to consent to see so little of you; but even a little is better than nothing at all."

"Oh!" she cried, in her desperation, "do not stop to argue about it. Don't you see—but you must see—that you are making me miserable? If there is anything you want, tell me; but oh, do not stay here!"

"What I want is easily enough divined. I want you, Margaret," he said; "and why should you turn me away? Let us not spend the little time we have together in quarrelling. You are offended about something. Somebody has been speaking ill of me—"

"No one has been speaking ill of you," she cried, indignantly. "Oh, Mr. Glen, even if I liked you to be here, it would be dishonorable to come when my sister Jean was away, and to impose upon poor Grace, who knows nothing, who does not understand—"

"Let me tell her," he said, eagerly; "she will be a friend to us; she is kind-hearted. Let me tell her. It is not I that wish for concealment; I should like the whole world to know. I will go and tell her—"

"No!" Margaret cried, almost with a scream of terror. She stopped him as he made a step toward the door. "What would you tell her, or any one?—that I—care for you, Mr. Glen? Oh, listen to me! It is not that I have deceived you, for I never said anything; I only let you speak—But if I have done wrong, I am very sorry; if you told her that, it would not be true!"

"Margaret," he said, with forced calmness, "take care what you are saying. Do you forget that you are my promised wife? Is that nothing to tell her? Do you think that I will let you break your vow without a word. There is more than love concerned, more than caring

for each other, as you call it—there is our whole life!"

"Yes," she said. Her voice sank to a whisper, in her extreme emotion; her face grew pallid, as if she were going to faint. She clasped her hands together and looked at him piteously, with wide-open eyes. "Yes," she said, "I know; I promised, and I am false to it. Oh, will you forgive me, and let me go free? Oh, Mr. Glen, let me go free!"

"Is this all I have for my love?" he said, with not unnatural exasperation. "Let you go free! that is all you care for. What I feel is nothing to you; my hopes, and my prospects, and my happiness—"

Margaret could not speak. She made a supplicating gesture with her clasped hands, and kept her eyes fixed upon him. Rob did not know what to do. He paced up and down the room in unfeigned agitation; outraged pride and disappointed feeling, and an impulse which was half generosity and half mortification tempting him on one side, while the rage of failure and the force of self-interest held him fast on the other. He could not give up so much without another struggle. He made a hasty step toward her and caught her hands in his.

"Margaret!" he cried, "how can I give you up? This hand is mine, and I will not let it go. Is there nothing in your promise—nothing in the love that has been between us? Let you go free? Is that all the question that remains between you and me?"

They stood thus, making a mutual appeal to each other, he holding her hand, she endeavoring to draw it away, when the sound of a steady and solemn step startled them suddenly.

"If you please, miss," said Bland, at the door, "there is a gentleman in the hall asking for Mr. Glen; and there is a person as says she's just come off a journey, and wants Mr. Glen too. Shall I show them into the library, or shall I bring them here?"

Rob had dropped her hand hastily at the first sound of Bland's appearance; and Margaret, scarcely knowing what she did, her head swimming, her heart throbbing, struggled back into a kind of artificial consciousness by means of this sudden return of the commonplace and ordinary, though she was scarcely aware what the man said.

"I am coming," she answered, faintly; the singing in her ears sounded like an echo of voices calling her. All the world seemed calling her, assembling to the crisis of her fate. She did not so much as look at Rob, from whom she was thus liberated all at once, but turned and followed Bland with all the speed and quiet of great excitement, feeling herself carried along almost without any will of hers.

The hall at the Grange was a sight to see, that brilliant summer day. The door was wide open, framing a picture of blue sky and flowering shrubs at one end; and the sunshine, which poured in through the south window, caught the wainscot panels and the bits of old armor, converting them into dull yet magical mirrors full of confused reflections. There were two strangers standing here, as far apart as the space would allow, both full of excitement to find themselves there, and each full of wonder to find the other. They both turned toward Margaret

11

as she came in, pale as a ghost in her black dress. Her eye was first caught by him who had come at her call, her only confidant, the friend in whom she had most perfect trust. The sight of him woke her out of her abstraction of terror and helplessness.

"Randal!" she cried, with a gleam of hope and pleasure lighting up her face.

Then she stopped short and paled again, with a horrible relapse into her former panic. Her voice changed into that pitiful "oh!" of wonder and consternation, which the sight of a mortal passenger called forth, as Dante tells us, from the spirits in purgatory. The second stranger was a woman; no other than Mrs. Glen, from Earl's-lee, in her best clothes, with a warm Paisley shawl enveloping her substantial person, who stood fanning herself with a large white hand-kerchief in the only shady corner. These were the two seconds whom, half consciously, half willingly, yet in one case not consciously or will-ingly at all, the two chief belligerents in this strange duel had summoned to their aid.

CHAPTER XLV.

THE strangers made their salutations very briefly; as for Randal, he did not approach Margaret at all. He made her a somewhat stiff bow, which once more, in her simplicity, wound-ed her, though the sight of him was such a re-lief; but even the comfort she had in his pres-ence was sadly neutralized by this apparent evi-dence that he did not think so charitably of her as she had hoped. Amidst all the pain and be-wilderment of the moment, it was a pang the more to feel thus driven back upon herself by Randal's disapproval. She gave him an anxious, questioning look, but he only bowed, looking be-yond her at Rob Glen; and it was Mrs. Glen who hurried forward with demonstration to take and shake between both her own Margaret's re-luctant hand.

"Eh, but I'm glad to see you, Miss Margret!" Mrs. Glen said. "What a heat! I thought I would be melted, coming from the station, but a's weel, now I'm safe here."

"Will you forgive me, Miss Leslie," said Ran-dal, "if I ask leave to speak to Glen on business? I took the liberty of coming when I heard he was here. I should not have ventured to disturb you but for urgent business. Glen, I have heard of something that may be of great importance to you. Will you walk back with me to the sta-tion, and let me tell you what it is? I have not a moment to spare."

"Na, na, ye'll gang wi' nobody to the station. How's a' with ye, Rob, my man?" cried Mrs. Glen; "you're no going to leave me the first moment I'm here?"

Rob stood and gazed, first at one, then at the other. The conjunction did not seem to bode him any good, though he did not know how it could harm him. He looked at them as if they had dropped from the clouds, and a dull sense that his path was suddenly obstructed, and that he was being hemmed in by friends as well as by foes, came over him. "What do you want?" he said, hoarsely. The question was addressed chiefly to his mother, to whom he could relieve himself by a savage tone not to be endured by any stranger.

"Me?" said Mrs. Glen; "I want nothing but a kindly welcome from you and your bonnie young lady; that's a' I'm wanting. But I couldna trust yon intil a letter," she added, in a lower tone—"I thought it was a great deal safer just to bring it myself."

"But I," said Randal, quickly, "have come upon business, Glen. Miss Leslie will excuse me for bringing it here, though I had not meant to do so. I have a very advantageous offer to tell you of. It was made to me, but it will suit you better. There is pleasant work and good pay, and a good opening. Could you not put off this happy meeting for a little, and listen to what I have to say?"

"Good pay, and a good opening? Rob, my man," said Mrs. Glen, "leave you me with Miss Margret—we were aye real good friends—and listen like a good lad to what Mr. Randal says. A good opening, and good pay—eh! but you're a kind lad when there's good going no to keep it to yourself."

"If Glen will not give me his attention, I may be tempted to keep it to myself," said Randal, with a smile—"and there is not a moment to lose." He had meant what he said when he pledged himself to serve her, to do anything for her that his power could reach. Nobody but himself knew what a sacrifice it was that he was prepared to make. And there was not a mo-ment to lose. It was evident by the look of all parties, and by the unexplained appearance of Mrs. Glen, that the crisis was even more alarm-ing, more urgent than he thought. The only thing he could do was to insist upon the prior urgency of *his* business. Could he but get Rob away! Randal knew that Margaret's natural protectors were on the way to take charge of her: he made another anxious appeal. "Par-don me if I have no time for explanations or apologies," he said; "you may see how impor-tant it is, when I have come from London to tell you of it. Glen, you ought not to neglect such an opportunity. Miss Leslie will excuse you—it may make your fortune. Won't you come with me, and let me tell you? I can't explain every-thing here."

"Eh, Rob," said Mrs. Glen, who had pressed forward anxiously to listen. "What's half an hour, one way or another? I would gang with him, and I would hear what he's got to say. We're none so pressed for time, you and me. What's half an hour? and me and your bonnie Miss Margret will have our cracks till ye come back. Gang away, my man, gang away!"

Rob stood undecided between them, looking from one to another, distrusting them all, even his mother. Why had she come here? They seemed all in a plot to get him away from this spot, where alone (he thought) he could insist upon his rights. "How did he know I was here?" he said, between his teeth.

As for Margaret, everything was in a confu-sion about her. She did not comprehend why Randal should stand there without a word to her, scarcely looking at her. Was this the way to serve her? And yet was it not for her sake that he was trying to take the other claimant—this too urgent suitor—away? As she stood there, passive, confused, and wondering, Margaret, standing with her face to the door, was the first to perceive, all at once detaching themselves from the background of the sky, two figures outside, whose appearance brought a climax to all the confusion within. In the pause within-doors, while they all waited to see what Rob would do, a brisk voice outside suddenly took up and occupied the silence:

"I think most likely they don't expect us at all. You never can be sure of Grace. Her very letters go astray as other people's letters never do. The post itself goes wrong with her. If they had expected me, they would have sent the carriage. But I declare, there are people in the hall! I wonder," said Mrs. Bellingham, in a tone of wonder, not unmingled with indignation, "if they have been having visitors—visitors, Grace and Margaret, while I have been away?"

No one said a word. Randal, who had been standing with his back to the door, turned round hastily, and the others stood startled, not knowing what was about to happen, but with a consciousness that the end of all things was drawing near. Mrs. Bellingham marched in, with mingled curiosity and resolution in her face. She came in, as the head of a house had a right to come, into a place where very high jinks had been enacted in his or her absence. She looked curiously at Rob Glen and his mother, who faced her first, and said "Oh!" with a slight swing of her person—a half bow, a half courtesy, less of courtesy than suspicion; but Jean was always aware what was due to herself, and could not be rude. When the third stranger caught her eye, she gave way to a little outcry of genuine surprise—"You here, Randal Burnside!"

"Yes, indeed," he said. "You must think it very strange; but I will explain everything to you afterward."

"Oh, I am sure there is no need for explanations; your father's son can never be unwelcome," said Mrs. Bellingham, guardedly. "Well, Margaret, my dear, so this is you! I think either you or Grace might have thought of sending the carriage; but you have been having company, I see—where is Grace?"

"Oh, dearest Jean!" cried Miss Leslie, rushing forward, "to think that you should arrive like this without any one expecting you! And oh, dear Ludovic, you too! I am sure—"

"You have been having company, I see," said Mrs. Bellingham; "I trust we are not interrupting anything. I will take a seat here for a little; I think it is the coolest place in the house. You had better ask your friends to take chairs, Grace."

"Oh, dearest Jean, it is Mr. Glen, the clever artist, you know, who—but I don't know the—the—" What should Miss Leslie have said? To call Mrs. Glen a lady was not practicable, and to call her a woman was evidently an offence against politeness. "I assure you," she said in her sister's ear, "I don't know in the least who she is."

Mrs. Bellingham sat down in the great chair which stood by the fireplace, a great old carved throne in black wood, which looked like a chief-justice's at least. It was close to the door, and served to bar all exit. Sir Ludovic had come in a minute after her, and he had been engaged in greeting his little sister Margaret, and shaking hands with Randal Burnside, whom he was

very glad to see, with a little surprise, but without arrière-pensée. But when the salutations were over he looked round him, and with a sudden, sharp exclamation, discovered Rob Glen by his side.

"Margaret," he said at once, "you had better retire; my dear, you had better retire. I don't think this is a place for you."

"I beg your pardon, Ludovic," said Mrs. Bellingham; "where her brother and her sisters are is just the right place for Margaret. I have not the pleasure of knowing the Miss Leslies' friends—neither do you, I suppose; but Margaret will just remain, and I dare say everything will be cleared up. It is a very fine day," Jean said, with a gracious attempt to conciliate everybody, "and very good for bringing on the hay."

After this there was a slight pause again; but Mrs. Glen felt that this was a tribute to her own professional knowledge; and as no one else took up the rôle of reply, she came forward a step, with a little cough and clearing of her throat.

"England's a great deal forwarder in that respeck than we are in our part of the world," she said. "It's no muckle mair than the spring season wi' us, and here it's perfit simmer. We'll no be thinking o' the hay for this month to come; but I wouldna wonder if it was near cutting here."

Meanwhile, Sir Ludovic had gone up to Rob Glen in great agitation. "What are you doing here?" he said. "Why did you come here? I never thought you would have taken such a step as this. I gave you credit for more straightforwardness, more gentlemanly feeling—"

"There has been enough of this!" cried Rob. Exasperation is of kin to despair. Amidst all these bewildered faces looking at him, not one was friendly—not one looked at him as the future master of the house, as the man who was one day to be Margaret's husband should have been looked at. And Margaret herself had no thought of standing by him. She had shrunk away from him into the background, as if she would have seized the opportunity to escape. "There has been enough of this," he said; "I do not see any reason why I should put up with it. If I am here, it is because there is no other place in the world where I have so much right to be. I have come to claim my rights. Margaret can tell you what right I have to be here."

"Margaret!" repeated Mrs. Bellingham, wondering, in her high-pitched voice.

"Glen!" cried Randal, interrupting him with nervous haste—"I told you I had an important proposal to make to you. When you know that I came down expressly to bring it, I think I might have your attention at least. Will you come with me and hear what it is? I beg your pardon, Mrs. Bellingham; I do not want to interfere with any other explanation; but I came down on purpose, and Glen ought to give me an answer, while I have time to stay—"

"Eh, bide a moment, bide a moment, Mr. Randal; gie him but a half-hour's grace," cried Mrs. Glen. "Speak up, Rob, my bonnie man."

Randal, though he felt his intervention useless, made one last effort. "I must have my answer at once," he cried, impatient. "I tell you it is for your interest, Glen—"

"I don't think, gentlemen," said Sir Ludovic,

"that this is a place to carry on an argument between yourselves, with which the ladies of this house, at least, have nothing to do."

"If you will not come, I at least must go!" Randal cried, with great excitement. He gave her an anxious glance, which she did not even see, and threw up his hands with a gesture of despair. "I can do no good here," he said.

Rob glared round upon them all—all looking at him—all hostile, he thought. He had it in his power, at least, to frighten these people who looked down upon him, who would think him not good enough to mate with them. He turned toward Margaret, who still stood behind him, trembling, and called out her name in a voice that made the hall ring.

"Margaret! it is you that have the first right to be consulted. Sir Ludovic, you know as well as I do that Margaret is pledged to be my wife."

"His wife!" Mrs. Bellingham sat bolt-upright in her chair, and Miss Leslie, with a little shriek, ran to Margaret's side, with the instinct of supporting what seemed to her the side of sentiment against tyranny. "Darling Margaret! lean upon me—let me support you; I will never forsake you!" she breathed, fervently, in her young sister's ear.

"Silence!" cried Sir Ludovic; "how dare you, sir, make such a claim upon a young lady under age? If you had the feelings of a gentleman—"

At this moment, Mrs. Glen stepped forward to do battle for her son.

"You may think it fine manners, Sir Ludovic, to cast up to my Rob that he's no a gentleman; but it doesna seem fine manners to me. Ay, that she is! troth-plighted till him, as I can bear witness, and by a document, my ladies and gentlemen, that ye'll find to be good in law."

"Mother, hold your tongue!" cried Rob. A suppressed fury was growing in him; he felt himself an alien among these people whom he was claiming to belong to, but of whom nobody belonged to him, except the mother, whose homeliness and inferiority was so very apparent to his eyes. He was growing hoarse with excitement and passion. "Sir Ludovic knows so well what my position is," he said, with dry lips, "that he has asked me to give it up; he has tried before now to persuade me that I was required to prove myself a gentleman by giving it up. A gentleman! what does that mean?" cried Rob. "How many gentlemen would there be left if they were required to give up everything that is most dear to them, to prove the empty title? Do gentlemen sacrifice their interests and their hopes for nothing?—or do you count it honorable in a gentleman to abandon the woman he loves? If so, I am no gentleman, as you say. I will not give up Margaret. She chose me as much as I chose her. She is frightened, and you may force her into abandoning her betrothed and breaking her word. Women are fickle, and she is afraid of you all; but she is mine, and I will never give her up."

"Margaret," said Sir Ludovic, taking her hand and drawing her forward, "give this man his answer. Tell him you will have none of him. You may have been imprudent—"

"But she can be prudent now," said Rob Glen, with a smile; "she can give up, now that she is rich, the man that loved her when she was poor. Margaret! yes, you can please them and

leave me because I have nothing to offer you. They say such lessons are easily learned; but I would not have looked for it from you."

Margaret stood in the centre, in face of them all, with her brain reeling and her heart wrung. She had a consciousness that Randal was there too, looking at her, which was a mistake, for he had left the hall hastily when his attempt was foiled; but all the others were round her, making a spectacle of her confusion, searching her with their eyes. What had she to do but to repeat the vehement denial which she had given to Rob himself not half an hour ago? She wrung her hands. The case was different: here he was alone, contending with them all for her. Her heart ached for him, though she shrank from him. She gave a low cry and hid her face in her hands: how could she desert him? how could she cast him off, when he stood thus alone?

"You see," said Rob, triumphantly, with a wonderful sense of relief, "she will not cast me off as you bid her. She is mine. You will never be able to separate us if we are true to each other. Margaret, my darling, lift your sweet face and look at me. All the brothers in the world cannot separate us. Give me your hand, darling, for it is mine."

"Stand off, sir!" cried Sir Ludovic, furious; and Mrs. Bellingham, coming down from her chair as from a throne, came and stood between them, putting out her hand to put the intruder away. Jean was all but speechless with wonder and rage. She put her other hand upon Margaret's shoulder and pushed her from her, giving her a shake, as she did so, of irrepressible wrath. "What is the meaning of all this? Put those people out, Ludovic! put this strange woman, I tell you, to the door!"

"Put us out!" cried Mrs. Glen. "I'll daur ye to do that at your peril! Look at what I've got here. I have come straight from my ain house to bring this, that has never left my hands since that frightened lassie there wrote it out. It's her promise and vow before God, that is as good as marriage in Scots law, as everybody kens. Na, you'll no get it out of my hands. There it is! You may look till you're tired. You'll find no cheatery here."

"Did you write this, Margaret?" said her brother, in tones of awful judicial severity, as it seemed to her despairing ears. They all gathered round, with a murmur of excitement.

"Marriage in Scots law! good Lord, anything is marriage in Scots law," Mrs. Bellingham said, under her breath, in a tone of horror. Grace burst out into a little scream of excitement, wringing her hands.

"Did you write this, Margaret?" still more solemnly Sir Ludovic asked again. Margaret uncovered her face. She looked at them all with her heart sinking. Here was the final moment that must seal her fate. It seemed to her that after she had made her confession there would be nothing for her to do but to go forth, away from all she cared for, with the two strangers who had her in their power. She clasped her hands together, and looked at the group, which was all blurred and indistinct in her eyes. She could not defend herself, or explain herself at such a moment, but breathed out from her very soul a dismal, reluctant, almost inaudible "Yes!" which seemed the very utterance of despair.

"Ay, my bonnie lady," said Mrs. Glen, triumphant, "you never were the one to go against your ain act and deed. Me and my Rob, we ken you better than all your grand friends. Weel I kent that whatever they might say; you would never go against your ain hand of write."

Rob had been standing passive all this time, with such a keen sense of the terror in Margaret's eyes, and the contempt that lay under the serious trouble of the others, as stung him to the very centre of his being. The unworthiness of his own position, the bewildered misery of the girl whom he was persecuting, the seriousness of the crisis as shown by the troubled looks of the brother and sister who were bending their heads over the paper which his mother held out so triumphantly—all this smote the young man with a sudden, sharp perception. He was not of a mean nature altogether. The quick impulses which swayed him turned as often to generosity as to self-interest; and all this while there had been films about this pursuit of the young heiress which had partially deceived him as to its true nature.

What is there in the world more hard than to see ourselves as we appear to those on the other side? A sudden momentary overwhelming revelation of this came upon him now. He did not hear the whispers of "compromise it"—"offer him something—offer him anything," which Jean, utterly frightened, was pouring into her brother's ear. He saw only the utter abandonment of misery in Margaret's face, the vulgar triumph in his mother's, the odious position in which he himself stood between them. In a moment his sudden resolution was taken: he pushed in roughly into the group, in passionate preoccupation, scarcely seeing them, and snatched the scrap of paper she held out of his mother's hands. "Margaret!" he cried, loudly, in his excitement, "look here! and here! and here!" tearing it into a thousand fragments. He pushed his mother aside, who rushed with a shriek upon him to save them, and tossed the little white atoms into the air. "I asked for your love," he said, his eyes moistening, his face glowing, "not for papers or promises. Give me that, or nothing at all."

Sudden tears rushed to Margaret's eyes; she did not know what had happened, but she felt that she was saved.

"Oh, Rob!" she cried, turning to him, putting out her hands.

Sir Ludovic sprang forward and took both these hands into his.

"Margaret, do you want to marry him?" he cried.

"Oh no, no, no; but anything else!" the girl said. "It was never he that did that. He was always kind—kinder than anybody in the world: I am his friend! Let me go, Ludovic! Rob," she said, going up to him, giving him her hand, the tears dropping from her eyes, "not that; but I am your friend; I will always be your friend, whatever may happen, wherever we may be. I will never forget you, Rob. Good-bye! You are kind again, you are like yourself; you are my old Rob that always was my friend."

Rob took her hands into his. He stooped over her and kissed her on the forehead: he would not give in without a demonstration of his power. Then he flung her hands away from him almost with violence, and turned to the door.

"It seems my fate never to be able to do what is best for myself," he said, looking back with a wave of his hand and an irrepressible burst of self-assertion, as he turned and disappeared among the flowering bushes outside the open door.

CHAPTER XLVI.

Rob issued forth out of the Grange discomfited and beaten, but without the sense of moral downfall which had been bowing him to the ground. His heart was melted, his spirit softened. He was defeated, but he was not humiliated. He had come off with all the honors of war—not an insulted coward, but a magnanimous hero. "All is lost but honor," he said to himself, with an expansion of his breast. His eyes were still wet with the dew of generous feeling: he had not been forced into renunciation; he had himself evacuated the untenable position. There was a little braggadocio in this self-consciousness—a little even of what in school-boy English is called swagger; but still he had a certain right to his swagger. He had taken the only possible way of coming out with honor from the dilemma in which he had placed himself. He said to himself that it was a great sacrifice he had made. All the hopes upon which he had dwelt so long and fondly were gone; he was all at sea again for his future, and did not know what to do. What was he to do? He could not return to the aimless life he had pursued in his mother's house; and by this time he had found out that it was by no means so easy as he had supposed to get fortune and reputation in London. What should he do? He could hope nothing from his mother. He knew well with what reproaches she would overwhelm him, what taunts she would have in her power. He must do something to secure himself independence, though for so long he had hoped that independence was coming to him in the easiest way—a rich wife—not only rich, but fair—the "position of a gentleman," most dearly cherished of all the gifts of fortune—a handsome house, leisure and happiness, and everything that heart of man could desire. The breaking up of this dream called forth a sigh when the first elation of his victory over himself was over, and then he began to droop as he walked on. No elevation in the social scale was likely to come now. Rob Glen, the son of a small farmer, he was, and would remain; not the happy hero of a romance, not the great artist undeveloped, not the genius he had thought. Thus the brag and the swagger gradually melted away: the sense of moral satisfaction ceased to give him as much support as at first—even the generous sentiment sank into a sense of failure. What was to become of him? He walked on, dull but dogged, going steadily forward, but scarcely knowing where he was going; and thus came upon Randal Burnside walking along the same road before him, more anxious and excited, and not much less discouraged and melancholy than he.

Randal's face brightened slightly at the sight of him.

"You have come, after all, Glen," he said; "I had almost given you up."

"I gave myself up before I came," said Rob.

"What do you mean? I suppose they were hard upon you—perhaps you could scarcely expect it to be otherwise; but with your good-fortune you may easily bear more than that," said Randal: then he checked himself, remembering that Margaret's horror of her lover's presence pointed to not much good-fortune. "Let me tell you now what my business was," he said, with a sigh. He was too loyal to depart from his purpose; but though (he thought) he would have given up life itself to serve Margaret, yet he could not make this sacrifice without a sigh. He told his companion very briefly what it was. It was an offer from a newspaper to investigate a subject of great popular interest, requiring some knowledge of Scotch law. "But that I could easily coach you in," Randal said. He went into it in detail, showing all its advantages, as they walked along the country road. The first necessity it involved was a speedy start to the depths of Scotland, close work for three months, good pay, and possible reputation. Rob listened to the whole with scarcely a remark. When Randal paused, he turned upon him hastily:

"This was offered not to me, but to yourself," he said.

"Yes; but you know a little of the law, and I could easily coach you in all you require."

"And why do you offer it to me?"

"Come," said Randal, with a laugh, "there is no question of motive; I don't offer it to you from any wish to harm you. To tell the truth, it would suit me very well myself."

"And you would give it to me, to relieve her of my presence?" cried Rob. "I see it now! Burnside, will you tell me honestly, what is your reward to be?"

"I have neither reward nor hope of reward," cried Randal; "evidently not even a thank-you. I would not answer such a question, but that I see you are excited—"

"Yes, I am excited—I have good cause. I have given her up, and every hope connected with her; so there is no more need to bribe me," said Rob, with a harsh laugh. "Keep your appointment to yourself."

"Will you take it, or will you leave it, Glen? What may have happened otherwise is nothing to me—"

"There is the train," said Rob. "No! I'll take nothing, either from her dislike or your friendship—nothing! There are still some in the world that care more for me than charity. Good-bye."

He made a dash up the bank, where a train was visible, puffing and pulling up at the little station—the legitimate road being a quarter of a mile round, and hopeless.

"Come back!" cried Randal; "you will break your neck. There is another train—"

Rob made no reply, but waved his hand, and dashed in wild haste over ditch and paling. Randal stood breathless, and saw him reach the height and spring into a carriage at the last moment, as the train puffed and fretted on its way. The spectator did not move—what was the use? He had no wish to take the same wild road: he stood and looked after the long white plume as it coursed across the country.

"He has got it, and I have lost it," he said; but Randal smiled to himself. A sense of ease, of relief, and pleasure after so much pain, came over him. There was no longer any hurry. Should he go forward? should he turn back?—it did not much matter; he had two or three hours on his hands before he could get away.

The rush and noise of the train was a relief, on the other hand, to the traveller. As it pounded along, with roll and clang, and shrill whistle, the sudden hurry of his thoughts kept time. He had not a moment to lose. Now and then, when its speed slackened, he got up and paced about the narrow space of the carriage, as if the continued movement got him on the faster. When he reached London, he jumped into a hansom and dashed through the crowded Strand to one of the little streets leading down toward the river. Arrived there, he thundered at a door and rushed up-stairs, three steps at a time, till he came to a little room at the top of the house, where the sole occupant, a young woman, had been sitting, looking wistfully out upon a glimpse of the river, which showed in dim twilight reflections at the foot of the street, for it was almost night. Her father was out, and Jeannie sat alone. She had "nae heart" to walk about the streets, to look in at the dazzling shop-windows, to take any pleasure in the sight of London. She was thinking—would she see him again? would he come and bid her farewell, as he said, "The day after the morn, the day after the morn?" she was saying to herself, sometimes putting up her hand to brush away a furtive tear from the corner of her eyes. That was the final day: after which, in this world, she should see Rob's face no more.

"Jeannie," he cried, coming in breathless, "I have come back to you as I said." Jeannie stumbled up to her feet, and fell a crying with a tremulous smile about her lips.

"Oh, I'm glad, glad to see you," she cried, "once mair, once mair, though it's naething but to say farewell! We're to sail the day after the morn."

"The day after the morn." He took Jeannie's hands, which gave themselves up to his as Margaret's shrinking fingers had never done, and looked into her pretty, rustic face, all quivering with love and the anguish of parting. Jeannie had made her little pretences of pride, her stand of maidenly dignity against him; but at this moment all these defences were forgotten. He had come so suddenly; and it was this once and never more, never more in all the world again. "The day after the morn," repeated Rob; "then there will just be time. I am coming with you; and if you will have a man without a penny, Jeannie, it shall be as man and wife that you and I will go."

She gave a cry of sharp pain and drew her hands out of his. "How dare you speak like that to me that means no harm? How dare you speak like that to me—and you another lass's lad, and never mine?"

"I am nobody's but yours," he said, "and, Jeannie, you need not try to deceive me. You never were but mine."

"But that's nae reason," she cried, wildly, "to come and make a fool of me to my face, Rob Glen. Oh, go, go to them you belong to!

I thought I might have said farewell to you without another word; but even that canna be."

"'There will never be farewell said between you and me, Jeannie,' said Rob, seriously, "never from this moment till death does us part."

When Rob Glen, stung at once by the kindness and severity of which he had been the object, took this sudden resolution, and with a wild dash of energy, and without a pause, thus carried it out, Randal was left alone upon the country road, all strange and unfamiliar to him, but with which he seemed all at once to have formed so many associations, with two or three hours at his disposal. He stood and watched the train till it was out of sight, idly, with the most singular sense of leisure in opposition to that hurry and rush. From the moment when Rob had dashed up the bank, Randal had felt no longer in any hurry or anxiety about the train. It did not matter if he lost his train—nothing, indeed, seemed to matter very much for the moment. He saw the carriage that contained Rob rush out of sight while he was standing in the same place: if he chose to spend an hour in the same place, thinking over the causes which had carried Rob away, what would it matter? He had plenty of time for that or anything else—no hurry or care —the whole afternoon before him. Would it not be better, more civil to go back, and pay his respects at the Grange as he ought? He had rushed into the house like a savage, and rushed out again without a word to say for himself. Evidently this was not the way to treat ladies to whom he owed the utmost respect. He would go back. He turned accordingly, and went back; still at the most perfect leisure. Plenty of time; no hurry one way or another.

He had not gone far, however, before he met a curiously-matched pair coming up along the road together—Mrs. Glen talking loudly and angrily, Sir Ludovic walking beside her, sometimes saying a word, but for the most part passive, listening, and taking no notice. Randal heard her long before he saw the pair on the windings of the road. Mrs. Glen did not know whether to abuse or defend her son. She did both by turns. "A fine son, to leave me, that has aye thought far ower muckle of him, to find my way home as best I can, after making a fool of himself and a' belanging to him! But where was he to gang, poor lad? abused on a' hands— even by those that led him into his trouble," she cried. There was no pause in her angry monologue. And, indeed, the poor woman, in her great Paisley shawl, with the hot sun playing upon her head, her temper exasperated, her body fatigued, her hopes baffled, might have something forgiven to her. "Gentry!" she cried, as she began to ascend the slope which led to the station, and which Randal was coming down; "a great deal the gentry have done for my family or me! Beguiled my Rob, the cleverest lad in a' Fife, till he's made a fool o' himself and ruined a' his prospects; and brought me trailing after him to a country where there's nae kindness nor hospitality—among people that never offer you so much as a stool to rest your weary limbs upon, or a cup o' tea to refresh you. Eh! if that's gentry, I would rather have the colliers' wives or the fisher bodies in Fife, let alone a good farm-house, and that's my ain."

"Mrs. Glen," said Sir Ludovic, "I am sure my sisters would have wished you to rest and refresh yourself."

"Ay, among their servant-women, no doubt —if I would have bowed myself to that. I've paid rent to the Leslies for the last thirty years —nae doubt but they durstna have refused me a cup of tea; but I would have you to ken, Sir Ludovic, though you're a Sir, and I'm a plain farmer, that the like o' your servant-women are nae neebors for me."

"My good woman!"

"I'm nae good woman to be misca'ed by ane of your race! Good woman, quo' he! as I would say to some gangrel body. You're sair mistaken, Sir Ludovic, if that's what you think of the like of me, that has paid you rent, as I was saying, and held up my head with any in the parish, and given my bairns as good an education as you or yours could set your face to. If ye think, after a' that I've put up with, that I'm to take a 'good woman' from the laird, as if I wasna to the full as guid a tenant as he is a landlord, or maybe mair to lippen to."

"Would you have me say 'ill woman?'" said Sir Ludovic, with momentary peevishness, yet with a gleam of humor. "You are quite right, Mrs. Glen; you are better off, being a tenant, than I am as a landlord. The Leslies never were rich, that I heard tell of; and if we were proud, it never was to our neighbors, the people on our own land."

"Well, I wouldna say but that's true," said Mrs. Glen, softened. "Auld Sir Ludovic, your father, had aye a pleasant word for gentle and simple; and if it was not for that lang-tongued wife down bye yonder—"

Sir Ludovic, though he was a serious man, felt a momentary inclination to chuckle when he heard his sister Jean, the managing person of the family, described as a lang-tongued wife. But he said, gravely,

"In such a question, Mrs. Glen, there is a great deal to be considered. You would not have liked it yourself, had one of your daughters been courted without your knowledge by a penniless lover. When you see your son, if I can do anything for him, if I can advance his interests, let me know, and I will do it. He behaved like a man at the last."

"Oh ay; when a lad plays into your hands, it's easy to say that he's behaving like a man," she said. "But she was mollified by the praise, and her wrath had begun to wear itself out. "I'll gie you a word o' warning, Sir Ludovic, though you've little title to it from my hands," she added. "Here's Randal Burnside coming back. If you've saved your little Miss from ae wooer, here's another; and my word, I would sooner have a bonnie lad like my Rob, with real genius in his head, than a minister's son, neither ae thing nor another, like Randal Burnside."

They met a moment afterward, and Randal recounted what had happened; how Rob had caught the train, but he himself, being too late, had intended to return to the Grange for the interval, and was now on his way there. Mrs. Glen, however, would not return; she was too glad to be deposited in a shady room where she could loose her shawl and bonnet-strings, and fan herself with her large handkerchief. Sir Ludovic, who had "a warm heart for Fife," as he himself expressed it, and who had been touched by Rob's final self-vindication, did everything that could be done for her comfort, before he turned back with Randal. But they had no sooner left her, than he fell to talking with an appearance of relief.

"Thank God, that's done with!" he said. "It was very foolish of poor little Margaret; but, after all, it was nothing—nothing in law. My sister Jean got a terrible fright. There is a panic abroad in the world about Scotch marriages; but a promise that is only on one side can never be anything. You don't seem to know what I am talking of."

"No," said Randal, who had gone out of the hall before the climax came. He looked with bewildered curiosity in his companion's face.

"You should have told me, you should have told me—what did you know about it, then? And what were you doing there, Randal? Excuse me, but I have a right to know."

"You have a perfect right to know. I knew that Glen had, by some means, engaged—her—to himself," said Randal, not knowing how to express what he meant, reddening and faltering, as if he himself had been the culprit. "I saw them together twice at Earl's-hall; and once she was good enough to speak to me about it. I had taken no notice of her when I saw them, thinking, as one does brutally, that she understood what she was doing, as I did. And in her innocence she asked me why? What could I say but that I was a brute, and a fool—and that if I could ever serve her I would do it, should it cost me my life."

"That is the way you young idiots speak," said Sir Ludovic, with an impatient gesture. "Your life: how could it affect your life? But you were neither a fool nor brutal, that I can see. Poor little silly thing, she thought you were rude to pass her, did she? and what then? Innocent! oh yes, she's innocent enough."

"And then," said Randal, "she sent to beg me to help her, to keep him away from her. I managed it that time; and this morning she sent to me again. She must have seen her mistake very soon, Sir Ludovic, and what it has cost her. But I hope it is all over now."

"And you came down here, ane's errand, as we say in Scotland, for nothing but to relieve her mind? How did you mean to do it? What was the business you were so anxious to tell him about? I thought it was a strange business that you were so anxious to talk over with Rob Glen."

"It was very simple," said Randal, coloring high under this examination. "He is a clever fellow; he can write and draw, and has a great deal of talent. I wanted to send him off on a piece of work that had been offered to me—"

"To relieve her?"

"Because I thought he could do it—and for other reasons."

"I understand." Sir Ludovic went on in silence for some time while Randal's heart beat quick in his breast. He had said nothing to betray himself, and yet he felt himself betrayed.

After a while, Sir Ludovic turned and laid his hand kindly, but gravely, on Randal's shoulder.

"Tell me the simple truth," he said; "has it ever been breathed between you that you should succeed to the vacant place?"

"Never!" cried Randal, indignantly; "nor is there any vacant place," he added. "Glen took advantage of a child's ignorance. She thought him kind to her. She was grateful to him, no more; and he took advantage of it. There is no vacant place."

"I see," said Sir Ludovic; then, after a pause: "Randal, you will act a man's part, and a friend's, if you will leave her to come to herself, with Jean to look after her. Jean may be 'a lang-tongued wife,'" he said, not able to repress a smile, "but she's a good woman in her way. She will take good care of our little sister. What is she but a child still? You will act an honorable part if you leave her to the women: leave her to be quiet and come to herself."

"I will follow your advice faithfully, as you give it in good faith, Sir Ludovic," said Randal, "if I can do so; but I warn you frankly that I will never be happy till I have told her what is in my heart."

"Oh yes, it needs no warlock to see what's coming," said Sir Ludovic, shaking his head; "and there's Jean's nephew, that young haverel of an Englishman—and probably two or three more, for anything I can tell. But let her alone, let her alone, Randal, I beseech you, till the poor little silly thing comes to herself."

It would be impossible to describe what hot resentment against such a disparaging title mingled with the softened state of sentiment and amiable friendliness with which Randal felt disposed to regard all the world, and especially this paternal brother, who was so much more like a father. "I will remember what you say, and attend to it—as far as I can," he said.

"That means, as far as it may happen to suit you, and not a step farther," said Sir Ludovic, once more shaking his head.

Margaret was not visible when they got to the Grange. She was supposed to be in her own room, and unable to see any one; and, what was more extraordinary, Miss Grace was actually in her own room, and unable to see any one—having wept herself blind, and made her nose scarlet with grief, over the separation of the two lovers, and all the domestic tragedy that had occurred, as Mrs. Bellingham declared, entirely by her fault. If ever there was a woman to whom the separation of true lovers was distressful and terrible, Grace Leslie was that woman; and Jean said it was all her fault! "When I would give my life to make darling Margaret happy!" cried the innocent offender. "They should have my money, every penny; I would not care how I lived, or what I put on, so long as dearest Margaret was happy!" and she had retired speechless and sobbing, feeling the calamity too cruel. As for Mrs. Bellingham, she was in sole possession of the drawing-room, where the gentlemen found her, walking about and fanning herself, bursting with a thousand things to say. The sight of an audience within reach calmed her more than anything else could have done.

"What have you done with that woman, Ludovic?" she said. "She was an impertinent woman; but I'm sorry for her if you walked her all that way to the station as you walked me. Did ever anybody hear such a tongue—and the temper of a demon! But I hope I have some Christian feeling; and after the young man was gone, if you had not been in such a hurry, as she is a Fife woman, and a tenant, I would have ordered her a cup of tea."

"I told her so," said Sir Ludovic; "but she is comfortable enough at the station, and I ordered the people at the inn to send her one."

"I would have done nothing of the kind," said Jean; "a randy, nothing but a randy; and just as likely as not to enter into the whole question, and make a talk about the family. And the way news spreads in an English village is just marvellous! Fife is bad enough, but Fife is nothing to it! So you have come back, Randal Burnside—oh yes, you young men are always missing your train. There's Aubrey would have been here with me and of some use, but that he could not get out of his bed soon enough in the morning. I am very glad Aubrey's coming; he will be a change from all this. And I never saw a young man with so much tact. Are you going up by the next train, Randal, or are you going to stay? Oh well, if you will not think it uncivil, I am glad for one thing that you're going; for I came away in such a hurry, and forgot one of the things I wanted most. If you would go to Simpson's—not Simpson's, you know, in Sloane Street, nor the one in the Burlington Arcade, but Simpson's in Wigmore Street, the great shop for artificial flowers—"

"You need not be at so much trouble to conceal our family commotions," said Sir Ludovic; "Randal knows all about it better than either you or me."

"Then I would just like to hear what he knows!" said Mrs. Bellingham. "I don't know anything about it myself, and I don't think I want to know. Randal, what time is your train? Will you be able to stay till dinner, or can I give you some tea? The tea will be here directly, but dinner may be a little late for Aubrey, who is coming by quite a late afternoon train. He said he had business; but you young men you have always got business. To hear you, one would think you never had a moment. And, Ludovic, just sit down and be quiet, and not fuss about and put me out of my senses. Now I will give you your tea."

Randal, however, did not stay until it was time for his train. Signs of the past excitement were too strong in the house to make it pleasant to a stranger; and Margaret being absent, he had small interest in the Grange. He took his leave, saying he would take a stroll and look at the grounds—a notion much encouraged by Mrs. Bellingham. "Do that, Randal," she said; "I wish I were not so tired, I would go with you myself, and let you see everything. And I'll tell Grace and Margaret you were very sorry not to see them, but time and trains wait for no man. You'll give my kind regards to your excellent father and mother, and you'll not forget the wreaths at Simpson's—plain white for Margaret. No, I'll not keep you, for my mind is occupied, and I know I'm not an amusing companion. Good-bye; I hope you will come another time, Randal, *when we expect you*, and when we will be able to show a little attention. Good-bye!"

Randal went away with a smile at the meaning that lay beneath Mrs. Bellingham's significant words. Should he ever come here as one who was expected, and who had a claim upon the attention she promised him? He looked wistfully up the oak staircase and at the winding passages, by some of which Margaret must have gone. Perhaps she would never know that he had been here. And at the same time, perhaps, it was better that he should not see her. She was rich, while as yet he was not rich, and he had no right to say anything to her; while, perhaps, if they met at this moment of agitation, it might be difficult to refrain from saying something. Thus sadly disappointed, but trying to represent to himself that he was not disappointed, he went through the shrubbery and out into the little park.

How different it was from old Earl's-hall! Glimpses of the old red house, glowing at every corner in some wealth of blossom, early roses climbing everywhere, wreaths of starry clematis twisted about the walls, and clusters of honeysuckle up to the very eaves, came to him through the trees at every turn he took. So full of color and warmth, and set in the brilliant sunshine of this June day, warm as no midsummer ever attains to be in Fife—the contrast between Margaret's old home and her new one struck him strangely. The old solemn gray walls, the keener, clearer tones of the landscape, the dark masses of ivy about the half-ruinous tower of Earl's-hall, came suddenly before his eyes. The scene was graver and colder, but the central figure had been all life and color there. Here it was the landscape that was warm, in its wealthy background, and she that was pale, in her dress of mourning.

He was thinking this, musing of her and nothing else, when he suddenly saw a shadow glide softly through the trees and stand for a moment upon a little rustic bridge over the small stream which flowed at a distance from the house. He started and hurried that way, striding along over the grass that made his steps noiseless. And, sure enough, it was Margaret. The fresh air was a more familiar restorative than "lying down," which was Jean's panacea for agitation as for toothache. She was standing watching the clear running water, wondering at all that had happened—her sob scarcely sobbed out, and apt to come back; her eyes not yet dry, and her lips still parted with that quick breath which told the unstilled beating of her heart. Poor Rob! would he be unhappy? Her heart gave a special ache for him, then quivered with another question: Was Randal angry? Did he think badly of her, that he would not speak?

She looked up hastily, when a step sounded close to her on the path, and that same fluttering heart gave a leap of terror. Then it stilled into sudden relief and repose. "Oh, Randal! you have not gone away!" she cried; and her face, that had been so passive, lighted up.

"I came back," he said; and the two stood looking at each other for a moment—he on one side of the tinkling water, she on the bridge. "But I am going away," he added: "Rob has gone."

"Oh, poor Rob!—he was very kind after all: it was a mistake, only a mistake. It was my fault. I did not like—to hurt his feelings. You should never let any one think a thing is true that is not true, Randal. It is as bad as telling a lie. It is all over now," she said, looking at him wistfully, with a faint smile.

"And you are glad?" He grudged her moistened eyes and the sob that broke, in spite of her, into her voice, and the tone with which she said "poor Rob!"

Margaret did not make any reply to this question; she looked at him once more wistfully.

"Were you angry," she said, "that you would not speak? I should not have troubled you, Randal, but my heart was broken. I was nearly out of my wits with terror. I did not know how to stand out and keep my own part. Were you angry, Randal, that you would not speak?"

"Margaret," he said, "why should you ask me such questions? I am never angry with you; or, if I am angry, it is for love; because I would do anything you ask me, even against myself."

Margaret smiled. Her eyes filled with something that was half light and half tears. "And me too!" she said.

Thus, without any grammar, and without any explanation, a great deal was said. Randal went to his train, and Margaret, smiling to herself, went home across the bridge. Both Jean and Grace heard her singing softly as she went up the oak staircase, and could not believe their ears. Grace cried more bitterly still to think that her darling Margaret should show so little feeling, and Jean was dumfounded that she should not be ashamed of herself—a girl just escaped from such a danger, and so nearly mixed up in a horrible story! Sir Ludovic, who had girls of his own, only laughed and shook his head. "She will have seen the right one," he said, with a gleam of amusement to himself. Perhaps he was all the more indulgent that Aubrey, who was clearly Jean's candidate, and far too much a man of society for plain Sir Ludovic, arrived with the cream of current scandal, and a most piquant story about Lady Grandton

and a certain Duke—"the same man, you know —all come on again, as everybody prophesied," that very night.

Rob Glen set off within forty-eight hours for the other side of the world, with Jeanie as his wife. He had not much more money than would buy the license that made this possible, and pay his passage, and would have faced the voyage and the New World without either outfit or preparation but for a timely present of a hundred pounds that reached him the night before he sailed. But he never spoke of this even to his wife, though his mother was aware of it, who—though she would not see Jeanie—saw him, and dismissed him with a stormy farewell.

"Sir Ludovic, honest man, might well say it was a heart-break to see your bairn throw himsel' away—little we kent, him and me, how sooth he was speaking," Mrs. Glen said. When it was all over, it gave her a little consolation to quote Sir Ludovic, what "he said to me, and I said to him," when she met him "in the South."

On the other hand, it cannot be denied that it was a great shock to Margaret to hear what had happened, and how soon and how completely the baffled suitor had consoled himself. "All the time it was Jeannie's Rob," she said to herself, with a scorching blush; and for the moment felt as deeply shamed and humbled as Rob himself had been by her indifference. And when Jean heard of these two or three words with Randal, which, indeed, as Mrs. Bellingham said indignantly, "settled nothing—for after an affair of that kind what is to hinder her having a dozen?" she was very angry, and planted thorns in Margaret's pillow. But Jean will not be supreme forever over her little sister's life.

THE END.

www.ingramcontent.com/pod-product-compliance
Lightning Source LLC
Chambersburg PA
CBHW030901050726
47500CB00009B/564